Book II
A FORGING OF AGE
Duology

TATIANA OBEY

Wanderlore Publishing LLC

The characters and events in this book are fictitious. Any similarity to real persons, living or dead, is coincidental and not intended by the author.

Copyright © 2022 Tatiana Obey
All rights reserved.

This book or any portion thereof may not be reproduced or used in any manner whatsoever without the express written permission of the publisher except for the case of brief quotations embodied in critical articles and reviews.

www.tatianaobey.com

Cover illustration by Asur Misoa

Wanderlore Publishing LLC
325 North St Paul Street, Ste 3100
Dallas, TX 75201

v 3.0

ISBN: 979-8-9856649-4-2 (trade pbk.)
ISBN: 979-8-9856649-3-5 (e-book)
ISBN: 979-8-9856649-5-9 (hardcover)

*to Tatiana, a younger me,
when the world weighs you down,
drag on*

"My analysis of the language concludes that the isolated culture of the southern wilds identifies four sexes and have no expectations regarding gender. All men, women, and those who exist within the spectrum and outside of it are valued equally with no distinct cultural, social, or economic differences. Undoubtedly, the most important societal divide is the chasm between childhood and adulthood—often demanding a bloody exacting sacrifice to cross."

—Vincent Alcantara, "The Becoming of Pronouns: A Study of Language and Identity," a thesis

Nico's Map

CHAPTER ONE

The warship thundered gloriously underfoot. The hull parted sand dunes with a battering roar, and the sails beat drums in the wind. If all the haters and naysayers could see Rasia now, no one would dare laugh, or mock, or claim what couldn't be done ever again. Only Rasia determined how her bones fall.

She rounded up her motley kull of losers. She pitched her feet atop the upper-deck railing, hands on her hips, and the high noon blazing heat overhead. Azan and Neema shaded their faces, while Zephyr rolled his judgy eyes. Kai gazed at Rasia into the sun.

"Listen up," Rasia announced. "We've got three days to slay this dragon, then twelve more sailing our asses off to reach the Grankull before the deadline ends. When the hard work comes, I expect hustle from everyone on this ship. Understand?"

"Yes, Han," they said, with various levels of enthusiasm.

Before they could scatter, she called out, "Zephyr, you're on steer."

Rasia hopped from her make-shift podium, and her leg buckled. She didn't right herself fast enough before Zephyr made it to the top-stair and turned those judgy eyes on her bandaged leg.

"You're barely standing."

"I'm fine," Rasia said. The tent kid's expression remained

unchanged. "Ugh. Watch the steer while I get some rest. A quick nap and I'll be good to go."

"I don't know how to steer a warship."

"You'll figure it out. Wake me when the wind changes." Rasia slapped Zephyr on his massive shoulder and peered down the stairs.

Unlike Zephyr, Rasia had ridden a warship before. She used to sneak on deck while Shamai-ta led kull drills. Everything had always seemed so huge when she was a budchild hiding from the crew, but apparently, a warship grew even larger when your ribs were burning coals between them. She took each stair a slow step at a time.

Smaller windships didn't have multiple decks to need stairs. Or a round wheeled steer. Or a dedicated Han's quarters. In the Grankull, a Han always slept with his kull, but a scavenger one didn't. The scavengers built the Han quarters to be luxurious and self-indulgent, but Rasia's favorite part was undoubtedly the sight of Kai collapsed across the immense bed of silk and linen. He cracked his eyes open as Rasia leaned against the doorway.

"There's nothing fucking sexier than you lying on the bed of my warship," Rasia teased.

"Your warship, Han?"

"Bet your shroud it is." If the warship survived the dragon, Rasia knew the Grankull would confiscate the ship the moment it neared the clawed checkpoints. But for now, she was the Han of this kull and that was Kai's shroud waving from the topmast.

Rasia lowered the drop bar across the door and finally surrendered to the pain of her injuries. Her leg had grown stiff. Her ribs burned at every motion. That jump during the dragon fight, when she wounded the dragon's ability to breathe fire, had re-fractured her previously injured rib. *Again*. It was amazing she hadn't punctured a lung by now.

Rasia limped over and dropped face-first onto the bed. She sniffed at the fresh lavender. The linen was a touch damp. "You washed the sheets?"

"We don't know what's been done on this bed," Kai grumbled.

Knowing Timar, probably everything. Rasia wished she had the energy to do the same, but all she could manage was to loosen the cords of the leather bodice she had plucked from a scavenger's corpse. Pretty clean and barely any blood on it at all. It was far tighter and more supportive compared to the makeshift wrap she had been wearing before, but it did hurt her back by the end of the day.

Kai massaged a hand up the thigh of her bandaged leg, and his touch had her warm and tender as if she had spent a drum in the steamed waters of the Grankull's public baths.

"You don't have to hide this," he said.

"They finally believe in me, but I know I'm not . . . Nico," Rasia muttered bitterly. For all Nico's faults, people followed her without question. "They're only following me because I can slay this dragon, but once they realize how wounded I am, they will start doubting me. Neema and Azan, they're both the type to panic when shit hits the hull. Then there's Zephyr, who's difficult no matter which way the wind is blowing."

Despite Zephyr's foreign blood, Rasia found him very much a tent kid in nature, with an instinct to constantly challenge the person in charge, always testing if you deserved his respect. Rasia sort of didn't want to lose it.

"There's no one right way to do a thing," Kai advised, echoing words Rasia had spoken to him a lifetime ago in the gorge. "You're never going to succeed doing everything 'Nico's way.' You've got to figure out the right way for you."

Rasia huffed at her own words thrown back at her. He liked to do that often. Use her own words against her. Probably because the only person with any common sense was herself.

Sometimes.

"Rasia," Kai said. "You need to be at your strongest against the dragon, and if that means trusting your kull so that you can get the rest that you need, you should. My shoulder might get in the way of steering, but I can keep the warship on track while you heal."

Logically, Rasia knew a brief nap couldn't fix everything

wrong with her. She knew the importance of pacing, but the closer they sailed toward the Dragon's Coast, the more wired and anticipatory her body became. It sucked when the biggest obstacle in a hunt was your own injuries.

"Okay," Rasia relented. Before, she wouldn't have trusted anyone else with such an important task, but somehow Kai had become as reliable as her pair of dragonsteel khopesh. She eyed his shoulder where the windship steer had punctured it during the crash. "Keep Zephyr at the steer. When we face the dragon, we need our windeka at his best too."

Kai nodded, and he shifted to lay on his back with his good arm settled around her waist. Rasia snuggled closer.

"I told Nico about us."

Rasia laughed at that and tried to imagine the look on Nico's self-righteous face when Kai revealed to his younger sibling that Rasia and Kai were *together* together. She wished she had been there to see it. "She threw a tantrum, didn't she?"

"Of course she did." Kai glanced over at her, after a time. "I've been thinking about us, and how it's going to work."

"What's wrong with how things work now?"

"I've given up all hope of you and Nico truly getting along, but you both are equally important to me. When it's just us, it's perfect. But the world is bigger than the two of us. Once Nico comes of age, she will become the head of my household. How can this truly work if I'm constantly stuck between the two of you? We need . . . rules."

Rules. Rasia silently voiced the word in disgust. Maybe this whole relationship thing was a mistake.

Kai swallowed, nervous, but voiced his rules anyway. "First rule: Don't call anyone out of their names. Not Nico. Not Zephyr. Not anyone. I know you don't like it when people call you Rabid Rasia."

"Ugh. Rules are the worst. Sometimes a skink is a skink, and you got to call that shit out."

"How about 'don't call anyone out of their names *without justification*'?" he nudged, compromising.

"Fine," Rasia huffed and rolled her eyes.

"Second: Don't attack first."

"What?" she twisted over, on her elbow. "Okay, I get the first one. I don't understand the second one at all."

"Rasia, you are a skilled enough fighter that you never need to attack first. You do so because you can. But it's easy to make mistakes that way. You can afford a pause." He noted the blatant doubt on her face and tried a different approach. "Think about it this way—if you're as good as you say you are, attacking first won't matter."

She narrowed her eyes at the challenge in his tone. "I guess I see your point."

"And last rule—don't diminish other people. There's no need to dim someone else's light. You shine bright enough on your own."

Rasia chewed over the rules as she stared at the wooden beams of the ceiling. She didn't believe in changing herself for anyone, but she knew if she couldn't find it in herself to soften her edges, Kai would end up being the one cut on them. Change didn't have to be conformity. Change could also mean growth.

"What if I fail?" she asked. "I'm not perfect."

"All I ask is that you try," he said. Rasia tucked her head under his chin, and he idly continued his massage up her scalp. She missed her hair sometimes.

"Fine. I promise," she decided. She didn't make promises lightly. You made a promise, you kept it. "But I have a rule of my own, and mine is absolute."

It was only fair that Rasia received something in exchange. She raised to her elbow, and her gaze pinned him to the bed with unyielding sharpness. She remembered the days when he shied away at every touch or tone of voice. Now, like the sun, he met her unflinching. "Never leave me."

Kai said easy like a breeze, "I promise."

Kai missed Rasia's mane of hair sometimes. It was growing back unevenly and served as a stark reminder of how he often didn't know what he was doing. Especially now that he was wading into his first committed relationship. He had been a little nervous when he dropped the 'rules' word, but he didn't see how this was going to work past the Forging without them.

Forging flames never last, they said, but Kai wanted to be the exception.

He tucked Rasia under the linen and then, careful to avoid putting any weight on his injury, sidled off the bed. He exited the Han's quarters and when he stepped out further onto the deck, Neema marched past, bumping into his wounded shoulder.

"Watch it," she gnashed.

Kai recoiled as the pain burned down his arm. Up until this point in his Forging, he had only interacted with Rasia, Nico, or Zephyr. He hadn't had any meaningful interactions with Azan or Neema since they'd set sail. They were out of his comfort zone, but he promised Rasia he would take care of things while she rested.

Kai rubbed at the faint scar on the palm of his hand. He pressed his anxiousness into that scar, then pushed himself toward Neema, daring to creep out of his well-established zones. "Neema, I understand you may not like me, but I hope we'll be able to work together."

Neema slashed Kai with a scathing glance, and he visibly flinched in response. "The only reason I'm here is to slay a dragon, but I am not about to kiss your ass because you're Rasia's fuck toy."

"I'm second-in-command."

"Watch yourself, runt. You are nothing without Rasia. I might need to act nice to get what I want, but I'll never forget what your tah has done. I'll never forget that you are the reason my jih is dead."

Kai rubbed that faint scar on his palm, again and again. His tah had murdered several children after he had been taken by the Council when he was a baby. Few have forgotten or forgiven the incident.

"Your days are numbered," Neema threatened. "Someone, someday is going to put the dagger in your back that you deserve. One day it might be me."

Then she whipped around and stomped toward the bow of the warship. She pointed at Azan. "You. Braid my hair."

"What?!"

She grabbed Azan by the bicep and dragged him over to one of the oar benches. Kai shuffled nervously and retreated. That was a stupidly bad idea. From now on, he would stay as far away from her as he could.

He ascended to the upper deck of the warship where Zephyr had two hands clutched tightly on the wheel. Zephyr glanced over when Kai reached the top-stair.

"What was that about?" he asked. This far up, Zephyr hadn't heard the words Neema had said but had seen enough to know that they hadn't been nice.

"It's nothing." Kai shrugged. He didn't really want to talk about it. "Rasia took some sleep powder, so she'll be out most of the day. The wind won't turn until later this evening, but she's given me permission to act as Han in her absence. How is the warship steering?"

"Like floating on clouds," Zephyr reported. When sailing Rasia's smaller windship you felt every groove and hop. On the warship, however, Kai felt neither the crunch of shrubbery nor a rock wobble the massive eight wheels. Zephyr shook his head. "Though, I have no hope if we need to make an abrupt stop."

"Hopefully we won't need to," Kai said. He leaned forward on the railing where down below, Neema was explaining to Azan how to braid her hair. A faint fog, thickened by the wind currents from the ocean, rolled over the sand dunes. Kai rolled his injured shoulder. "I talked to Rasia. Said she'd try."

Earlier that day, he had told Zephyr how he and Rasia were officially a couple.

"But I don't know," Kai said. "Who am I to dare ask her to change?"

Zephyr snorted. "You can ask her these things *because* you are in a relationship. If she cares about you, she'll respect your boundaries. My tahs are kulani, but that doesn't mean it has always been easy for them. Things that exist in my father's language don't exist in my tah's. It's easy to get frustrated, but they've promised to be patient with one another. They've promised never to raise their voices at one other. They've promised to talk through misunderstandings. It's work, Kai. If you want it to last, it's work."

"But if you're . . ." Kai glanced at Zephyr, self-conscious. "If you're, maybe, hypothetically, *kulani*, then shouldn't it work out on its own? Not that I'm saying that Rasia . . . but . . . I . . . if she's the one, then it's supposed to be forever, right?"

Zephyr studied him for several uncomfortable moments as if Kai had horseshit all over his face, and the smell of it disgusted him. "Because my father is a foreigner, no one believed my parents could be a kulani pair. Some people still don't recognize their union. I'm not going to judge you as everyone else will, but you don't deserve to name her your kulani if you can't say it with conviction."

Why was it so hard to outright say it? He had almost told Nico back at the Graveyard, but even then, the word got caught in his throat at the last vibration.

After a thoughtful silence, Zephyr continued, "Your tahs are kulani. Was their relationship perfect?"

"No," Kai said. "It . . . was complicated. From what I understand, they separated after I was born, and they made several compromises when they got back together. One of the rules tah established was that I wasn't allowed in any room with Kenji Ilhani in it."

"That's . . . fucked up. Did you tell Nico about Kenji-shi?"

Kai's hands tightened on the railing. There had been a perfect moment to bring it up with her in the Graveyard, but Nico was finally starting to trust him to make his own decisions. He hadn't wanted to ruin that.

"*Kai*," Zephyr said, exasperated. He wiped a hand down his face, and then decided on something. His expression blanked into an impassive shroud. "When I joined my father's caravan last year, he had warned me away from same-sided relationships. But I didn't listen. I pursued a flame that had caught my interest, and when discovered, his family stoned him to death. It was . . . the worst thing I have ever witnessed in my entire life."

Kai could hardly breathe through his horror. The worst Grankull offenders had their faces burned off alive and their corpses tossed to the carrions, but at least they were dead before the latter. "Are you okay?"

"I'm . . ." Zephyr paused, ". . . better. The whole point I'm getting at is that I could have sworn his father was the nicest person I've ever met, but it was his father who threw the first stone. After it happened, I began to question everything. I began to wonder if my father had warned me away not just because he feared what would happen, but also because he believed in the prejudices too. Up until that point, I never considered there might be a part of me my father didn't want. When I asked him, he told me that he knew my sexuality could be a possibility with where I had grown up as if . . ." Zephyr looked Kai up and down with such intensity, a flush heated Kai's face. "As if it isn't something that's a part of me. As if it's an option. But I'd be all-sided no matter where I'm born. The only difference is that in the Grankull, most are allowed to be who they are, or they are allowed the journey to figure it out." He shook his head. "I idolized my father, and it took the worst day of my life to realize he wasn't perfect. He came for me. He protected and defended me . . . but he might never understand me. It took a long time to reconcile with that."

"Your tah—*father*," Kai said, enunciating the foreign word carefully. "Might never understand, but he came for you. At least he cares."

"Exactly. What hope do you have when they don't?"

Kai blinked blankly. That hurt. More than all of Nico's entreaties and arguments. More than the Lake of Yestermorrow and the false illusions. It smelled too much like truth.

"I don't mean to hurt you," Zephyr said, "but for people like you and me who are born into hate that is so . . . unjustified, we've got to keep our faces clean. You need to be more honest with yourself regarding Kenji-shi."

During the conversation, Zephyr had loosened his grip around the wheel, and remembering himself, clutched it tighter.

Kai wiped at his face and mumbled, "You're going to break it, if you're not careful."

"I am not going to be the reason that we all crash," he said, determined. He licked sweat from his lips and glanced at Kai with furrowed brows. "Has Rasia told you the plan?"

He tried keeping a straight face.

"We are a day out from the Dragon's Coast, and she has no plan? She hasn't said anything?" If you listened closely, you could hear the undercurrent of panic in Zephyr's voice even though looking at him, you'd never guess he was anything but calm and collected.

"I think she's waiting until we get there to figure it all out," Kai said. Even if things didn't work out, Nico always had a plan. But Rasia . . . well . . .

"If we die, you owe me."

Kai nodded. "That's fair."

CHAPTER TWO

1

Everyone talked of rain, but it had been the same overcast high noon for the past few days, nothing but parched air and an endless sweep of clouds that passed them by.

Nico and the other Forging kids had stopped for a break at the base of the mountain range a couple of days out from the Yestermorrow Lake. Nico walked away from camp, both to scout the area and avoid Suri's ever-present scrutiny. The sand shifted under the soles of her gonda leather sandals as she sat on her haunches and spread the Grankull map across her thighs. Nico drank from her water gourd and spat with intention over the map.

The magic-infused droplets landed at disparate places in every direction, coalescing in five distinct globs of spit. She marked the places with charcoal circles. A sudden wind blew, and her last circle ripped the papyrus along the dampened fault lines. The Grankull-issued map, given to every kull at the beginning of the Forging, split into two rough damp pieces.

"You need a new map."

Kelin stood over her shoulder. His eyes scanned the ripped markings, and his initial amusement fell to an expression of concern. "What are you doing?"

Nico sighed. Well, she couldn't hide her intentions forever.

"These circles indicate all the other Forging kids that I sense out in the Desert."

". . . so?"

"We have four gonda, Kelin. That's enough for twenty, and there's twelve of us."

Kelin looked at her, in disbelief for a moment, before throwing up his hands. "We've only got fifteen days before the end of the Forging and look at those circles! The windships left from every direction of the Grankull. We can't possibly save them all."

"I know that. But shouldn't we at least save as many as we can?"

"They could be scavengers! There's a price on your head, if you don't remember. It's a risk, and even if they are Forging kids, some of them could be from the Tents. I can assure you I'm not the only faction that was hired to take you out."

"I changed your mind. I can change theirs too."

The brass of Kelin's feather earring glinted in the sun as he turned his head to look out at the sand dunes. He had a habit of always carrying himself sharp and lean, like a jackal on alert. "This is the moment I was going to assassinate you. Right here. On our way back with the gonda. Away from everyone. You and me, alone."

"You're a terrible assassin."

"I am a great assassin. It's not my fault I was given an impossible task. I was expected to kill you *and* kill a gonda. I'd like to see any other Tent assassin take down a fucking gonda. I've eaten one, sure. I've seen one dead, sure. But I never would have guessed the sort of crazy it took to take one down. And then there are the giant fucking scorpions, and the giant fucking spiders, and the giant fucking dragons. I once laughed at the kullers and their Forging. Thought it easy, compared to Tent life." He clicked his tongue. "I'll never laugh again."

"Well, we've got our gonda. What now?" she asked.

"Now?" Kelin said as he crumpled into a pile of arms and legs beside her. "*Now*, I'm a terrible assassin."

She smiled and swept her high ponytail of dark brown hair to her other shoulder to see his face.

"It was the perfect plan," he said mournfully. "Except you were nothing I expected you to be. It's not some act. You . . . care," he glanced down at Nico's torn map, "*about everyone*, even at your own expense. But I'm tired, and I want to go home. Do you know what it's like to deal with the fretting of twenty-six tahs? It's endless."

"That's why I've planned to go off on my own. I can't ask you or anyone else to further risk your Forging for me. I'll find as many as I can and meet back up with you at the northern oasis. Without the gonda to weigh me down, I should be able to move a lot faster and cover more ground."

"You can't steer a windship by yourself."

"With magic, I can. I'll figure it out." Nico noted the conflict on Kelin's face. "You're going to worry about me?"

He scoffed, but when she nudged his shoulder, he broke into a begrudging smirk. He quirked an eyebrow. "Are you going to tell your little embers about your plan?"

"I have no idea what you're talking about," Nico said, pretending she wasn't aware of all the kids tripping over themselves to cater to her every whim.

"Poor Ohan, charring bones wherever you go." He touched her shoulder and hissed, wagging his finger as if the touch had burned. She laughed at his dramatics and swatted at his hand.

"Oh, you shut it," she teased. She sincerely valued their relationship and the surprising ease of it. "We'll remain friends, right? Even after the Forging and everything changes?"

"What else would I have to brag about?" he asked, with that sharp cutting laughter he clutched tight around himself like a protective cloak. Then, for a moment, his shoulders dipped and that tension ready-to-reach-for-a-dagger-at-any-moment gusted out of him. He looked so young suddenly. Kelin said to himself, surprised, "I don't think I've had a friend before."

It was said that forging flames never last, but forging friendships are forever.

Nico did her rounds of the camp, checking in with everyone as they rested. She was concerned for some of them. All, except Suri and Kelin, have been traumatized by their experiences with the scavengers. Some bounced back the closer they came to the Grankull, some pretended it never happened, and others, like Loryn, preferred to sleep all day.

One person was missing. Nico had to reach out with her magic to find him. She climbed one of the windships and then scaled further up the mast. Faris sat folded into the small circular space of the scout's nest.

Not wanting to intrude if she wasn't welcome, she simply asked, "Are you okay?"

Faris glanced at her, then scooted to make room. Nico joined him. She stretched her legs out of the rim and her toes pointed toward the stars, but Faris kept his legs pleated underneath him like a baby bird, his arms wrapped tight around his knees. Together, they overlooked the camp.

All but this windship were overturned, which hadn't been needed with their meager numbers. The other ships created makeshift camps out of the wingsails and comfortably sheltered everyone down below. Under the translucent sails, the campfires danced like fireflies. Too many ships. Too much gonda. They had enough to share.

"Do you want to talk about it?" Nico asked. Faris didn't respond immediately, which was alright. Nico was learning how to accept silence when it was given to her. But he did respond eventually, when the clouds grew heavy in the sky and shrouded the gibbous moon.

"I was supposed to protect them."

"You did all that you could," she said, to both herself and to Faris.

"I watched so many of them die," he said. "From the heat or lack of water. Many didn't make it out of that windship hatch alive. I still have the stink of their bodies clogged in my nose. So many cried for their tahs in the end. I don't . . . after this, I don't think I'll ever step on a windship again."

Faris had lost a lot of that strength and confidence from when Nico first met him at the oasis, but from what she had heard, he was the one who kept the others going. She pressed a gentle hand on his arm, and after further consideration, pulled him into a hug.

"You got them this far. You made it," she told him, and he shook in her arms. "Let me carry the rest. It's okay. I've got it from here." He compressed further and sobbed, hiding his face in the darkness.

It wasn't fair what these kids had to go through, all because of politics, all because someone on the Council had a vendetta against her. Nico promised that she would find out who placed the hit on her head and somehow, give these kids justice.

"Sometimes I wanted to give up," Faris said, his voice a tiny broken thing, "but I couldn't because they were all depending on me. How do you do this? How do you lead so effortlessly?"

"Trust me, I don't," she said. Her thoughts lingered on the first half of her Forging and how she spent most of it chasing after her jih. "It's all mistakes and lessons learned. I didn't get here easily, either."

"How is this supposed to work?" he asked. "We didn't hunt these gonda. It was your kull that lured the gonda into the Graveyard, trapping them all. It was your kull that ultimately killed one. Even if we make it home, the Council might not approve our faces."

"No. I refuse to allow the Council to deny your face because of their machinations. We play their scheming game, and we beat them at it."

"I could tell my granta the truth," Faris said. His granta was the Claws Councilor of the Council.

"Would he grant you your face, knowing?"

"No," he admitted. "He'd be angry and upset since I didn't kill a gonda myself. I'll never be an adult in his eyes. I don't . . . this doesn't feel earned."

"Slaying a gonda doesn't make you an adult," Nico said, bitingly. "Nor does slaying a dragon. It must be more than that. You have faced Death, Faris, and survived. You deserve your face. You deserve a name that recognizes the strength and resilience of your bones, and I won't stop fighting until that is true."

"I . . . thank you," he said. He unfolded, stretching his limbs like the falcon in the stories he was named for. They perched together atop the nest and watched the dark horizon.

A drop of water landed on Nico's cheek. She startled, surprised.

"Is this you?" Faris asked as the drops grew in weight and frequency.

Nico could move water, shift it from one place to another, but she couldn't create it out of thin air. Her powers were as limited as what the Desert provided.

"No, it's not me," she said, delighted. "It's the first rain of the season."

A shout rolled through the camp. Sleepers jolted awake and, one by one, people poured out from under the wing-sails. Kids who were haggard and feeling defeated by the scavengers came alive under the warm shower of rain. In the Grankull, no matter what time, no matter what you were doing, when that first rain fell—you danced.

Nico and Faris climbed down from the scout's nest to join the drenched crowd. They spun, twirled, and swiveled their hips. Someone overturned pots and added rhythm to the symphony of notes that played every time a raindrop struck the ground.

In the sea of merriment, Nico spied Suri watching her dance. The reed-thin young female stood still amid the revelers, and Nico's eyes wandered over the soaked clothes that clung to Suri's body. No. Nico deflected her eyes and reminded herself that they were not friends anymore. That relationship ended because of Suri's prejudices against the Tents. To this day, Suri still hasn't apologized to Kelin for it.

Suri disappeared behind the thickening sheets of rain. But the joy was too infectious to be weighed down by broken friendships. The First Rain always came gentle and warm; not yet one of those ferocious downpours that caused flash flooding deeper into the season. In the stories, the First Rain represented new hopes and new beginnings and the cleansing of the dust from the past.

Nico unabashedly cupped Faris' face. Tears trailed the lines of laughter around his mouth. "We can't save everyone," she said. "Doesn't mean we shouldn't try."

Then Nico held her breath and jumped the raindrops, leaving the camp behind. She climbed each droplet like stairs and sailed the fertile clouds across the sky. She surfed the First Rain to cover vast distances and landed at one of her map's charcoal circles.

She stepped across the crunch of saltpans. She dipped her head underneath the wing-sail of a broken windship and two children scrambled up at her appearance. She offered her hand.

"I am Nicolai, and I am here to help."

CHAPTER THREE

Kai tasted salt on the wind. The familiar ochre cliff formations of the Desert had given way to the dark stratified blue of basalt and volcanic rock. The Dragon's Gate, a tunnel created by an Ohan long ago who wanted an accessible pathway through the cliffs to the coast, yawned open in the distance. But distance was always funny in the Desert, and what seemed close might be days away.

"Don't give up now! We're almost there!" Rasia yelled on high from the steer. Kai and Zephyr rowed the left oar. Azan and Neema rowed the right. They spurred the wheels forward as Rasia tacked them around a merciless wind.

"You said that a hundred times ago!" Azan complained. Azan's arms trembled, and he was the child of a blacksmith. Kai only had one arm to contribute to the effort, while Zephyr's face grew steadily red at the exertion.

Rasia pounded her hand on the wheeled steer and took up song to keep them on beat. She had an off-tune singing voice, but one that never wavered:

Oi-yo!
We sail the storms of the golden sea
Row, friends, row

The wheels roll a'thunder
For Death is out hunting my kull and me

Zephyr picked up the words, then Azan and Neema. Kai had never heard the shanty before, so it took a few passages to understand the pattern. He had never raised his voice in song before. He had never added his timbre to a chorus. A thrill of exhilaration zapped through him as he sang at the top of his lungs, a voice among many. This must be what it felt like to be part of a kull.

Oi-yo!
We roar the waves of the golden sea
Row, friends, row
The ground is asunder
For Death is out hunting my kull and me

They entered under the shadow of the Dragon's Gate and darkness swallowed them. The tunnel formed a wind funnel. It made the ship difficult to maneuver, and Kai was forced to use both hands and apply all his strength to make sure they didn't veer into the rocky walls. The pain in his shoulder returned with the strain of the grueling and punishing pace.

It was slow going and every grain hard fought. They rowed through the darkness, closer and closer toward the growing light. Even though Rasia was rough in the way she led her kull, it didn't make her any less good at it than Nico. While Nico's kindness encouraged everyone to give their best, Rasia's sheer prowess demanded everyone to match her greatness. Their arms burned and hot air lashed their faces, but Rasia kept them going. The wind howled, but they howled louder. Their song echoed off the rocks, adding more voices, as if they weren't five rowing this massive warship, but a hikull of chanting hunters.

Oi-yo!
We sing the might of the golden sea

Row, friends, row
Farewell to all I know
For Death has caught my kull and me

OI-YO!

They burst into the light. What Kai thought to be drums beating in his imagination had been the sound of rolling waves and the ocean crashing in the distance. Dark water scraped at a snaking sliver of black sand. The sky flashed with distant lightning, for thunder to boom and shake the world vibrations later. For a moment, Kai wished that Nico-ji was here to see this. The Desert often restricted her power's potential, but in this place where she could wield oceans and storms, he had no doubt she could take down a dragon single-handedly.

Various dragons swooped and swept through the sky. An emerald dragon dove into the ocean and impaled a fish the size of a warship on their talons. Then, as the dragon lifted into the air, the waves burst apart for an enormous sharp-toothed whale the likes Kai had only seen in the sketches of the library. The dragon barely got away with their catch. The whale fell, causing visible waves that exploded throughout the coast.

"Whoa," Neema said. Azan's jaw dropped. Even Zephyr, the only one other than Rasia to have ever seen an ocean, had his eyes wide.

So stunned and overwhelmed, Kai had forgotten about the oars. It was a good thing the wind had turned and they no longer needed to row. Rasia adjusted the sail, and the large warship sailed over rocks unimpeded. The rocky coast stretched five vibrations to the ocean.

A dragon of lapis lazuli swept towards them. Neema scrambled for her spear but barely got it in hand before the dragon flew past. The resulting draft of air pulled at their sail, and the entire warship tilted toward the steep cliffs that bordered the beach, which had been smoothed by thousands of years of storm winds. The dragon disappeared into one of the many dens clawed out of the cliff face.

"What was that?" Rasia asked Neema, unimpressed.

Neema tightened her hands around her spear and defended, "That dragon was coming straight at us. What if they ate us?"

Rasia laughed. "We're not even a snack to a dragon. They're not bothered by us."

"But what about Aurum? They attack kulls all the time."

"That's because Aurum is a kulo. Most dragons don't leave these hunting grounds," Rasia said. Neema huffed as she sat back down at the oar bench but continued to hold the spear in her lap.

Rasia wheeled the warship toward a cove, and as they approached, she ordered a stop. Everyone glanced at each other in panic, and they scrambled to figure out how to stop this thing. The warship halted slow and dragging, and they almost crashed into the cliff. Kai had no idea how they were going to maneuver this hulking warship against the dragon when they could barely get it to stop with their meager kull of five.

He looked to see if Rasia had any of the same concerns on her face, but she gave him that mad grin, that same one she gave him when he stepped out of the oasis reeds. It had been a wild ride ever since. He grinned in turn, maybe with one as moon-mad as hers.

She cheered, "Let's slay a dragon!"

Rasia figured everyone would collapse the moment they disembarked, but they found a second wind to draw them toward the ocean. She remembered the first time she had seen the roaring black waves, felt the thunder of it rolling through her chest while she stood beside her tah and jih at the end of the world. Judging by her sense of time, it was high noon, but the clouds were so dark they cast perpetual night over the coast. The kull stared at the waters in awe, too scared to cross the shifting boundary clawing and raging at the shore.

Then Kai stepped forward, daring, and he watched the water sweep his sandaled toes. Rasia smirked at the sight of him, hair and shirt whipping in the fierce winds, his clothes hugging the lean strength of his body. Then he threw off his shirt, pulled down his pants, and discarded his loincloth. Rasia had seen him naked for the first time under the harsh high noon sun, and so many times since then, but never like this—tattooed by lightning and cloaked in wind.

He looked over his shoulder and a flash illuminated his face. He raised his brow as if to ask, '*What's taking you so long?*'

Kai raced into the sea.

"Wait," Neema cried out. "Is that safe?"

"Nope," Rasia said as she yanked off her clothes and then raced after Kai. Her bare feet ran over seashells and pebbles. The salt wind cut at her lips.

"Nico would never let us do this," Azan said, awed.

Rasia leapt after Kai and caught herself on his back. They splashed into the water. Briefly, she flashed back to the Yestermorrow Lake, to the pull and strength of current and tide. But this time, when she lifted out of the surge, she found Kai drenched and grinning. She caught him in her arms, and they kissed till a wave swept them aside.

The others were more hesitant in following. It was Azan who finally cursed, threw caution and his clothes to the wind, and went streaking into the water. Azan swam out past them to deeper depths.

"Careful!" Rasia yelled after him. "Don't go too far or the waves will pull you out to sea!"

The warning had been pointless as Azan was immediately thrown off his feet by a powerful wave, which turned dark and seductive by the time it reached Rasia and Kai. Neema stretched a toe into the water. Zephyr gave one distrustful look and plopped down on the shore.

Without warning, Kai splashed Rasia in the face. She laughed at the audacity, and then quickly chased after him. She almost touched him, but at the last vibration, spun and tagged Neema wading through the waves. Neema tagged Azan climbing his way above water. Azan poked Zephyr on the shoulder.

"I'm not playing," Zephyr said. "We don't know what's in these waters. This ocean . . . it's not normal."

"Oh, come on!" Rasia yelled. Soon, everyone took up the cry, taunting Zephyr into the ocean. His shoulders crumbled bit by bit, until he finally gave in and dived after Azan. Everyone cheered.

The tag returned to Rasia (it does get kind of boring being too fast to get caught), and then she very blatantly went after Kai since he started this game in the first place. She tackled him along the shore, and they wrestled to find the upper hand in the shallows. She lost her breath when Kai wrapped her legs around his waist, playfully, but Rasia shuddered when his hips rolled. It felt like forever since they'd been intimate. The need for it curled in her belly. Their hips crashed, and he was a slick wave away from slipping inside of her.

Kai froze, looking down at her, hot and brimming with anticipation. Even out here in this gloom, his eyes cut through the darkness like a beacon, calling to consume her like a moth to flame. He dug his fingers into the sand and shook his head, dislodging cold droplets onto her skin. Right. They had agreed on abstinence until the Naming Ceremony, but Rasia didn't think getting a little handsy would hurt any.

"Here, let me," she said, reaching between them.

Neema screamed—no, wait—that high-pitched shriek had come from Azan. "Something touched my leg!"

Azan raced past them. Neema looked to be running because Azan was running. Zephyr hadn't gone too far out and backed up cautiously to shore.

Kai's eyes flashed. "Something is out there. Something big."

Kai and Rasia scrambled to their feet and ran out of the water as the ocean crackled and lit with blue lightning. Amid the blinding luminescence, Rasia spotted the shadow of a slithering snake in the waves before the waters again went dark.

The ocean continued to roar.

Through the citrine tinted view of the eyeglass, Rasia spotted a dragon launching from one of the cliff dens. Soundless lightning reflected bright off the dragon's gold scales before they disappeared into the dense miasma of clouds. *Odd.* Most injured dragons clung to their dens to recover. Rasia hadn't thought Aurum would be out hunting so soon.

Perhaps Aurum wasn't as injured as Rasia thought? Perhaps Aurum have already recovered their fire-breath from when she shot a bone-spear through their throat at the Graveyard? Regardless of the speculation, this provided an invaluable opportunity.

Rasia descended from the top of the cove where they had made their camp and waded through ankle-deep water to reach the entrance. The cove was a kull camp and had been used for generations in preparation for a dragon hunt. Inside, the sand ended, and the rock flooring climbed to high enough elevations that parts of the cove remained dry no matter the tide.

"Aurum just left to hunt," Rasia announced to the kull huddled around the campfire. They had dressed in their spare clothes and hung the wet ones to dry across a line.

"What does that mean for us?" Zephyr asked.

"It means that this might be the only chance we have to scout out the den and determine if it's better to trap them there or somewhere else. If Aurum returns with a sizeable meal, they could dig themselves in for several days and we'll lose the opportunity. Start erecting those bone shields on the windship and finish off-loading the supplies. We need that warship moving as light as possible. Kai, you're with me."

Before they could yammer her with questions, she spun back toward the beach. She grabbed her climbing equipment from the windship while she waited for Kai to follow. Before, Kai had been dressed in the shirt and pants she had gifted him, but with those now wet, he wore the clothes he had stripped from the scavenger Han, Timar. They didn't fit him well, but he couldn't exactly go hunting for dragons in his worn linen caftan.

Rasia and Kai set off at a brisk pace along the beach. Seaweed decorated the dragon bones washed along the shore. Flocks of seagulls roosted atop the bones and giant crabs peeked out from underneath to watch Kai and Rasia as they trekked the black ocean sand.

Rasia glanced over at Kai as they walked together, quiet. A sapphire dragon flew overhead, but Kai hardly flinched. She wondered at his thoughts.

"Are you scared?" she asked him.

Kai combed back his hair and eyed their destination—those towering imposing cliffs that punctured storm clouds. A pair of amethyst thunder dragons weaved through the lightning. So far, Rasia had only spotted four or five distinctive dragons on this side of the coast, but hundreds ranged farther headward, some of them probably of breeds no one had ever seen before. She wondered if one day Kai would be willing to help her discover them.

"I feel nothing at all," Kai finally said, drawing Rasia away from her musings. "I feel as if I should feel *something*. Maybe I'm not allowing myself to. I don't know. For so long, the dragon has felt the end of a long journey, but beyond it is darkness. That darkness, the after—seems unknowable. Earning my face and names, trying out for the kulls—it's still not real. Not yet. It's still the illusion from the Yestermorrow Lake. This is the moment it all becomes true. This is the moment that frees me. And I feel nothing at all." He glanced at Rasia, knowingly. "You're *excited*."

Rasia was always excited right before a hunt. She turned her face into the wind. "In moments like these, you know who you are. I've always strived to be everything that I can be. I am each new experience, each new piece of knowledge," Rasia looked at Kai considering, "and each new relationship. If it all ends here, at least I'll go out with the all of me."

"And if we win?"

"If we win," she smirked, "then there's always the next hunt."

Rasia offered her hand, and her heart jumped stupidly when Kai took it and tied their fingers together, a promise.

She walked hand-in-hand with the person who made her heart do backflips, while stamping their footprints into the end of the world. It couldn't have been more . . . romantic? Rasia laughed at herself. Whatever. The dangerous ocean, the fierce storm, the dragons, the impending sense of Death hunting after them, and best of all, Kai walking at her side—to Rasia, it was perfection.

Aurum's den was a hollow hole in the cliff face, most likely built before Aurum ever popped out of an egg. Many of the dens were larger than their occupants, evidence of how dragons have become smaller with every subsequent generation.

Rasia and Kai tied ropes to each other. Rasia started first. She hammered hooks into the black basalt and used them as leverage to climb up the smooth rock face. She took care not to near any of the other dens and aimed straight for the one half-way up the cliff.

Sweat beaded her forehead. Pain trembled through her thigh. Her foot slipped, and Kai reached up to steady her with a hand on her leg. Rocks crumbled down into the unrelenting ocean below.

"Are you okay?!" Kai yelled over the buffeting winds. He flinched as he withdrew his bad arm from her leg. He had been primarily using his good arm to climb.

Rasia bit down on the agony and focused on finding the next handhold. *I am Rasia. I am invincible. Nothing is going to stop me.* She repeated the mantra in her head. If she said it enough times, maybe her body would believe it. A fall from this height and she'd be dead. All of it over. The only thing to do was to keep going, so that was what Rasia did.

She heaved herself up into the den's mouth with a gasp of relief. After several breaths, she reached down and helped Kai the rest of the way up. He certainly was not as light as he used to be. Probably all the scorpion jerky he was swallowing down recently.

She retrieved the driftwood from her back and used a strike of flint to illuminate the cave and all the bountiful bones decorating the home.

A pool of silver shifted, and then a head popped up from a flutter of wings.

Rasia froze at the sight of the baby dragon.

"Shit."

A spark jolted through Kai's veins when he met the eyes of the infant dragon, then it fizzled out just as quickly when Rasia's fluting whistles caught the dragon's attention. They bounded over and slipped on their wings before straightening and craning their neck toward Rasia in curiosity.

"Hey beautiful," she said. She boldly allowed the dragon to sniff her hand. Once she had gained their trust, she caressed the silver translucent scales. Then she bounced back. She laughed as she twisted, and the baby dragon chased her around the cave. They tripped and rolled over, and Rasia knelt and rubbed at their soft underbelly.

"*This* is why the Desert is starving," Rasia said, "because of this little one. I should have known, but I didn't think . . . Aurum currently presents as male, which is why none of the hunting kulls have suspected. But I should have known. Dragons don't act weird for no reason."

Dragons are bimale—the fourth sex. Even though Aurum currently presented as male, dragons are male and female, often transitioning between both in their lifetimes. Usually, they weren't male so soon after a hatching, and if there was one fact about dragons the temple library always emphasized is that the hatching of a baby dragon endangered the local food population. They required almost five times their body weight in food in order to survive. Because of the resources required to raise one, many didn't live past infancy, or they grew up to be smaller than their predecessors.

"Dragons tend to give birth to their corresponding color. This little one must have been adopted. That explains a lot." Rasia rubbed the baby dragon all playful and gentle, but her voice held none of it. "You do understand what this means, right?"

Her words sent a cold shiver down Kai's spine. The understanding settled heavy in his gut. "But they're a baby."

The baby dragon chirped out of Rasia's lap, then ran behind a stalagmite out of view and returned playfully rolling a ball across the floor. Kai's stomach churned when he realized it wasn't a ball at all, but a human skull.

He took a moment to look around. His throat tightened at the sight of broken windships parts and at the human bones mixed with the animal ones. Rasia picked up the skull and used it to coax the dragon back into her lap. She petted over the silver scales.

"Their existence is starving the Grankull, the Graveyard, and the entirety of the Desert. For whatever reason, the coast is not providing the dragons with enough food. That, or their population has grown unsustainable. Historically, when dragons have threatened our hunting grounds, our hunting kulls have restored the balance. The environment we live in is too fragile and delicate for compassion. Besides," Rasia gave a strained grimace. "We're from the Grankull. We cull babies all the time—those not yet born and those who can't survive."

Kai squeezed his eyes closed. He knew that all too well. Still, he argued. "We could let them go. Perhaps just killing Aurum will restore the balance enough in our direction."

"Maybe. Maybe not. And who's to say they will survive without a parent? A quick death is better than a long hungry one. Sometimes, compassion is crueler."

Kai knew that all too well, also. He knew first-hand the scars of a life born out of compassion. He should have been culled the moment he exited Ava-ta's womb. No one thought he would survive past infancy. No one thought he would survive his first Forging. Even Kai, many times, didn't think he'd survive.

"I'm still here," he said. Maybe he was barely scraping by most days, but he was still here. And that mattered. "Back home, I'm the monster. I'm the villain in everyone's stories. My existence is an inconvenience to everyone around me. But it was you who taught me that ultimately, I determine my own fate. I write my own story." Kai crouched down, as careful with his motions as he was with his words because he knew that the moment Rasia made up her mind, the harder it was to budge it. He had no doubt she could plunge a knife into the dragon's underbelly without hesitation or guilt. "This doesn't have to be the end of theirs."

Rasia argued, "Maybe we leave, and they live, and they survive—then that's a problem for someone else on a different day, but it's still a problem. Sometimes, this is what it looks like to save the world. It's not always pretty."

Kai squeezed his hand over hers. "Tomorrow might be a necessity but today, right now, is a choice. We don't have to."

Rasia sucked in a sharp breath and snatched her hand from the dragon's belly. "Fine. The Desert will decide." She stood up, then motioned toward the dragon. "Okay, pee on him."

"What?"

"It's much easier for you to whip it out. Hurry up, pee on him." Then her lips cracked into a smile, and Kai rolled his eyes. "Fine. You don't have to pee on the dragon, but you've got to pee on something. Dragons are territorial. Claiming Aurum's territory is a surefire way to get that dragon coming after us in a fury. And you're the windeka. The plan hinges on Aurum coming after you."

"Right. I'm the bait."

"It was your idea."

Kai turned away from Rasia and the baby dragon. He didn't know why he was so embarrassed about this after everything he and Rasia had done together. He chose a dirty corner that smelled dank of refuse. He pulled his dick from his pants. His eye twitched as the warm stream splattered the rocks.

The baby dragon hissed at him, quickening Kai's task. He was more than relieved to tuck himself back in and re-adjust his clothes. No one could ever deny he didn't contribute to this hunt. When Kai joined Rasia at the mouth of the den, she climbed down first.

Realizing that they were leaving, the dragon whined after them, much the same way Rae had cried when Kai left for his Forging. Kai glanced at Rasia, already a distance down the rock. He hoped climbing down was much easier than climbing up.

Out of Rasia's view, he sucked in a breath and released the magic he held tightly to his chest. He sent a gust of wind dancing through the den, and the dragon chased after the stray leaves and dust, attention diverted as easily as a budchild's.

Kai and Rasia reached the ground and hiked back to their camp along the beach. The stench of droppings, entrails, and thick animal musk clung sticky to their skin.

"Thank you," Kai said.

"I'm convinced they're going to die, either now or later. We also could have used the hide. You need a good pair of pants since Timar's are too loose on you," Rasia shrugged. "But it was just as much about you as the dragon."

"You think I'm wrong?"

"I like dragons. They're not pure instinct like most animals. They get angry, and grow fond, and seek vengeance. They're intelligent. That's what makes them such worthwhile hunts. That baby dragon will remember you. They will mourn their parent. Perhaps they will be grateful you spared their life. Or they will hate you. Or they will suffer. Whatever happens, that's on you. That's your weight now."

"I'll carry it," Kai said decisively.

She nodded. "If I didn't think you couldn't, I'd have never let you choose."

Going into this hunt, Kai had considered himself forged by either his success or failure to slay Aurum—that the dragon would somehow remake him. He had hoped to finally prove himself greater than the runt of the Grankull. As Rasia had said—moments like these show you who you are. But perhaps a different moment would define him.

Maybe his hunt was always a different dragon.

CHAPTER FOUR

1

Nico viewed the curved spine of the Great Elder through her eyeglass. Palm groves ringed the yawning Lakejaw, one of the largest bodies of water in the entire Desert. The wingspan stretched across fields, and the tail curved a knobby mountain range in the distance. They should reach the Grankull by tomorrow.

"Nico, we've got a problem."

She sighed. She had almost made it back home without hearing those words. She tied the eyeglass to her belt and turned toward Suri's approach. They had already made camp for the night, the watch rotations were assigned, no one had called out any warnings, nor did she sense any predators nearby. Nico had no idea what trouble to expect.

"What's wrong?" she asked.

"It's best if you come," Suri said.

Their four windships formed a ring barrier around the dried and salted gonda at the center. Many of those she had rescued from various parts of the Desert were severely dehydrated and heat sick, and Nico had used her magic to get them home as quickly as possible. She greeted the kids on watch and followed Suri inside a windship hatch. A clay oil lamp burned atop one of the shelves and highlighted the red rimmed around Loryn's eyes.

Faris, head crooked against the side-ceiling, turned as Nico bent her way inside.

"What's going on?" Nico asked.

Suri shut the hatch door.

"She's seeded."

Shocked, Nico stared at Loryn. It was Rasia all over again. But Loryn, whose jih hadn't survived his Forging, wouldn't have risked hers in such a careless manner. Something else was going on here.

"Was it the scavengers?" she asked softly.

Loryn began to cry.

Nico had been of the understanding the scavengers hadn't touched the oasis kids. Faris crouched down and rubbed circles along Loryn's back. He soothed, "It's okay. Nico will help."

Loryn glanced furtively at Faris before whispering against her scarred knees. "It happened at the oasis. When they were rounding us up. I was with Tarick, but he had fought back, and they killed him. I was all alone and they—they—I thought I was going to die."

"You don't have to say more," Nico said.

Suri, Faris, and Nico looked at each other, fully understanding how much of a mess this was. Whether Loryn consented or not, the Forging allowed none of the participants the protections usually afforded to children. Judged as an adult, the Grankull would punish Loryn for a choice she never made.

They needed to get rid of it.

Nico, Suri, and Faris regrouped outside of the windship for privacy. She leaned her head toward Suri. "Can it be done?"

"I don't know," Suri whispered. "I've only apprenticed with the healers, and they keep the recipe for gonom on a need-to-know basis. I'd be guessing at it. We have plenty of gonda venom, but we could end up with another Rasia situation on our hands if we're not careful."

"*Rasia?*" Faris whispered.

"*Forget it,*" Nico stressed to him. The fewer people who knew about Rasia and Kai the better. Faris immediately nodded.

"Even then," Suri continued, "whatever gonom substitute I could mix might not be effective. If this happened at the oasis, then she's what? About two blinks seeded? Even with gonom, the amount needed to poison a more developed seed might poison her as well. Especially without the resistance most adults develop after taking gonom for years."

Nico rubbed at her face and looked at Faris. "Did you know? Why didn't she say something sooner?"

Faris' shoulders hunched to his ears. "It was only a suspicion at first. At the oasis, she was the last one chained into the hatch, and I thought it took so long because they had a hard time finding her. I didn't know—I—I noticed her bleeding, but I thought—I thought it was her deathsblood. It was only after . . . Loryn stopped acting like herself. I knew something was wrong. She started getting sick, and it was all the signs we were taught in school, but I still wasn't sure. I tried to talk to her about it, but she denied everything. She finally told me this morning. Now that we're almost to the Grankull, she doesn't have a choice but to face it. She almost drowned your jih at the beginning of the Forging and feared you might not help her, so she came to me. I've been convincing her to talk to you all day. She finally agreed to get Suri to at least look at her and confirm it."

Nico sighed. "What about doing it physically?"

"Again, it'll be guess-work," Suri said. "But I can try."

"Okay. Let me talk to her."

Nico returned to the hatch where Loryn waited with her forehead on her knees. She crouched against the bunker slab. "Loryn. There aren't many options. None of us have the medical ability to take care of it in the ways of the alley, but Suri is willing to try. She can also try to mix a substitute gonom, but there's no guarantee it won't kill you as well as the seed. The third option," she said, slowly, "is my magic. I've never tried this before and there's no guarantee. It might fail, but I do feel confident it's the likeliest option to leave you alive by the end of it. But you'll have to trust me."

Loryn's jaw locked, and her fists clenched so tightly she drew blood. "I can't even demand a blood price for this . . . this shame. My triarch can't defend me. No one will shed blood or give their lives for what has been done to me. I—I—was so weak. I didn't even fight back."

"That's not your fault, Loryn. None of this is your fault. Suri, Faris, and I—we will never say anything. No one will ever know."

"*I'll know*," Loryn hissed out. She looked up at Nico. "I want you to do it."

"Do you want anyone with you? Faris?"

Loryn shook her head.

"Do you want to do it here?"

Loryn peered around the hatch and shivered. "Those scavengers stuck me into a windship hatch bleeding, with barely any air, and hungry for days. If this doesn't end well, I don't want to die in this darkness. Anywhere but here."

Nico said, without hesitation, "It's your choice."

⁘

The endless expanse of cold Desert enveloped Nico and Loryn in its vastness. They trekked over the dune until the mountain of sand veiled the lights from the campfires. Stars orbited the overhead gibbous.

"Here," Loryn said finally, decisively, when a wind blew up a haze of sand and whipped at the loose fabric of their clothing.

"It would be easier for me if I'm touching you," Nico said, doing her best not to treat this situation as awkward and as uncomfortable as it was. "We can do this however you want."

Loryn switched positions several times, testing them, until finally settling between Nico's legs. Nico reached under Loryn's arms, under her shirt, and placed her hands below Loryn's bare belly. Nico sensed the life there now that she was looking.

"I'm sorry," Loryn said suddenly. "I'm so sorry, for what I did to your jih."

"I'm not the one owed your apology," Nico said. "Tell him yourself, and we're balanced. Ready?"

Loryn squeezed her eyes shut, and nodded, a movement Nico felt against her chest. She hugged Loryn and focused. It shouldn't be harder than filtering gonom poison through Rasia's bloodstream, but at that moment, Nico had been saving Rasia's life. This was different. She weaved her magic through the fluid-filled amniotic sac protecting the embryo, a small thing barely rooted.

Nico often wondered at the difficult choice Ava-ta made when Kai came into the world. It was the one choice she never blamed her tah for. The rest, all the bloodshed that came afterward, Nico could never forgive. And yet, she had killed someone for the very first time back at the Graveyard. She held Rianis dying in her arms. She had blood on her hands, now. How much more was she fated to carry?

Emotionally, this was one of the hardest things she had ever had to do.

Except it had to be done. This seed belonged to Death, but Nico refused to give it over violently. Her magic sang soft, beckoning like a lullaby, and soothed the passing. Most likely, they would bury it, planted in the ground as done with all seeds.

Loryn's sobs of broken relief howled into the wind.

CHAPTER FIVE

"I have a plan!" Rasia announced.

"Thank Elder," Zephyr said when Rasia and Kai returned from scouting the dragon's den. The mention of a plan lured Azan and Neema away from their dinner. Kai had to admit he was also curious at what she had come up with.

Zephyr and the others had finished off-loading the warship and setting up the "shields," the loose bone plates of the dead dragons Rasia had gathered from the Graveyard. Along with the battering ram made of teeth, the warship looked even more imposing. They also had finished cranking down Rasia's windship from the warship's side.

Rasia dramatically clutched her hands to her chest. "Zephyr, I can't believe you would have so little faith in me."

"*What is the plan?*"

Rasia smirked and then dropped to her knees to draw scribbles in the sand. She explained the markers. A conch shell represented the warship, a clam shell the windship, rocks for each member of the kull, and a small sand crab for the dragon, but it kept scuttling off. "Okay, so. Using the den is out. Complications arose, but while we had the chance, Kai very helpfully planted the bait. So we have about . . . whenever the dragon gets back from its hunt to get everything in place. Maybe a few drums at most?"

"*Wait, what?*"

"I thought you said we'd have at least a day to prepare?!" Azan whined. Neema suddenly looked ill. Everyone, even Kai, thought they had more time. Again, that deadened nothingness seemed to consume him.

"Change of plans. Happening now," Rasia chirped. She squinted at Azan and Neema. "How many arrows and spears did you manage to make from the Graveyard bones?"

"Several quivers full," Azan said, in a reedy whisper. "Five throwing spears."

"That'll work," she said.

Rasia finally, *finally*, explained the specifics of her plan with the same confidence and experience of a storyteller weaving intricate plotlines on the fly. Kai listened, amazed at the way it solidified before their eyes. Rasia knew all the dragon stories and twisted their tropes easily. She colored in the setting and built her world with observations from today's scouting expedition and the memories of her childhood. She took the characters and tools given to her and created the likeliest arc to culminate in a happy ending for all. Rasia herself hadn't known the exact plan, until she did.

"Okay," Zephyr said, squinting at the sand squiggles, and nodded. "I got it."

"I don't," Neema said, panicked.

"Just don't freeze this time," Rasia said as if that should have been obvious.

"Can we go over it maybe one more time?" Azan asked. "I don't want to mess up."

Rasia flung up her hands, becoming visibly frustrated and unable to understand why Azan or Neema didn't immediately get it. But they weren't used to keeping up with the speed of Rasia's run-on sentences when she was excited, nor were they familiar with the ad hoc vocabulary she used for specific parts of the windship.

"I'll go over the plan with Azan again," Kai interjected. "Rasia, why don't you finish any extra preparations we might need?

Zephyr, go over the motions with Neema. Help her drill it down so she'll feel ready and less likely to freeze when the time comes."

"What he said," Rasia flung her hand in Kai's direction, then walked off in a huff. She scooped down to grab her bow and the string wax as she left.

Zephyr nodded at Kai and took Neema to the side, while Kai crouched down with Azan. Kai added words and steps to many of Rasia's pictographs. The crab had crawled away. Really, Azan just needed the reassurance, but it helped to go over the plan until Azan could recall it from memory. It felt like no time at all had passed when Rasia came racing back, chest heaving, several drums later.

"I spotted Aurum in the clouds," she said. "I'd say at least half a drum out. It's happening now."

Everyone lingered, waiting on Rasia to give something more—a little more direction, a little more instruction, a little more *something*. Kai nudged Rasia in the arm and whispered, "Maybe say something encouraging."

"Seriously? We don't have time for this."

He nudged her again.

Rasia clapped her hands together. "Don't die."

Kai lowered Rasia's clasped hands. Someone needed to say something. He glanced at Zephyr, but Zephyr only glared back at him, urging Kai to speak. Kai's mouth suddenly dried, but time ticked down and every vibration mattered.

With a dry swallow, he forced words out of his mouth. "Many of us are here for different reasons—for glory, for family, for doing the right thing—but regardless, we're all here together. Whether or not we succeed today, no one can ever question the mettle of our bones. Even though the dragon can't breathe fire, as far as we know, doesn't make it any less dangerous. We go in with everything we've got to give because anything less won't be enough. Never forget—all hunters are hunted."

"All hunters are hunted," they repeated and broke to their stations.

Kai moved towards the windship, but Rasia snatched a hand

around his neck and he curved eagerly into her lips. This was it.

Everything they had to give.

The moment Aurum returned from their hunt, they roared a fury so loud the sound rippled the ocean and the black sand vibrated.

Rasia's heart ratcheted up in anticipation. She lived for this moment—the vibrations right before a hunt, knowing you've done all you could in preparation and yet knowing all your carefully laid plans could still come tumbling down around you. She got here as fast as she could. She prepared as much as she could. She rested as well as she was able. She had thrown her bones as hard and as far as possible.

Now it was time to see how her bones would land.

Rasia stood at the back of the windship, facing the cliffs and the dragon bearing towards them. As predicted, the dragon charged in their direction, chasing Kai's scent like a well-trod path and shattering clouds in all directions.

Rasia looked at Kai over her shoulder, where he stood with his good arm on the steer. She trusted Kai to get them where they needed to go and hoped that the others were in position.

She turned back toward that incoming dragon and braced herself with one foot between the railing. She pulled a bone-shard arrow from her quiver and nocked it to her bow. She aimed for the dragon's massive outline and waited for Aurum to breach her range.

The ship wobbled, so powerful the flap of the dragon's wings displaced wind currents. The wobble made it hard to aim, no matter how much Kai tried to steady the ship. Her first arrow veered off.

She grabbed another arrow and anchored herself against the railing. She watched patiently for her opening as the dragon swooped down with gleaming talons. Those talons were sharp enough to rend through the entire ship, crush the mast, and impale both her and Kai all too easily. And yet, she waited.

The talons neared.

Three vibrations.

Two vibrations.

Rasia loosed her arrow. It struck true, hitting the center of the right talon, but the dragon didn't slow. Rasia released another one, this time aiming for the fiery smoldering eye. She never got the shot off as the windship abruptly turned.

Kai dropped his weight against the outrigger and maneuvered the ship underneath the dragon's incoming talons, causing the dragon to overshoot. Aurum crashed against the ground. The windship, although untouched, shook at the nearby impact.

Kai straightened the ship and moved them back on track toward the Dragon's Gate. The dragon thrust off the ground and continued the chase. The shadows through the gate tunnel shifted, and out of the shadows came the warship on a collision course.

"Hurry!" Rasia yelled when Kai maneuvered around the large warship. Kai slowed, and Rasia pulled at the rope cast off from the warship's side. Neema, Azan, and Zephyr slid down from the warship's deck, quickly evacuating onto her smaller windship as they passed.

The warship rammed straight into the dragon flying on their heels. The large battering ram, made from dragon bone, cracked and ripped and splintered. The dragon screeched, clawed, and wrestled the massive warship.

Rasia smiled, triumphant. There are many ways to stop a warship.

Kai brought them back around to survey the damage. The ram had impaled the dragon's ribs, but the dragon had wounded themselves further when they had ripped the warship through their right wing to get free.

Rasia had fought many of the creatures that populated the Desert. She knew their strengths and weaknesses, but to defeat a dragon, all Rasia had were kull stories: *Bad steel will break against a dragon's hide. Have a good kull that you trust at your back. Limit its ability to fly.*

With the dragon now grounded, they accomplished the hardest part, but the fight was far from over.

Rasia, Neema, and Zephyr pelted the dragon with arrows as Kai circled with the windship. Some glanced off scales, but others punctured the tough hide. The head swiveled toward Kai, nostrils flaring, and growling. Blood leaked from one eye, and the right translucent wing had collapsed inward. Aurum roared, and the sound quaked through Rasia's limbs.

"Straight ahead," Rasia ordered, never taking her eyes off the dragon.

Kai, her beautiful brave Kai, never hesitated. He charged full speed ahead. Aurum opened their large maw, out of desperation or instinct, Rasia didn't know. She saw deep down the dragon's throat and could see the bone-spear broken off within. All evidence so far had proven to her that the dragon could no longer breathe fire, but when you're staring down that fathomless abyss, you're never truly certain.

"Behind the shields!" she ordered.

Rasia ducked behind the bone-plate shield that had been tied and looped through the railing. Zephyr erected a shield in front of both him and Kai, who had no immediate defenses as the windeka. The dragon exhaled scalding fumes and choked the air with thick brackish smoke. Rasia left the protective shield and raced into the blinding clouds of ash that burned her eyes and throat. Blindly, but knowing every board of her ship like the back of her hand, she retrieved her pair of khopesh from the open weapons hatch.

A raised talon cut a path through the smoke.

Kai crashed the ship. Intentionally. It fell on its side, slipping forward under the talon. It came to a stop right at the dragon's shoulder.

It was close enough. The others covered her sprint with arrows. With the khopesh in both hands, Rasia raced along the date palm mast, now as horizontal as the rest of the ship. She vaulted off the end and landed atop the wing with a roll. She raced uphill, heart pounding in her ears, and her eyes burning. The closer she came, the more the smog thickened and obscured her vision. She reached the edge of the wing, then the shoulder, and blindly leapt.

Rasia planted her khopesh into the dragon's neck, ripped down the narrow nape, and beheaded it in one fell swoop.

Her leg buckled when she landed. Her chest heaved. Her ribs ached. It burned to breathe. But Rasia felt none of it. The gibbous moon glowed a spotlight on the aftermath. Gold bled white. The wind cheered. The ocean applauded. Forever the stars would be her witness.

Rasia roared in bloody triumph.

CHAPTER SIX

1

The birds frolicked and gossiped in the early morning before sunrise. After almost two blinks of their absence, Nico woke instantly to their tweeting. She peered through the sun-slats of the inner wall: at the garden, the flitting birds, and the blooming chrysanthemums waving her awake. She had missed waking to the smell of herbs and flowers, compared to the parched and cracked shrubbery of the Desert. There was life in the Desert, if you knew where to look, but she missed being enveloped in the lush greenery of home.

Nico returned to her headrest and stared up at the ceiling, at the painted tiled mosaic of a colorful oasis and all the animals peeking at her from the papyrus fronds.

"Good morning, beautiful ibis. Good morning, tenacious camel. Good morning, noble addax," Nico began, greeting every animal on her ceiling in a childish ritual she had done ever since she could remember. At the end of it, she usually extended the greeting to her family. Her magic could sense far better and clearer in the Grankull, but her heart dipped at the hole of Kai's absence. Kenji-ta also wasn't home. Rae was at tajih's place, and Nico had been too tired to inquire why when her hikull pulled into the Grankull last night.

She was all alone.

She finished, lamely, "Good morning, Nicolai."

Then, she got up and started her day. She pulled water from the well to refill the washbin. She washed her face, underarms, and legs in the citrine reflection of the wall-length dragonglass mirror of her bedroom. Ugh. She had stress pimples. Hopefully, they'd fade before the Naming Ceremony where she was expected to show her face to the entire Grankull.

Nico entered the dojo and sat cross-legged atop the woven reed mats. She didn't know what to expect of the bloodrites, but going through her breathing exercises could only help. The Forging had certainly taught her that she needed better control over her magic, which allowed her to shift any liquid. Water was always easiest. Blood was difficult. Poison, apparently, was the hardest.

Traditionally, the bloodrites had always been scheduled for the night of the Hunter's Eye that concluded the Forging. Judging by the moon, she didn't have much time to prepare for a test she didn't know the format or criteria of; a test where failure meant death.

Nico slowed her breathing and sank into her magic, exactly the way her tah once taught her. She listened to her water-swollen cells, the water-song of the underground cistern bellowing below, and the percussion of the dripping irrigation in the wingfields. She listened to the Elder's song, a light plucking melody that reminded her of an ilhan's chords.

Then she jerked from her meditation at the sound of the windchimes, which tugged at the bells throughout the hallways. Tajih must have heard of her late-night arrival. Nico smiled as she rushed through the hallways to greet Rae and her tajih. She had missed them both so much.

Nico threw open the door and opened her arms for a hug. Rae, her little jih, stood next to tajih bouncing in anticipation. Then they blinked, and their expression dropped. Rae looked around Nico's outstretched arms.

"Where's jijih?" Rae demanded.

Nico dropped her arms and felt a little hurt by Rae's indifference.

She explained, "Kai is still on his Forging."

Rae squinted at her, then planted their feet, and Nico could already feel the incoming headache. Then they screamed at the top of their lungs as if that could compel Kai to appear out of thin air.

"Enough!" Nico snapped. She was not in the mood for a screaming tantrum. Gone for only a blink and a half, and the kid lost all sense. "You are too old for this nonsense."

Rae flinched at the volume of Nico's voice and rushed to cling to tajih's leg. Tajih shook them off with an unimpressed huff. "Your jih just got back home from her Forging. Give her a break."

Rae looked at Nico with bottom lip undoubtedly quivering behind the half-shroud. Ugh. She was turning into Ava-ta. Nico crouched and said more gently, "Kai has got some things to do, but he made me promise to come home and make sure you're being good. Have you been good?"

Rae blinked away crocodile tears and nodded.

"Then I know Kai will be home soon."

Nico certainly hoped so. She had been tracking Kai's progress. When she checked last night, he had barely left the Dragon's Coast. She hoped he made it back home in time, but she didn't let any of those concerns show on her face.

Nico beckoned Rae over. They crept from behind tajih's leg, and then rushed forward into Nico's arms. There was that hug she had been waiting for. She squeezed them tight, before hefting an arm under Rae's rump and standing with them settled on her hip.

"Where's Kenji-ta?" Nico asked her tajih. "And why isn't he looking after Rae? Nor did he come to greet me last night when I pulled in."

Tajih winced. "I've been watching after Rae in the evenings. Your tah . . . he's—he's been drinking a lot. Kulani has gone to look for him. He usually does a good job of locating his jih."

"How?" Nico asked, displeased by the news. "We barely have the bone chips for him to be throwing it away on alcohol."

"You know how it is. When you've got names, people feel

compelled to pour you a drink, and then it's one drink too many. Kulani has spoken with the kulls about enabling him, but Kenji-ji can barely walk down a street without someone wanting to hear a story."

"That's no excuse. He's not some new-face fresh from his Forging. He was supposed take care of Rae," Nico said, careful with her words. She didn't want to disparage their tah in front of Rae any more than she had to. "Thanks for looking after them."

"Of course. I hope jipoh is alright?" Tajih questioned, searching for some answer as to why Nico was in the Grankull without Kai.

Nico didn't want to mention the dragon, in case it alarmed Rae. She carefully hedged her words. "Apparently, Kai and Rasia have crossed paths."

"Huh. Interesting. Well, if anything she'll take care of him." Tajih gave Rae a parting kiss on the forehead. "I'm off to work. Make sure you get some rest. The bloodrites are soon."

"Is there anything you can tell me about it?"

"Honestly, I'm the Mythkeeper and I barely know why the ritual succeeds or fails. Whatever happens, it's between the magicborn and the Elder. Just . . . get some rest," Tajih advised, and then she left down the road.

With a sigh, Nico brought Rae into the house. She did some cleaning and prepared breakfast, and she suspected that the alley cat had stashed kittens somewhere in the house. She planned to hunt for them after breakfast, but the windchimes rang out while she and Rae ate at the serving table.

The front door creaked open. Nico stood to her feet at the sight of Kenji-ta hanging off the shoulder of his twin sibling, head clutched in his hands, and obviously suffering from a hangover.

"Jipoh," Anji-taji greeted. He threw off his sibling's arm and Kenji-ta went sprawling across the floor unconscious. Rae giggled. Tajih asked, "How was the Forging?"

"The worst," Nico muttered. She glanced at her unconscious parent with a sigh, "Can you carry him to his bed?"

"He usually sleeps fine on the floor," her tajih said and then paused at her expression. "Okay. Okay."

He picked tah off of the floor that Nico had just dusted. Before dragging his twin down the hallway, tajih said, apologetically, "I know it might not seem like it, but he's trying."

Trying wasn't good enough. Nico should be able to go on her Forging and not have to worry about affairs back home. She had hoped with both her and Kai away from the Grankull, that tah would rise to the occasion and take care of things, but he only seemed to have gotten worse. This wasn't the reception she expected when she returned home.

The windchimes rang again.

Nico checked the front door and found two messengers jostling each other in competition to deliver their letters. She cleared her throat, and they both thrust out their scrolls. The first scroll had the time for her interview, scheduled for this evening, where the Council would pick over her Forging story.

The day before returning to the Grankull, Nico and the others had gone over their story extensively to make sure it passed the Council's inspection. They had cut most of the end, which meant she would likely sacrifice most of her earned names, but names had never truly mattered to her.

Nico's face dropped at the contents of the second scroll. The end of the Forging usually coincided with First Harvest, the harvest of the cold season crops. Usually, children returned from their Forging were exempt from work until the Naming Ceremony, but no one was prepared for last night's large gonda haul. It was a race against time to preserve the meat. With the sudden influx of food, the Grankull had drafted everyone from school children to the elderly to help, including Nico.

Nico turned to Rae, who peaked their head through the shroud room. Kenji-ta was in no shape to look after them. "Looks like you're coming with me to the wingfields."

With a shout of glee, Rae rushed to grab their sandals and their shroud. Nico rolled her eyes. "Oh, now you're excited."

Nico wiped sweat from her forehead as she stood ankle-deep in the fertile soils of the wingfields. Water dripped from the engineered wings overhead. The drip-rains were a specific sort of song that imprinted on Nico's bones ever since she first apprenticed to the Grankull's leading botanist, sounding like a ballad that never ended.

The wings, covered by dragon leather, protected the fields against extreme conditions—whether from the cold, heat, or duststorms—and tucked them in a warm humid embrace. A dragon's wings were often three times the size of their body, and from where she stood, she couldn't see the end of the fields beyond the swaying wheat and sorghum.

The reapers cut down ripe ears of corn with a swish. Nico walked behind them, alongside many others to gather the fallen crop. The children made a game of collecting the most ears, and Rae took to the task with much seriousness. Usually, Nico would be working under her Han, learning how to organize and manage large numbers of people for such massive operations, but since she had Rae with her, she didn't hesitate to roll up her caftan and get dirty in the fields with everyone else.

Most Ohans usually took up some sort of management role in the Grankull. With Nico's magic, working the wingfields made sense as she was able to easily move water around in a hurry, if need be, but she was also grateful that she adored the job. She liked rubbing elbows with other people and contributing to the chatter, gossip, and laughter. She liked the jaunty work-songs, the smell of fresh vegetables, and the dirt and sweat of hard-work.

"Nicolai."

She turned and spotted her supervising Han, Dulcae Wingroot, approaching with a belly as round as the ripe melons. Han's pregnant belly had become so much bigger since Nico left for the Forging. She glanced over at Rae, and one of the workers in charge of watching two other rambunctious youngsters, nodded at her.

She gave her thanks and quickly jogged over to Dulcae Han. Her Han rubbed a hand against her chest, and said, "I'm not feeling well."

"What's wrong? Is the baby okay?" Nico asked.

"It's just heartburn, I think. I talked to one of the healers and she suggested I go home and rest. Says I shouldn't have been out here anyway but," she shrugged. "We need all the hands we can get. From what I heard, they're still working on all that gonda you brought in, but that doesn't change the fact that we need to get all this harvested and the next rotation of crops planted before the floods hit. You might need to oversee the maize fields."

"But . . ." Nico said, shocked. "I'm not an adult yet."

"No choice. No one else is trained for this." Han said softer, "I'm sorry. It seems you've always been thrust into adult spaces too soon."

"No, that's fine. You need the rest," Nico said. It was her Han's first child, and she wanted to do her part to make sure it was a healthy birth. A couple might only be approved for one or two births in their lifetime. Every pregnancy was a special occasion.

Han placed both hands on her lower back and stretched. She looked out at the fields and shook her head at the amount of work still left to do. "I don't think I'm running again for the Council next season."

That worried Nico, but she tried not to let it show. She didn't know who she could trust on the Council, but at the very least, she trusted her Han wouldn't knowingly bring her harm. The absence of her support could mean even more opposition against Nico in the future.

"I just . . . I can't do both anymore, and I want to have time for the baby."

"I understand. I've got things from here," Nico said, determined. She'd figure something out regarding the Council. She'd manage the maize fields and meet the quota. Even though she was tired, she always managed to scrape up the strength from somewhere. She promised, "I won't let you down."

Her Han smiled.

"You never do."

⁒

Nico didn't finish the day's harvest quota until later that evening. With Rae on her back, she raced across the Grankull to the Heart Temple. She practically threw Rae into tajih's office and bounded into the interview room with barely a vibration to spare.

The interviewer, the Neck Councilor and Suri's tah, grilled Nico endlessly about her Forging. Every sentence she recited had been inspected and picked over. Her head hurt by the end of it. Finally, she trudged home with Rae dragging behind her.

Nico entered the darkness of their house, helped Rae take off their sandals and shroud, and began lighting the oil lamps in the serving room. She checked the kitchen and froze at the emptiness of it.

"I'm hungry," Rae said, echoing the same grumbling thoughts as Nico's stomach.

"I'll fix something," she said. She looked for today's rations. She frowned as she searched the empty shelves and cabinets. Did Kenji-ta not pick up their rations today? She sensed for him and found him . . . still in bed.

Nico's chest heated. She stormed through the hallways before she could stop herself. He lay there on the bed in the same place his jih had deposited him that morning. In a fury, she sent a wave of water atop his head and completely drenched him, the bed, and the floor.

Tah shot up and reached for his sword—who knew where that was. After grabbing futilely at empty air, he paused and blinked at her through the darkness of the room. "Caterpillar? When did you get back home?"

"Last night!" Nico snapped. "I've been back for an entire day. Have you truly done nothing but sleep? Did you not answer the work summons? Did you not pick up rations for the day? Did you not cook dinner at all?!"

"Nico," tah said, sitting up. He looked like a bedraggled bedsheet caught in the rain. "I'm sorry. I tried to get up."

"No! I don't want to hear it. Watch Rae while I grab our rations." At this time of night, the line would be snaking down the Neck. Nico turned on her heel and marched out of the house.

One thing at a time. One thing at a time.

As expected, the ration line extended all the way down the vertebra steps and Nico was disheartened staring uphill at the base of it. She was exhausted by the time she stumbled home later that night with their rations in hand. She mechanically pulled everything from the ration pack that could be eaten raw to forego the time it took to start a fire or heat the oven.

They finally increased everyone's rations. That, at least, was a relief.

Nico dropped the plates onto the serving table where Kenji-ta sat apologetically with Rae in his lap. Judging from the smell, Rae was fresh from a bath, but Kenji's meager effort barely soothed her bad mood.

She had chopped and mixed lettuce, radishes, and corn into a salad and drizzled on top a sauce of vinegar and grapes. It was simple and quick, and the fresh vegetables crunched between her teeth.

"The bloodrites are soon."

"I'm aware," she said with a flat crunch.

Tah said so softly, and she had been so unfocused she almost missed the words, "What if I lose you too?"

"Ava-ta trained me well. I do not fear it," Nico said, lying. She was terrified, but she refused to show it lest it worried him further. At that moment, it occurred to her that her tah was also terrified, but fear was no excuse not to take care of your family.

Kenji looked down at Rae in his lap and cradled his hand over their hair. "To think you can raise a child for fifteen years only to have them taken away from you—by the bloodrites or the Forging—doesn't matter, all parents prepare themselves for the pyres. I survived the death of my kulani, but I don't know . . . I don't know if I'd be able to prepare yours. I couldn't live in a world without you, caterpillar."

"You've been drinking," Nico said. She didn't like this conversation. It terrified her for reasons she couldn't put into words. She was used to Kenji-ta's silence and his melancholy, especially after Ava-ta died, but this was something else. If something should happen to her, she feared tah would never get out of bed again.

She couldn't afford to fail the bloodrites. It wasn't an option. Nor was there an option to delay it. The Grankull had been without an Ohan, a conduit for the Elder's magic, for two years.

"Put Rae to bed, please?" she asked and finished her dinner.

Nico returned to the training room to resume her breathing exercises. She had barely sunk into her magic, before snapping to her feet and grabbing one of the spears from the wall. The tip of the polearm had dulled because no one had been keeping the weapons sharp. Ava-ta would be aghast. Nico marched through the halls and up the ladder to the rooftop terrace.

She readied the spear as a dark figure landed lightly between the pottery. Although dulled, the spear point greeted the intruder. The figure stumbled back to the edge of the roof, a push away from being shoved off the roof entirely.

"Fuck. Guess I am a terrible assassin."

Nico pulled back and reprimanded herself for not slowing down to determine if she recognized the intruder's water signature. To be fair, normal people used the door. Kelin straightened and checked to make sure she hadn't ripped any of his clothing.

"What are you doing here?" she asked. "You're not allowed into the Grankull until the Naming Ceremony."

"I figured it was worth the risk. Didn't think I'd get thrown off the roof for the effort." Nico didn't know what face she was wearing, but Kelin quickly ended his joking. "I came to warn you. The Flock received an anonymous "suggestion" to assassinate you during the bloodrites. I'm sure other factions have received the same. Thought you should know."

She stared at Kelin, absorbing the news. An overwhelming pressure, one that had been building at every bad turn of the day and unable to bear any more weight, finally exploded. Nico burst into tears.

At that moment, she never missed Kai more. If he had been here, there would have been someone to greet her on the doorstep after a long day of work. If he had been here, Rae wouldn't have had to be dragged around on all of Nico's errands to end the day tired, hungry, and cranky. If he had been here, she'd have someone to rant to about Kenji-ta and express her growing concerns that something was really, really wrong with him, a type of wrong Nico couldn't blame on Ava-ta's death anymore. If only he were here, then when she received the news that the Grankull was trying everything in its power to keep her from succeeding an already nigh impossible task, it wouldn't hurt so damn hard.

But Kai wasn't here. And she was on her own.

"You're crying?" Kelin said, alarmed. He stood there, utterly useless and as awkward as a kid taking off their shroud for the first time in public. "You don't really do that. Usually, it's other people crying around you."

"It's been a long day," she sniffed.

"Do . . . you, um, need a hug?"

"I doubt you'd know how one works." Kelin proved her right as he stepped forward a foot at a time, and then wrapped his arms straight around her. His hilarious awkwardness, more than anything, made her feel better. Nico was often the shoulder people leaned on, often the lap people cried on, and often the hug when people needed one. But sometimes, even Nico, needed someone to hug her.

She considered the promise she had made to Kai—she had promised to take care of things back home so he could finally do something for himself without guilt or worry. After all these years, she owed that to him. If Nico had learned anything from today, it was that once the Forging ended, that ride was over and all the problems you left behind were still here waiting for you.

Kai should enjoy his peace.

Nico wiped at her face and straightened out of Kelin's rigid arms. It didn't matter how exhausted she was. It didn't matter how terrified she became. It didn't matter how stressed or overwhelmed she felt. She mustered the stubborn strength to keep going because she didn't really know how to do anything else.

Nico faced Kelin and said, "I think it's time I met your tahs."

CHAPTER SEVEN

Rasia had little time to soak in her hard-earned victory. The moment the battle fever left her, she wasted no time instructing everyone on how to butcher a dragon. The dragon's bulk created too much drag, so they wrapped it in a package of its own wings to glide smoothly atop the sand. They had the dragon hitched to the warship by sunrise, then they unbolted the damaged ram and left that dead weight behind.

Ever since they left the Dragon's Coast, they'd been rowing their arms out. Rasia rested for three days, primarily because at one point she had collapsed in exhaustion, and then she took shifts with everyone else. She didn't care if she broke another rib. The dragon didn't matter if they didn't make it back home in time. Despite days of the same grueling pace, no one complained.

But as the moon grew full and the days ticked down, the truth became harder to ignore.

Rasia threw her calculations against the wall of the Han quarters, hoping she had missed something the first, second, or third time she did the math. (Different answers every time because math wasn't her strong suit, but did every answer have to be so wildly off the mark?) She stormed out of the quarters and snapped at the kull to finish their break and get back to the oars. She ascended the steps to where Kai guided the warship through too gentle winds. She glanced down as the others stretched and shook out their arms, preparing for yet another relentless drive that wouldn't be enough.

"We're not going to make it, are we?" Kai asked. Rasia wasn't surprised he had figured it out. He had a windeka's sense in his bones and was better at math with enviably precise calculations.

"No, we're not. We were on schedule, but the dawnward winds have come early this season. With the dragon's weight and the shift in wind, we'll miss the deadline by two days. Or three. Either way, it's not looking good. We were so close, Kai. *So close.*" Rasia tightened her hands on the railing. "I have to tell them. That's my responsibility, right? I'm the Han. I've failed them . . . I just . . . I was hoping I was wrong. But I know I'm not."

Kai kept his face toward the horizon, continuing to steer as he nonchalantly mentioned, "What if I told you I could get us back home before the end of the deadline?"

Rasia raised both brows and turned to scrutinize him. He combed back the hair that the wind had blown into his face. "What are you talking about?" she asked.

"I can control my magic."

She jerked away from the railing and straightened to stare at him. She tried to remember all the past instances of Kai's magic. They had been accidents, hadn't they?

"When? How? Why haven't you said anything before?"

"Since the Yestermorrow Lake," he admitted. *What the fuck?* This whole time and Rasia hadn't noticed? Kai glanced at her out of the corner of his eye and shrugged. "If everyone knew, I feared they would pressure me to use it against the dragon. If I used my magic against the dragon in any type of way, I knew you would regret it. You would always wonder if we could have succeeded without it. It would have agonized you. When people asked, I wanted to be able to say that *we* did it—no shortcuts, no cheats—that we did it on our own." A small smile lifted at the corner of his lips when he finally faced her. "We did it, Rasia."

Those four words swept her off her feet and flipped her world around. She fell into the sky, and she wholly and unequivocally embraced the descent. She leapt into his arms. He caught her solidly, no wobble, and she kissed him to soften the landing. She laughed, breathlessly, buzzing helplessly with giddy excitement. She floated on his faith in her, and she never wanted to walk the ground again.

"Kulani," Rasia branded the word to his lips. "*Kulani.*"

Many people committed years to each other before ever daring to use the word. She didn't need years. At that moment, she knew. He could have chosen the easier path. So many people would have done so if given the option. But he chose *her* path. He faced down a dragon with her, and they did it on their own.

A throat cleared insistently above them.

Kai and Rasia reluctantly pulled apart enough to glare at Zephyr, who crossed his arms and asked, "Are we leaving or not?"

"Why do you got to stop them?" Azan complained, from where he sat on the oar bench watching the show. "That was hot."

Rasia returned to her feet, weak-kneed, having yet to get her ground legs back. Kai turned to Zephyr and explained, "I think I can use my magic to get us home."

"Then what are you waiting for?" Zephyr asked.

Kai glanced at Rasia, uncertain. "Is it okay with you?"

She understood what he was really asking. How much magic was she willing to use to finish her Forging? "Fuck that. If it weren't for the Council and their stupid hit on Nico, we would have made it back with plenty of time. Let's go."

"I've never tried something this big before, but just in case, you should hold onto something," Kai advised.

He moved to the space in front of the wheel and gripped the half-wall in concentration. Rasia considered Kai's advice and cheekily locked her arms about his waist. Zephyr repeated the order to the others.

"Let's finish our Forging," she encouraged.

Kai nodded. Under her arms, she felt him take a deep breath. His skin warmed under her hands. His gold eyes glowed brighter.

A deep grumpy bass rumbled through Rasia's ears.

The entire Desert woke up, as if it had been sleeping for thousands of years, and only now it had reason to stretch itself awake. The sand dunes undulated like ocean waves, and then a tsunami of sand roared from behind and launched the entire warship and its dragon load into the air.

As if the very Desert carried the warship in the palm of its hand, they sped forward when the Desert stretched its arm across the sky. They flew over the Graveyard, joined formations of birds over the Lake of Yestermorrow, followed herds of ibex leaping across the gorge, skipped over nesting skinkos, and swayed past the oasis. The Grankull rose out of the sand in the distance.

"*Stop!*" Rasia called out.

They stopped, suspended briefly, before the Desert begrudgingly placed them back onto the ground. They landed light as a feather without nary a jostle. Then the Desert shifted, turned over a blanket of sand, and went back to sleep as if nothing had ever disturbed it.

They all stared in awe. Zephyr's jaw seemed to have come unhinged. Neema placed a hand before her face, and Azan laughed breathlessly. It took a moment, even for Rasia, to gather herself. The sand had come alive in the shape of Kai's hand and had ferried them across the Desert in the space of a drum. She had no words. She had witnessed a god walk.

"Why did we stop?" Kai asked, confused. "I could have gotten us closer without anyone seeing."

Rasia cracked open stiff fingers from around his waist. She leaned against the steer and pressed a hand to her racing heart. This was how she felt when her tah first brought her to the Dragon's Coast, or when she climbed to the tallest peak of the Desert to claim the top of the world, or when she experienced the eye of a sandstorm for the first time. She felt this overwhelming sense of awe that only nature in all its grandiosity could invoke.

"Rasia?" Kai asked, uncertain.

"That—" Rasia stuttered. "*That* was awesome!"

Kai soon had his arms full of Rasia. He didn't hesitate to pull her closer and then whisked them away atop a breeze of wind to the Han's quarters. Rasia blinked and looked at their sudden change in surroundings. To her perception, they were just standing at the steer, but in actuality Kai had teleported them off the deck with his magic.

Her eyes narrowed, calculating, "Why didn't you do that to the warship?"

"I wanted to impress you."

Rasia laughed, and Kai's magic whipped around them, tousling things off the shelves, and upturning wicker baskets. He had held it in for so long. It felt good to finally breathe all the magic to the surface, and Rasia stood unafraid at the center of the calm, with all the world raging around them. Utterly fearless. Kai swept her onto the bed, planting kisses. They'd been hustling so fast across the Desert, neither really have allowed themselves to feel the triumph of their victory over the dragon. But Kai felt it now, mixed with the thrill of his magic and the exultation of 'kulani' on Rasia's lips.

With a flick of his hand, the strings of her pants came undone. Another flick, and her pants were swept clean off. He wrapped her legs around his head and dove into her wet heat. Her fingers clawed at his scalp.

"*Kulani.*"

The word vibrated through his chest. He couldn't say it. Kai had this lock on his throat, this deep-seated fear that if he said the word aloud, the world would come tumbling down around him. For now, he kept the word in the joints of his bones where it would be safe. He hoped to show her, instead, everything that he felt. He hoped to fold them into one weave, subsist off nothing but her fire and sex, and suck out her soul.

Kulani. His soulmate. *His*.

She tensed, tighter and tighter, till finally shuddering and melting into a puddle of soft limbs. He withdrew and reached down between them. Rasia joined his fingers, stroking to finish him off, together. Kai didn't resist as both his climax and magic punched out of him. The walls shook. Distant shouts raised alarms. The warship floated back to the ground.

Kai wiped his hands at the edge of the bed, and they collapsed, breathing. They both wallowed in the release. It felt a lifetime since they've had sex.

Then he remembered why.

"We broke the 'no-sex' rule," Kai mumbled out, embarrassed, and covered his face with his forearm. They were supposed to have waited until after the Naming Ceremony. It was not that he didn't understand Nico's alarm for his recent lack of self-control. It alarmed him too, sometimes. Even though he knew their recent tryst had no chance of seeding her, certain dangers still existed. What if he bruised her and made a suspicious mark on her thigh? The Grankull might find out, and it could be all over for the both of them.

Rasia grinned cheekily. "We gave an admirable effort."

Kai playfully pushed her, and she laughed. He liked it when she laughed on top of him, when he could feel her joy in his chest.

"You're right," she said, and punctuated the laugh with a sigh. "It's about more than seeding now. One stray mark and we could be in trouble. We've got to be more careful, especially now we're so close to home. But fuck, I needed that. I can't wait when we don't have to worry about this shit. When I'm officially on gonom, and we don't have to hold back, and I can write my fucking name on your skin."

Kai couldn't wait for that day either. Now that they had slayed the dragon, that day wouldn't be too far from dawning. He could almost reach out and touch it with his fingertips.

"Why did we stop?" he asked.

"No point in being back before we've got to be. Once we

return to the Grankull, we go back to the shrouds and the caftans and the no touching until the Naming Ceremony. Now, we've got three whole days before the deadline. We've got time to enjoy ourselves."

"We've already enjoyed ourselves too much."

Rasia laughed and kissed up his neck. Then she lifted on her elbow and eyed him, expectantly. "Magic. Explain."

Of course, she wouldn't let him get away without an explanation. He pressed his hands to his face and breathed in a deep sigh. "You were right."

"I am always right. But what exactly am I right about?"

"Kenji Ilhani was not the first vision the Yestermorrow Lake showed to me. I wanted answers too. I wanted to know the truth about my magic. I wanted to know why I am the way I am, and why neither healer nor historian could figure out what was wrong with me. Then the Lake gave me the answers I wanted, and I didn't believe them. Not even afterward. Only when I became desperate and didn't have any other choice."

"What did you see?" she asked.

"I was born a twin. I had a twin that didn't survive the childbirth, but their magic didn't die with them. It passed to me. The reason my magic has never been right isn't because it's broken, it's because I have too much of it." Kai released a self-deprecating laugh. "I thought it was horseshit. How did I know if what the waters showed me was true or if they were just answers I desperately wanted?"

"Your tah is a twin," she said, connecting the dots far faster than he had been willing to. "Your cousins are twins. It makes sense. You've said before that you've been unable to feel your magic, but when you think about it—you take a gourd and fill it half-way, you hear the water sloshing around. But fill it up full, you can't hear anything because it's so near to bursting. There's no space to move. Shake it up enough and water starts leaking from the top. That's why your magic did all those random things. You were leaking."

Kai nodded slowly. He had come to the same conclusion,

eventually. He turned over on his good shoulder to face her. "I have two elements—both wind and sand. *Two*. That's unprecedented. There has never been an Ohan in the history of the Grankull with two. That would mean . . ."

Rasia leaned forward. "Say it."

He looked at her, eyes wide and scared of the implications. "That would make me the most powerful magicborn to have ever lived."

She smirked, smug and immensely pleased. "Of course, you are. You are my kulani."

He snorted at her. "Your ego knows no bounds." Then he said more seriously, softer. "I don't feel powerful."

One by one, Rasia locked her fingers with his. He didn't pull away, and they both stared at their interlocked grip. His hands were long and corded with a strength that hadn't existed a blink ago. He had gone from malnourished bones and skin to a lean youth with a pebble of muscle from rowing the warship oars.

"You look healthier than you were before," she said.

"I was sickly because a human body is not supposed to hold so much magic. You were right. Out of everyone in the Grankull, you were right. I needed to *eat*. Magic requires energy to function and without a sufficient amount of food, it fed off off me instead. I need to eat five times more than the average person."

Rasia's eyes widened at that number. "How powerful are you?"

Kai could make the Desert walk, and it hadn't exhausted or chilled him as magic does to Nico when she performed huge displays of it. It frightened him that he couldn't imagine the borders of its potential. His eyes opened wide and round as he answered, "Powerful."

"Shit." Rasia laid back and clicked her tongue, thoughtfully. "Wait until the Grankull hears of this."

"No. They can't know. No one can know. We have to tell the others not to say anything about my magic."

"What? Why not?"

"I'm not going to eat five rations more than everyone else. It's different out here where we've had plenty of food, but the

Grankull can barely sustain more than a ration pack. I'm no different than that baby dragon, except I understand better. I can't starve out the Grankull."

"But you're my kulani. I'm not going to let you starve. We can hunt outside of the Grankull and smuggle in what we need. And when you try out for the kulls and become windeka, you'll be out in the Desert again and you can eat as much as you want. You are the most powerful magic-born to have ever lived. Don't you want to know what you're capable of? Experience your full potential?"

"I don't think the Grankull could ever support my full potential," he said, honestly. "Sometimes it's okay not to always be everything. I'm okay if this is all the magic I'll ever be able to do."

"But—but—how could you live like that?" Rasia sputtered as she sat up. "Why would you ever want to live . . ." She scrunched her face. "Less than? You shouldn't have to limit yourself because of the Grankull's stupid rules. You deserve to live every bit as amazing and as brilliant as the person you are. Don't dim your light because you're too bright for people to look at. Fuck that."

"Rasia," Kai soothed as he stroked his hand down her arm. "I've slayed a dragon without my magic. *I don't need it.*"

"What about the other part?" she snapped. "What about the part where your magic feeds off you? You also need food to keep you healthy."

The thought had crossed Kai's mind, but he had thought it a small sacrifice. He never wanted to be so bright that he inadvertently blinded people. "It doesn't matter."

"Fuck you." Cross-legged, Rasia slapped her knees. "The way I see it, there are two issues here. You don't want to be defined by your magic. I get that. If it's not you, it's not you. Regardless, it affects your health as well. Despite your guilt, you need to eat. We can keep your magic a secret if you want, but you allow me to do whatever I've got to do to keep you fed."

"I can't possibly ask that of you." He crushed his hands to his face. "I don't want to be a burden to you."

"Lani," Rasia said, and Kai's heart tightened at the endearment.

She tugged his hands away from his eyes. "You are not a burden. You are my kulani. You are my ride-or-die. Anyone who fucks with you, fucks with me. It's you and me, always."

The bones Kai threw all those nights ago sailing away from the oasis have finally landed. They've clicked into place. *This was real.* It was not a dream he had stuffed down and hidden away. It was not an illusion of the Yestermorrow Lake.

His soulmatch was a star of boundless laughter and twinkling mischief. She was sharp edges that melted in his hands. She was the wild gust under his wings. She was the Han to his windeka, and they sailed worlds together.

Kulani. A kull of two.

CHAPTER EIGHT

1

"Are you sure you shouldn't warn them that I'm coming? It seems like a bad idea to come unannounced," Nico asked Kelin. They passed through the outer ring of Flock territory, known as the business sector, where feathered veils entreated customers. Kelin waved a dismissive hand over his shoulder that didn't make Nico feel better at all.

Many of the Grankull thought the Flock was a group of whores who sold themselves out in the Tents, but in actuality, the Flock managed a sophisticated business empire that dominated a chunk of the Tent's economy.

Kelin had taken off his shroud when they reached the large maze of interconnected tents that populated the heart of Flock territory. Walking the tent maze was like walking the back alleys of the Grankull, but one made of gonda leather walls, scorpion carapace ceilings, reed fringe doorways, and colorful rug walkways. Nico marveled at the world inside of a world inside of a world.

What surprised Nico the most were the intimate scenes she passed: gossiping siblings doing each other's hair, parents rocking newborns to sleep, children causing havoc racing through tents, and elders stitching a dress of feathers while they spun old memories into tales. Several people paused upon seeing Kelin and greeted him with hugs and warm kisses to the forehead, revealing

Kelin's physical awkwardness to be more of a personality trait. Everyone knowingly teased him, and he took it all in stride. Somehow, he had acquired a budchild on his hip, who blinked sleepily at Nico before falling asleep in the crook of Kelin's neck.

She had been wrong. The Flock might have been a business, but it was a family too.

"Why haven't you been home?" Nico asked. Judging by his family's surprised reactions, this was the first time they had seen him since the Forging.

The toddler in his grip jostled when Kelin shrugged a sharp shoulder. "I failed. I might have done the right thing, but I've never failed before. I don't know. I guess I didn't know how to face their disappointment. Most here are insulated from Grankull gossip, but the tahs knew you were still alive the moment we checked in at the gate last night. And now I'm bringing you right to them," he laughed. "At least one or two will appreciate the irony."

"How did you know about the bloodrites, then?"

"This is my territory. I know everything." Nico raised her eyebrow, unconvinced. Tent territories were often very segregated. She further placed her hands on her hips, then his lips cracked into a weak smirk. "You can never allow me to be mysterious, can you? My ex told me. He's in Vulture territory."

"So that's where you've been hiding?"

"Hey. I survived dragons, scavengers, and gonda. I deserved some dick."

"That is all you did during the Forging!"

"*What*???" Kelin blinked, wide-eyed and a poor parody of innocence.

Nico glared at him like some imposing elder sibling, and they stared at each other. Then they both simultaneously broke into laughter. She couldn't tell herself why. It was all just ridiculous in that moment, and she clutched at the levity. A sibling came walking between them and looked at Nico and Kelin as if they had smoked a whole waterpipe. They smartly decided to take the sleeping budchild off Kelin's hands.

Nico wiped the tears from her eyes and straightened. She had an important meeting with Kelin's tahs, and she needed to be prepared. He offered his elbow. She smiled and looped her arm through his. They faced the door together—a door made entirely from a curtain of heron feathers. Kelin hadn't provided much information about the room where most of the tahs gathered. She had so many wild expectations going in. She imagined a room of business that calculated numbers and profits like the library study of Nico's home, or a room of politics where one decision single-handedly decided the fate of the Tents like the veranda where her mother received visitors, but when Nico stepped inside, the expansive room reminded her of the comforting familiarity of the lounging room, filled with family enjoying each other's company.

The leaders of the Flock sat eating bread, drinking beer, smoking waterpipes, and discussing day-to-day events at a volume Nico only experienced when the extended family got together on the holidays. Someone plucked a cheery tune on an ilhan to provide background noise for the boisterous conversations. She identified persons of all sexes, some scarred and some with hands as soft as silk, some wore basic linen and others the current fashions of the Grankull, and some were the most stunning persons Nico had ever seen and others humbly plain and non-descript.

"Kelin-po!" Someone shouted.

Nico blinked and Kelin was gone. A flurry of motion immediately ensued. The closest set of arms grabbed him, kissed him on the forehead, and then he was summarily rotated around the room. Some of the greetings were perfunctory, but many were warm, and several crushed Kelin in excited arms. He endured it all with mild resignation.

"Who is your guest?" Someone asked. Nico had waited patiently for an introduction. "Not exactly your type, eh?" Several laughs went up throughout the room. "Take your shroud off child. Didn't poh tell you? There are no shrouds worn here."

Of course, Kelin had not told her. She swore that he enjoyed throwing her into situations uninformed because he found her reactions amusing. Not wanting to be rude, she unwrapped the shroud.

She hadn't expected the silence that followed. They recognized her, but Nico had no idea how they all knew her face. She had always entered the Tents shrouded, even when she walked the relative safety of Zara-shi's territory.

Kelin finally escaped the round of familial greetings. He stood at her side, sweaty and nervous. He hadn't anticipated their recognition either, and it worried him. He said with a gulp, "She is my friend."

Finally, someone laughed, and their laughter jostled their necklace of heron feathers and stone beads. A few others followed, but most scrutinized Nico with an intensity she hadn't felt since Ava-ta was alive.

"You know my face?" Nico asked.

"Child, you have been here before," the one who had first laughed explained. "Your tah brought you to us when you were a budchild. You've run through these tents before."

Kelin spluttered out a laugh at the sheer irony. It was common knowledge that Kenji-ta had learned to play the ilhan from tent whores, but that could have meant anything. The Grankull often didn't understand that knowing tent whores and knowing the Flock were two very different things, nor had Kenji-ta ever elaborated on the legend. Whenever Kenji-ta had brought her into the Tents, it had been to Scorpion territory to visit Raiment and Zara-shi.

"She is supposed to be dead," someone else commented. "And you, Kelin-po, should have reported to us the moment you returned home."

The room grew solemn. An elder with feathers braided into their hair patted the sitting mats beside them. "Come. Sit, Kelin-po. It seems you have a story to tell."

Nico politely folded to her knees beside Kelin. Several in the room adjusted their seats until a circle of listeners had formed. Now, it was business.

Kelin started from the beginning but left some parts out. Most notably, he hadn't told them about Azan. When he finished, feather-necklace said, "You have done well. We did not have all the information, and you have protected the Flock. The purge is a threat to us all."

"It is good to hear that the child has so much of Kenji Ilhani in her. He has done a good job in raising her," someone else said.

Nico thought of her tah in his day-old clothes that smelled of stale alcohol. She bit her tongue on her immediate response. Instead, she carefully curated her question, and then realized she didn't know anyone's names. Kelin had failed to make those introductions. A Grankull conversation always began with naming introductions, but the Tents sometimes forwent them completely. Still, this was a business meeting. They knew her name, and it was only fair that she knew theirs if she was to be acknowledged as an equal.

"I'm sorry," Nico spoke up. "I didn't catch your names."

"They are all named Heron," Kelin said, with an amused sharp glint in his eye.

Nico looked at all twenty-six of them in shock. She had never met anyone who shared a name.

"Thank you, Heron," she said, quickly adjusting to the concept. Heron was many, and Heron was one. "Now that you have more information regarding the Council's machinations, are you agreeable to calling off your assassins from the bloodrites?"

Heron began to argue with themselves.

Nico was tempted to interject, but Kelin shook his head. Let this play out, his expression suggested, and give the many voices time to become one. Although, they all were fiercely protective of this bubble of safety that they have carved for themselves, they disagreed on the how, and it took time for them to make a decision.

"The vote to send an assassin after her during the Forging was not unanimous. There are debts we owe her tah."

"We did what we had to do."

"This is getting messy."

"I say we stay out of it."

"Let's not forget the debts that need to be settled with the names of her other bloodline. They have oppressed us for generations. Her granta led the last purge. Why should we care about her life? We are owed blood prices."

"The price on her head is immense and has only grown since the Forging. Regardless of whom owe what debts, we could use that money. We need to protect our own."

Nico remained silent and tempered her reactions throughout the discussion. These people have experienced much harm, at times caused by her own ancestors. She didn't blame them for not trusting her or acting in their own self-interests.

"Obviously, the child has evaded a few assassins already. Would it be worth trying to kill her compared to those we could lose?" Heron turned to Kelin. "Could you kill her?"

Kelin looked at Nico with serious consideration. "If I caught her off-guard maybe."

Nico deflated. She had hoped that once the Flock knew the truth, they would take her side. But of course, it could never be that easy. Despite her growing anxiety, she sensed that it still wasn't her time to speak up. She didn't know if they would ever give her a chance to participate in the conversation but worried any interjection would be unwelcomed. She didn't want to give them further reasons not to help her. Luckily, she had someone within the community to advocate on her behalf.

"Perhaps I can make a suggestion," Kelin offered. "She is interested in hiring our services for that night of the bloodrites." He looked at her, and Nico nodded slowly even though she had no idea what he was talking about. She didn't have the money to hire Flock assassins, but she trusted him to know the room better than she did. "The dragonscale I mentioned that she hid out in the Desert? She is willing to give us that location to pay for her protection. Of course, she can't possibly give us the location of it if she's dead."

"Yes," Nico caught on, and confirmed her agreement, "I'll be more than willing to give you the scale's location after I have survived the bloodrites, with your help, of course."

"And she is telling the truth?" Heron asked. "Have you seen this dragonscale, Kelin-po?"

"I have. She's good for it."

Heron looked around the room, at each other. "This is good. We'll settle the debt with her tah, ensure the protection of the Tents, and we'll get paid for our services."

Heron nodded as one.

÷

"You didn't have to do that," Nico said as they walked towards the border. "That wasn't what I had intended the dragonscale for. It was supposed to be a gift."

"This is the Tents," Kelin shrugged. "Nothing is free."

"You could have let me know the plan."

"And miss the look on your face?" he smirked. "Besides, I came up with it on the spot."

"Liar. You at least had the idea of it when you recited your Forging story. I wondered why you had skipped over the location of the scale but figured you were going to mention it later. I didn't want to buy them. I wanted to gain their trust."

"Gaining Heron's trust is hard."

"I have certainly learned that." She sighed. Guess she should start somewhere. If she survived the bloodrites and delivered the scale, at least they would know they could trust her word. She had to make sure she differentiated herself from the two very different views they had of her parents.

"Just don't forget your promises," he advised.

"I won't," Nico promised.

She followed curiously when Kelin led her away from the border checkpoints. He lifted one of the vertebra plates at the bottom of the Tail. Ah. A smuggler's tunnel. Nico crouched down and crawled under the bone to the other side.

The Elder's tail circled to form an immense stage the Grankull used for celebrations. They paused for a moment to take in the hunched mountainous figure of the Elder.

"Do you mind if I ask you something?" Nico asked. "You don't have to answer, but why are you so uncomfortable with touch?" It took a while for many of the Grankull to become accustomed to public touching once the shrouds came off, but she had never seen such an aversion with one's own family.

Kelin pushed up and sat down on one of the vertebra plates. Nico joined him. "I think," he said slowly. "It was something I had developed when I was an orphan. The Flock didn't adopt me until I was nine-till, or so we think; I don't really know how old I am. A few have been trying to break me of the aversion ever since."

"Please let me know if anything I do makes you uncomfortable."

Kelin tilted his head and smirked. "You're the second kuller to have told me that."

"Azan?" she asked, taking an educated guess.

"Being with my ex really drove home how achingly sweet that kid is," Kelin sighed, and did that soft sigh sound a little like heartbreak? "But he's a kuller."

"Look who has a flame now," Nico teased. Kelin snorted but didn't disagree with her. He didn't seem to want to elaborate so she changed the subject. He could be prickly about things until he was ready to talk about them. "So . . . you think can kill me?"

He laughed. "I said *maybe*."

She swung her legs over the boneplate. Despite all of Kelin's playful machinations of the truth, she trusted him. She couldn't say the same for many others of the Grankull.

"I'm scared," Nico confessed out loud for the first time.

"Good to know you're human. You are the crazy person that regularly steps in front of dragonfire."

She chuckled at that. She had never considered that worthy of appreciation. "Even so, *thank you*. Tonight meant a lot to me. I like to fool myself that I can do it all because I don't have the choice not to, but I'm only one person against the entire Grankull. I can't do this on my own. Thank you, Kelin-kull."

Kelin sucked in a harsh breath, and Nico wondered if she had mis-stepped. In the Grankull, using the address was the ultimate seal of friendship, but the Tents were so distrusting that they rarely used it. Ideologically, they rejected the idea of belonging to any kull. She had meant it sincerely but had forgotten all the complicated Tent implications.

Kelin nodded and looked away. He wiped at his eyes, and grumbled, "Don't call me that in front of my tahs. They might make fun of me."

Nico smiled and placed a gentle hand on his knee. She said, more formally, "You may call me Nico-kull."

CHAPTER NINE

The warship deck smelled of scorpion jerky, cooked gonda, kebabs of skinkos, grilled sandsnake, and anything else Rasia could empty out of the warship's stores. All day, she conscripted the kull's help to prepare a feast for their last night of the Forging. They rolled out barrels of scavenger moonshine and decorated the warship with flowers and strings of dragonglass. Crackling energy followed their heels all day and they finally gathered around all of their hard work.

Rasia overflowed the brim of their gourds with scavenger moonshine. Kai had seen this stuff take down the stoutest of Timar's facehunters. It crept up on you and the next thing you knew, you were on the ground.

Zephyr sniffed at the drink. "I'm pretty sure this is going to kill someone."

"A kid from the Tents is afraid of scavenger moonshine?" Rasia asked.

"I'm saying this kid from the Tents is going to watch all of you drop by the end of the night."

"Don't bet on that," Azan said. "My jihs have been sneaking me drinks since I was five-years-till. I can drink all of you under the table."

"Is that a challenge?" Rasia crowed in excitement.

"I guess this will be good practice for the namepour?" Neema asked slowly.

"Exactly." Rasia winked at her. "You don't want to be the one vomiting after one drink."

Most people consumed alcohol for the first time during the namepour, and new faces must learn quickly how to hold their drink. You couldn't buy food in the Grankull, but you could buy alcohol. You purchased it as a gift for when you're visiting someone's home, meeting a friend you haven't seen in a season, courting gifts for flames, and celebrating every birth, death, new job, lucky windfall, and stubbed toe. Celebrations are called a pouring because the alcohol flowed faster and quicker than water.

Rasia handed Kai his gourd so full that the drink spilled down his arm. It gathered in a pool at his feet, pale and milky like the overhead gibbous. The dragonglass chimed twinkling songs in the wind. The oil lamp glowed off the mast posts and encased them all in a citrine glow.

Rasia raised her gourd and toasted, "To the best kull this Desert has ever seen. Tonight, we celebrate our hunt, we celebrate each other, and we celebrate ourselves. Thank you to all of you, both stupid and brave, who followed me on this hunt. We killed a *ta-fucking* dragon!"

"Oi-yo!" Everyone drank.

Kai took small sips. He knew he wouldn't be able to keep up with everyone else otherwise. He learned that the hard way back at the gorge. When he swallowed, he thought he knew what to expect, but he gagged on the trail of fire that burned down his throat.

"Shit," Azan coughed, then doubled over and coughed some more.

"My throat is *still* burning," Neema hacked.

Zephyr watched, smug. Rasia rolled her eyes at the dramatics.

"Suck it up. This is a kull toast. We've got four more to go," Rasia reminded them all. "Lani, your turn."

Kai blushed deep red at the address, nor did it go unnoticed. Azan glanced between Rasia and Kai. Neema snarked, "You two do know that Forging flames never last?"

"They also say it's impossible to slay a dragon within a Forging season, but we beat those odds," Rasia said.

"You two are like, *together*?" Azan asked. "You're not wearing any namesakes. How am I supposed to know if you're together if you're not wearing any namesakes? I've been flirting with you all day!"

"Is *that* what you've been doing?" Rasia scoffed and patted Azan's shoulder, consolingly. "Flattered, but his dick can do magic."

Far from being put off, Azan rose his brows intrigued. "Are we talking about literally or figuratively? Or both?"

Kai hid his face in his hands, while Rasia whispered loudly, "*both*."

"Ugh. Too much information," Neema complained.

"Try being stuck on a windship with them for half your Forging," Zephyr grumbled.

Rasia cackled and nudged Kai in the arm. "Come on, toast. At this pace, we're never going to eat."

Kai cleared his throat, shoulders up to his ears, embarrassed to face them all. Most people would be proud of the fact they could satisfy their partner, and Kai should be proud Rasia boasted of it—but he was still embarrassed. More than ready not to be the center of attention, he lamely mumbled out, "To the kull?"

"That toast sucks," Rasia said. Because of course, she would never let him get away with that half-ass attempt. "Come on. Try again. *Make me wet*."

Zephyr took a drink without prompting. Azan looked entirely too invested. Neema blanched. And Kai realized, at that moment, that none of the others mattered. He killed a dragon. What did he have to be embarrassed of? Kai focused on Rasia. He raised his drink, and the movement sloshed most of it down his arm.

"A toast—to all the hunts awaiting us, to all the horizons we've yet to reach, to all the nights we've yet to sail, to many more ends and many more beginnings, and all the journeys in between. This is a promise to you, Rasia."

"Oi-yo," Rasia purred in response. She hid the curling of her lips over the rim of her gourd, but her eyes visually stripped him of his clothes. He sipped at his gourd and eye-fucked her with the same intensity. He barely noted the second burn of the alcohol.

"You two are so weird," Neema muttered.

"What do you think of a threesome?" Azan asked.

"Is food and sex all you think about?" Neema asked, exasperated.

"*Yes*. Why? You interested?"

"Not my type."

"You mean your type for small, curved, and sharp?" Azan joked, referring to Neema's obsession with her daggers.

She gave Azan the 'V' of her fingers. "My type is someone with a job, and established, and with status."

"To the Tents, to prosperity, and to better seasons," Zephyr toasted, interrupting them all.

"Oi-yo!"

Azan toasted, "To all the faces we're going to fuck on our Naming night!"

"Oi-yo!"

Neema toasted, "To glory! To a name remembered!"

"Oi-yo!"

They drank. Both Rasia and Zephyr emptied their gourds. Neema looked to have the same idea as Kai, sipping at safe mouthfuls, while Azan finished half of his. Even with small sips, Kai wobbled as they gathered around the feast and attacked the endless spread of food. Per tradition, it was Rasia's duty as Han to make sure the gourds were always topped off, and she certainly took the job seriously.

It was said that those who eat the heart of a dragon die as legends. Many lived their entire lives without a taste of dragon meat, and only a handful of hunters have ever eaten the heart. They didn't have the time to celebrate the day they slayed Aurum, but Rasia had sun-dried and salted the organ to eat on their last night of the Forging. They all sat in reverent silence with that dragon heart on their tongue. Even though dried, it melted like butter in their mouths.

"I don't feel any different," Azan said when he finished.

"Of course not," Rasia said. "It's food like everything else."

"Yes, but it's *magic* food."

"It has never given anyone magic to have eaten it," Rasia said. "Shamai-ta killed two dragons, and he was never any different."

"They say you live longer," Neema piped in.

Rasia said darkly, "You don't."

"I always thought the magic was in the bones, not the meat," Zephyr said.

All at once, they turned to Kai for clarity. Transport one warship across the Desert and now, suddenly, he was an expert on magic.

"He's right," Kai explained. "There's no magic in the heart, only the bones. Bones are . . . magnets for magic, but that doesn't mean all bones hold magic, or can hold magic at the same capacity. Magic prefers dragon bones because dragon bones remember magic the most, but that doesn't mean the magic won't transfer if there is a more appealing container. Magic might prefer dragon bones, but it also prefers living ones. Eventually, the magic will be recycled somewhere else."

They all squinted at him.

"Huh. Are the throwing bones really magic, then?" Azan asked.

"Kind of? Because the throwing bones are made from the bones of the magicborn, they attract more magic than normal bones, but I wouldn't say they contain a lot. I can't speak to how much they affect a greater divine plan, but at the very least, they stay in the air a little longer." Kai shrugged.

Rasia guffawed.

The throwing bones were supposed to be sacred and held the secrets of everyone's destinies. Kai sometimes forgot that the Grankull didn't perceive things the same way. Nico constantly reminded him that the truth was not always the truth. Sometimes it was false for a reason, and sometimes it had been stretched over hundreds of years to become something new.

"We probably shouldn't mention this in our interview," Neema grumbled into her cup. "After everything, we wouldn't want the Grankull to fail us for blasphemy."

"We'll need to omit quite a bit from our interview," Rasia said. "No one should mention anything about Kai's magic either. We caught a lucky wind and made it in time. That's that."

"Why don't you want the Grankull to know about your magic?" Zephyr asked Kai.

"That's Nico's thing, and I don't want the Grankull to expect it of me when I might not always be able to perform it."

"But why should we have to lie to the Grankull on the runt's behalf?" Neema asked.

Rasia surged through the crumbs and dishes. She swiped up a bone, chewed meat still clinging to it, and brandished it at Neema's throat. "He killed a fucking dragon. You put some respect on his name."

Kai was so used to Neema calling him runt, he hadn't realized this was the first time Neema had said it in Rasia's presence. Neema reached for a dagger, but Rasia already had that bone shoved so hard against Neema's throat she could barely breathe. She gave a reluctant stubborn nod up.

Rasia shifted enough for Neema to breathe in air, but kept her glare pinned on Neema in case Neema had the gall to call him a runt a second time.

"No one complains when it's Nico," Rasia complained. "None of those oasis kids killed a gonda on their own. Those gonda were our kills. They haven't earned their Forging, but Nico made us all agree to lie for them. That's the one thing I respect about you, Neema. You didn't take the easy way out. You killed your hunt. Don't ruin that by playing the fucking snitch." Rasia plopped back down and pointed to both Azan and Zephyr. "And that goes for both of you. Anyone spills about Kai's magic, or anything about me and Kai, and I swear no one will ever find your bones."

Azan said after a moment of silence. "You know, Rasia. You

can be kind of a bully sometimes. Of course, we aren't going to say anything. We wouldn't be here without you."

Neema's dark glare told a different opinion, and Rasia didn't miss it. She dragged the bone across her neck in warning.

"*Okay* . . . anyone up for a game of rattle bones?" Azan asked in an attempt to lighten the air.

"Ooh, we should play the drinking one." Rasia brightened and tossed the bone over her shoulder.

Azan jumped to his feet in excitement and then stumbled back. Zephyr caught Azan by the shirt and stabilized his footing.

"I'm fine. I'm fine," Azan said. He rushed below-deck to grab his pouch of playing-bones.

Zephyr shook his head and helped Rasia clear the deck of the empty earthenware. Kai didn't exactly feel comfortable trying to stand right now. For a moment, Neema and Kai sat across from each other, alone. The alcohol pulled the words from his lips. "I'm sorry," he said. "For your jih. And I'm sorry for what happened back at the scavenger camp. I wasn't strong enough to save you."

"I never thought you could," Neema said. "But Rasia is right. You sailed that windship against the dragon like one of the best. You are no longer the runt of the Grankull. You've outgrown that. Doesn't mean I still don't want to see you dead."

"I understand."

Neema nodded, sharp and quick.

Azan slid between them. The pouch fumbled out of Azan's grasp and the bones rattled. Kai moved to catch them before they rolled across the deck. He placed the bones back into Azan's hands and found himself surprised when Azan latched onto his wrist. Azan's thumb rubbed the top of his hand.

"Are you double-sided? All-sided?" Azan asked.

Kai snatched his hand away. "I d-d-don't know."

"I've got experience. I'd take good care of you. You tell Rasia that."

Neema gagged. "Ugh. He's a *stick*."

"You're only mean to him because you know he's pretty. I've

seen you staring when he's at the steer," Azan said to Neema before turning back to Kai with a drunken wobbliness. "You become a whole different person when you're steering the windship. It's so fucking hot. Sometimes, instead of the steer, I imagine my dick in your hands."

Kai slapped his hands to his face. "If this is you flirting, I don't understand how Rasia missed it."

"*Me neither*. She laughed at everything though. Maybe she thought I was joking."

"That's because Rasia has eyes for only one person," Neema scoffed. "Why you would get yourself so entangled with one person right before the Naming is beyond me. She's the last person I'd peg to be the hit-it and commit-it type."

"Didn't her jih choose a kulani after only a year? Maybe it's a family thing."

"Maybe I just give good dick."

Azan and Neema swiveled their heads towards Kai, both struck speechless by the unexpected boast. Azan exploded into laughter.

Huh. Kai didn't mean to say that. But he was not taking it back.

Azan's eyes grew heavy, looking him up and down. Kai had no doubt Rasia would be up for it, but he didn't want this night spiraling out of control. He needed to establish boundaries before he couldn't consent to them anymore. He placed a placating hand on Azan's forearm, and it took a lot of courage just to do that. The difference was a stark reminder of how much he trusted Rasia, unequivocally.

"I appreciate your interest, but I don't think . . . I'm not ready."

Azan gave a sweet endearing smile. "I'll be here when you are."

Kai flushed, noticing for the first time how handsome Azan was when he smiled.

"Can we play?" Neema groaned. "All this flirting is making me sick."

Azan grinned unapologetically, then began setting up the game. "Do you know how to play rattle-bones?"

"I've never played before," Kai admitted. He had observed a few family games. His cousin, Ashe, the math genius, was infamously banned from the gambling houses. He glanced up when Zephyr and Rasia emerged from below-deck, sniping at each other as they often did.

Thoughtfully, Kai said, "You might roll a better hand with Zephyr."

Azan dropped the bones, again, clattering them over the deck. Kai caught the ones that rolled in his direction. Azan swiveled his head toward Zephyr.

"It's pretty obvious he has a thing for Nico," Neema said. "*Why* does everyone have a thing for her?"

"He's trying to get over her, not very successfully," Kai said, "but he's open."

"I pegged him for a top," Azan said, thoughtfully.

"He's a bottom," Kai corrected. He tossed the stray bones at Azan. Azan barely caught them, distracted, as he watched Zephyr and Rasia walk over. It was a wonder that Azan hadn't lost any of the pieces yet.

Rasia hopped into Kai's lap, and asked, "You don't have the game set up yet?"

"I'm working on it," Azan said. Finally, with everyone's help, Azan got all the bones together into one pot. "Each round, everyone but the winner drinks. Someone rolls a red, everyone drinks."

"Those are only the drinking rules," Zephyr said, and then helpfully explained the regular non-drinking rules. The tent kid seemed far more stable than the rest of them. Even Rasia, often balanced to an extreme degree, rolled off Kai's lap and plopped to the deck with a squeak. He scooped her up, settled her a little more solidly between his legs, and wrapped a stabilizing arm around her. Rasia smiled up at him, and Kai smiled at her in turn.

"No," Azan corrected Zephyr's explanation of the rules. "Those are the kull rules. We're playing Tent rules. Tent rules are better."

"Since when do you know Tent rules?"

"Kelin taught me." Azan's eyes narrowed on Zephyr, trying. "Kelin taught me a lot of things."

"Roll, Azan."

The bones clattered into the pot. Kai sort of got the hang of the game as best he could but felt the worst of the alcohol brewing like an encroaching storm. To everyone's surprise, Rasia was disastrous at the game. Her number guesses were wildly off. She took a shot every round and got drunk much faster than anyone expected.

"This is stupid!" Rasia shouted. At another loss, she leapt off Kai's lap and overturned the pot. She scattered the bones around with her body, wiggling like a sand-snake in retribution.

Azan whined. "I was winning!"

"What the fuck is your math? I was winning," Neema said.

Azan squinted and counted his bones. He counted several of the same bones three or four times. Zephyr shook his head at how utterly out of hand the game had gotten. Kai secured Rasia back into his lap. She pouted as she slumped against his chest. "It's not fair. I hate this game. *I never win.*"

The more Rasia began to lose, the less she cared about the game, and the more her hands roamed underneath Kai's clothes. He threw his bones. A lap full of Rasia. Time tilted sideways. The next thing he remembered, he had Rasia in his mouth and a dick hard and throbbing in his pants.

"Kai?" Zephyr's voice floated at the edge of his periphery. Whatever Zephyr wanted, it hardly felt as urgent as the pressing heat of Rasia in his lap. Kai tightened his hands around her ass, clutching at the friction as she humped him like a rabid drunken bunny.

"Are they fucking?"

"Skip 'em."

"They are worse than my tahs."

Kai's senses exploded into awareness. His heart pounded in his ears at the end of a race he didn't remember. Rasia lay loose and content against him. Wet fingers chilled cold in the night air. He had made a mess in his pants.

"I'm sticky," Kai complained. He tapped Rasia on the behind. She rolled off him and flopped to the deck.

Kai got to his feet and wondered why the warship was moving. He stumbled over to a more secluded area and grasped at the railing for dear life. The warship kept lurching underneath him. He pissed off the railing, and then used the rest of the water in his gourd to clean his hands, thighs, and groin. Behind him, he cringed when an exultant cheer rang out as Neema won the game. She jumped up, then quickly crashed back down. Laughter, then worry, then more laughter followed.

Once Kai felt adequately presentable, he swayed a meandering path toward the food. He dropped down and stuffed his face, starving even though he had eaten a lot a few moments ago. The food settled his stomach and rounded the sharp edges of his drunkenness. He ate while Neema and Azan argued over who won.

Zephyr joined him and scooped up a bowl of olives. He popped them into his mouth and looked at Kai shrewdly. "How are you feeling?"

"Drunk."

Zephyr offered his gourd of water. Kai took deep sips of it. He wiped the droplets from his mouth, lowered the gourd, and was met with Zephyr's serious expression.

"One of you needs to stay sober," he said. "No more alcohol tonight."

Before, Kai would have chafed at the command and complained that he could take care of himself, that he didn't need anyone looking out for him. But he was also the dumbass who got Rasia pregnant, and it would be just his luck to mess up again so close to the Grankull. He ceded. "'kay."

Kai looked at Zephyr owlishly. "I . . . thank you. For being a friend."

They had a rocky start, but Zephyr had always tried to respect him, and had more often than not learned from his mistakes. He tried to give space and understanding when Kai needed it, and, in turn, Kai had begun to understand Zephyr's own peculiarities.

Zephyr just . . . talked like that, to everyone. Kai learned not to take it too personally. Even though his relationship with Rasia was one of the momentous things to come out of this year's Forging, just as importantly, he also gained a friend.

"I might have suggested to Azan you could be interested," Kai said.

"I picked up on that."

Kai concentrated on making sure his words made sense. "I know you haven't had sex since your last flame, and I can't imagine how hard it must be to move on from that," he said. "But . . . you deserve to get laid." Kai swore he was trying to say something far more eloquent. Zephyr was right. He had got to stop drinking.

Zephyr pouted. "True."

"Let me be the responsible one tonight," Kai said. "Have fun. I owe that to you."

"You owe me so many." Zephyr slapped him on the back, leaving his water gourd with Kai, and went to go piss over the railing.

Kai ate and focused on sobering up. Rasia had disappeared off somewhere. She showed back up whatever-time later. She carried something behind her back, but he couldn't get a good view of it before she crouched in front of him. A shy smile spread across her face.

"I made you a gift," she declared.

Rasia presented an ilhan. Some things started making sense. She had gone off on her own yesterday morning before everyone woke up. She brought back a huge sand-snake for the feast, but Kai had suspected she had other motivations, or she would have invited him along.

"I found it in the hold. It was in a bit of a rough shape, but I've replaced some of the materials. Considering I broke the last one, I figured you could use a new one. And this time, it's *yours*." Rasia grabbed his hand and placed his fingers along the neck. He blinked at the carved letters written into the palm wood. It was too dark to see the lettering, but he traced the letters with his fingers: Rasia's name.

It was a namesake—a courting gift. Kai couldn't help the smile, and the ridiculous backward way they always managed to do things.

"It's not exactly a traditional namesake that you can wear, but I figured—I thought you would like this better. When I earn the rest of my names, I'll add those too, all down the neck, which means you'll have to play it, so people will see my name and know you're mine."

"I . . ." Kai's throat clogged with emotions. "Thank you."

"Play me a song."

"I can't actually play, Rasia."

"What does that matter? I'll dance to any sound you make."

How could he possibly refuse?

High on the confidence of alcohol, Kai sat atop an upturned calabash bowl. He pulled the ilhan between his legs and curled his fingers around the handposts. They were a little bit uneven, the top of the left post chipped off. He strummed his thumbs forward along the strings. Rasia hadn't known how to tune it, but despite the off-note sound, she shimmied to it anyways.

He knew exactly the song he wanted to try. Rasia, Azan, and Neema drunkenly cheered at the unmistakable notes. Without further prompting or even the right chords, everyone raised their voices to sing the infamous kull shanty, which over the centuries had turned into a rowdy song no proper celebration could go without.

Drink another gourd for me
The Han of winds I obey
A fortnight apart from my kulani
The hunt got us blowing away!

Clap. Clap.

Drink another gourd for me
And dance the ilhan sway
A fortnight returned to my kulani

and now I can't wait to get away!

Clap. Clap.

Rasia pranced and danced around the deck with Azan. Neema spun effortless circles. Zephyr flipped over a few more dishes and accompanied Kai with makeshift drums. They glanced at each other with foolish grins and played off each other's cues. Music had always fascinated him, at the way sounds could be woven into beautiful shrouds. He had seen Kenji Ilhani thread music from air and compose tapestries of songs dedicated to Ava-ta, Nico, and Rae. All he had ever gotten was silence.

Now, Kai played his own songs.

Clap. Clap.

A strong wind jerked Rasia awake, then she jarred her elbow. She blinked at the sight of Kai's old shroud fluttering overhead. She stretched out from under a blanket tucked around her, peeked out over the rim of the scout's nest, and winced at the long way down. Her head hurt. She didn't really remember how she got all the way up here.

But her mouth was dry, and she was thirsty. She clutched the handholds and climbed down naked from the mast. What had been a faint sound of music, which she had initially thought had been a lingering memory of last night, grew louder as she climbed down.

Dawn lit the horizon a stratum of blended orange and yellows. When she reached the deck, Rasia stretched her arms, popping bones and waking up muscles. The morning air felt great on her bare skin. When they returned to the Grankull, they'd have to go back to the shroud and the restrictive white of the caftan until they received their names during the Naming Ceremony. Rasia wanted to bask in this freedom for as long as possible. They had to be in the Grankull by sunset. Plenty of time for everyone to sleep off the alcohol and wash up all evidence of illicit activity.

Rasia trudged into the Han quarters, looking for her gourd, and froze at the sight of Azan and Zephyr splayed out haphazardly on the bed. Huh. Azan did have a pretty dick. But comparing the two of them, and Rasia would die before ever admitting this out loud, she thought Zephyr the more attractive one. It had always been rather irritating.

Rasia shuffled through the mess on the floor, found her back-up gourd, flung it over her shoulder, and left them to their sleep.

Kai strummed the ilhan at the bow-tip of the warship, his hands exploding with music. He played without pause. Breathless. Leaping freefall from one song to the next. He claimed that he didn't know how to play, that he had never put fingers to an ilhan before that night in the gorge, but his fingers pressed along the strings at a frantic pace, like someone afraid to forget the steps. Those are Kenji-shi's songs, Rasia knew. Kai played almost perfect renditions, and Rasia realized with sudden clarity that Kai had memorized the finger placements. He played through the songs with a forcefulness, with such a determined reclamation Rasia couldn't bring herself to interrupt. Was this how Kai's ability to observe and perfectly mimic was born? By watching Kenji-shi play music?

Fingers slipped and a sharp note halted the song. Kai shook out the strain in his hands.

"Have you been up all night?" Rasia asked.

Kai jumped in surprise. She sat down at his side, took a drink of water, and then wiped the sweaty strands of hair out of his eyes. Someone needed a haircut. It had grown longer than his shoulders. All he needed now was one of Nico's dragonglass hairbands.

"I . . ." Kai paused and squinted out at the dawn. "I think so."

"You must have watched Kenji-shi play a lot."

"I . . . yeah," he said to himself blankly. He looked down at the ilhan and said, "The Lake showed me this, too. It was in my dreams. Me and him, playing music together, forever and ever until the end of time. I'd always hoped if I ever got the chance to show him who I am, and fix things, that he would teach me how to play. I've been waiting for it my entire life without any hope of it ever coming true." He shook his head, and his fingers tapped a song atop the deck. "Sometimes, there's no time to wait on people. Sometimes, you've got to teach yourself how to play."

"I get that. When Ysai-ji refused to come into the Desert with me, all the plans we had laid unfinished. We had planned to slay a dragon together. It had been *our* dream. Then tah died, and Ysai-ji's plans changed. You can't wait on people. You move on." Rasia settled a hand over Kai's tapping fingers. "This was better, anyway."

He threaded his fingers through hers, and they sat watching the dawn.

"How did I get all the way up in the scout's nest?"

"I magicked us up there."

"What happened to my clothes?"

"You took them off. Claimed you were hot," Kai smirked. "But you were just trying to get in my pants."

She laughed. "Did we fuck?" She didn't feel any of the familiar soreness, but she wanted to be sure.

"I took care of us," Kai said.

Rasia released a sigh of relief, then dropped her head against his shoulder. This was the first time she had ever blacked-out while drinking. She didn't like the idea of empty spaces in her memory, but it made her feel better to know Kai had taken care of things. It had been so long since she had someone she could rely on so implicitly.

Rasia watched dawn spread light over his goosebumps. She knew the difference now—between attraction, and a flame, and *this*. She didn't know when it happened or how—when this kernel lodged in her chest grew to consume her.

No word could contain a feeling so vast.

She swept her fingers across the planes of his face and held him as if she had personally molded his angles out of clay. She marveled at the color of his golden skin alongside her sun-burnt copper, at the way the colors bled together in the shadows. Kai held her hand, and his thumb pressed gently between her knuckles. She surged up, and he caught her in his arms, and she knew it'll always feel like flying.

They kissed until the sun broke the horizon.

"I've got something for you," Kai said, as dawn combed through his hair. "I've got to go get it."

"Sure. Meet me on the deck of the windship."

Kai got up and paused to look over her nakedness. "Do you want me to grab your wrap?"

"Nope. I'm good."

He pecked her lips, hauled the ilhan into his arms, and rushed toward the Han quarters.

Rasia yelled after him, "Make sure you don't trip over Azan's huge dick!"

Kai stumbled in laughter. Rasia smiled and admired his striking silhouette as he disappeared into the cabin. She stretched up to the tip of her toes, rolled her shoulders, and pulled at her hamstrings. Her windship was hitched over the warship's side, creaking at a particularly strong draft of wind.

Rasia skipped down the chains and landed on her dangling windship. She greeted the familiar bumpy texture of her deck. When Kai shimmied down the chains and joined her, she immediately searched him for the surprise. There was only one thing it could reasonably be.

"Is it a namesake?"

Kai sighed, more amused than exasperated. "You can at least act surprised."

Rasia practiced her best surprise faces. Kai snorted at her attempts. He pulled the item from his belt, unwrapped it from a sheet of cloth excruciatingly slowly, and her smile dropped at the sight of the glass bauble in his hand.

It was a necklace, a pretty traditional type of namesake to give, but Rasia was expecting something a little more . . . exciting. (The namesake she gifted had definitely been better.)

"That's it?" Rasia picked it out of his hand and lifted the necklace by the tightly woven jute braid. The sun gleamed off the clear glass and the deposits of sand trapped within. "It's . . . *nice*."

Kai crossed his arms, face revealing nothing. He said her name, "Rajiani."

The trapped sand whirled. The bauble warmed, then flew from her hand of its own accord and tugged headward, parallel to the Grankull.

"Oh."

"Say my name."

Rasia smirked at the suggestiveness. She said, with a hint of playful teasing in her voice, "Kailjnn."

The namesake flew back into her hands.

"I made it while practicing my magic yesterday. When you say your name, it'll always point headwards. No matter where you are, you'll always find your way. When you say my name, it'll always come back to you, no matter what. That way, you'll never lose it. I don't want people to know about my magic. It doesn't belong to them. They don't get that part of me. It's mine to choose who I give it to, and I choose to give it to you."

Overwhelmed, Rasia spun on her heels to hide the sudden heat in her cheeks. Kai tied the magical compass around her neck. The entire kull voiced concerns last night regarding Kai and Rasia's relationship but fuck their opinions. She glanced at tah's name inscribed on the mast. After Shamai-ta's death, she never thought she could feel this way ever again. *Happy*.

Kai stepped back and smiled at the sight of the necklace around her neck. The glass sat warm on her skin. It was odd—to carry something of someone else. "I intentionally made it look worthless, so the sentries won't confiscate it when we return to the Grankull. No need to smuggle it in your vagina. But if you want to go that route, I'd still be willing to help."

Rasia laughed and kissed him. When she stepped back, she unsheathed Kai's dagger from his waist. She waggled it at him, and he tilted his head in question. "There's one more thing I need to do before we return to the Grankull."

She stood before the mast, pressed a hand to her tah's name, and then stabbed the palmwood underneath it. She performed the movements of the kah to find the last letter.

Below her tah's name, Rasia wrote another.

Ysaijen.

"I get it now," she said. Kulls weren't forever. She promised herself no more waiting on people. She was ready to move on. "Eventually, they have their own ship to sail."

"Very wise," Kai nodded and pressed a kiss to her scalp. "You're an amazing Han."

Rasia smiled, smugly. "I am."

They said the parting words together.

"Paths diverge, and split, and end. Till we meet once more again. Forever this ship ferry your name. All hunters are hunted, but the kull remains."

It was ironic how Rasia ridiculed Ysai for his certainty that Jilah was the one, and now she was carrying the namesake of someone she had known all of a season who had become the steer to her windship. Rasia thought she knew better than jih, thought him dumb, and an idiot, and a fool. She thought she knew everything.

If there was one thing she had learned from her Forging—that for all her vast experiences, for all her skills, and all her accomplishments—Rasia knew nothing at all.

CHAPTER TEN

10

The drums beat a message through the Grankull: calling all sentries to report immediately duskward. People froze with their scythes and plows in their hands, on alert in case they needed to evacuate to the shelters. Children came rushing toward their parents. Rae emerged through the eggplant trees, shaking the lavender flowers. Nico swooped them up in her arms and dirt flew from the soles of their bare feet. The fieldworkers waited with bated breath, and all searched for the first hint of a vibration through the ground.

"It's a ship!" Someone shouted, running into the fields. "A scavenger warship!"

Nico dropped her shoulders and then rolled her eyes. She had initially worried about the fact that Kai's kull had stopped right outside the Grankull's view for the past three days. She feared some sort of injury, but as the deadline of the Forging drew near without movement, she could hazard a guess who was behind the delay. Normally one more windship racing the Forging deadline wouldn't draw attention from anyone other than anxious families with children who haven't made it home, so of course, Rasia had to return with drums announcing her arrival.

People whispered to each other and glanced at Nico none too subtly. Already, workers were beginning to drift away in curiosity.

She knew they couldn't afford the pause but there was no point damming the flood. She raised her voice and ordered everyone a break. The order echoed down the wingfields.

Woven baskets of olives dropped to the ground. Stalks of wheat were thrown onto the backs of carts and left behind. Everyone surged excitedly duskward, carrying their assumptions. Not every day did you hear of scavengers openly approaching the Grankull, and since the battle drums hadn't sounded yet, it was reasonable to assume the threat level wasn't very high. The sentries hadn't called Nico for battle, and a barrage of arrows and projectiles from the Spine could take out a lone warship before it ever got too close. Their curiosity swept Nico up in the stream.

"What is it?" Rae asked, clinging to her as the size of the crowd grew and squeezed them both. The wide streets, usually able to accommodate at least two lanes of camels, goats, and carts, swelled as different rivers of people converged on one another.

"It's jih," Nico said. "He's come home."

Rae's eyes lit up, and they bounced in her arms, urging her to go faster. Which, in fact, made it harder for her to go faster.

They reached the duskward edge of the Grankull. Again, Nico rolled her eyes. Kai and Rasia had been coming from the dawnward direction, from the Dragon's Coast, and should have arrived near the dawnward wingfields, but Rasia had circled all the way around the Grankull just to have the sunset behind her. Perhaps Rasia should perform plays with her affinity for the dramatic.

Initially, Nico couldn't see anything over the crowd, but she sensed Kai drawing closer. To her right, a line of kull ships waited for the Forging's end to launch and gather all those kids who didn't make it. They would not find anyone, for Nico had picked up all the stragglers she could find alive in the Desert. Rasia and her kull were truly the last ones out.

The crowd of onlookers atop the roofs and at the height of the Spine shouted and pointed. Against the backdrop of sunset, a mast peeked over the horizon. It expanded until that small speck transformed into the massive size of a warship. A dirty off-white shroud waved from the topmast, triumphant. Strapped at the very front of the ship, unmistakably, was the head of a dragon.

Out of caution, the sentries formed a protective line in front of the spectators. More and more people gathered. They hemmed and hawed as the giant scavenger warship approached. Standing amid the crowd, the excitement was palpable. Nico had no doubt the Grankull would remember this moment forever.

The setting sun lit the sky afire.

÷

Rasia stuffed on her shroud as the Grankull reared out of the sand. Despite what Kai claimed, she had never heard those Elder bones sing. They were dead and hollow to her ear, and the corpse looked ever more cramped and smaller than the last time she left it behind. But Rasia knew no greater high than the sun setting over the Forging, the drumbeat of the massive warship rumbling underfoot, the billowing crunch of sand churned beneath creaking wheels, and the heavy dragging baritone of her dragon. Like Kai, Rasia made her own music.

Alarmed by the warship, sentries rushed from their posts to form a defensive line at her approach. People crawled out of holes and crevices like frenzied ants over an upturned hill. They chittered and gathered and gossiped and gawked. Glory tasted of nothing but sand and wind, but it filled her belly full.

"Anchor!" Rasia shouted.

The sentry line wavered as the warship came to a trudging stop. She grabbed a piece of rope, which had already been looped around the railing, and swung down to raucous cheers.

Kiba-ta stood before the line of sentries, arms crossed, unmoved and unimpressed that she had to gather her entire sentry force *for this*. The crowd waited for a sign from the sentries, and the sentries waited for a sign from Kiba-ta, and Rasia swore, her tah was deliberating whether or not to release the arrows. Rasia could never win with her. Just look at that dragon!

The impasse broke when one sentry bravely broke the line.

Rasia grinned and raced to meet the lone figure. She jumped. Ysai met her low. The ground fell from beneath her as she flipped over his back. They turned and came together in a twirling boisterous hug.

"Fuck, Rasia. Of course, you'd choose the dramatic entrance, arriving at the last vibration. You had me worried for a moment." Ysai tossed the ground back to her feet. The movement sent Rasia's shroud spiraling loose from around her ear. Out of habit, he moved to fix it, then paused and rubbed an amazed hand over the short strands of her hair. "About time you cut that bird's nest off. What happened? It got caught in the tree where it belonged?"

"Ha!" Rasia ducked under his hand and shoved off his teasing. She adjusted the shroud before Kiba-ta could say something about it and squinted up at her big jih. After staring down a dragon, he didn't seem all that tall as she had once imagined. "I didn't break Shamai-ta's record."

"No, you didn't. But bones, you did better. A dragon, Rasia? A fucking dragon. You did that shit."

She waggled her eyebrows. "Come on, say it. I want to hear it."

"Ugh," Ysai hunched and ate the words. "Rasia is the best there ever was, the greatest of all time, a legend till the end of memory—and her jih is a loser."

"You're damn right."

Kai and Zephyr watched the crowd surge around Rasia from the railing of the warship. Neema and Azan had already scrambled down the stairs toward their families. Azan immediately disappeared under a tower of jihs. Neema approached her family cool and collected, but she broke down the moment her tah hugged her. Zephyr's family wouldn't be down there waiting for him. Once everyone cleared, the sentries would escort him around the Grankull to the Tents.

"Where's Nico?" Zephyr asked as he scanned the mass of people.

"Still making her way through the crowd," Kai answered. "She must have been working the dawn wingfields."

Zephyr scanned his eyes over the Grankull, almost wistfully. Even now, after killing a dragon, he was still not allowed in, not until the Naming Ceremony which coincided with the solstice. They also had to complete the medical examinations and the interviews first. None of them, not even those who arrived earlier, were considered adults until then.

Kai's attention drifted to a group of hunting kull ships. At the end of the Forging, the kulls always sent out a few parties to find any survivors. Kenji was on one of those ships. Zephyr elbowed Kai to get his attention and motioned to where Nico pushed out of the crowd. A weight fell off his shoulders to see her. Then Rae's shrouded face caught a glimpse of him, and they broke free from Nico's arms.

Kai pushed off from the railing and rushed down the warship's stairs. The warship had a lot of stairs. He subtly dropped, and the wind caught his fall. Then he raced forward, faster than when he had a skinko and scavengers at his back. He slid to his knees and caught Rae in his arms. Rae's fingers smeared dirt into Kai's shroud and tightened their arms around his neck. Kai valued the opportunity to do something on his own for once, but there were those he left behind, and he was ready to come home.

Rae cried, pulling back. "I missed you. Don't leave again."

Kai tightened his grip, chest heavy. He thought of the oasis and how he had tried to kill himself at the beginning of the Forging. For some stupid reason, he had allowed the Grankull to convince himself that he wasn't important. That no one would miss him. That Rae would move on and forget he ever existed as easily as replacing a new toy. It took Rasia to remind him that he mattered. Kai had come so close to breaking all of his promises.

"I won't. I'll never leave you again," Kai promised anew,

meaning it with every bone in his body. He'd never give up again. He'd never run away again. He'd never let the Grankull dictate his worth ever again.

He looked up when Nico's shadow engulfed them. He reached out an arm. Nico dropped to her knees and sort of plopped into their joint embrace. She dug her head into his shoulder, and he could feel her exhaustion. Unlike Rae, it had only been a couple of weeks since he saw Nico but even that brief time apart had aged them both. The three of them embraced until night dispersed the lingering wisps of dusk.

Nico pulled away and glanced over at the kull ships launching out from the Claws. "About Kenji-ta . . ."

"I know," Kai said. There was no reason why he should have expected Kenji to be waiting for him like the rest of the families, but his chest ached from his small crushed hopes.

Nico helped him stand while Rae clung to his arm. Behind them, the sentries crawled over the warship. After giving them space to reunite, Zephyr drifted over once they pulled apart.

"Good to see you," Nico said to Zephyr. They glanced at each other, and Kai could tell they longed to hug one another, but they were back in the Grankull now. Children couldn't touch anyone outside of their family.

"It's tonight, isn't it?" Zephyr asked, brows drawn together.

It was the last day of the Forging, the eve of a night significant only when there was an eligible heir to inherit the mantle of Ohan. The Hunter's Eye gaped in the sky.

It was the night of the bloodrites.

THE NAMING

CHAPTER ELEVEN

I

Deafening silence suffocated Nico as she entered the Heart Temple. The temple sounded peculiar without the familiar sounds of whispered footsteps, the endless scritch-scratch of scribes, and the brush of gossamer curtains. During the day, a thick duvet of reverence reigned over the halls. Down one corridor, scribes recited stories for the budchildren of the Grankull, and down another, they argued over archaic facts. In the main chamber, people lost themselves to scrolls in the reading nooks while seeking that spiritual rapture of a good story.

Vendettas and conflicts were supposed to be left at the temple doors, but that wasn't always the case. Tonight, the scribes have barred all but Nico from entering the temple to prevent any disturbance to the bloodrites. Not even the Councilors were allowed entry.

The scribes, all with shrouded faces, lined Nico's way to the Heart Chamber. Because weapons weren't allowed inside the temple walls, scribes were well-versed in hand-to-hand combat. Nico didn't know if the Council had any spies planted among them. Sweat crept at the base of her neck as she walked deeper inside, through solemn hallways lined with diagonal slats filled to the brim with scrolls that reminded her of a beehive, with combs of words, instead of honey.

Finally, at the center, before the bone curtains of the Heart Chamber, Nico's tajih—no, on this night using her title felt more appropriate, the Mythkeeper awaited her.

Nico took off her sandals and dressed in the provided ceremonial robes before entering the chamber. She stepped down into a pit of sand. When scribes entered the Heart Chamber all they heard was silence. But Nico heard a symphony—various bones all performing in harmonic orchestra. The performance vibrated pitch around her as if she stood at the center of a bell.

Unlike the adobe mud-houses of the Grankull, the entire Heart temple was built of dragon bone. Soon, the bones of Aurum would undoubtedly reinforce existing spires or build new ones. Further surrounding her were rows and rows of rectangular urns engraved with the names of the deceased. They spiraled around her on tiers, higher and higher, up through the Heart temple's main spire. Some urns were taller than others to accommodate a longer tower of names. One glimpse at the tallest among them, and Nico could identify the legends.

Through the center of the Heart Chamber, the fractured sternum of the Great Elder curved out of the ground, cutting a bone walkway across the room. The throwing bones hummed inside a basin at the center of this bone altar.

The Heart Chamber not only served as a powerful magical amplifier but also held the greatest store of magic in the entire Desert. The chamber's capacity grew more and more powerful with the dead. Only the Ohan, one connected to the Dragon's Heart, had the capability to wield it.

"Nicolai, you have come before the Great Elder to offer yourself as candidate." The Mythkeeper removed the basin and stepped aside. "Lay atop the altar and remove the shroud."

Nico hadn't gotten much sleep these past few days due to being run ragged with her responsibilities to her family and the wingfields. She felt unprepared. Doubts weighed her down. What if she wasn't strong enough? What if everyone was wrong and the chosen one should have been Kai all along? He was born ahead of her. The opportunity to face the bloodrites should have been his first. Despite everyone's beliefs that his frailness could never survive the rites, Nico knew better.

She clamped her eyes shut and admonished the doubts as she lay down on the sternum altar. She could feel the Elder's latent magic thrumming underneath, yearning for connection. She had theorized that she might need to expend her magic until she was close enough to death for her bones to attract the stores of magic within the Elder. Up through the spire, the Hunter's Eye peered at her through the funnel.

With shaking hands, Nico unwrapped her shroud and for the first time in her life, exposed her face to a full moon. Her heart pounded in her chest. The moonlight reflected an eerie light off her gold and white robes.

A dagger flashed in the darkness.

Nico barely had time to react when the Mythkeeper stabbed a dagger into her heart. For a moment, she feared the Council's machinations had somehow infected her tajih. Then, realization struck her.

The bloodrites did not end with death.

It started with it.

The Mythkeeper bowed her head and prayed, "All hunters are hunted, and Death is the greatest hunter of them all."

Blood dripped down the altar. Nico followed the trail of it with her magic as it leeched through her clothes and slid down the altar. A weight, like a heavy cloak, pressed down on her chest. At the last vibration, her instincts fought back. She clawed for life with frantic tears and desperation. She needed to live. She had to live. She had so much work to do.

Nico inhaled darkness.

CHAPTER TWELVE

I

You never forgot the face of Death. You never forgot the way it pierced you through the round reflection of a dying child's eyes—or the ragged gasps of scavengers clutching open wounds—or seeds planted in infertile ground—or the last gasping billow in Nico's lungs.

Death had many faces.

A fiery sun flared and burned away the darkness. Nico winced at the sudden brightness. Then another, a second sun, winked into existence. She stood before two large eyes, and then in realization, bowed to her knees as the Elder lazily blinked awake. She felt like a pebble to a mountain. She never imagined she would meet the Great Elder, but it made sense that the Elder could be found here, in this murkiness between life and death.

The gargantuan body stretched and the Elder extended massive luminescent wings. Nico could barely see over the Elder's snout. Living in their bones could not compare to the heft of skin and flesh, or the awe-inspiring sight of their iridescent scales. Every motion birthed rainbows.

It has been a long time since someone has come to visit me. The Elder lay their head onto thick forearms, looking down at Nico. The great tail swayed. **Tell me a story.**

She blinked. ". . . what?"

Thinking perhaps the Elder confused, she faced those two impossible suns and formed arguments and entreaties in her head. "I am the child of Avalai Ohan. I am here to humbly entreat you to bind me to your magic. It is imperative that I become Ohan, for if I do not, many could die. The Councilors wish to purge the Tents and-"

The Elder huffed, uninterested. **I want a story.**

Nico's brain froze. That couldn't be right. Where was the test of character? Or a trial to prove herself? Or a gauntlet of challenges and a twisted confrontation of her own fears? This had to be some sort of trick or clever test. Yes. Perhaps the story she chose would somehow determine why she was deserving of such great power. She attempted to meet the Elder's unexpected demand, but Nico had never done well being put on the spot. And right when she needed her wits about her the most, her mind went blank.

Completely and utterly blank.

She wracked her brain for a story—a fable—an anecdote—anything to satisfy the centuries-old dragon. She lived surrounded by stories but at that moment, she couldn't think of *one*. Her fists tightened. She squeezed her eyes shut and tried to control her rising panic. She needed to calm herself. She needed to think.

"There was once a horse, a spider, and a hawk," Nico began, retreating to one of the first stories that children learn from the scribes. It was a silly tale of an unlikely friendship.

The Elder snorted. **I've heard that one.** Their snout turned away, and the two blazing eyes began to set.

"No!" She cried out in alarm. The bottom collapsed underneath her, and she fell. She clawed at the smothering darkness.

"I have a story!" she screamed. "It's the best story you'll ever hear!"

She landed abruptly, jarring her elbow. Two suns dawned open. The Elder looked down at her insignificance with smoking nostrils.

"The story starts . . . It starts . . ." Nico began again. Her hands curled into fists. She had come too far, put in too much sweat, and pushed through too much to fail. People's lives balanced on her shoulders. There were too many dreams to plant, to water, and to help thrive. Desperate and without a clue as to what sort of story would entertain the generations-old dragon, she mentally flipped through the stories of scribes, legends, and Forgings but none of them seemed enough.

Scrap this. If the Elder wouldn't grant her their magic, then she'd take it instead. Nico sprinted toward the blazing irises.

Sometimes, you couldn't wait to be chosen.

You chose yourself.

Nico dove into the fire. A burst of white consumed her. Out of the radiance came color and images. She watched her life flash before her, and a presence watched it all unfold beside her.

Nico smiled when Ava-ta nodded approvingly at one of her spear forms. Nico hummed the lullaby Kenji-ta sang as he rocked her to sleep. Nico and Kai played dolls and re-enacted their favorite stories. Nico rescued puppies with Zephyr. Nico and Suri helped each other with homework. Nico gossiped and lounged in mud masks with Jilah. Nico enjoyed the smell of petrichor, fresh vegetables, and herbs. She enjoyed dirt on her hands, dancing in the rain, and the smell of cardamom in her tea. So many moments and sensations that defined her over the years—all the small details that made life worth living.

Why didn't you tell your own story? the Elder asked.

"I didn't think you would be interested."

It never occurred to her. She wasn't exciting like Rasia. She wasn't the scrappy underdog like Kai. She was boring and imperfect. Her story was the chapters you skip over to get to the exciting parts. Her story was broken clay wheels and digging in the dirt. It was stress pimples, and responsibility, and putting in the work. It was mistakes, and learning, and sometimes three steps back for two steps forward. It was watching a garden grow.

Like so many times before, she had been wrong.

Her story mattered.

With sudden inspiration, she said, certain, "This story deserves a better ending, don't you think?"

I suppose it does. Make it a good one. I look forward to seeing how it ends.

Nico exhaled light.

CHAPTER THIRTEEN

I

Dying hurt. Living hurt worse.

Nico awoke as one would burning atop their own funeral pyre. The Elder's magic blazed through her veins, pumping too full through her previously dead heart. The magic stretched her skin until it crackled and curled. It zapped her mouth with lightning. Her ears filled with the screeching ring of her own screams searing her throat.

Shadowed figures flitted overhead, blurry in her vision, but sharpening as they rappelled down the spire. A flash of steel, and with great effort, she bucked and toppled off the sternum altar. The dagger she narrowly avoided chinked into the bone and provided the only sound to mark the assassin's landing.

Nico spied the red flash of the Mythkeeper's hair, and the assassin disappeared behind that blur. But more assassins roped down the spire. Instinctively, she knew she needed to remain connected to the Elder. She stretched out her arm, trembling under the weight of her agony, and touched the bone sternum just in time.

Nico's heart burst.

Then she opened her eyes again, gasping with life, revived yet again. The magic healed, and then destroyed—trapping her in an endless cycle of death and rebirth. As long as she remained touching the altar, she would come back, dying and gasping, dying and gasping, until her body finally accepted the immense store of magic that the Elder offered. But if she lost the connection, she would stay dead.

A shrouded face pushed into her field of vision. She shuffled stiff fingers through the nearby basin, then stabbed the bone of a poor ancestor into the assassin's neck. Blood spilled down her arm. It rushed in her ears. She blacked out against the altar, dying again, and then came to with the weight of her attacker dead on her chest.

Steel flashed in the corner of her eye. On instinct, from years of training, she twisted a hand under the assassin's wrist and flipped the dagger out of their grip. She stabbed it through the assassin's chin and thrust it up into the brain.

She shoved off the assailant and yelped when someone grabbed her by the hair. An assassin stood atop the altar and pulled her up off the ground. Nico got an arm underneath the hold before a strong bicep wrapped around to crush her neck. She dropped down, off-balancing her attacker, and with a helpful assist from momentum and gravity, flipped the attacker over her back. Her attacker landed neck crooked at the base of the altar. She remained crouched atop the bone sternum, barefoot, in her bloody robe, hair tossed about her face.

Then lightning struck her. Finally, *finally*, the magic imprinted—branding her bones, and tattooing her from skull all the way to the phalanges of her small toes. She finally connected to the Elder's immense well of magic. The supply of it felt endless. If she had been a river before, now she was an ocean.

Nico whipped her head toward the remaining assassin locked in vicious combat with the Mythkeeper. She stepped off the altar, stretched out her arm and found her senses far sharper than they had ever been before—she felt the weight of two molecules in the air. Instinctively, she bonded them together.

Water formed in her palm.

Not moved. Not shifted. But created.

The Mythkeeper took a blow to the gut, then the assassin

turned toward Nico and charged. Nico inhaled.

Blood ripped from the shrouded figure, like a bloody flag waving, to splash and paint the surrounding bones, walls, and the Mythkeeper's face in a mad mosaic. The assassin slid across the sand pit a desiccated husk.

Silence suffocated the chamber.

The Mythkeeper stood. The Ohan didn't recognize this Mythkeeper and sneered when the Mythkeeper cautiously approached.

"Nico, this is the last endurance," the Mythkeeper said. "You've been accepted by the Elder, you've bonded with the Elder's magic, and now the memories of the other Ohans are overwhelming you. Find yourself. Remember who you are."

The Ohan's vision filled with fire, screams, and burning tents. The stench of death burned their nostrils. The person that the Mythkeeper called Nico threw their head back at the agonizing pain of childbirth. They collapsed back against the altar and widened their legs. Push. Push. Push. They've birthed many children. Held them in their arms. Eaten their placentas. Suckled babes at their breasts and pressed them to their chest with joy, at times sadness, at times melancholia.

They've killed many people. Ripped them apart with lightning and fire. Poisoned guts, cracked bones, and entombed souls alive. They've waged war, led purges, and died many, many, many times.

They've inhabited many bodies. Known many kulanis and many more flames. Have rocked on seas of skin and crested atop waves of pleasure. They've laughed mightily. They've hurt deeply. They've cherished joys.

Memory after memory, one life after another—an endless circle. They knew all of the stories ever told.

CHAPTER FOURTEEN

÷

Avalai Ohan was breastfeeding when the gondas attacked. The war drums sounded through the Grankull, calling all sentries to the frontlines as the ground began to vibrate. Ava identified five gonda incoming from the dawnward side of the wingfields. It had been a long time since a group of gonda attacked the Grankull, but the enduring drought made all the animals desperate.

She sat in her warehouse office where she oversaw the management of rations, her primary day-to-day job. She also worked evenings on the Council. There had been a time when Ohans were not expected to work, but past Ohans have learned that distance from the people bred bitterness and discontent. As if that mattered with Ava. They all hated her anyway. With good reason, but she had no regrets. She glanced at Kai reading in the corner of her office. No regrets.

He looked at her wide-eyed once the vibrations started. She had to get the children to a shelter. She pulled the thirteen-year till budchild off her lap. To maximize rations, most try to breastfeed their children for as long as possible. She had dried up early from stress with Kai, had been slammed with work and too busy to stay consistent with Nico, but with Rae, her sweet little Rae, she managed to keep them fed and healthy for the past two years. She was proud of that small achievement.

She fixed the half-shroud on Rae's face, hefted them on her hip, and motioned for Kai to follow her out of the office. The warehouse whirled in a state of chaos and panic as people gathered their things to leave for the shelters. Ava snapped out a disapproving word, and they all froze in place. They should be ashamed of themselves. Every season, they underwent drills to prepare for such an event. Ava soon had them following her orderly out of the warehouse.

As she stepped outside, Ava sensed for her third child and found Nico in school, where she was supposed to be. Nico's teachers would get the school children to safety. Ava wished she could hand off Kai and Rae and go fight at the front lines, but she didn't trust anyone with Kai. She needed to see them to the shelters first and then she would go help.

Ava whipped around at a sudden creak. The warehouse teetered. Cracks webbed along the wall, threatening to buckle. Someone behind her screamed. She thrusted out her free hand and full-grown palm trees sprouted from the ground to stabilize the wall. When she turned back around, a cloud of dust had formed from where the workers had fled down the street. Ava grabbed Kai by the hand, tightened her grip on Rae, and rushed toward the nearest shelter. There was one in every neighborhood.

A roar boomed through the sky.

The sound shocked Ava to a stop. Was that a dragon? There hadn't been a dragon on this side of the Desert in a long time. A distant shadow flew through the clouds, reinforcing the fact that yes, it was a dragon. Had the dragon followed the gonda all the way here, waiting for their chance to feast? The sentries wouldn't be prepared to handle this situation, not a dragon and five gonda. She looked down at Kai and knew there was no time to get them to a shelter anymore.

Ava glanced around for somewhere safe. She spotted a crack in the stone road, ripped along the edge of the vertebra steps that curved a hill up the Elder's neck. Ava pointed at the small crevice. "Get in."

Kai glanced at the hole, then back at her as if hoping her

command would change. Sometimes, the child had no self-preservation and no awareness of how frail he was compared to the other kids, an awareness she had hoped he would develop as he got older. Instead, her child was thick-headed and stubborn and would stand straight as lightning hits him. Only when she narrowed her eyes, did he scramble to squeeze into the crevice. She reached down and placed Rae into Kai's arms, and the children tucked against the curve of the large vertebra. She allowed one look back to ensure they were safely concealed. Elder protect them.

Then Ava shot off into the sky, propelled into the air atop a carpet of blooming pink tamarisks, and landed at the top of the Elder's half-turned skull. Most of the sentries stationed in this area had been drawn toward the gonda.

Ava planted her feet and took a stabilizing breath. Her long earrings of gold and lapis lazuli rattled in the wind. The scarab beetle and turquoise rings weighed heavily on her fingers. She had ruined her silk dress in her rush and breastmilk had stained the cloth. All those small annoyances and hindrances faded away. Connected to the Heart, she drew on the well of magic generations have stored in the Elder bones.

Ava summoned a date palm spear and launched it into the air. It missed, but it caught the dragon's attention. Dragons were territorial, but so was she. This was magicborn territory, and this dragon should certainly know better. The gold dragon exhaled fire, and Ava erected a wall of large expansive sycamores. Then she pulled up their roots and tossed them all into the air. One clipped the dragon's wing. Several fell into the Lakejaw, creating waves and flooding the banks. Another crushed a patch of orchard trees that Ava knew people would complain about later.

The dragon swooped around. They pressed their wings to their side and aimed straight toward her, talons out.

Ava wove a chord of papyrus stalks as the dragon neared. The sound cracked the air when Ava whipped the dragon's hide. Once. Twice. The dragon huffed, aborted the dive, and retreated into the clouds. They hung a shadow in the air, calculating, before finally retreating.

Ava held her breath just in case. This could be a ruse. Dragons were too crafty and intelligent to celebrate too soon. She tracked the dragon across the Desert and only released her breath when she was certain that she had succeeded in repelling the attack.

Eager to locate her children, Ava skipped down from the skull on a rain of hibiscus flowers. A fearful rage boiled her insides when she spotted Kai running toward her up the neck, with Rae half his size in his arms.

"I told you to stay!" Ava yelled at him. Kai flinched at her tone. He paused in the street and then his eyes went wide at a sight over her shoulder. She turned around to find one of the nearby granaries teetering, the one filled to the brim with wheat grains. In alarm, she dived toward the children.

The granary shattered against the stone ground, cracking sharp like a wind chime of a thousand broken pottery shards. Dust and sand filled her vision. Ava had erected a sphere of tightly woven tomato vines. Some of the tomatoes had time to ripen, and when crushed, had splattered red all over her clothes. She lifted off Kai and Rae, who had been knocked unconscious underneath her. Grain showered the ground around them. She tugged. Her right leg was trapped under a large debris that had breached her defenses. She couldn't feel any pain. That wasn't good.

Ava spotted movement in the dust and called out for help, hoping to find someone who could run for the nearest healer. She feared moving the debris without a healer nearby.

Kibari Oshield, the Ribs Councilor and Han of the Sentries, apparated out of the dust with an arrow knocked to her bow.

"The dragon?" Kiba immediately asked. Of course, Kibari would be running toward the dragon.

"Gone. I chased it away," Ava answered. They both shared a moment of relief, and then slowly, came the realization that they were alone, together, with all of their shared messy history. Kiba looked down at her bow. Ava tensed.

Ava deflected the arrow with a grape vine, then quickly followed by shooting the debris off her leg with two beams of doum palms. The debris launched straight at Kiba. The idea was to get herself and her children away as quickly as possible, but she hadn't been prepared for the agonizing pain that consumed her leg once the debris came free. A wave of nausea hit, and she fought to stay conscious.

Kiba's hands wrapped around her throat. Her head slammed back against a bed of scattered grains and crushed tomatoes.

"You don't have your magic to protect you anymore," Kiba snarled, squeezing tighter on Ava's throat. Ava fought for breath and clawed futilely at Kiba's arms. "You have owed me this blood price for a long time. I never forgave you for what you did. How dare you take my child away from me?"

"You took mine away from me first!" Ava gasped out. It was precisely because of their past friendship that she had planned to save Ysai for last. Fortunately for Ysai, it only took the public impaling of four children to convince the Council to finally give hers back.

"You think you are the only one to have lost children?" Kiba pressed. "The only one forced to make a choice? You aren't special. You had no right to cheat Death. No right at all. I hope this blood price satisfies all the children that you have slaughtered."

Ava punched Kiba in the face, hitting her with all the sharp jewels of her rings. The scarab caught Kiba in the eye. The blow loosened Kiba's grip and afforded Ava enough air for one final breath. The effort burned down her trachea. With her ruined leg, and up against the Sentry Han who had knowledge of how Ava's magic worked, she knew she was dying today. Might as well go out with a bang.

Don't ever let it be said that Ava didn't go out as petty as she lived.

She sensed through the Grankull, for Kiba's kulani, and found him among the adobe spires of the ribcage. Roots wrapped around the building and crushed the base until it came tumbling down.

Kiba froze at the sight of the distant spire collapsing. The resulting crash caused a boom so loud that it creaked the Elder bones. A lot of people probably died, but Ava didn't care. She never truly cared about any of these fools who never gave a shit about her.

"Was that you? What did you do?" Kiba whispered in horror.

Ava offered a crooked bloody grin. "You should probably check on your kulani."

Kiba stared down at Ava, and Kiba's previous anger cooled into calm resolve. "One day, I'll see your entire family wiped from the sands. No one should ever wield such power. The Grankull will be far safer without you and your ilk."

Kiba reached down and with both hands, picked up a large slab of rock broken off from the granary. She lifted the stone slab over her head. Dust and bruising marked her face.

"I'm paying my blood price," Ava wheezed. "When will you pay yours?"

Kiba slammed down the rock and Ava splattered against the cobblestones.

CHAPTER FIFTEEN

I

"Nico! Remember who you're fighting for!" A voice echoed. "Remember who you are!"

It didn't matter. Nothing the healers said mattered. Ava stubbornly clutched her tiny newborn to her chest, rocking Kai with the tired hope that the babe would finally stop crying. The healers thought something was wrong, but they didn't know anything. Just small was all. Ava was determined not to lose another one.

Ava killed the Councilor's child quickly, without pain, with more mercy than they'd ever give to Kai. The families watched on the temple steps in horror, sobbing out, but Ava didn't care. They took her child, so she took theirs.

Ava rocked her beautiful baby in her arms and teared up at the chubby health of her little Nicolai. Against her shoulder, Kai stared. Ava touched Kai's nose playfully and wrinkled his placid expression.

"Your name is Kailjnn, named for the sandstorm of your birth. This is your little jih, Nicolai, named for the First Rain after a long drought. You two have to protect one another, okay? The burdens you'll know will be uniquely yours, but you'll always have each other."

Nico looked up, chubby legs kicking out, to stare with a

newborn's curiosity. A light reflected in jih's eyes. There. In the glimmer, she found herself.

She couldn't stay swimming in her tah's memories. She couldn't linger over the lives of other Ohans. Those previous Ohans were the past. Their mistakes and knowledge and triumphs were the past. Their chapters ended, and what mattered was the story that she wrote now.

She stepped away from the bloody altar. Tajih asked, defensive and uncertain of the person standing before her, "Who are you?"

The answer came without a doubt.

"I am Nicolai Ohan."

CHAPTER SIXTEEN

1

A rattle banged down the Heart Spire.

Nico spun and crouched into a fighting stance when a corpse bounced off the altar, followed by the lithe landing of a shrouded figure. Bright eyes looked around and noted all the corpses scattered around the chamber.

"Now, those are terrible assassins."

The tension drained from Nico's shoulders. She straightened. "You were supposed to stop those terrible assassins. What happened?"

"Remind me not to make you angry," Kelin said as he tiptoed into the blood pooled around the altar. "We had more company than expected. Me and mine intercepted most of them. I didn't realize some were coming down the spire until it was too late."

"There were truly that many?" she asked.

"Most were free agents. But that one," Kelin motioned to the shriveled corpse she had stripped of blood, "is from the Jackal Han. Apparently, he couldn't afford to reject the offer but decided to send his 'worst.' I suspect the others calculated the same."

Nico had sent the other Tent Hans a message regarding the purge, hoping that the information might sway their involvement with tonight's assassination attempt. Admittedly, after her meeting with the Flock, her hopes hadn't been that high.

Nico swept her hand over the floor and washed away the blood. She wiped the blood from her skin and wrung it out of her ruined robe. Kelin wiggled his boots, and she cleaned them too.

Her tajih, the Mythkeeper, glowered at the defilement of the most sacred space in the entire Grankull. Nico did her best to clean up the blood, but some of the urns had been knocked over, and the throwing bones were scattered all over the floor. Something also had to be done about all the corpses.

"We need to report this," tajih said. "Assassins have never breached the bloodrites before. This cannot go unpunished."

Nico gave a deep sigh, a sound much too old for her age. "We can't. Rasia and Kai killed the dragon. The Council has no more justifiable excuses for a purge, and this was their attempt to create one. We report it, and the Tents will be blamed for this. Whether succeeded in killing me or not, either way, it is a trap. No one can know about tonight."

"They've gone too far," tajih hissed. "Someone let these assassins into the Grankull. Someone paid them. Someone told them about the spires. Who would think to rappel down them?"

The Han of the Sentries, Nico thought immediately, but couldn't say it out loud. A former Ohan had been so paranoid of being assassinated by his siblings that he had cast a spell of silence over the whole ceremony, which was why to this day, the ceremony was shrouded in such mystery. Nico couldn't reveal the truth she had learned of Ava-ta's death. But at least she finally had a name and a motivation. There were probably more perpetrators, but she was too tired to go searching for snakes in the sand tonight.

"Will you deal with the bodies?" she asked.

"They'll be taken care of," tajih said. Nico started for the door, but tajih caught her by the arm with those same bare hands that crushed an assassin's windpipe but a short vibration ago. "If you want to keep this a secret, the scribes outside cannot know. He must go out the way he came."

Right. She was getting too tired to think straight. Kelin looked up into the dark spire he had roped down, doubtful. "I don't think that's possible."

Nico grabbed him around the chest, and before he could protest, jetted up toward the moon. Kelin's startled scream echoed within the spire as he scrambled to wrap arms and limbs around her waist. She forgot to put her shroud back on, but that thin scrap of linen seemed laughable now. She spun toward the moonlight, toward that wide gaping eye, unafraid.

All hunters are hunted.

Even Death.

Nico and Kelin studied every shadow with suspicion as they cut through the temple gardens. When she stepped in sight of the front door, Kai came running out, barefoot in his rush, and shoved her into his arms. Almost immediately, he pulled back, and his perceptive eyes noted every rip in her caftan and every strand of hair out of place. Good thing he wouldn't have the chance to see the bloodied and torn ceremonial robes she had left behind for tajih to dispose of.

"What happened?" he asked.

"Oh, you know, just another night in the Grankull," Kelin chirped, his easy-going voice in direct contrast to the alert tension in his stance. He spun his pair of talon daggers with a casual air but stayed ready to throw them at any moment.

Then suddenly, Kelin attacked a large shadow that lumbered down the roof ladder. The weapon missed Zephyr's ear by a pinky finger. Kelin scrunched his nose, disappointed. "You do not flinch."

Zephyr frowned, unamused, as he approached. Nico had feared that assassins would be sent after her family, too, so Zephyr had agreed to guard the house. She mourned the fact that this had to be his first night in the Grankull.

"A few assassins made it past Kelin and his friends. They came down the spire," Nico explained to both Kai and Zephyr.

Zephyr glared at Kelin. "I guess the Flock's reputation isn't what they say it is."

Kelin straightened and raised his chin. "Excuse you. I thought your people were supposed to be monitoring the smuggling routes. How did so many get in?"

"They didn't come in through the illegal channels. According to tah's spies, there was a mix up of the sentries' schedules. Unofficially, it could have been anything—bribery, coercion, blackmail." Zephyr frowned. "Someone let them in."

"I appreciate both of your help," Nico said and placed a hand on each of their shoulders. Out in the Desert, they had generally been on each other's side but once returned to the Grankull, their Tent loyalties had become more pronounced. "We might never know the truth of what happened without an official investigation—but they probably know that. They know I'm not going to report this. But that doesn't mean tonight was a failure. They had the chance to assassinate me during the Forging and failed. They had the chance to assassinate me during the bloodrites and failed. Now that I am connected to the Elder, they must know it will be almost impossible to kill me. I'm too powerful now. They lost their last chance." Nico looked at both Zephyr and Kelin. "They're still trying to get rid of the Tents. They're still trying to justify their purge, but we won't give them a reason. Tonight, at least, we've won."

"Still Tent blood spilled in the end," Kelin said, sourly.

Right. Nico had washed off the blood, but she could still feel the sticky tack of it on her skin. Her attackers had been nothing but puppets on someone else's strings. She rubbed at her eyes, and those she killed flashed behind her eyelids.

"Good night," Kai said, decisively, speaking up.

"Think I'll hang out on the roof, though. Just in case," Kelin said.

Zephyr glanced at Kelin, who no doubt had the same idea. "It's going to be a long night, isn't it?"

Kelin fluttered his eyes.

"And Kelin-kull, Zephyr-kull, thank you," Nico said. She didn't know if she could have made it through the night without the both of them watching her back.

Zephyr smiled dimples. Kelin winked. Those two disappeared into the shadows behind the house.

Nico considered inviting them inside, but Kai insistently pulled her by the arm to the front door. The moment she hit the shroud room, she dropped to her hands and knees. Shaking. The magic singed like the pain of a fresh tattoo, still lingering long after the wound. She had made it this far on sheer force of will, but now she had gone as far as she needed. She didn't think she could move from the serving room floor.

To her surprise, Kai crouched down and lifted her onto his back. He had been weak and malnourished a blink and a half ago, and although still lean and skinny, he had gained a modest bit of strength. He balanced her weight and carried her through the house.

"I should have been there to protect you," Kai said, breathing through the effort.

"You know competing heirs are forbidden in the temple during the bloodrites."

"Technically, I'm not an heir."

"A technicality we couldn't risk. You were exactly where I needed you." Nico trusted Rae with no one else. "Is Rae asleep?"

"Just put them to bed. They were too wired from excitement now that I'm home, but Rae could tell something was going on." Kai deposited Nico onto her bed and then sprawled out next to her, chest heaving at the exertion. "You're heavier than Rasia."

Nico used what little strength she had left to knock him on the temple. He smiled and then pressed an intent hand to her forehead. "You should refrain from working the wingfields tomorrow," he said. "I'll send a message to your Han in the morning and explain that you're sick."

Nico's thoughts were as far away from work as they could have been at that moment. She had to tell him somehow about

Ava-ta. He needed to know the truth about their parent's death. He had been carrying around tah's death for far too long. Nico tried to pick her words carefully, attempted to circle around them or choose replacements, but no matter what angle she tried to approach the revelation, she couldn't break the spell of silence.

All spells were fallible. They were created from a person's will, but humans made mistakes, especially when overcome with emotion, and even with careful planning and logic, no one could foresee every circumstance or loophole. They were imperfect, and as such, so was the silencing spell of the bloodrites to the cursed spell of the Yestermorrow Lake. Rasia must have inadvertently found a loophole that had gotten her out of the Lake, although Nico couldn't guess at it. She needed a loophole now, but she could only manage a strained croak.

"You need to rest," Kai insisted. Then he reached for the edges of her caftan. With a defeated sigh, she stretched out her arms for Kai to pull the caftan over her head. She curled up and pressed her breasts to her knees while he crossed the room to retrieve her night shift from the chest at the foot of her bed. She submitted to being taken care of, and eyes half-lidded, followed Kai's gentle commands as he dressed her and combed her hair.

She yawned. Kai withdrew and returned the evory comb to the vanity, and she fell back against the headrest. "Tomorrow, when I'm more awake, you're going to have to tell me about the dragon."

Kai climbed into the bed next to her and tucked himself under the covers. He stared up at the ceiling. At night, glass pieces shone like stars through the oasis painting. "Aren't you going to do the thing?"

Nico's cheeks flushed, embarrassed. "I'm the Ohan now. I shouldn't waste time on such childish habits."

Kai blinked at her, waiting.

Fine. Nico rolled her eyes and said, "Good night, beautiful ibis."

Kai said, in turn, "Good night, tenacious camel."

"Good night, noble addax."

"Good night, fierce hawk."
"Good night, wild horse."
"Good night, laughing jackal."
"Good night, clever fox."
"Good night, mighty crocodile."
"Good night, big jih."
"Good night, little jih."
"Good night, Great Elder."
Good night, Nicolai Ohan.

CHAPTER SEVENTEEN

—

"Jijih, someone's in the house."

Kai jolted awake, hooked Rae under his arm, rolled to the ground, and squeezed through the trap door under his bed. His heart pounded as hard as the time he once watched Ava-ta eviscerate an assassin sent to kill him in his sleep. He remembered the sound of tah's vines ripping through flesh, and the intruder's startled dying gasp. He remembered how the blood spread across the stone floor to drip through the cracks of his hideout and rain down on his head.

Kai licked at the salty sweat above his lip as they stewed in the dark. He dared to whisper, "Is Nico up?"

"Sleep."

"I'm going to go get her. Stay here."

"No!" Rae shouted.

Kai quickly pressed his hand over little jih's mouth, but Rae leaked faint whines through Kai's fingers. If discovered by an assassin, Kai wasn't sure he could protect them. He slayed a dragon. He was supposed to be stronger, but he was not willing to bet his jih's life on it.

"We'll go together," he decided. He knew these halls better than any intruder. "But you have to be quiet."

Rae nodded against the thin linen of Kai's sleep shift. Kai hiked

Rae tighter to his chest and rocked his balance to his thighs. He prepared to spring from under the bed, swipe his dagger from the top-shelf, and sneak his way to Nico's bedroom. He lifted the trap door the exact moment a shout rang throughout the hallway. "Kai! Where the fuck are you? Is this another dead-end?!"

At the familiar voice, Kai crumpled against the sharp edge of the trap door's entrance. "It's Rasia," Kai told both Rae and his frayed nerves. "It's just Rasia."

And yet his heart still pounded. His throat remained tight. His body refused to uncoil.

"Who Rasia?" Rae asked.

Rae peeked out as if under the covers after a nightmare looking for monsters. Kai hooked an arm around his little jih and climbed out of their hiding spot, which used to be a wine cellar in the storage closet of Kai's room. He tried to place Rae on their feet, but the kid refused and wrapped their arms gonda-tight around his chest.

"It's okay," Kai soothed. He hefted the eleven-year-till more securely onto his hip, and then hunted Rasia down to confront her about the intrusion. The relief of the situation had washed away, and anger took its place.

He followed the sounds of Rasia's vocal frustrations at the intentional maze of their home. Thousands of years ago, a magic-born had erected and designed these walls specifically to ward off intruders, because although an adult's magic is powerful, the children not yet come into their magic are still vulnerable. The layout made sense to those who had been raised within its walls, but guests and intruders, and even Kenji on brief occasions, were endlessly lost. Kai was grateful for the small measure of protection, but he had seen it fail far too many times to feel entirely safe.

"Why is this the same dead fucking end?!" Kai found Rasia kicking a wall.

When they returned from the Forging, Rasia had been carried away on the tide of her family and triumph. After hearing nothing from her in days, Kai honestly thought he had been forgotten.

He was admittedly caught off-guard that he wasn't. Tucked within his small corner of the Grankull, it was so easy to believe the Forging had been a distant dream. But here was Rasia, like a splash of cold water.

She turned with a groan on her heel. Then her eyes brightened and greeted him with unreserved excitement. Kai's anger wavered, but Rae's outright terror kept it from dissipating completely.

"You should have checked-in with the sentry," he said.

Rasia's sprint to reach him slowed, petering off as the smile dropped from her face. She gave a wry sharp-edged laugh. "Check-in with a sentry? Why the fuck would I do that?"

"You scared Rae."

You scared me, but Kai didn't want to admit to that.

She glanced at the young budchild. "They'll get over it. Let's hangout."

She walked down the hallway, expecting him to follow. Kai's jaw tightened as he struggled to keep pace with her while holding at least ten bricks of another person. He knew this was a huge ask. Most households didn't have assigned sentries, and this was Rasia, with little patience and always doing what she wanted. And yet, most people didn't invade other people's homes without warning either.

"Rasia, you need to check-in with the sentry," he insisted.

"You mean the one asleep at your front door?" she spun around a corner, the wrong one. He could barely catch up to correct her. "Why is this place such a maze? Anyway, I was thinking we could swing by the market today, and then the training fields to get some practice for the kull tryouts. We still have a lot to do to get you ready. I know-"

"Rasia, stop," Kai snapped.

She halted, *finally*.

He didn't know why it was all too overwhelming—why now Rasia was suddenly too much. He needed a moment of pause. He needed time to adjust to the interruption of his carefully maintained routines. He was *still* fucking light-headed from her unannounced entry.

Her annoyed glare shifted to one of concern as she took him all in. She slackened, and then pouted. "I just . . . wanted to spend time with you."

"I know. *I know.*" Kai knew he didn't sound convincing. At the crack in his voice, Rae jumped from his arms and charged at Rasia.

"Meanie!" Rae punched her in the stomach.

Kai scrambled after Rae and tugged them back. Rasia looked shocked at first, as if all this time Kai had been carrying a doll around and not a real person that might come to life at any moment. Then her eyes narrowed. She pointed at Rae. "Next time, I'm going to bite you."

"Enough," Kai said. "Rasia, I still need to feed Rae breakfast and give them a bath before we can do anything. Rae, hit her again and no toys for the rest of the day."

"What's going on?"

Nico peeked her head from the adjoining hallway. Her hair frizzed sleep-mussed around her head. She looked so much better than the days following the bloodrites. His memory still lingered on the paleness of her on that moonlit night, as if she had seen Death and had been cursed from describing it.

Rae raced from Kai's arms to Nico's. The toddler climbed around her like sprouting vines on a trellis and proclaimed, "She was being mean to Kai!"

"The brat punched me in the stomach!"

Nico gave Rasia a half-awake stare. "You probably deserved it. Why are you here? It's hardly past first drum."

"I'm here because I was going to blowjob your jih awake, but I couldn't find his fucking room."

"Rasia!" Nico slapped her hands over Rae's ears.

Kai snatched Rasia's hand and pulled her down the hallway. Rasia cackled madly as he wound her back around to the front of the house. He kissed her to attention in the serving room.

"Good morning to you too," she said and licked her lips with a hyena grin.

"If you refuse to go through the sentry, let me at least show you how to get to my room." Because he had to face it—Rasia was never going to have the patience to check in with the sentry, and if she was going to flit about as she saw fit, she might as well know how to get to him without scaring his little jih half to death. He led her through the maze and narrated the twists and turns.

"What have you been up to?" Rasia asked.

"I've been here, watching Rae. Nico was conscripted into helping with the Forging haul. She has been working the wingfields."

Everyone had been excited to see the dead dragon, at first, until it dawned on everyone the amount of work it required. From what Kai understood, they were still chopping up Nico's gonda when the dragon arrived. Then there was First Harvest and all the preparations needed for the Naming Ceremony. Children were pulled from classes to help the tanners. Sentries were re-assigned from their posts. Everyone, from weavers to brick-makers to merchants, had mobilized to organize the sudden influx of food and resources. With Rae on his heels, Kai had assisted tajih with scribe work, while most of her employees cataloged the dragon bones.

Thankfully, all the chaos had finally calmed.

"I figured you were busy with the same," he said.

"*Technically.*" She shrugged. "The healers were running low on a few herbs. But they didn't have the staff to send a kull out for it, considering all the help needed with the haul and all the kids recovering from Forging injuries and whatnot. On behalf of the Council, tah volunteered jih to go after more. I decided to join him. I wasn't going to stay here and deal with all the haul-madness. I tried looking for you before I left, but the sentry said you weren't in."

"Oh," he said, surprised by the fact she had come looking for him. "I might have been with tajih. I was helping her at the temple."

Rasia ran her hand along the sepia brick wall. Her fingertips danced over tapestries and the colorful mosaics. She peeked her head into all the rooms they passed: the library, the storage, the lounging rooms. Kai automatically hooked an arm around her waist and pulled her from wandering into the dojo.

"We'll come back," he promised.

Rasia walked backward atop his feet and clung to his hips. "How did things go with Kenji-shi? How did he react when he found out you killed a dragon? I bet he was real impressed."

"He doesn't know."

"He doesn't know?"

"He left with the hunting kulls once the warship pulled in."

"Oh. That sucks. Well, I'm sure it will be fine once you tell him how you slayed a dragon. Kenji-shi always listens."

"He'll be back tomorrow. I'll tell him then." The moment that they had slayed the dragon, Kai began imagining all sorts of ways how the conversation would go. He was equally both terrified and anxious, and tried placing as few expectations on the conversation as possible. Maybe, Kenji would finally call him by his name.

When they reached Kai's room, Rasia threw her hands up in exasperation. "I might need to make a map."

"At least it's not behind the secret door."

"Wait. There's a secret door?"

". . . yeah? It leads to the inner chamber where Nico sleeps."

"I'm making a map."

Rasia wandered around his bedroom. He followed her nervously, suddenly self-conscious of the cramped and narrow space not even big enough to accommodate a window. It was odd, having Rasia in his room. To have her roaming her fingers over every surface and exploring it through her endless curiosity. His stomach churned with anxiety.

What if she asked why he lived in an obviously re-purposed storage closet? Or why he didn't sleep in the inner chamber with his other siblings? Or why it was in a random nonsensical corner of the maze? His makeshift bed, built atop a shelf for earthenware, barely accommodated Kai and Rae, much less Kai and Rasia. Kai didn't know how she fit—in his bedroom, in his routines, or in his life. He feared it would not be big enough for her.

Over her shoulder, webbed the cracked wall where Kenji had thrown him the day before the Forging. The adobe brick floor where she stood, at the edge of her heel, tinted dark from the blood of the intruder his tah had once killed. No. Rasia didn't fit wandering the wicker and mudbricks of his nightmarish existence. He suddenly and urgently didn't want her in his room anymore.

"Rasia," Kai called out. He moved to grab her, but she had already turned and flounced on his pallet of linen stuffed palm-leaves. With a jackal grin, she roamed her eyes down Kai's figure, interested in only one thing in the room. Her face dropped in confusion. "What's wrong?"

"Nothing," he said quickly. He stuffed away all the fear and anxiety. She didn't seem to care about the details or the obvious questions he didn't have answers to. With a relieved sigh, he fell upon her on the bed. Despite all the chaos she brought with her, it was one of her traits that he appreciated the most. He missed the ease of her underneath him. He missed the soft smiles she only gave to him. He missed their tangled limbs. Rasia was easy in a way the rest of his world wasn't.

"I don't know if I'm ever going to get used to this," Nico said.

Kai peeled away from Rasia, flushed and lip-bitten, to find Nico at the door. Rae's brown curls peeked from behind Nico's legs. A little distance seemed all the permission for Rae to come jumping into the room. They leaped onto Kai's lap and squeezed Rasia out of the way. It was painfully obvious how Rae was unaccustomed to being anything other than the center of Kai's attention.

Nico glanced at him, and immediately he knew what she was thinking. He subtly shook his head, but Nico was too prideful not to be a good host. She asked, "Would you like to join us for breakfast?"

"Yeah, sure, whatever," Rasia agreed. He winced at her thoughtlessness.

"Kai, why don't you give Rae a bath? I should be done with breakfast by then," Nico said and rushed from the doorway before Kai could take back Rasia's words.

He sighed, then looked down at Rae, who harrumphed at the idea of bathing. He tickled their sides until the grumpiness broke into rolling giggles. "You heard her, bath time."

"NO!" Rae rolled, slid down Rasia's back and, as if they didn't do this every day, ran screaming out the door.

"Rasia, do you mind?"

"Gladly." She pounced up and raced out of the door.

Kai sat there, taking a much-needed moment. He clutched his head, still feeling a little faint and dizzy, and hoped if he sat still long enough, the room might stop spinning. He soon heard a screech. His cue to get up.

Rasia met him, jogging down the hallway, with Rae kicking over her shoulder. "I don't get it. All my little cousins run away from me too. Am I really that scary?"

"Depends on the day," Kai answered diplomatically. He up-righted and grabbed Rae from her arms, who sobbed betrayed and faux-traumatized.

"Where are we taking them? To the lake? To the bathhouse?"

"No, we have a bath here," he said.

Her brows rose.

Kai led Rasia through the maze toward the inner chamber. He pressed the patterned tiles in the wall and the secret door receded. Compared to the rest of the house, the space and opulence of the inner chamber reflected a by-gone era when the Grankull had no Council and the magic-born had ruled absolutely. Very few non-family members had ever stepped inside of it.

Murals of histories, of wars, and legends that gradually turned the land more arid and stained with magic, decorated the walls in bright splashes of color. A magic-born from a long time ago had carved the artwork. It still buzzed with magic at night, sometimes shifting images and scenes in the corner of the eye.

"Is this . . . us?" Rasia touched the painting of a warship sailing toward the Grankull. Kai studied the image over her shoulder and was unsurprised by its appearance. It must have shifted last night—perhaps the only thing in this entire house which anticipated Rasia's arrival.

"It does that. The wall reflects the past, even that which happened a few days ago."

Rasia slid her hands along the images, pointing out scenes from stories she knew and studying others she didn't recognize. Eventually, they made it to the bath. Red flowers from the large poinciana tree that grew on this side of the house floated atop the water. Rays of sunlight cascaded over the room, blooming warmth through the patterned ceiling slats above.

"You have your own private lake," Rasia said, astounded. "I didn't know this was a thing that could exist."

"Some great-great-great-granta used his magic to funnel water from the cistern to the bath." Kai walked around the corners to burn the kyphi incense. They didn't have much left and only used it for special occasions, but the bath soon swelled full of the relaxing aroma—warm and sweet, and a little spicy. The smell always reminded him of his tah. She always wore it thick in her hair and on her skin.

"Your house is so . . ." she scrunched her face. "Magical."

He had never thought of it that way. Except for his tajihs' place, he had never been invited over to someone else's house to compare. Until the Forging, all he knew were these adobe walls.

Items clinked and clanked to the floor. Kai dunked aside the splash Rasia made as she jumped into the bath. She swam naked laps around the pool. A scattered trail of clothes, leather belts, her khopesh, and daggers trailed the floor in her rush to undress. She moved a lot better now, and he noted that her Forging injuries had finally had some time to heal.

"What other cool things do you have back here?" she asked. The necklace he had given her sparkled wet between her collarbones.

"There are some old relics and stuff, but for the most part it's just the bedrooms."

"How come your bedroom isn't with the others?"

He froze. His tongue felt heavy with the answer. Rae

exclaimed beside him, "To have a place where I can hide from my nightmares!"

Kai physically felt his bones soften. He ruffled Rae's cloud of curls. "That's right, grubworm."

Rae beamed, absent a front tooth that Kai had missed falling out. They saved that tooth to show Kai after he returned from the Forging. Sometimes, he felt guilty for missing so much. Rae had begun to follow him around the house to make sure he wouldn't leave again, and while it did feel stifling at times to take care of jih every vibration of the day, that was little sacrifice for the unconditional adoration he received in return. This morning, Rae ran to Kai first, when they should have run to Nico. To Rae, Kai was never the monster, or the runt. He had always been bigger in his little jih's eyes.

Kai gently knocked their foreheads together, then stripped Rae of their clothes and sat them in the shallow side of the bath. They grabbed for their toys while Kai gathered the soap and towels.

"Are you getting naked?" Rasia leaned over the side and watched him with that ever-present mischief in her eyes. She reminded him of some wild thing he somehow convinced to follow him home. He stared at her, dramatically tied his robe up at his thighs, then sat down on the shallow step behind Rae.

"Boo, at some point we've got to defile this bath."

"Trust me, it already is." Kai did not doubt that generations of magic-born have fully enjoyed all of the benefits of this bath.

Rasia laughed, then splashed over a wave of water. Rae perked to attention and pointed. "She splashed! You're not supposed to splash!"

"You're not supposed to splash *me*," he amended.

Rae crowed, then kicked their feet to splash at Rasia. It became the first shot in a bitter war that left Kai the drenched casualty. But he didn't mind. He settled into the mirth and allowed the warmth of their play to balm his anxieties.

During the Forging, Kai hadn't allowed himself to imagine what it would truly be like for Rasia to be in his life, but he could see it now. He imagined many more disrupted mornings and many more shenanigans. He imagined waking up to Rasia's laughter every day. He imagined adventures on kull hunts, walking the streets proudly hand in hand, and a family. The images hit him all at once and with such speed, he felt dizzied by them.

Water splashed his face. Both Rae and Rasia laughed. The walls resonated with their joy, and Kai's chest swelled with happiness. He hugged his arms around his hopes. Yes. He could get used to this.

CHAPTER EIGHTEEN

—

Breakfast included a plate of spongy flatcakes drizzled with date syrup, a shared bowl of gonda noodles, and cups of cinnamon black tea, with warm camel milk for Rae. Nico cut the two flatcakes into fours. She prepared what they could spare, but it paled in comparison to any meal Kai had out in the Desert.

"Is that it?" Rasia asked, without any sort of tact. Since her clothes hadn't survived the splash-war and were currently hanging on the line to dry, she sat at the table in one of Kai's old caftans. "I thought they increased the size of everyone's rations since the Forging?"

Kai grimaced. Nico stiffened, and embarrassment flushed her cheeks.

"Everyone's portion has increased, but I still don't get rations," he explained. "And I won't until after the ceremony and even then, until I get a job."

"Oh." Guilt marred her face. "I forgot. I should not have gone with Ysai-ji. I left you here to starve."

His teeth clacked down on her words. He hated their implication—as if he were some helpless baby bird who needed someone to feed him. "It's not your fault."

"But I'm your kulani," she said.

"*What?!*" Nico swiveled towards Kai. "You're calling each

other kulani now?"

Rasia sat on his right, but she spun the full way around on the woven seating mats to face him. "You didn't tell her?"

"Are you two insane?" Nico asked before Kai could meep out a word. "Couples together for years barely call themselves kulani. Many don't even dare without a signing ceremony. Don't you think this is moving too fast?"

"What does it matter when I'm apparently the only one who cares about him?" Rasia snapped. She motioned toward the food. "You're the triarch. What the fuck is this?"

"She said bad word!"

Kai dropped his face into his hands.

Nico slammed her hands onto the table, standing up. She pointed at Rasia. "*How dare you*. You don't get to charge into this family and criticize me. You have no idea what I have sacrificed to keep this family afloat for the past year. Don't you, especially you, fucking *dare*. You didn't have to stay for breakfast."

"*You invited me.*"

"*Read the room!*"

"Nico. *Please*," Kai begged. Her eyes narrowed, and she stiffly sat back down. Rae crawled from Kai's lap, under the table to Nico. She hugged them like a pillow.

Rasia crossed her arms with a huff. "I won't stay if you don't want me here, but I won't allow your *negligence* to bring Kai any more harm. Who knows how this week could have affected his magic or his health?"

"What are you talking about? What does any of this have to do with his magic?"

Rasia swiveled hotly back to Kai. "*You haven't told her?!*"

He kept his face a blank mask, careful not to leak anything while the right side of his cheek was hot with Nico's scrutiny. He narrowed his eyes at Rasia in a futile attempt to remind her of the promise to keep his magic a secret. "There is nothing to tell."

"Tell me what?" Nico crunched every word.

"Kai figured out the secret to his magic," Rasia revealed without pause. Did she not understand any of his minute eyebrow wiggles? Had she forgotten their promise already? "Apparently, Kai's magic is so powerful it's almost parasitic. He needs food to fuel it. Without food, his magic feeds on him instead. It's why he used to be so sickly before. He found all this stuff out in The Lake of Yestermorrow."

"You promised to keep it a secret," Kai hissed out.

"I have."

"You just told Nico!"

"She's your jih. You said not to tell the Grankull, but Nico is your jih and your triarch. How can she make sure you're eating if she doesn't know these things?"

"Jih is the main person I didn't want to know!" Kai checked his raised voice and turned in horror to Nico's shadowed face. She had her shoulders up, in that way, when she was hurt.

She whispered, "You were never going to tell me, were you? All these years, and no one could figure out what was wrong with you. This whole time, you suffered because we couldn't provide for you."

"That is exactly why I didn't want to tell you. This isn't your burden to bear."

"Of course, it is," she snapped. "I am to be the triarch. All of you are my responsibility. You should have told me."

"You're dealing with enough as it is, and I am done watching you all suffer because of me."

"You are my jih and we are a family. Despite what you've gotten into your head during the Forging, you need to realize that you can't do everything by yourself. Nor can I. No one can. I can't take care of this family alone."

"How many meals have you missed this week?" Rasia's words knifed sharp through the conversation. He didn't like the way she studied the lines of his face. "I thought something was off this morning. You've lost weight."

Kai didn't answer.

"How many meals have you seen him eat, Nico?" Rasia asked.

"We eat dinner together, but I leave for the haul before Kai and Rae wake for breakfast in the morning." Nico paused, catching on. She turned to their little jih, and sweetly asked, "Rae, is Kai being good and eating all his food? Or does Kai need all his toys taken away?"

Rae shifted wide-eyed to Kai and back to Nico. Loyally, they whispered, "It's a secret."

Both Nico and Rasia shouted. Kai hunched under their raised voices, blending at times to create a monster fused from Nico's disappointment and Rasia's outright anger. What was happening? How had the alliances shifted so suddenly? One moment Nico and Rasia were at each other's throat, and the next they were ganging up on him. He could hardly keep up.

They could yell at him all they wanted, but they haven't had to swallow down the guilt and live a parasitic existence off their own family. Kai had no regrets. The next he tuned in, both Rasia and Nico had shifted from yelling at him to figuring out solutions.

"We talked about this. There are options. You don't have to starve yourself. I'm going to take the windship out," Rasia declared.

"Or maybe there would be more rations for everyone if certain persons didn't keep illegally smuggling in food for themselves," Nico argued. "Every hunt is for everyone."

"Except for Kai. *He gets no rations*. So, we should do what? Let him starve for your morals?"

"I didn't say that." Nico turned to Kai. "I'm selling tah's stuff."

Thus far, Nico had sold off her own personal items for the family. They hadn't touched any of Ava-ta's stuff for a reason. They feared upsetting Kenji.

"No. We won't do any of that." Kai rejected them both. "No smuggling. No pawning. I'll eat. I promise." That was a lie. Rasia bought it, but Nico knew better. "I'll make do until the kull tryouts. As a windeka, I'll be out of the Grankull for most of the year with the kulls. I'll be able to eat my own hunt, and therefore won't be a burden on anyone else. It's the best-case scenario."

"What? I thought you had given up on the tryouts?" Nico asked. "You haven't mentioned it at all since you've been back, and you've been spending all this time helping tajih with scribe work. We both know that's a guaranteed job for you."

"I was going to mention it," Kai mumbled. Nico was always rushing out of the door for him to really have a conversation with her about it. Or he kept putting it off because to talk about it meant he was really going to try out.

"*You haven't told Nico about that either?!*"

"Welcome to my life!" Nico said. She rubbed her temples and squinted at Kai from the table. "Is that what you truly want? To be a windeka?"

"I'd like to try."

"Then I'll support you. I've promised you that. But have you considered everything? *Are you sure?*" Kai knew the question jih tried to couch in softer words. What if he failed?

"Tajih offered me a job as a scribe if I fail the tryouts. I've already talked with her." It would be nice if the Forging wiped away all his problems and made all his dreams come true, but he also felt better with a fallback plan. Visible relief washed over jih's face. She nodded, mollified.

"Fuck that scribe shit. You're passing the tryouts," Rasia declared. "And you're eating."

"She said bad word!"

"Rasia, don't curse in front of Rae."

"Then don't fucking starve yourself," she snapped out. "You're coming with me to the market. I can get you some food. People owe me."

"What do you mean people *owe* you?" Nico asked.

"Don't ask questions you don't want the answers to," Rasia swiveled back to Kai. "You need to eat. There's no point preparing for the tryouts if you pass out halfway through. You also need a new pair of pants. The ones you picked up from Timar are ripped, and the ones I gave you are getting short at the ankles. You need a pair that truly fits you."

"We don't have the money to-" Kai said, but quieted when Rasia gave him that same look when she threatened Neema with a jawbone.

"We'll stop by my place and grab some of jih's old pants. Think he was going to give them to a younger cousin or whatever, but you need them more. We'll have them resized for you. It won't cost as much as buying a new pair."

"He needs new shoes, too," Nico said, eyes alighting in tentative excitement.

"Hmm. I have an idea for that. We'll go once my clothes are dry." Rasia glanced over at him, at the table of practically untouched food, and then tossed her plate at him. "*Eat.*"

At the order, everyone remembered breakfast. Nico rolled the flatcake in her hands, and the rest of them followed suit. Rasia gulped her tea and watched Kai with an intensity that threatened him with every bite. They cleared the plates, and Rae licked at the date honey on their fingers.

"Rasia, when is your interview?" Nico asked.

"Tomorrow. Why?"

"Do you remember the story we all agreed on? Maybe we should go over the details again. Everyone else's interviews went off without a hitch, but your kull is the only one left for questioning."

"I honestly thought I'd never see the day perfect little Nico would be so willing to lie to the Council."

"They tried to kill me. Several times at this point."

Rasia's brows rose. "Have they sent more assassins since the Forging?"

"They tried to attack Nico during the bloodrites," Kai said.

"But not after you?"

". . . no?"

"Okay then." Rasia shrugged, unconcerned. "Nico can handle a few assassins. How close did they get? Did they nick your hair?"

"This isn't funny. We need to make sure you get your story straight."

"Fine, whatever. Tell me the story again. I might have forgotten some of the details."

"I kept it as simple as possible. After our initial kull fell apart, I traveled to the oasis and got several teams together to take down a bunch of gonda at once. The Council mustn't know I had any run-ins with the scavengers. I don't want them to know that I know about their involvement. As far as you and I are concerned, after our falling out, we both went to the oasis. I found my team and you found yours. We went our separate ways and did our own thing from there. How you tell the rest of the story is up to you."

"But *I* can talk about the scavengers, right? They are going to want to know how I got the warship."

"Feel free to take the credit for defeating the scavengers all by yourself."

"I basically did." Rasia nodded. She turned to Kai. "We might have to talk to the others and make sure we are all on the same page."

"Not much needs to change, I think," Kai said. "The easiest thing to do is start with the moment you recruited me. Instead of just me, you recruited everyone who was involved with the dragon hunt at the end. We ran into trouble with the scavengers, got the warship, and killed the dragon. We . . . streamline the story."

"You know, this would be a whole lot less stuff to remember if we just kill the whole Council."

Nico scrutinized Rasia at that comment. "That includes your tah."

"Especially her."

"No," Nico said, even though she said it with a hitch of hesitation. "The one time a magic-born indiscriminately killed Council members, they killed him in turn. I need to be smart about this. If the Council learns that some might not have earned their hunt, they'll no doubt blame it on me, but more importantly, those kids won't have a chance to show their faces. I picked up more, you know, after the Graveyard. I brought back anyone left alive that I could find."

"You picked up everyone?"

"There was enough gonda."

"What are the hunting kulls going to think when they don't find any survivors? They are going to be suspicious. That was a needless risk."

"They won't suspect a thing. People are already calling it a lucky year—what with your dragon and all the gonda—this will only support that," Nico defended.

Still, Kai was a little worried about the plan. Ava-ta had been powerful, too. She had those she trusted around her, too. But she still died long before she could see any of her children succeed in their Forging. Kai remembered how weak and ill Nico had been after the bloodrites. How could he possibly add his own mess on top of that?

"It'll work," Nico said, determined, "if we're all in it together. If we do this right, the Grankull will never know."

CHAPTER NINETEEN

—

Rasia tossed her shroud about her face, messy and unhinged and ready to unravel at any moment. Kai wrapped Rae in their half-shroud, slow and careful, and tucked in all the loose ends until only the bright copper of their eyes showed. Since Rae was a budchild, not yet reached puberty, they could get away with a half-shroud and a white loincloth in public. Kai finished wrapping his own shroud and then stared at the open doorway with a trembling breath.

He never ran errands by himself. Not anymore. Not since the incident. Sometimes, when he didn't have a choice, he would bring Rae because it meant the sentry would accompany them. But the sentry wasn't always attentive and often saw this job as easy rations. Rae sensed his jitters, and as instructed whenever they go outside, held tightly onto Kai's hand.

He and Rae emerged from the doorway and found the sentry snoozing atop the swinging bench of the veranda. Still holding Kai's hand, Rae leaned forward and poked the sentry's arm. The sentry snorted awake and blinked blearily at them.

"We need to go to the market today," Kai said.

"Not right now," the sentry grunted and settled back down. His butt hung off the bench while his back lounged against the house. The sentry's spear laid carelessly against the trellis.

"The fuck did he stutter?" Rasia asked, emerging from the doorway.

The sentry glanced at her and laughed. "I don't answer to some cunt desperate for skink dick. Go home."

Her eyes narrowed through the slit of her shroud, the only warning before Rasia leapt over the porch table and pottery. The sentry reacted, shooting up at the sudden action, to fall back off the bench when Rasia slammed the sentry's head to the ground and twisted his arm. It popped.

"Too bad you can't effectively do your job anymore with that broken arm. Looks like you need to request a replacement. Tell them Rasia, child of Kibari Oshield, sent you." She released him. The sentry scrambled up and wind swept through the chimes at how quickly he bolted down the road.

Kai had never seen that sentry move so fast.

Rasia slapped rolls of gonda leather onto the tailor's table. Kai's eyes widened at the sight of it and at the casual way she pulled the rolls from under her caftan and unstrapped them from her back. He spotted other things under her caftan she was not supposed to have—her twin khopesh, sheathed and strapped to her curves by buckles and straps, vials of various animal materials clipped to a belt along her waist, and a pair of pants cut to the knees.

Kai knew Rasia illegally smuggled food into the Grankull, but it made sense she was smuggling other parts of the gonda as well. Every hunt belonged to the Grankull for the Council to appropriate to various sectors, nor were they allowed to wear pants again until after the Naming Ceremony. He remembered all the items scattered alongside the rim of the bath, but the implication didn't hit him until now. Every inch of Rasia, from head to toe, could be considered illegal.

"I want a pair of pants in his measurements," Rasia indicated

Kai. "A rush-order. We need it in time for the Naming Ceremony. As usual, the leftover leather should be enough to buy your silence."

"Always a pleasure doing business with you," the tailor said. He grabbed the rolls of illicit leather and tucked them away. The tailor licked over the metal ring in his lip. "Did you manage to snatch any of that dragon leather?"

"You don't want those problems," Rasia reproached. Dragon leather was often used for ceremonial purposes and was rarely available for public purchase. Because of it, the Grankull tracked and monitored it more closely than any other resource.

"You're right," the tailor grumbled.

The tailor indicated Kai to come over. Kai ducked under a curtain of suspended leather pouches and weaved through the displays of linen pants with detailed stippling on the waistbands. He admired the green snake leather, the gold speckled pattern of gonda, and the scorpion black that gleamed red in the sun. Towers of white linen were stacked in the back of the shop. Rae held tightly onto his hand, never letting go since they had stepped out of the front door of their house.

Kai stopped where the tailor indicated. It was the first time he had ever been measured for anything. He watched the tailor wrap a notched string about his waist.

"The little one is going to have to let go."

Kai nodded to Rae. They separated to allow the tailor to complete the circle around Kai's waist and once released, Rae raced to touch everything in the shop. Before Kai could stop them, they disappeared into a cavern of leather.

"Rasia, can you get them?"

"Let them have their fun." She tossed an uncaring hand over her shoulder. She leaned atop the tailor's table. "Maybe make the pants a little looser? He'll be gaining some weight soon."

"I thought we were going to alter your jih's pair?" Kai asked her when the tailor left to grab a different measurement string.

"That's what I told Nico. This business," Rasia circled her hand around the store, "is between us."

"Like how my magic was supposed to be between us?"

"She's your jih."

"As if you tell your jih everything."

Rasia laughed at that. "Oh, I do."

The tailor returned and finished measuring Kai's frame with a more knotted string. The tailor didn't write anything down but memorized the numbers in his head. "I'll make sure the pants are ready for pick-up the morning of the ceremony."

"Perfect."

"Is it true?" the tailor asked. "That he killed a dragon?"

"He's standing right in fucking front of you. You can ask him yourself."

The tailor's neck hinged, notching several vibrations at a time to finally look Kai in the eyes for the first time since he entered the shop. The tailor's smooth professionalism dropped for a moment to stare at him in gross fascination. He bowed his head under the scrutiny and waited for the question, but it never came.

One of the linen towers toppled.

Almost in relief, Kai rushed to retrieve Rae from underneath the falling sheets of white. He peeled one of the linen cloths from Rae's head and revealed their cheeky face. He held out his hand. Obediently, they locked back their fingers. By the time he returned to the front of the shop, the tailor had moved on.

"What's next for you?" the tailor asked Rasia. "Following Shamai Windbreaker's footsteps to become a kull hunter?"

"Of course. Don't know what happens with the business after that, but I am my tah's kid. It'll be a kull's life for me."

"I reckon with you in the hunting kulls, the Grankull will never starve again. Stay wary the Hunter."

"Wary the Hunter," Rasia said. She took two steps out of the store, when she suddenly stopped. Kai ran into her, then looked past her shoulder. The sun gleamed a crown atop the head of a giant, who peered down at her, with an unimpressed expression.

"*What did you do this time?*" Ysai asked.

"That sentry sucked at his job, and he made fun of Kai's dick. He had it coming."

"Yes, but," Ysai indicated Kai and Rae, "they can't be out in public without a sentry. The Grankull will think we're not doing our jobs."

"Trust me, you weren't." Rasia nudged Ysai with her elbow. "Tah sent you, as usual, to clean up my mess? You're the replacement sentry?"

Ysai huffed. "Yes, I'm the replacement sentry."

Rasia cheered. Then she grabbed him by the arm and dragged him over to Kai. "Ysai-ji. Kai. Ysai-ji. Kai's grubworm."

"Rae," Kai said, automatically, faintly.

Throughout the Forging, Rasia had jealously complained of Ysai's height, but there was nothing like experiencing it first-hand, like the difference between spotting an enormous sand dune in the distance and finally standing at the base of its shadow. Kai felt utterly small in comparison. Ysai towered over not only him, but most of the crowded market. Most of Ysai's dusty brown hair had been gathered into a braided snake down his back. He wore the typical armor of the sentries: a gonda leather vest, a dragonsteel spear, and a carapace shield.

Ysai grinned, an odd replica of Rasia's own, and said, "I've heard a lot about you these past few days. *A lot.*"

Rasia stuck out her tongue.

Kai remembered her words back in the tailor's shop—how she tells her jih everything. His face warmed, and an anxiousness jittered through his limbs. Surely, Rasia didn't tell him *everything*.

Ysai asked him, "tell me a little bit about this job? Obviously, I haven't had time for a proper orientation."

Ysai walked at Kai's side and provided a convenient shield. Groups of shrouds walked around the tall adult, while messengers ran around him like an obstacle in the road. You didn't move someone like Ysai easily.

"Historically, the Council has assigned one sentry to the magic-born family to prevent ransoms. Usually because," Kai swiped a hand over his eyes. "Some of us are born with the eyes, and we stick out regardless of the shrouds. When Rae is with me, people know who they are and can target them. They are your priority.

There have been . . ." Kai didn't know how much Rasia told Ysai about Nico and the danger to the family, but he was wary of speaking it aloud in the middle of the market. "We want them safe."

"Got it." Then the tower of Ysai crouched down in front of Rae and whispered conspiratorially. "Want to ride on my back?"

Their eyes widened in excitement, then stared at their interlocked hand, and up at Kai for permission. He nodded. They cheered.

Ysai laughed and Rae hopped onto his shoulders.

They bounced down the market street and Kai wondered at the view—if Rae could see a pattern to the merchant tents, artist carts, and the sitting rugs of the hawkers? Weavers worked giant looms right along the street, showing off their skill weaving linen and silk. Pottery makers, evory and calabash carvers, basket weavers, papyrus soakers, perfume extractors, and all other tradespersons crowded under the belly with shouts of deals and discounts that zig-zagged through the air.

The market was unusually busy today, now that people had more rations and some extra money to tackle their various to-do lists. It was almost suffocating squeezing through the crowd. As they walked, Kai drew several eyes—a change considering most willfully avoided him. Hushed whispers traveled in his wake. His shoulders hunched to his ears as he tried to ignore them.

With Ysai and Rae a little way ahead, Rasia slyly pushed Kai out the river stream of people and toward a store. He stopped in the doorway once he eyed the merchant's wares. Sex tools of all sorts hung on display around the tent. A string of dildos, of several sizes and materials, hung from the beams. High grade palm oil sat in stacks on the shelves. Brass rings and beads sparkled like jewelry. Most of the items Kai had no idea what they were for, but he was sort of curious to figure them out. The store had available every tool an adult could hope to have in their inventory.

The merchant ran forward to shoo at them. "Out. No children in the store."

Rasia reached into her shroud and proudly pulled out her Forging seal, issued to all those who successfully returned to the Grankull from the Forging. "We're not. We're Naming candidates, and we are here to peruse your wonderful array of wares."

The merchant crossed his arms and glared. "You are no adult until you have more than the name your tahs gave you. Come back in two days. Now, out!"

Kai fled backward and bumped right into Ysai's leg. Ysai placed a hand on his shoulder to steady him, and quickly released him.

"You really thought that was going to work?" Ysai asked, who had circled back around to find them.

"Eh, it was worth a shot." Rasia tossed a hand over her shoulder, and without pause, popped over to a booth that sold cheap medicine for those who could not afford the healers. She crouched down, as if correcting her shoe, then came back up with one of the vials attached to the belt under her clothes. He recognized it as the leftover paralytic they extracted from the scorpions. As before with the tailor, Rasia crossed her hands over her shoulders, almost as a form of identification, and the vendor quickly swooped up the vials. Kai listened as they bartered in low voices.

He found himself engrossed by the way Rasia finessed the market compared to the barterers and hagglers who spend all day driving down the prices. The latter never worked for Kai. Sometimes they would intentionally sell to him at marked up prices, and it took years for him to find the ones willing to be fair.

"Are you . . ." Kai didn't know the words he was after and gave up trying to find them once Rasia hopped to another booth and used sleight of hand to exchange skinko eyeballs for bone chips.

He knew she did some illegal stuff from time to time, but this was the first time he had witnessed the extent of it. Her smuggling venture was a lot more organized than he ever imagined. This was a whole other side of her that he didn't know existed.

Ysai noted Kai's conflicted expression and explained in low tones as they walked, "Shamai-ta promised himself that he would never see his family starve. It was initially his idea, but Kiba-ta developed the business behind it all. She formed relationships with the sentry guards, often those she trusted in her employ, and cut deals with the merchants. We did turn in plenty of kills to the Grankull and gave a lot of it away, but we kept just enough for the family that by the time the Grankull hit hard years, the tahs were already the leaders of a small smuggling ring."

"So . . . the Han of the sentries is the leader of a smuggling ring, while in charge of destroying and breaking up everyone else's smuggling ring?"

"Essentially," Ysai said without a hint of remorse or guilt. Although they've had little interaction, Ysai had always treated Kai equitably over the years. In that time, the affable adult had never come across as the reliable left arm of a crime family. Kai found that Ysai and Rasia's moral compasses were oddly aligned.

"The herbs that you and Rasia retrieved on behalf of the Council?"

"We got enough of what the healers needed, but we pocketed some of it," Ysai admitted. "Kiba-ta will wait until the off-season when the herbs grow scarce and then sell it for ten times the price. At the same time, the Council didn't pay me any extra wages for the effort. The healers didn't have to risk their own people. It's a win all around."

They caught up to Rasia inspecting a shoe booth. She leaned over to the vendor, made the sign, and said, "I want to see your back inventory."

She disappeared into the store.

"What's the back inventory?" Kai asked.

"Tent kids sell him shoes they've stolen. The cobbler refurbishes them until they're unrecognizable, then sells them at a marked price—but still reasonable for a pair of leather shoes. The shoes in the back are the ones not yet furbished, but some of them are in good condition. We sell him our scraps of leather sometimes."

"You're a terrible sentry."

"Probably," Ysai said, and then inclined his head toward two full-shrouded figures who held hands between the narrow alley of the stalls. The rules for half-shrouded budchildren were looser, able to hold hands or ride on someone's shoulders without criticism, but the fully shrouded were banned from all touch in public. Ysai walked up to them, made a single disapproving face, and the underaged kids screeched before scattering in different directions. He laughed all the way back to Kai's side.

"Sometimes I look the other way," Ysai smirked. "Sometimes I keep secrets. The Grankull, it's not . . . kind. But tent kids got to eat too."

Kai had heard those words before, once or twice from Zephyr. He mulled over the phrase, and then it hit him in a flash, in a blinding realization—why Rasia never fit so neatly into the Grankull rules and didn't care to; why she prioritized the people closest in her circle far more than she ever would the Grankull at large. All the stories of their tah, all Rasia's actions, and even Ysai's temperament—it all made sense once you found the missing page.

"Shamaijen Windbreaker was from the Tents."

"Yeah," Ysai said, proudly. "Tah was a tent kid. He broke the Grankull's Forging record and earned his face, but the Tents never really left him. He was determined to teach us how to take care of ourselves because he knew that sometimes the Grankull often failed to do so. He taught us about windships, and taught Rasia and I how to hunt. He shaped a lot of who we are."

People often spoke of Shamaijen Windbreaker with respect and awe. No one mentioned how he used to be from the Tents, as if the place he had come from didn't matter after the Forging, but it was obvious Shamaijen had continued to carry his birthplace, and this had informed all his decisions and actions since.

Kai wondered if that would happen to him—after the Naming would everyone forget who he once was and who he had been, although he would be the one to carry his past for the rest of his life?

Rasia returned with a pair of shoes she bought for three chips, and Kai stared aghast at the cheapness of them. She shoved the shoes at him and told him to try them on. They were the first closed toed pair of shoes he had ever owned. They fit well, but he couldn't help but wonder who they were stolen from.

Rasia gave an approving nod and then set off toward another booth that displayed hand-carved evory, also known as processed gonda chitin. Kai recognized the voice of Neema, the shrouded vendor Rasia had stopped to talk to.

Neema's family was most famous for their secret technique in fashioning gonda chitin into evory statues. They've always been masterful artists, but they didn't get rich until Zephyr's tah came to town. Evory was in high demand in distant countries, and that demand propelled Neema's family to one of the richest in the entire Grankull, so much so they had to fend off rivals who wanted to steal their secret techniques.

The more intricate designs weren't on display—probably hidden in a locked chest somewhere—but the stall's inventory included necklaces of small animals, hoops of teeth, and delicate rings. Most popular was the carving of a stylized sun, a charm people wore to ward off the Hunter's Eye. Sometimes, people clutched their charms when Kai passed them by—as if his mere presence symbolized bad luck and bad omens.

"Got the story down?" Rasia asked.

"Yeah, I got it," Neema said, her chin on the palm of her hand.

Rae popped up from under Kai's arm to peek at the display, startling him, for he had missed when Rae had scrambled down Ysai like a date palm. They marveled at the intricate dragons carved into majestic poses.

"You want something? It's on me," Neema said.

"Really?" Rasia asked.

"You did get us back home."

Rasia reached for the dragon in mid-flight, but Kai caught her hand. Beside him, Rae hit a disappointed chin against the stand. He explained, "It's fine. We don't need anything."

"Let the kid have something nice." Rasia swiveled her wrist out of Kai's grip. She grabbed the figurine and threw it in the air, to both Neema's and Kai's horror. Rasia caught it effortlessly behind her back, then handed it over to Rae with a smug look. "See? I am fun."

"Perhaps this exchange can be the start of a mutual business relationship, you know, in case you happen to have any chitin on hand," Neema suggested.

"Nope," Rasia said. Neema jerked back at the word. "Your family is thriving. You don't need any more than what the Grankull has portioned for you."

"My family creates more value from it than any other artist in the belly market, and the Grankull gets a cut with every sale. We're singlehandedly keeping this placc running."

"Cute," Rasia popped the word and then strolled off down the street.

Neema's eyes narrowed after her. Kai grabbed the dragon from Rae and moved to return it. She glanced at it, and then snapped, "Keep it."

The dragon thudded at the force Kai placed it back onto the booth. He gathered up his jih and followed after Rasia. Two years ago, while at the market, Rae had run over to look at the carved windships. When Kai had pulled Rae away, Neema accused him of stealing and stabbed a necklace straight through his hand. It went all the way through.

He doubted Neema remembered it. Automatically, he rubbed his hand where the scar still lingered after all these years.

"You okay?" Ysai asked as he scooped Rae back onto his shoulders.

"I'm fine."

They turned down a small but infamous street called the Lungs, where the blacksmiths turned scorpion carapaces and dragon-scales into weapons. From a distance, you could see the smoke curling over the buildings, huffing like some living creature. They entered the largest shop on the block where the symbol of Azan's blacksmith clan hung out front. Ysai swung Rae off his shoulders to bend down and enter through the doorway.

Aden, Azan's older jih, stood at attention once Ysai walked through the front door.

"I thought you'd be out with the kulls?" Ysai asked, rushing forward and clasping Aden along the arm. Aden melted at the touch and returned it with a soppy smile.

"Supposed to have been, but the Council commissioned more sentry armor and the family needed the extra help." Aden looked over Ysai's shoulder at Rasia, Kai, and Rae. Kai held onto Rae's hand to make sure they didn't touch any of the sharp weapons displayed around the shop. "What's the occasion? Please don't tell me she's here to buy another sword. She broke another one?"

"Ha! I do need to replace some stuff I lost during the Forging, but I'm here to see your jih. The youngest one."

Aden yelled toward the back. "AZAN! It's Rasia!"

Rasia's brows went up when Azan came out, shirt off, and sweaty—along with two other half-naked and sweaty muscled jihs. Many perused the store's wares just for the view.

"The crazy dragon kid? Oh, the runt is here too," one of the jihs said gleefully.

"It's Kai!" Rasia corrected, before hooking an arm around Azan's shoulders and pulling him outside so his jihs couldn't eavesdrop on the fabricated lie they'd created for the Forging.

"Azan says you're like hot under there?" One of the jihs said, coming from around the corner to study Kai like a sword on display. Kai froze at the scrutiny. The same jih looked up at Aden and waggled his eyes before shoving Kai toward the desk. "Just your type, right, Aden-ji?"

"Leave him alone."

Another jih chimed in, "You did used to have the biggest flame for Kenjinn Ilhani."

"By the Elder, shut up." Aden slapped his hands to his face. "Get back to work."

"I remember when you'd come back home from a day of apprenticing with him and then jerk off—urgh—" Aden leapt and wrestled him to the ground. A sword display clattered down when they knocked into the wall, luckily narrowly missing the knot of limbs.

"They can't be together for one vibration before a fight breaks out," Ysai said as he guided Rae and Kai out of the chaos. They stepped outside to Rasia and Azan conspiring in the street.

"Don't fuck this up, Azan. You got this?"

"Yeah, I'll remember everything. I promise."

"Good," Rasia pointed at him as she walked away. "Also, Naming night. Orgy. Invite all your jihs."

"I'm not having sex with my jihs!" Azan shouted at her, causing everyone in the street to turn towards him in shock. Rasia cackled and motioned Ysai and Kai back around the corner, a turn away from the main street. Rae complained of how their feet hurt, and Kai automatically scooped them up in his arms. They left behind the bustling market.

Rasia turned left toward the Hindlegs, but Ysai caught her by the shoulder. "Whoa, where are you going?"

"The Tents," she said. "We've still got to run by Zephyr's to make sure he knows the story."

"Rasia, we're not taking them into the Tents."

"We'll be fine. Kai can hold his own."

"It doesn't matter how many people he can fight; it only takes one inopportune mistake, one knife, and the youngest heir is dead. The Grankull will be in an uproar, and tah will have my neck. They cannot go into the Tents."

"Fine." Rasia shuffled through her clothes and handed Kai a wrapped package. Then pulled forward quick, before anyone could see, and kissed his shrouded lips. "I'll meet up with you both after high noon for training. Jih, you know which field. See you later!"

As quick as the whirlwind she rode in on that morning, she spun and ran off down the road.

CHAPTER TWENTY

—

Ysai escorted Kai and Rae back home to drop off the items Rasia bought from the market. When Kai unwrapped the package Rasia had given him, he found it full of scorpion jerky, gonda meat, and dried vegetables. He had no idea when in the market she had acquired all this food and, quite frankly, didn't want to know in case the sentries came calling.

Kai cooked lunch for the three of them. He felt obligated to feed Ysai as well, considering the food had been illegally acquired. Plenty of food was leftover to supplement other meals, but after some consideration, he scraped a little off his plate, not very noticeable, but it made him feel less anxious.

After lunch, they left for the training fields.

The practice fields were fairly empty since most of the hunting kulls were out of the Grankull and everyone else was still busy with preparations for the upcoming ceremony. Rae had brought their toy windship and slid it down the hills of sand to chase it to the bottom. Watching them, Kai wished he had more opportunities to take them outside to play instead of being stuck in the house all day.

"How about we warm up a bit?" Ysai suggested. He shuffled through the dulled practice blades piled into a large carapace bin for general use.

"Oh, sure," Kai said, more than a little intimidated. Ysai and Aden had often competed for the top marks of their generation—which would have been Kai's generation, too, if he had succeeded in his first Forging.

"Show me first position of the scorpion path," Ysai said when he tossed Kai a blunted practice sword.

Kai caught the sword upside down by the worn hilt and stared at it, hoping the blade could somehow tell him what Ysai was talking about. "Rasia didn't teach me any of that."

Ysai's eyebrows furrowed, and then he bent over a great bellow of laughter. Kai clutched the sword to his chest, uncertain if he had already done something wrong. Ysai straightened and wiped at tears in his eyes. "Of course, she didn't. She is the person who showed you how to steer a windship only one time, and then left you to figure out the rest on your own. I don't know how you managed. What sword fighting has she gone over with you?"

"She said there wasn't a lot of time to teach me the basics, so she . . . attacked me and I tried to survive?"

"You're a good sport," Ysai said amused. "She's not wrong, *per se*. You don't have a lot of time to catch up, but throwing people off a cliff doesn't always work with everyone. Rasia doesn't comprehend how talented she is sometimes. She'll watch something, and move through it, and *get it*. Because she can figure out things on her own, she assumes everyone else is the same way, and then finds herself frustrated when they aren't. I'm impressed you've been able to keep up with her, but you're lacking so many of the basics that it has probably been more time-consuming for you to flounder on your own. Come at me."

The balance of the practice sword differed from Rasia's dual-khopesh and tah's dragonsteel blade. It was a lot heavier than what Kai was used to. It didn't sit comfortably in his hand, but Ysai stood there waiting, and Kai didn't want to disappoint him. He lunged forward.

Ysai angled his torso and Kai's attack swept past. He almost stumbled when Ysai's sword tapped flat against his back. But unlike Rasia, who would have continued to press her attack, Ysai paused to correct Kai's stance. "When you lunge, most of your momentum should come from your back leg. Keep your elbows up. Bend your knees. Now, again."

Kai tried the lunge again. This time, he snapped forward faster. When Ysai evaded and aimed for his back, his body no longer fought against him. He had the stability to quickly switch and evade the blow.

They exchanged several more strikes, and every time, Ysai paused to correct Kai's mistakes. Against Rasia, Kai had been fighting a vicious tide where he barely managed to keep his head above water, but sparring with Ysai was like being tossed a floating palm to learn how to swim. He adjusted, widened his stance, and loosened the tension from his shoulders. He started correcting himself before Ysai had to tell him.

Kai saw an opening. In that brief moment, it was Rasia's brutal lessons that had his body reacting long before his thoughts processed the practice sword had slashed across Ysai's arm. He stilled in surprise at the hit.

Then Ysai flashed a brilliant grin and sweptCed Kai off of his feet. He hit the ground and squinted up into the sun, until Ysai blocked the blinding light and offered a hand. Ysai hefted Kai up and called for a water break.

Kai was relieved for the momentary pause. He breathed heavily, yet Ysai hadn't broken a sweat. In the span of a drum, he had learned more technique than Rasia had ever taught him, if any. Kai kicked at the hard-packed dirt of the fields and admitted, "She's a terrible teacher."

Ysai laughed, bright, with the same tone of Rasia's carefree abandon.

"I don't know if I have the bones to break it to her," Kai said, mostly to himself, but it sent Ysai off into another roll of laughter.

Ysai snickered. "If you ask me, that mountainous ego of hers can bear to be knocked down a little."

"How did you ever survive growing up in the shadow of it?"

"By being taller than her."

A laugh cracked out of Kai, and they both shared knowing smiles. Most people didn't like Rasia, and their complaints and criticisms were often harsh and pointed. It was refreshing to joke around with someone who genuinely cared for her.

"Do you think I have a shot at the kull tryouts?" Kai asked.

Ysai stretched his arms and thought for a bit. He said, "Some of these kids have held practice swords since they were ten-till. I can teach you all the technique that I can, but you're never going to catch up by the time of the tryouts. But, you only need to win two fights, and I think you have what it takes to surprise them. After all, I've heard you've beaten Rasia once or twice. You and I can work on the rest."

Kai blinked at Ysai, surprised by the offer. "I wouldn't want to impose."

Ysai shrugged and looked over at Rae playing in the sand. "Today has been far more interesting than I thought it would be. I'm thinking of transferring posts. Of course, if that's alright with you."

A knot swelled in Kai's throat. To have a sentry who saw this job as more than an easy paycheck, who carried Rae on his shoulders and spoke to Kai like a person, was more than he could ever hope for. He tentatively said, "If it's not too much trouble. You should know, Nico has a growing number of enemies."

"Oi-yo, Rasia mentioned that. Aden-kull might have more names than I, but I can still knock him off of his feet. My skills are wasted standing guard around the shipyards, and your family needs the protection."

"Honestly, you'll probably end up carrying Rae on your shoulders most of the time."

"The perfect practice for more important things," Ysai waggled his brows, and Kai couldn't help but to smile. Ysai and Rasia even wag their eyebrows the same way. It reminded Kai of being around his twin cousins, Jilah and Ashe. Even though they weren't identical, their expressions often had a shared language all their own.

"You and Jilah-shi are putting in an application for a child?"

Kai asked.

"We would like to. We want to move out of the house first, but there have been some complications with our housing application. Someday, we hope."

Ysai signaled the end of their break. They resumed their sparring while they waited for Rasia to meet them. Ysai stopped correcting Kai so often and let Kai paddle around on his own to get the rhythm of it. Out of nowhere, the rhythm sped up too quickly, a brutal reminder Ysai had been going easy on him. He struck an unrepentant knee into Kai's groin.

Kai's eyes watered, and he collapsed to the ground at the pain. He didn't think it was possible for someone to have their balls kicked into their stomach, but Ysai certainly tried. Ysai grabbed the top of Kai's shroud, catching hair as well, and twisted Kai to face him. His easygoing swagger flipped to a vicious terrifying sharpness. This sharpness Kai hadn't seen before, different from the hot rage of Rasia's temper.

"I like you. You've got a good head on your shoulders. Rasia needs that. But if you fucking seed my little jih again—if you ever again put her in a position where she has to poison herself or risk the back alleys, I will cut your dick off and shove it down your throat till you die choking on it. You understand me?"

Kai swallowed down the pain and faced Rasia's big jih. It didn't feel right to shake and quiver in terror, not when her jih's anger was wholly justified. He collected himself, looked Ysai in the eye, and promised, "I understand."

Ysai released Kai's shroud.

"I know Rasia isn't easy, and I'm glad someone is looking out for her. Even after the Naming, even after the Grankull prescribes her gonom, you've got to be *sure*. Rasia gets so caught up in things, *she forgets*. Despite her best efforts, that's who she is. You need to remind her every morning to take her gonom. *Every morning*. I don't care if you've got to slip it in her tea."

"I will."

"And if you have any questions about sex, please don't make any more fucking assumptions. I am here. Ask me. There is no question in the world that I haven't heard from Rasia already. I will not tolerate any more mistakes. No more fuck-ups. Got it?"

"I understand, Ysaijen the Unbowed."

"Ysai-ji," he corrected.

It was more than a correction. It was acceptance and approval from the most important person in Rasia's life. Kai wanted nothing more than to consider this face a friend, but he found it hard to accept. "Isn't that too presumptuous? What if Rasia changes her mind about me?"

Again, Ysai laughed. "A lot of people claim Rasia gets distracted easily. They don't know her. She gets distracted with things she doesn't care about, but when she has a mission in mind, she'll stop at nothing to see it through. Nothing could have stopped Rasia from slaying that dragon, but she stopped for you after the lake. Do you know how many people in Rasia's life she is willing to stop for? You're jih's kulani. I believe it."

"But that's not what I want. I don't want her to stop for me. I want to keep up."

Ysai leaned forward, as if to tell Kai a secret. "You might be the only one who can. Don't mean I won't kill you though. You might be her kulani, but she can do fine all by herself."

"I'll do better. I promise," Kai said, spine straight. "No more fuck-ups."

"Good, 'cause Rasia will hate me for it. She seems rather attached to your dick."

"I am rather attached to it, too."

"She said you were funny," Ysai smirked. Then he nodded up.

Kai scrambled to his feet, and they returned to their sparring match. Except this time, every hit left a harder bruise than before. Ysaijen the Unbowed was nice enough to teach you how to defend yourself, *then* he would kick your ass, and smile while he did it.

CHAPTER TWENTY-ONE

—

"He kneed you in the balls?" Rasia laughed, later that day, as they shared dinner in the middle of the training grounds. They had been out here most of the afternoon, so long that Nico had sent the night sentry to find them. Rae had cried and threw a tantrum about going home, but Ysai had scooped them up and returned them to Nico, while Kai and Rasia stayed to continue practicing.

Rasia raised Kai's arm, dropping the long sleeve of his caftan, and inspected the bruises Ysai swatted onto his skin. "Ugh. The Naming Ceremony is tomorrow. He could have gone a little easier on you."

"I've gotten more bruises sparring with you."

"But he's supposed to be the nice one . . . sometimes. Guess it could have been worse. The day I told him about the whole seeding thing, he was absolutely furious and would have run you through with his spear if you had been there. Luckily, he's calmed down since then."

"You really do tell your jih everything?"

"Of course. Although, it's much easier to admit to anything when you're sailing out in the middle of nowhere Desert. Gives him plenty of time to calm down."

Kai wondered if Ysai and Rasia had the normal sibling relationship, or if his was as fucked up as he had always feared.

There were whole parts of Kai's Forging that Nico still didn't know about.

Even Rasia looked at him askance. "It makes sense now why you spent most of your Forging running away from your jih."

She finished off a honeyed-oat bar and licked the crumbs from her fingers. Kai chewed at a piece of flat-bread. Rasia wrapped her arms around her knees and watched him eat. She studied every twitch of his jaw. "Are there things you don't tell me?"

Kai stopped chewing. Rasia frowned at his hesitation and crooked her jaw. "Oh."

He swallowed a large piece of bread. It traveled slow and obtrusive down his throat. He said quickly, hoping to save the situation, "It's nothing important."

"So why not tell me? I remember when you needed to wake up from the Yestermorrow Lake, and I realized how much I didn't know about you. I still don't. I don't know your favorite food. I don't know your favorite song. I don't know your favorite color, or if you even have one. For all the times we've had sex, I don't know your favorite thing to do. You're my kulani, but you're so guarded sometimes."

Kai looked down at the half-eaten bread in his hand. He'd never given his favorite food any consideration, not when the aim of his existence had been to survive off as little as possible. He had a favorite song, but it was a song no one knew but Kenji and the kulani he wrote it for. And the rest didn't matter. So much of Kai quite frankly wasn't worth knowing.

"I like making you orgasm," he offered. He liked the way her body released, the sound of her breathless from all the air he took away, and her exultant face when she clung to him. It made him feel powerful.

Rasia blinked and threw up her hands. "But that means you like everything we do!"

She lay on her side and kicked her feet in the air. She dragged a finger, writing katas into the skin of his leg where the caftan didn't cover. "What about tomorrow? During the bodika? If someone else pleasured me, you wouldn't like that?"

Kai had forgotten all about the bodika, which happened at the tail-end of the namepour. He said diplomatically, "If that's what you want."

"*See*. That's what I'm talking about. Just say, 'no, I would be super crazy jealous if you fucked someone else.'"

"The bodika is a big deal," he said. "Most kids look forward to it their entire lives. They save themselves just to experience their first time at that moment. I would never ask you not to."

"I can't take your feelings into consideration if I don't know them," Rasia said frustrated as she sat up. "Do you want me to participate in the bodika or not?"

"You can if you want."

"Are *you* not going to?"

He froze. The idea of involving other people terrified him, especially with random strangers of the Grankull. He didn't know them or their intentions, and he feared that no number of names could abate people's hatred of him. He could barely walk in a crowded market without a sense of dread. But he didn't want to admit that fear. He had slayed a dragon. Nothing was supposed to scare him anymore.

"I'll do it," Kai said, hoping he would find the courage by then. "We'll do it together."

Rasia nodded, appeased. Then her lips smirked in that wicked smile and leaned forward conspiratorially. "How about you spend the night over at my place?"

Kai had never imagined himself as that kid climbing through windows. The runt of the Grankull would certainly not spend the night underage at someone else's house. But he had slayed a dragon, he kept telling himself. He wasn't that person anymore. "My interview is first thing tomorrow morning. I need to be up at first drum."

"I'm not going to let you miss your interview. Come on." He shoved the rest of the bread into his mouth, before Rasia rushed up behind him and wrapped her arms under his armpits. She pulled Kai to his feet with a heave. "I can't wait to have you in my bed. We haven't truly fucked since the gorge."

"Rasia," Kai said, legs moving in the direction she pulled him. "I promised your jih we would be responsible. We only have one more day till it's legal."

"I can steal gonom from tah. The Elder knows she doesn't use it. It'll be fine."

"We should wait."

"Fine." Rasia blew out her breath in disappointment. "We'll make do without."

"And what about your tah? Won't she be home?"

"She always pulls an all-nighter before the Naming Ceremony."

They left the training grounds and wound back onto the streets of the Grankull. Rasia released her grip on his hand. This was probably a dumb idea. What if Rasia's tah caught them?

"Maybe we shouldn't," he said, losing his steam. "I don't want to risk a bad first impression with your tah."

Rasia broke into laughter. "Kai, no matter what you do, tah is going to despise you. She doesn't *like* Jilah, and she's as perfect for jih as you can get."

"Oh." There was reality hitting him in the face again. Of course, no parent would be happy if their child brought him home to be introduced, but being in Rasia's orbit always made him forget. Stare at the sun too long and the edge of your vision develops blind spots. "Even if she hates me, shouldn't we have an Introduction Dinner? We might not be legal yet, but I'm still courting you."

"Absolutely not. I wasn't going to tell tah about you until after you've got a face, after you've got a job, maybe even after our Signing Ceremony. If she meets you any time before then, she'll probably try to kill you."

"Then why am I going to your house?!"

"Because she won't be there. I wouldn't bring you if I wasn't certain it was safe. She is the Han of the sentries, and she always stays late working on the security details of the Naming Ceremony the night before. Trust me, Ysai-ji has snuck Jilah through the window plenty of times on a night like tonight and has never gotten caught."

If there was one thing Kai had faith in, it was Rasia's ability to get up to no good. He should turn around and make the smart decision, but all that's behind him are the walls that have kept him contained for almost seventeen years. With Rasia, there was freedom. If he could just take hold of it again, it might be enough to blow him over into adulthood. He'd shed this fear behind him. He'd have a face, and a name, and a job with the kulls. They'd have their Signing Ceremony—*wait, what?*

Kai swiveled to Rasia with her words a squall through his head. "You want to introduce me to your tah after our Signing Ceremony?"

"Duh. What's the point of calling ourselves kulani if only we recognize it?"

A lot of people call each other kulani before legalizing it. A Signing Ceremony was only a formality but a requirement for the application paperwork, such as applying for housing or a child. Kulani was the only name you chose for yourself, and once signed to paper, the only name you would ever be able to have children with. You must be sure. No doubts. Most wait ten to fifteen years after their Forging to decide. Rasia hadn't been overreacting when Ysai and Jilah chose to carry each other's names only a year out of the Forging. It was unusual. It was a choice the Grankull encourages years of deliberation over.

"If I carry your name, if I legally claim you as my kulani, Kibata might be less inclined to kill you. I only get the one. It might give her pause."

Kai's stomach twisted at the urgency in her tone. He hadn't given much thought to their potential Signing Ceremony, figuring that was years ahead in the future. "How soon do you want to have it?"

"The day after tomorrow."

"*What?!*"

Nico was going to thunder the moment she heard about this. Kai couldn't think of a single story of anyone participating in a Signing Ceremony a day after their Naming. It wasn't done.

"I was going to bring it up with you after the Naming

Ceremony," Rasia said. "It can be a private thing. Just you and me. We'll ask the Mythkeeper to oversee it, we'll sign each other's names in the Book of Names, and it'll be official."

"Don't you think we're moving a little too fast? We should wait at least until after the kull tryouts. This is a big decision. We have to be sure."

"I am sure."

"Maybe we should give it a year."

"Why wait? You're my kulani."

Kai opened his mouth to argue, but what was he going to say? That no, he was not her kulani? That she had it all wrong and she was moving too fast, and she was making the biggest mistake of her life? Because maybe, just maybe, he might not be who she thought he was.

Suddenly, the hairs on the back of his neck pricked up. Thick darkness cloaked the Grankull once the colors of dusk dispersed from the bones. Other people navigated the streets at casual gaits, laughing in the starlight or stumbling drunk from the dancing stages and gambling dens of the Pelvis. Even though he had Rasia right beside him, his heartrate increased. The lateness of the night reminded Kai of when he had accidentally got behind time at the market and took a shortcut to get back home. That decision left him with a scar forever on his stomach.

"Rasia," Kai whispered, drawing closer to her. "Those faces are following us."

Rasia blatantly turned around and studied the three shadows trailing after them. One of them fell over, and the others barely caught their drunken friend from hitting the cobblestones. She scoffed. "They can barely follow their own feet."

Maybe she was right. It could all be in his head. He hadn't been on the streets of the Grankull at night in years.

The streets narrowed. An upturned cart with a broken wheel blocked their path. The loose wheel creaked. He didn't see any evidence of what the cart had been transporting. It had been stripped and abandoned.

Rasia narrowed her eyes. "Cute."

She made a sharp turn down the alley. The only alley. Blood swelled in Kai's ears. Darkness ate at the pathway, chewing at its end, and swallowed it down like the hungry insides of a gonda's throat.

"Rasia . . ."

"Hurry, Kai." She insisted, with that brow arched, in excitement. They could turn around and face the three behind them. Or they could climb over the cart. But Rasia chose the alley because she was a hunter.

Kai opened his mouth and couldn't voice the fear locking his limbs in place.

"*Come on.* What is wrong with you?" She grabbed his hand and dragged him into the alleyway's maw. He reversed their grip, tightening his hold, afraid of losing her and being left to float alone in this darkness.

Two strangers stepped into the alley in front of them. The lantern light that illuminated a wider street ahead glowed around the outline of their figures. The three following them blocked their exit from behind.

"Oh no, a trap," Rasia gasped dramatically. "Whatever should we do?"

"My first-named child is dead," one of the shadowed figures spat, "but that thing is allowed to cheat his way through the Forging? Over my dead body."

"Move aside, Ohan. We don't want to involve you in this," another said.

The assumption had Rasia cackling. "I'm not his jih," she corrected. "I'm his kulani."

Kai's bones stiffened at the declaration. It was one thing to say it to each other, but it was another to announce it in the middle of an alleyway of people trying to kill him. It had him wanting to give his name over to her right then and there. The declaration shocked their ambushers, but the mourning parent only grew angrier. "Where are your parents, child? Step aside or die with him."

Rasia swatted Kai's shoulder. "This will make great practice for the tryouts. Okay, go."

"*What?*" The last time Kai was cornered in a dark alley, it had been by a bunch of rowdy kids. This time, five grown adults were looking to kill him.

"Oh kulani, defend my honor." Rasia faux fainted against the grimy wall and pressed her hand to her forehead. No one would ever employ her to perform any of the great epics.

"Something is wrong with you," one of the attackers said.

Rasia tossed Kai one of her swords from underneath her clothes. It clattered at his feet. His brain had been too slow to even attempt to catch it. He stumbled back as the grieving parent charged him. The parent's sword glinted off the lantern lights the same way the kid's dagger did two years ago. The blade swiped toward him, and Kai tripped against the alleyway wall, evading the worst of the sword stroke but his arm had been nicked by the end of it.

"Fucking pathetic."

The parent spat in Kai's face. The wad sloughed down Kai's shroud and into the corner of his eye, but he barely had the strength to breathe right now much less wipe it off. That night, two years ago, had been the first time Kai had killed someone. It was all a haze of sensations and images in his nightmares, but the memory came back in startling clarity. The stench of stale breath. The faint glow of an oil lamp overhead in the high windows, unable to penetrate the suffocating darkness gnawing away at him. The sound of his head cracking against the adobe walls. The blows of their knuckles. The pain in his lungs.

He couldn't breathe. Panic overcame him. It pulled him under, taking him down like the Yestermorrow Lake.

"Kai? Kai? *Fuck.*"

Rasia's voice echoed off the worn mudbricks. Then her hand grabbed him and pulled him forward, out of the darkness. They emerged running onto the wider street toward the lantern lights. Blood dripped down Rasia's blade and splattered Kai's caftan as they ran. She led him through twists and turns and physically dragged him forward when his exhaustion weighed him down.

She pushed him up ladders and jumped a roof. They climbed the partitions and ducked into one of the wind-catcher towers. The tower was filled with sand and dust and needed to be cleaned out, but the ventilation whipped at Kai's hair, and cool air funneled toward the homes below.

Rasia leaned out of the tower to make sure they had lost their pursuers. Then she turned on her heels to snap at him. "What the fuck was that?"

Kai flinched and hunched down into his arms where he had collapsed against an inside corner of the tower. She dropped the anger and followed up with, "Are you okay?"

He didn't know how to answer that question. If only the panic had stayed in the alleyway, but it had relentlessly chased him down. It kept pace around corners and over rooftops and attacked with a vengeance, and his thoughts buckled under the weight of its blows. He didn't want Rasia to see him like this. He never wanted her to know this truth. But no matter how hard he tried, how hard he clung to Rasia's gravity, the truth careened free anyways.

The Forging was a lie.

"*Don't touch me*," Kai snapped.

Rasia snatched back her hand as if bitten. He immediately regretted the outburst and drowned under another wave of panic. He couldn't *breathe*.

"I don't . . . I'm sorry . . . I don't know what's wrong with me. It won't stop." Kai slapped his face, frustrated, angry, again and again until Rasia forcibly clasped her hands around his wrists to stop his self-immolation.

"DON'T TOUCH ME!" he screamed. Rasia retreated, something he had never known her to do. His voice diminished to a creak. "Leave me alone."

She crossed her arms, and her gaze burned the top of his bowed head. "I'll be outside. Let me know when you've got your shit together."

Kai laughed hollowly at that. He didn't think there had been a moment in his life when he had ever had his shit together. But it helped when Rasia left him to crumble without the pressure of her judgment.

The world blanked out.

Sensation returned sluggishly slow. Wind whistled in his ears. He focused on breathing. He felt wrung out and exhausted by the time his panic washed him back ashore, after having tossed and turned all his previous notions of himself. He felt embarrassed and ashamed. So much so, that he sat motionless in the tower with the apprehension of Rasia waiting on the other side.

She had seen his true self now. She had pulled off the shroud and finally found the weak, shivering, and sniveling monster at the core of him. He would rather face down another dragon than face Rasia with the truth in her eyes.

But he couldn't stay here all night. He had his interview in the morning. He wiped at his eyes and pushed himself onto unsteady feet. He tucked the incident deep down, chunking the messy parts of himself away to leave it all behind. He would pretend it never happened, and tomorrow, he'd be someone else. Someone Rasia could look at and know was her equal.

He walked through the narrow slats of the tower. He sort of hoped Rasia had left, but instead, he found her perched on the nearby edge of the roof.

She scrutinized him with those sharp perceptive eyes. "I should take you home."

"*No.*" This was a detour. Nothing more. It never happened. "We go to your place."

Rasia raised her brows at the demand, and as always, couldn't leave well enough alone. "Something is wrong with you. All day. Ever since this morning to Neema's stall in the market. You froze in that alleyway. You never freeze. You've gone against much bigger and much tougher things than some thugs. I don't know what is going on. This isn't you."

Kai couldn't stop himself from laughing out, which descended quickly into a pathetic sob. "*This is me.* I'm not that person from the Forging. I'm not the Kai from the Lake or the gorge. I'm not your kulani!" Rasia's face shattered with hurt feelings, but nothing could stop his tirade. "This is the real me—constantly terrified of everyone and everything. Maybe if the circumstances of my birth had been different, maybe the me that hadn't been sick, the me that could have been—that's your true kulani. I'm nothing but his broken shadow. You deserve better than me."

"Shut up, Kai. None of that's true."

"It's all true!"

"You slayed a dragon! There's nothing truer than that. I don't know what else to say," Rasia said, throwing up her hands. "I thought maybe at first all of this was because you were nervous about the tryouts, but I don't know anymore. I don't know. Can't we just fuck and forget about all this shit?"

Finally, something Kai agreed on.

Rasia lived in one of the tallest spires poking through the ribcage. She could step out her front door onto the literal Spine Road of the Great Elder. It was the highest Kai had ever traveled in the Grankull. Rasia tugged him through the window of her bedroom, a simple step away from the neighbor's roof, and they tumbled onto her bed.

Their mouths clashed and wrestled. She shoved at him. He bit her lip. Her nails clawed into the skin of his back. The usual ebb and flow of their joining struck like a dry storm; full of flash fires and hard thunder. Anger and frustration bolted lightning heat into his chest. They grappled on the bed, falling hard on the floor of scattered items that dug into his shoulder in the dark. She yelled at him, and Kai bore all that vocal frustration in silence.

Her right arm slipped from his grip and slapped him. He slapped her right back. She slapped him harder. Kai licked at the blood on his split lip, then licked at his palm and reached for his dick. He frowned. He licked his hand some more. He tugged and twisted and stroked and grew all the more angrier with himself.

"Are you fucking kidding me?" Rasia said above him. She slammed both hands against his chest, throwing him off balance, and sent him crashing to his elbow. Rasia turned away from him. The shame of failure rang red around Kai's vision. He beat at his dick, but no matter what he did, it wouldn't rise.

"I can eat you out."

"No."

Rasia never said no.

Kai collapsed back to the floor and curled in on himself away from her. He felt the burn of her scratches on his arms. The pain in his chest where she had shoved him. This hadn't happened before. They always had been able to rely on sex to communicate. It had always been the place where they could meet in the middle. Sex had buried his initial lack of confidence. Sex kept his head floating above water long after he had been pulled from the Yestermorrow Lake. It was the pedestal of their victory over a dragon. It ferried them here.

"I don't get it," Rasia said, brokenly. "It was so easy during the Forging. Why is this so hard? All we've done today is argue."

All Kai's hopes and dreams from that morning lost color. He thought it would take only a few adjustments on his part to fit their lives together, but it was far harder than he could have ever imagined. Kai felt Rasia slipping through his fingers, and he didn't know how to hold on to her.

They say Forging flames never last.

"How do we fix this?" he asked. He didn't want to give up on this relationship. She was the best thing to ever happen to him. How could he let it crumble without a fight?

"I don't fucking know. You're the one that froze."

"You're the one who treated the whole thing like some game."

"That was the perfect opportunity to get some practical experience with your swordwork," she argued. "Against the skinko, you didn't freeze. Against facehunters, you didn't freeze. Against a dragon, you didn't freeze. But a group of date-climbers and stall hawkers who can barely hold a sword scares you? At first, I thought *you* were joking."

Rasia stripped off all the articles of clothing he never got the chance to. She reached behind her back and unbuckled the leather straps that held down all the illegal items under her clothing. She tossed off a shoe and unbuckled a belt of daggers from around her ankle. She left on her wrap, a new one she must have recently bought that offered better support with thicker straps. She tossed on a night robe, stepped over him, and stretched out grumpily across the reed frame of her bed.

He felt guilty in that moment. He needed to tell her the why, but he found it so difficult to give voice to his nightmares. He had lived his entire life where his best defense had always been his silence. Zephyr was right. If Kai didn't want to lose this, he would need to work for it. No matter how much he didn't say, Nico would always be there for him. Rasia . . . might not be.

Kai stared out her window at the stars and said aloud for the first time, "I got caught up haggling at the market. The merchants were skinks. We needed a new cooking pot, and they all refused to sell me one at a fair price, but we couldn't afford to waste our money. I went home with nothing. In the end, it was all for nothing. It had gotten dark, and I took a shortcut through an alleyway and got jumped by . . . I don't know how many there were."

Rasia had shifted at this point. He felt her eyes on him, but he continued to talk to the stars, unable to face her.

"I don't remember much of it. I don't remember if they wore shrouds or if it was just the darkness. All I remember is stabbing one of them in the throat. The rest fled after that. I remember sitting there, in the quiet, with a dagger they left in my stomach and thinking that I couldn't do this anymore.

But giving up meant that tah died for nothing. Giving up meant that Kenji was right about me. I remember thinking I had a few blinks until my Forging, and everything would change, and everything would be different, and I'd show everyone. But within the first few vibrations of my first Forging, my kull tossed me out of the windship. I gave up after that and existed from one day to the next, waiting to die.

Then you happened. I'm not so naïve to think that everything should have changed after the Forging, but I thought... I thought *I* had changed. Today was the first time I've been back to the market since that happened, and I still froze in that alleyway. It all seemed that everything: you, the dragon, the scavengers—had been for nothing. For some stupid reason, I thought I wouldn't be scared anymore."

It wasn't the behavior of others Kai had hoped the most would change. Ultimately, he was disappointed in himself. He was an idiot to have believed that somehow his debilitating fear of every sudden movement, of every rustled shadow, of every unexpected visitor, and every unknown stranger, would somehow disappear. He thought he had finally outgrown the runt of the Grankull.

"You're right. You haven't changed," Rasia said, finally. "That brave and smart kid from the Forging is the same brave and smart kid from before it and the same brave and smart kid after it. A gang of stupid kids jumped you, and *you got back up*. You failed your first Forging, and yet you threw your bones on me. I don't know what I have to do or what you need to do to prove to yourself the truth. If a dragon isn't enough, then I don't know what is. But tomorrow, you're going to stand in front of the entire Grankull and show them your face, and that brave and smart kid will become a brave and smart adult."

Kai crumbled at the words. He never thought anyone would interpret that nightmarish scene of weakness and helplessness as one of strength. He found it so hard to be strong in the Grankull, in this place where nightmares crept around every corner, anxiety wracked every decision, and panic awaited him in ambush. The reed frame of the bed creaked, and Rasia joined him on the floor. When she wrapped her arms around him, tears slid down his cheeks.

"If I had known," Rasia said, "I would have taken the confrontation a lot more seriously. I would not have left you to fight on your own. But Iani, I still would have chosen that alleyway. Spears and longswords aren't effective in an alley because of the limited space. The walls limit the number of sides a group of attackers can come at you at once. The alley is a daggers game, and you excel at those. Next time you're being followed by a group of people out to do you harm, run toward the alley. Not away from it. In the small dark spaces, it is you they should fear."

Leave it to Rasia to do what she did best by turning his whole world upside down. She turned traps into opportunities, and fear into lessons, and maybe even the runt of the Grankull into a brave and smart adult.

CHAPTER TWENTY-TWO

—

Kai lay awake. His brain churned, so paranoid about missing the sound of first drum that he kept going in and out of a superficial sleep. It gave him a lot of time to think, to count the puffs of Rasia's breath against his neck and stare out the window from her bed. He didn't have a window in his small bedroom back home, but even sitting outside on his veranda, the stars blinked distant overhead. He wondered what it would have been like to grow up as Rasia did, to have the stars so close in reach.

At the tallest spire, the Elderfire scout whistled at the first sight of sunrise. Then the drums rolled, beginning at the center, to deploy down the spine in both directions. Sometimes in the Desert, Kai had lain awake waiting for first drum, only to realize its absence once the sun had risen. But he had never experienced first drum like this, so close to its origin that the sheer volume physically boomed through his skull and along his vertebrae.

"Morning," Rasia said, awake and bright underneath him. She licked her lips and coiled. Kai braced himself as she flipped on top of him to greet him with a morning energy he found hopeless to match. Warmth rushed through him, and as one, both Rasia and Kai looked down at his waking dick. Her lips twisted, amused. "Morning to you, too."

Then their eyes met again, jolting a spark down his spine and twisting the air with tension. He wanted her so badly in that moment and desperately wanted to make up for the disaster that had happened last night, but he also hadn't been in the right headspace. He saw clearer in the morning.

Kai grabbed her hips and shifted her higher. "My interview is at second drum, and I promised your jih to be more responsible."

"But I can get gonom right down the hall."

"We've waited this long. We can wait for tonight. It'll be safer for the both of us when it's legal and you have your own gonom." He soothed a hand up her thigh. She crossed her arms and collapsed sideways onto the bed. He could feel her anger stewing beside him.

Five kulls. Twenty-five vibrations.

The time ticked down.

"Rasia," Kai said nervously and licked his lips. "Can you escort me to my interview?"

He hated the fact that he needed so much handholding for basic activities like walking down the street. But he didn't know this neighborhood, and he feared another incident like last night could keep him from reaching his interview on time. But what if Rasia was too mad at him?

"Of course," she said, and flopped her legs as if she were going to get out of bed but stayed horizontal like that with her head on his stomach.

Kai didn't know why he had expected the worst. He felt so insecure around her lately. Yet, she had held him last night as he told her one of his darkest secrets, and she had thought him brave. The thought gave him the courage to ask, "Are you angry at me?"

Rasia released a heavy huff. "I'm *frustrated*. I finally have you in my bed, and we can't do anything about it. I hate . . . I just want people to stop telling me what to do. I want my names already. I want you. I want to be free to do whatever I want with you."

He released a breath and said, truthfully, "I don't want to do the bodika."

Rasia turned on her elbow to give him a flat stare. "*I know*. You don't have to force yourself to do something you don't want to do."

"I just . . . I thought you'd think me weird for not wanting to do it and it's a lot of people and I'm afraid I might have another . . ." Was there a word for what had happened to him last night? "I have these . . . episodes."

Rasia sat up, wrapped her arms around her legs, and placed her chin on her knees. She studied him in the close light of morning. "It was scary," she said. "You couldn't breathe."

"It's usually not that bad. I don't know. I handle it better when I'm by myself, I think," Kai whispered, and hung his head between his own knees. He couldn't describe to her the mixture of panic and anxiety that demanded inexplicably that he freeze. He felt so stripped open and scared that she would judge him, that she would determine he was too broken to keep around. He held himself and his edges went numb with the waiting.

"Okay." It all popped when Rasia kissed him on the forehead. "It's my morning at breakfast. I need to ask Ysai-ji to cover for me."

"Wait, no, if you need to stay-"

"It's fine. Your interview is important. We got cornered by five losers last night. I am not going to let anyone make you late."

Then she pushed off of the bed to her feet. She picked up caftans from the floor to sniff at them, and then quickly discarded them over her shoulder. Her brows rose when she grabbed one by the bed, smelled it, and then moved to toss it on.

"Wait, Rasia, that one's mine."

"Oh," she laughed at that and tossed it to him. Eventually, she found an acceptable one. She threw it on, inside out, judging by the stitching. "I'll go update jih on the situation and bring back water from the pump so you can clean up."

She disappeared through the beaded curtain of her doorway. Kai took advantage of the moment alone to collect himself and process everything that had happened. He had opened up to her, and she hadn't run away. Finally, having reached a sort of equilibrium, he uncurled from the bed. He took the moment to look around the room.

Last night, while he lay awake, everything looked like imposing shadows and unknown borders, but now, the sliver of sunlight rising through the window illuminated the contents of Rasia's bedroom. The dragonglass beads of the curtain, still swaying from when Rasia displaced them running out of the room, caught on the light, and spun sparkling stars atop her belongings.

Several clothes littered the ground, while well-tended swords and spears rested in racks on the walls. Rocks ranging in different sizes and colors were scattered with purpose atop a dresser. Spread across her desk was a large map, larger than the one she carried on her person, with lines drawn in and landmarks marked, a work in progress and years of dedication, with as much craft and beauty as the murals in the baths of his home.

Kai again began to imagine their futures together but this time with sharper details. He wouldn't want to move out of his house with Rae still so young, but perhaps Rasia would be willing to move in with him into a room big enough for the two of them? He saw how all her belongings could fit like puzzle pieces.

"Rasia!" He jumped at the sound of Ysai's voice down the hall. "*What do you mean he's here? He spent the night?!*"

"Calm your tits. We didn't do anything. We were disgustingly responsible."

"You have got to get him out of here before tah gets home."

"*Are either of you finally going to tell me who he is?!*" Kai froze at the familiar voice of his cousin. Logically, in his head, he knew Jilah lived with Ysai, but that fact hadn't occurred to him when he accepted Rasia's invitation.

"Shush the both of you. His interview is at second drum. We've got to get going."

The volume of the voices lowered. Kai stood over Rasia's map and inclined his head toward the hallway, trying to pick out any words. Soon, she came back, charging around the corner with a basin of water on her hip and a towel slung over her shoulder.

Kai washed quickly. He threw on his caftan. She wrapped his shroud around his head and practically pushed him out of the window.

"This way. I know a few shortcuts."

Rasia led him down Spine Road. Luckily very few people were up and about. While first drum typically signaled everyone to wake up, second drum signaled everyone to get to work. Since a lot of people were off for the holiday, their way was practically clear.

Spine Road arched over the world below. All his life, Kai had viewed the Grankull as buildings that bent over him and narrow alleyways that threatened to steal him away into the shadows. From the top, with his feet on the wide berth of the spine, Kai for the first time felt tall.

Then Rasia froze, her entire body shuddering at the force she used to come to an abrupt stop. Someone had turned the corner of a distant street. He sucked in a breath, because no one in the Grankull could ever mistake those eyes of steel.

Named Kibari Shamaikulani-Spearedge-Undefeated-Sentry Han-Ribs Councilor-Oshield. Kai knew her names.

In a vibration, the Han noted the color of his eyes to the inside-out of Rasia's caftan. The confusion that twisted through Kibari Oshield's face smelted into something heated and dangerous.

Rasia snatched his hand and ran toward the closest side-street. She led them down ladders, jumped across rooftops, and descended stairs until they made it to the relative safety of the ground. She pressed against him where they paused in a narrow alley. Kai's throat burned, and he gathered a few breaths of air.

"Are you in trouble?" he asked.

"I'll deal with tah. You focus on your interview."

"Is she going to hurt you?"

"She won't *kill* me," Rasia laughed, and then frowned when she searched his face. "I was joking. Tah has never hurt me. I'll deal with her. Trust me."

She moved to pull away, but he held her against him. He rested in the crook of her shoulder, not ready to let her go.

"Thank you," Kai said, "For last night and this morning. Thank you, kulani, for taking care of me."

Rasia's focus narrowed on him, surprised. Kai had imagined the setting would be a lot more romantic when he finally said the word aloud, instead of in the middle of an alleyway bleeding red with the sunrise, but it felt right at that moment.

"It's difficult sometimes for me to say things, but I don't want that left unsaid. You deserve to hear it. And tonight," he stamped her lips with a promise, "I'll take care of you."

Rasia grinned wickedly, then she tapped her hands on his chest. "Say it again."

"Kulani."

She lit up pleased, and he felt so full of warmth. She had patiently waited all this time for the moment he was ready to say it. It truly hit him that he was safe with her. Come alleyways or dragons, he found safety in her arms.

Then Rasia snorted, breaking the moment, but unable to fully wipe away the blush that peeked through her sloppily wrapped shroud. "We're so fucking sappy. Come on. Let's get you to your interview."

They stopped outside the temple steps. Out of all the buildings in the Grankull, Kai had been in and out of these temple doors the most. It was where tajih taught him to read and then further allowed him to help with scribe work. It was also where the Council tried to beat his magic out of him. Later this evening, on these very steps, he'd show his face.

He looked over at Rasia. "I'll see you . . . later?"

She wiggled her brows and teased, "Unless you want me to walk you home afterward?"

His house squatted only a block away, with the winding temple gardens practically his front yard. The walk between his house and the temple was the only one he felt confident taking alone.

"I think I can manage."

Rasia leaned in the wind's direction. "My interview is at high noon, and then Jilah is helping me get ready. I might not catch up with you until the ceremony. Make sure you eat breakfast."

He nodded. "Be careful. Your tah looked mad."

She winked at him and then left, racing off. Kai stood on the steps where Rasia left him, staring up at the towering doors.

Second drum echoed around the Grankull and rumbled like a bellowing yawn this far to the ground. He took a deep breath and pushed into the temple. He didn't need the scribes to tell him the direction to the interview room. He had been imagining this day for the past sixteen years.

Kai finally got the chance to tell his story.

CHAPTER TWENTY-THREE

O

Rasia did not go through the front door when she returned home. Instead, she went around back and climbed in through her bedroom window. It was more of a mess than it usually was, tossed apart from trying to get Kai dressed, and generally not cleaning it for the past year.

She pulled on a pair of pants and flipped her caftan right-side out again. With a further moment of consideration, she packed up all her items of import—her money and her maps, rolled up her leather smuggling belts, stuffed a few clothes into her scorpion armored vest, grabbed a couple of weapons, and pushed it all out of the window.

Then Rasia left for the kitchen and grabbed the bread and the bowl of gonda noodles Ysai had set aside for her and entered the serving room. Kiba-ta sat at the head of the table. Jilah and Ysai sat on the longer side. Rasia sat down on Kiba-ta's left. Tah didn't say a word as she ate. Across from her, Ysai communicated with well-practiced eyebrows and discreet eye gestures.

'*Why the fuck is tah so mad?*'

Rasia tilted her head out the doorway, wiggled her brows, and rolled her eyes. '*I got got.*'

'*Why didn't you take the down streets?!*'

They all flinched when tah's soup ladle slammed atop the

table—her breakfast finished. Rasia braced herself.

"You are mere drums away from your Naming Ceremony," Kiba-ta began, "and yet you risk losing all that you have achieved on some defective skink? If any of the neighbors had seen the two of you last night, your entire Forging would have been up for forfeit. You have shamed me before, you have embarrassed me before, but I never thought you'd be so carelessly foolish."

Kiba-ta moved a hand to one of her pockets and sent an object flying at Rasia's face. By reflex, Rasia caught it one-handed out of the air. She looked down at the almost empty vial of gonom. "We didn't—"

"Drink it," tah commanded. "Death knows the day you get seeded by the runt of the Grankull is the day I kill you myself."

Jilah coughed, then literally choked on her food. She mouthed, '*Kai*?' at Ysai in question.

Guess it couldn't hurt. Rasia swallowed the gonom and then almost retched. It tasted too much like the gonom venom it was diluted from. For a moment, she flashed back to the taste of vomit in her throat and the excruciating pain. Her hands shook. Under tah's hard stare, she forcibly swallowed down the contraceptive. Then she snatched for her tea to wash down both the taste and the memory.

"Today was your morning for breakfast," tah continued. "While you are still living in my house, you will not neglect your responsibility to this family, regardless of any late-night proclivities. Understand?"

"I understand."

"There were reports yesterday of you buying things for him at the market," tah said, with a disgusted sneer. "Is this some kind of arrangement? Are you buying him things for sex? I'm not surprised he'd turn out a fucking whore."

This was exactly why Rasia didn't want Kai anywhere near Kiba-ta. His self-esteem was already shit, and she didn't need her tah tearing it further apart. She never feared physical harm from her tah, but conversations could be more vicious and dangerous than any Desert skirmish. Rasia had seen her tah eviscerate adults to tears.

"You're wrong about him, Kibari Oshield," Jilah spoke up in her cousin's defense. "He helps Juno-ta with scribe-work all of the time, and he's rather accomplished at it. It is my understanding he'll be a scribe after the Naming."

"You might be sitting at my serving table, but I never invited your opinion to this conversation. Close your mouth or stick poh's dick in it for all I care, but do not interrupt me again."

Jilah immediately quieted and shrunk.

"Tah," Ysai began but one glare, and he folded in half beside Jilah. He once used to defend Jilah against every cutting remark but learned the hard way that tah treated Jilah even worse afterward.

"Jilah's right," Rasia said, uncowed. "I bought him things yesterday because I like him."

Tah raised a disgusted lip. "You can have anyone you desire, and yet you choose the biggest embarrassment of the entire Grankull? I wish I could be more surprised, but when have you ever chosen anything conventional? You're the first child in my entire family who didn't attend school and instead ran around like some untrained child from the Tents. You embarrassed me by throwing your bones halfway across the Desert. Now, you're entertaining a flame with the one kid who should have been scraped from his tah's womb in a back alley. I'm hardly surprised by anything that you do anymore. The one comfort I have is the certainty that your attention never lasts for long. You'll get bored. You'll throw him away, like you do with everything else."

In the corner of Rasia's eye, Ysai shook his head. The way to survive a conversation with tah was never to rise to the bait. Rasia could overlook the brutal name-calling, but she gritted her teeth and found it difficult to let tah's accusation go unchallenged. Because in the deepest recess of her joints, she did fear a day she got bored of Kai. Thus far, he'd defied all expectations but what if her attention didn't hold? What if he *was* a passing flame?

Rasia raised her chin stubbornly, and said, as much a declaration as to dispel her own doubts, "He is not a phase nor a passing flame to throw out the window. Kai is my kulani."

Kiba-ta physically and mentally froze. Rasia found it almost satisfying to find tah so startled for failing to predict every twist of a conversation. Simultaneously, she worried about tah's reaction. She had intended to keep Kai a secret at least until the Naming Ceremony. It was an easier truth to swallow if Kai had a face, and Rasia had seen firsthand the abuse Jilah suffered because of tah's disapproval.

Finally, tah released a twisted sneering laugh. "Real funny."

It was an out. Rasia could have taken it. She should have taken it. But she refused to be ashamed of Kai. "I'm serious. He is my kulani, and I won't hesitate to defend him. You will not talk to my kulani. You will not touch him. You will not call him 'runt' or 'skink' or any derogatory term anymore. If you do, I will take all our contacts and all our receipts to the Council, and I will destroy you, and I will destroy this family."

That got tah's attention. Tah's fists clenched at the threat, but it had to be made. Rasia would not see Kai suffer the same way Jilah had. Tah turned to Ysai, a last-ditch effort to expose this for the prank she thought it was.

Ysai glanced helplessly between Rasia and Kiba-ta. "They are well-matched. He seems a good partner for her."

To tah's credit, she took the sudden world shift in stride. Plenty of people would have laughed at Rasia, would have questioned her capability to match with anyone. But she was Kiba-ta's child, and her steely cold-blooded tah had matched souls with a face from the Tents. Their experiences weren't all that different. . . Okay, maybe a shortened version of it. Shamai-ta had courted Kiba-ta for three years, then they committed for two years before legally carrying each other's names.

When Kiba-ta was ready to settle down, she had reviewed her options and picked the person she wanted to see the most in her children. Kiba-ta had wanted her children to have Shamai-ta's ambition and ingenuity, and her steel and pragmatism. That was it. That was Kiba-ta's cold logic. Rasia didn't think Kiba-ta had anticipated how good Shamai-ta would be for *her*. They had been a good match in the end. All Rasia wanted was the same.

"You're not your jih," tah said. "For all your faults, you're not some child who stupidly believes that the first person to make you cum is your kulani. Whatever this is, it's not forever. It's a flame. A *Forging flame*. It's not going to last. The stories have you believing that a kulani is about destiny and fate—but it's hard work, responsibility, and commitment. We are not born with a soulmatch, we learn to live with one. And you, my dear child, are not ready."

"Maybe I'm not, but we're figuring it out," Rasia argued. "I choose him. Like you chose Shamai-ta. Kailjnn is my equal."

Tah laughed. "I was there when that runt was born. I guarded the Ohan's family for five years. That pile of skin and bones is not worth a face."

"I don't care what you think. We're both going to be adults by the end of the day and after the Naming, we're free to carry each other's names. I don't need your approval. I never expected to have it."

"You killed a dragon," tah snapped out, frustrated.

"He killed one too!" she snapped, just as frustrated.

"You have your choice of job available to you. You could have anyone you want. Anyone you set your eyes on will worship you. Explore your options. Make mistakes. Live your life. You think you know what you want, but you don't. You can barely stay in the Grankull for more than a couple of days. What makes you think you can take care of a kulani? What you're experiencing right now? It's a flame. It'll peter out. That's not a kull-of-two, and eventually, with more experience, you'll learn to know the difference."

"I know the difference."

"You know nothing. The only reason you want to carry his name is to prove me wrong."

Rasia narrowed her eyes and bit out, "It's not always about you."

"Isn't it? I tell you not to do something and you do it anyway. That's how it always goes. It's pointless to tell you to stay away from him, so I'm not even going to waste my breath. But if this is the path you choose, then you walk it alone. You are no longer my child, and you are no longer welcome in this house. Make your mistakes and learn the hard way. Go be an adult."

Rasia pushed herself up from the table. She had anticipated this moment since she returned to the Grankull with Kai's namesake around her neck. Kiba-ta had never approved of any of her choices. It did not surprise her that Kai would be the breaking point.

"Tah, how is that fair?" Ysai argued. "You didn't kick me out when I introduced Jilah."

"She might not have been what I wanted for you, but at least you weren't permanently tying yourself to the biggest mistake of your life."

"Too bad giving birth to me is the biggest mistake of yours!"

"Get out!" tah bellowed.

Rasia didn't hesitate.

"So . . . that happened," Rasia said as Ysai and Jilah joined her atop the neighbor's roof a short time later. Even though Rasia had been the one kicked out of the house, both Ysai and Jilah stood in silent contemplation.

"She caught you with Kai this morning?" Ysai asked, to confirm aloud.

"Dead center of the Spine," she spat, annoyed. She and Ysai had come up with several contingencies on how to deal with Kiba-ta, but none of them included the possibility of tah finding out about Kai before the Naming. "The plan doesn't change. We knew she wouldn't approve of him. We knew this could happen. I'll sleep on the windship."

"I don't want to live here anymore." Jilah's small hurt whisper shocked both Ysai and Rasia. *That* wasn't something either of the siblings foresaw.

"*I know.* I'll put in another housing application." Ysai sighed. Without saying anything aloud, they all knew it wouldn't make much difference.

Every time he applied for housing, his application was denied. The administration office considered a lot of factors—the number of years worked, your value to the Grankull, and how much money you could slide under the table—but ultimately, they both knew tah influenced the application because she disapproved of Jilah and wanted to keep Ysai close to home.

Rasia, on the other hand, was finally free.

She honestly felt bad for them both. In the beginning, Jilah moved in with Ysai hoping to eventually win over Kiba-ta. She had stubbornly refused to listen when Rasia told her that was a lost cause.

"I don't want to live here anymore," Jilah repeated, again. "I'm tired of being treated like some flame you're fucking around with. I'm tired of being afraid of her. I'm tired of you being too afraid to defend me. And if you do . . . then you're kicked out and excommunicated from the family like Rasia? It's ridiculous. We're moving in with my parents."

Ysai opened his mouth to argue, then deflated at Jilah's glare. Honestly, Rasia was impressed Jilah had endured for this long, but in the end, Kiba-ta gave an impossible test that Jilah could never have passed.

"Wait," Rasia said. She rushed behind the house and scooped up her pile of belongings from under the window. When she returned, she shoved the blatant clack of bone chips into Ysai's hands. "No matter how much tah has threatened the administrative office, this should be enough to bribe them."

"Rasia, this is all your savings. You might need this."

"I'm free. No one deserves to be stuck with tah forever."

Before, Rasia had reveled in the way their tah treated Jilah. She had secretly hoped Jilah would turn tail and run for the dunes. But something had changed. Jilah wasn't the enemy anymore.

Ysai broke into a watery smile and shoved Rasia into a hug,

one of those hugs they used to have, when it was her and Ysai against the world. For so long, she thought she had lost her jih, thought she'd never get him back if Jilah had her hooks in him.

In the end, it was Rasia who had lost her way.

"Thank you," Ysai said.

"I'll always have your back," Rasia promised, and then with a twist of her lips, snarked, "even if that includes Jilah-ji."

Ysai pulled back to look at her, surprised. "Did my little jih finally have a change of bones?"

"My bones have been doing a lot of twisting and turning these days." She looked at Jilah meaningfully. Jilah gave a tentative smile, then rushed forward to join the hug. Ysai melted happy and content with his arms wrapped around them both.

"This isn't over, you know," Ysai whispered seriously between them.

He was right. This was far from over.

Kiba-ta never let go of things easy.

CHAPTER TWENTY-FOUR

O

"But I slayed a dragon!"

"That may be so, but it isn't your greatest accomplishment," the Mythkeeper countered, because of course she had to be Rasia's interviewer. "The rarity of an incident is also considered, and you are the only person on record to have ever survived the Yestermorrow Lake of your own volition. Your Last Name is Yestermorrow."

As tradition dictated, the scribes recorded a person's names with their greatest accomplishment last. The Council had since determined that the new name of 'Dragonblood' would be awarded to those who had slayed a dragon for their Forging. The name was awesome and badass, and everything Rasia worked so hard for. She didn't come this far for the order she wanted to be denied to her.

Rasia crossed her arms, thinking, and watched her tea as it grew cold. They both sat on floor cushions across from one another in the interview room, a half room with the entire backwall replaced by a curtain of beaded dragon bones. The wind barely moved them, but when they did, the bones clashed together like a tempest. Sometimes, it distracted her attention.

"This last name is uniquely yours. I figured you would be happy."

"But it isn't earned," Rasia argued. "I worked for that fucking dragon, and I'm proud of it. But the Lake is magic, and magic has no rules. I never had any control over what happened. I would like to think it was because I'm a ta-fucking badass, but the truth is, I don't know why I survived."

"Language, Rasia. You're not of age yet."

"The point is, I'll never know why."

"Exactly. Sometimes, one doesn't understand the significance of an action the moment it occurs. All have drowned, except you. You survived and people will always wonder why."

"Then they can jump in the fucking Lake and wonder at it themselves! It was the Lake's choice, not mine. I understand that not all names are glory and triumph. Some are mistakes and hard-earned lessons, but at least they are *my* mistakes, *my* lessons. I should be known for my choices."

"Rasia, you might throw your bones as far and as hard as anyone has ever thrown them, but in the end, you still have no control over how they land. Sometimes, fate is just fate."

"Fuck that shit. I refuse to be identified by some stroke of accidental luck. I am more than that Lake."

"You *are* more. That's why you have *other* names. You have collected more names than anyone else in the history of a Forging season. Isn't that enough?"

"No." It would not be enough. Not until Rasia got what she deserved. "When a hunting kull slays a dragon, all the members of that kull are given the name Dragonslayer. *But*, the Han of the expedition receives the name of Dragonsbane because the Grankull recognizes how difficult it is to lead such an expedition. Therefore, shouldn't I earn my own unique name for being the undeniable leader of this Forging hunt? And if so, wouldn't the uniqueness of that name be as equal to the uniqueness of 'Yestermorrow?'"

"I suppose," the Mythkeeper said, so far unconvinced as Rasia gave her pitch.

"And certainly, you would agree that a person's 'greatest' accomplishment could be a matter of opinion? Sure, the

Yestermorrow Lake might be the easy story. Those who haven't slayed a dragon can't fully grasp or appreciate the hard work it requires. On top of that, we did it in a season—a feat that no other kull has accomplished, which exponentially increases the difficulty. Only a fellow dragonslayer can truly appreciate the monumental accomplishment of my Forging hunt. In the end, if it's all a matter of opinion and perception, then isn't the order of my names a reflection of what the Grankull should value most? Should people strive to put in the hard work to hunt a dragon threatening the Grankull's livelihood? Or should people strive to jump in a magic lake and drown like idiots? Which is the better story?"

The Mythkeeper considered Rasia for a long time before expending that relenting sigh Rasia knew all too well. Her lips curled in a pre-emptive grin. "It's a shame you refused to apply all this philosophy to your schoolwork. You've made a good argument. What name, exactly, do you believe you have earned?"

Rasia had the perfect name in mind.

CHAPTER TWENTY-FIVE

O

"Rasia!"

She swiveled the moment she exited her interview and barely had time to brace when Jilah slammed into her. She blinked, confused by the sudden hug, then Jilah remembered herself and sprang a step back. Rasia was underage for a few drums more and still disallowed public touch.

"Rasia, it worked! Our housing application was approved!" Jilah exclaimed.

Several of the scribes, and several behind the reading curtains, viciously hushed her. Jilah blushed and rushed Rasia out of the temple doors.

After so many attempts of Ysai and Jilah trying, Rasia hadn't thought the bribe would actually work. Guess you should never underestimate the power of money, especially several pouches full.

"Lani wanted to tell you himself, but your interview went on for so long. He's at our new place right now cleaning it. I told him I'd bring you over once your interview finished."

"Where is it?" Rasia asked and followed Jilah down the temple steps. Since Ysai was a sentry and Jilah a scribe, they were only eligible for housing in the Ribs and Heart district. It was no surprise which one Ysai preferred—as far away from their Kiba-ta as possible—but Rasia knew he'd be willing to take whatever he could get.

"It's in the Ribs, but it's several spires away from your tah."

"Thank goodness for that. I should grab my stuff from the windship. How long is your break?"

"Who says you're staying with us?"

Rasia glared at Jilah, and Jilah broke into a grin. "Let's go get your stuff since I'm off now. Yours was the last interview to finish. I don't have to report back until the ceremony."

"Perfect." They headed toward the shipyard to retrieve the clothes and valuables Rasia had stashed in the windship earlier that day.

"Why by the Elder was your interview so long?" Jilah asked as they walked the bustling Grankull streets. A sharp whistle cut the air behind them. Jilah and Rasia moved to allow the messengers to run past them down the streets. Many, except for the goats along the road, automatically moved out of their way.

"There was a slight disagreement over my Last Name," Rasia said.

"What's there to disagree about? I thought all the kids who killed Aurum are to be named Dragonblood?"

Rasia inclined her head toward Jilah and wondered if she needed to explain the whole Lake business. "How much do you know about my Forging?"

Rasia told Ysai everything, and most likely he had mentioned bits and pieces of it to Jilah, but probably not all of it. Ysai was well aware his kulani liked to gossip. He would have kept Rasia's more private experiences to himself.

Jilah blushed and admitted, "I got it all from Nico, way before you ever returned to the Grankull. Lani has since filled in some of the holes, but neither he nor Nico said anything about you and Kai, so apparently, I'm still missing a lot. I'm sure you've omitted a lot more from the official record too."

Rasia laughed at that and gave Jilah a sly shrug. "I kept certain parts to myself, but I was honest in my relationship with Kai. I named him my kulani several times."

"You called him your kulani on record? That's . . . wow. Good. Kai deserves someone brave enough to say it."

Rasia froze. She frowned as she peered into the distance of the shipyard. She knew that distant view intimately—the windship builders on the right, the resource vessels, the private ships. Something was off. She scanned over the bustle of activity, and her eyes snagged on the emptiness of *her* windship lane.

Where the fuck was her windship? Rasia broke into a sprint, and Jilah shouted in alarm behind her.

She slammed into the closest sentry. She had been at the shipyards not a few drums ago, stashing away all her clothes, armor, and spare weapons. "What happened to my fucking windship?! Where is it?"

The sentry looked at first baffled, and then gathered his wits when Rasia drew her swords on him. "It was taken to impound. A tip came in that payment was overdue." He paused to look at her shroud and then her swords and wisely didn't say a word about a child illegally carrying weapons.

"Do you know whose fucking ship that was?" she demanded. "It belongs to the Sentry Han's dead kulani. Payment for the ship comes out of her paycheck. It's not possible for it to be overdue. Who the fuck authorized this?"

The sentry shook his head helplessly. "It was the Sentry Han herself who authorized it."

With a snarl, Rasia stormed through the Grankull. She thought she was prepared for anything, but she hadn't anticipated their morning feud to spill over to the windship—Shamai-ta's windship that he had built with his bare hands.

This was war.

"TAH!" Rasia yelled as she charged into the sentry's administrative office. She hopped the greeting desk and thundered into the back towards Kiba-ta's office.

Rasia kicked open the doors and demanded, "WHERE THE FUCK IS MY WINDSHIP?!"

Kiba-ta, sitting at a low-desk full of paperwork, glared annoyed as if Rasia were one of the new recruits lost in the wrong part of the building. The sun shone through the diamond slatted window-wall to speckle tah with shadows. "I thought I was clear this morning that you are no longer entitled to this family's resources, which includes paying the rent space for your toys."

"How could you? That was tah's windship!"

"And now your responsibility. I'm certain once you get a job, you can go down to the shipyard office to pay your tab and get this cleared up, *or* you can pay it with your secret stash of money. If you still have it, or is that the reason why Ysai-po's housing application was suddenly and swiftly approved without moving through the proper channels? If anyone finds out the truth and reports him, he could be revoked rations."

Rasia crossed her arms. "I'm sure you'll cover it up, the same as you've covered up all the times you made sure his application failed."

"I've done nothing but try to protect you both. Abandon the runt, and I could have your windship freed immediately."

Rasia slammed her hands atop tah's desk, her knees hitting the ground harshly. "You can't do this. You can't disown me. You need me. You need both me and the windship. I'm the foundation of this entire family. What are you going to do? Stop the smuggling business?"

"Thanks to you, the dragon is dead, which means we should expect a good hunting season. Smuggling is only a good business when food is scarce. It was only meant to be temporary to get us through the hard years. But you wouldn't know a thing about sacrifice."

Rasia snarled, leaned closer to Kiba-ta, and threw another threat out of her smuggling pockets. "Discharge the windship, then maybe I won't tell the Council *everything*. You think I don't know that you're the one who put the hit out on Nico? Your last name is Oshield because you once saved an Ohan's life, and now you're hiring assassins to kill one?"

"My job is to protect the Grankull, not the Ohan. The magicborn are powerful but not perfect. I learned that lesson when the runt came into this world, and I refuse to allow the

Grankull to suffer because they can't make the hard choices. I protect the Grankull, even from itself."

"I almost failed the Forging because of the scavengers you hired! You went through all the trouble of paying for Nico and me to be on the same kull, and then you send assassins after us?"

"The Forging hunt is the one thing I never doubted of you. I never paid to put you on the same kull. The bones did that."

Rasia paused and took a moment to be smug by the fact that Neema had been wrong about her tah's involvement. She knew her tah wouldn't waste money on a sure bet. "It's still a whole bunch of money wasted considering she's alive."

"She's lucky you killed that dragon. She's weak like Avalai Ohan, and that weakness could kill us all. She is a foolish naïve child who knows nothing."

"She's not wrong to stand up for the Tents. There are good people there. Tah was from the Tents."

"Kulani earned his name. But most in the Tents live and die feeding off the Grankull like parasites. They do nothing but steal and swindle away the resources we desperately need."

Rasia scoffed. "*You* have been supporting the Tents all these years. Tah sent money back, you know, 'cause there were people in the Tents worth giving a shit about."

"Your tah was as subtle as . . . you. Of course, I knew everything he got up to. But those were different days and a better season. Until you slayed that dragon, there was no hope that things were getting any better. Sometimes you make the hard choice, for your family, for your employees, and for the Grankull. Everything I have done, I did for you and your jih. Kulani and I worked hard to give you children a good life. He never wanted you to know hunger, and I'll destroy half the world to make sure you never do. But no matter all that I have sacrificed for you, how much I have protected you, you've always thrown everything back in my face. You are so brilliant and talented, but you've always squandered your potential on these frivolous flights of fancy. Kulani should never have encouraged you. All I wanted was the world for you."

"You wanted *your world* for me," Rasia spat. "All I've ever wanted was for you to support me and the things that make me happy. But I'll never throw my bones like everyone else. My kulani will never be like anyone else. I'll never be the face that you want, and if you can't accept that, if you can't accept me, then we have nothing to do with each other. I don't need you. I'll live my life on my own terms."

"Then go live it, but I'll no longer save you from your fuck-ups. Life isn't what you think it is."

"I SLAYED A DRAGON!" Rasia bellowed.

Rasia swept her arms along the desk, scattering all tah's paperwork along the floor. She used the momentum to turn on her heels and rampage out of the room.

⸻

"I hate her," Rasia complained to the only person who understood and shared her hatred for her tah.

"Kibari Oshield is an asshole," Jilah agreed. "But you're also an asshole. You get it from somewhere."

Rasia gasped, offended, and swiveled atop the ottoman. Jilah jerked back with the heated porcupine needle aimed at Rasia's ear. "Rasia," Jilah complained. "You've got to sit still."

"You're saying I'm like Kiba-ta?"

"Is this a surprise?"

"I am nothing like her."

"You are everything like her. Do you not remember the disaster of the Introduction Dinner when lani formally introduced our courtship? Kibari Oshield was bad enough, but you were even worse. You told lani that he was ruining his life, and you'd pay for a tent whore if he were so worried about keeping his dick wet."

"Huh. I don't remember that."

"I do, *vividly*." Jilah shoved Rasia's head to the side and decisively punctured Rasia's right ear with the needle. "Some people are like . . . Nico, who can't help but care about everyone. Then there's you. You care about who you care about and don't give a shit about anyone else. Kibari Oshield is the same way."

It was odd for Rasia to hear Jilah describe her and Kiba-ta in such similar terms. Side by side, all she could see were their differences. She never considered their similarities. Maybe she could see how Jilah kinda had a point.

"Kibari Oshield is capable of compassion," Jilah said. "So are you. But she is also cruel; so are you."

Jilah pulled the needle all the way through. She discarded it and then picked up a bronze bar with a dragon glass bead on the end. She dipped the bar in alcohol, pinned it through the newly created hole in Rasia's ear, and fastened another bead onto the open end. Without her hair, Rasia felt bare. She missed having *something*. Jilah stood out of the way for Rasia to inspect the piercing in the mirror of Jilah's new bedroom.

"I'm sorry," Rasia said to the mirror. She only had scattered memories of that night. It hadn't been nearly as important for Rasia as it had been for Jilah. "I should have had jih's back, no matter how I felt about you. I hated you for all the wrong reasons. I was jealous. I'm not good at making friends, and Ysai-ji was all I had."

"I know," Jilah said. "You will always be important to kulani. Yours are the only opinions that truly matter to him. He respects you so much. That'll never change. I could never take your jih away from you, but if you're ever feeling insecure or lonely or neglected, he doesn't have to be your only friend. I'm here too, if you ever need me."

It was a nice offer, but Rasia honestly could not imagine them as friends.

"Thanks. I just . . ." she shrugged. "We don't have much in common other than Ysai-ji. Could we do the friend thing? How would we get there?"

"You and Kai are friends," Jilah pointed out. "And that, quite frankly, seems all the more impossible to me."

"Kai was easy," Rasia huffed. She thought back on the Forging and tried to figure out that thin line when Kai and Rasia had stumbled over into friendship. "I wasn't even trying to befriend him. I was just being myself, and somehow . . . he fell into my vagina?" Jilah curled over laughing. "I don't know! I guess there were other parts in between."

Jilah wiped tears from her eyes as she straightened. "How about you tell me all the stuff you left off of the official record?"

"So, all the sexy stuff?" Rasia grinned. "You perv."

"Hey, I've got," Jilah visually counted, "three more piercings to go. The least you can do is entertain me. Who kissed who first? I need to know."

Rasia rolled her eyes and told Jilah about the gorge and all the sexy stuff that followed. She omitted all the magic stuff, since Kai was so sensitive about it, but Jilah still found all the salacious details quite entertaining. Jilah gasped, and laughed, and encouraged. Rasia found herself enjoying Jilah's reactions to the twists and turns of the story. Ysai wasn't nearly as fun and nowhere near as engaged.

"Even in the shroud," Jilah commented. "I can tell he's sprouted drastically over the Forging. His old clothes hit his ankles now, and soon he'll be earning his own rations. He keeps this up, he'll be as tall as Kenji-shi by next year. The healers are going to be beside themselves. They never looked past the illness. Tah and I always hoped it was something he could outgrow."

"There is something I've been meaning to ask. I haven't been able to with Ysai-ji since he's one-sided and all. Does a big dick really make a difference?"

"It's harder on the mouth, that's for sure." Both Jilah and Rasia snickered. They were going to get along fine. All Rasia ever had to do was give her a chance.

Jilah placed a hand on her shoulder, and said softer and more seriously, "In my experience, the best partners are the ones that listen."

Then Ysai sprung from the doorway. "Are you two seriously comparing dick-sizes? It hurts our poor feelings when all you do is talk about our dicks."

"Only when you don't know how to use it!" Jilah teased.

Rasia leaned back and greeted the sight of all her clothes and weapons in Ysai's arms. He had argued that it would be far better if he talked to the sentries at the impound and explained how all her clothes for the ceremony were stuck inside the ship than for Rasia to sneak in and risk getting detained. He hit her atop the head as he passed by and dropped the clothes.

"Oh yeah?" Ysai said as he charged up under Jilah and lifted her off her feet. Jilah giggled as they went crashing and rolled onto the nearby bed frame.

"Come on, you're supposed to be helping me dress for the ceremony," Rasia complained. She kicked Ysai's butt, toppling him over, as she passed them. She shuffled through the pile of clothes for *the* pants. They were the same pants Shamai-ta wore for the signing ceremony with Kiba-ta, and the same pants Ysai wore for his Naming ceremony. Rasia had to order several alterations, but they fit perfectly when she fastened the beautiful white dragon leather waistband. It laid smooth atop her skin. It was the same leather from their tah's first dragon kill. Very few families could afford dragon leather clothing, and even if they could, it was only worn for momentous life events.

Rasia spun toward the mirror. The blood-dyed linen of the pants swished like a skirt around her legs and ended cropped at her ankles. She pressed the scorpion carapace to her chest and glanced over her shoulder at Ysai and Jilah making out behind her. This was why Rasia got annoyed so easily. Sometimes Ysai and Jilah wrapped themselves in their own world and left Rasia out alone in the rain.

"*Help.*"

"Okay, okay." Ysai rolled over and up behind her. He grabbed the leather cords to tie the red carapace halter. Scorpion carapace was normally used to make armor, but this piece was purely decorative. While others would no doubt wear beaded and woven dresses, Rasia liked the chest piece for its sleekness. It gleamed with pieces of dragonsteel to give it a glittering depth. She remembered the day she saw it in the market and how she had smiled. The edge pressed into her breasts, lifting them, and provided enough support that they weren't too cumbersome. It showed off her new bellybutton piercing nicely. She smiled at the red and white of blood and bones—the hunting colors.

"Bones, Rasia. You've got tits like tah."

"They look great," Jilah approved. "Glad you finally got rid of that wrap."

"Kai cut me out of it."

"I bet he did," Ysai snickered. Rasia shoved her hand back at into his face, but then he wrapped his arms around her from behind and squeezed her tight. "I know it's not the same, but that's from Shamai-ta."

"Thanks," she said, watery. She stared at her reflection, at the face Shamai-ta never got to see. She wondered if he would recognize her without the hair. She still felt the ghost of it sometimes, when she futilely searched for it to give her direction.

But she was also lighter now.

"You're beautiful," Jilah said.

"Ugh, really?"

"She means you look badass," Ysai chirped. Then he reached forward and adjusted the carapace halter, tightening it a little to further hike up her breasts. He gave an approving nod. "There you go."

"You're a real one, jih."

Rasia strapped her swords to her hips with satisfactory finality. She tied Kai's namesake around her neck. For the first time, she didn't have to hide anything under her clothes. She didn't have to wait for the border before she could jump into some pants. She could finally walk through the Grankull as herself.

Rasia put on the shroud for the last time and walked out the door.

CHAPTER TWENTY-SIX

O

The temple plaza was so crowded that people spilled over to the adjoining streets and rooftops. As a Naming candidate, Rasia arrived early to get a place at the front of the steps, but she and Ysai had managed somewhere near the middle. It was not her fault they severely underestimated the size of the crowd. These numbers were unprecedented. Everyone in the Grankull attended the namepour, the big celebration afterward, but the actual ceremony usually only interested immediate and extended family members. Apparently, everyone was excited to see the faces of those who slayed a dragon. And, also, Nico, the Ohan, or whatever.

"Do you see him?" Rasia asked as she tried to pick Kai out from the crowd. She could barely see over everyone's heads when she stretched to her tiptoes. She only had a clear view of the rising temple steps that staged the ceremony.

"Maybe. I think that's him by Kenji-shi."

Rasia gave Ysai's shoulders a considering look. Knowing her thoughts, Ysai raised his eyebrows.

"Come on, I practically bought a house for you."

"You know the rules."

She sneered. "Oh, amazing and physically superior jih of mine, can I please borrow your shoulders?"

He grinned and crouched down for Rasia to climb up. She smoothly hopped onto his shoulders and balanced herself for the lift, then she rose out of the crowd, far higher than everyone else except for those on the rooftops. Someone behind them complained, and she threw a 'V' over her shoulder.

"They're over there," Ysai pointed, "to the right of the stage."

She spotted Nico by the steps, because of course, Nico came early. Next to Nico, Kenji-shi carried Rae on his hip, while Kai stood almost hidden between them. Rasia waved to get his attention, but he kept his head down. She had hoped to meet up with him before the ceremony, but that became nearly impossible in the thickening crowd.

Azan caught sight of her wave and waved back where he stood with his siblings and his parents off to the left. Rasia spied Zephyr, Suri, and Neema. She couldn't find Kelin but had no doubt he was around.

The Ceremony started with a rumble of drums. Ysai tightened his grip on her thighs as the crowd surged forward, jostling him and rocking Rasia in turn. He elbowed the person who shoved into him and glared until they backed off. Rasia snickered in amusement. She undoubtedly had the best seat in the entire Grankull.

The Council and scribes proceeded to the stage. Ysai waved as Jilah walked behind the other scribes, as if she had any problems spotting them both sticking out of the crowd. Jilah smiled in their direction and then focused on the task of carrying the Book of Names to the pedestal atop the stairs.

The Mythkeeper stood before the podium, and her voice boomed, amplified by the acoustics of the temple dome over the courtyard. "We are gathered here today to welcome new faces to our kull. These individuals braved the Forging to feed us with their hunt and have earned their place among us. Those that endure remain."

The Mythkeeper read the first name from her list. Traditionally, they called names in the order of who returned first from the Forging. That could have been Rasia if she had beaten Shamai-ta's record, but as it was, her kull would be called last.

"Child of Avalai Ohan and Kenjinn Ilhani," the Mythkeeper announced, halfway through the ceremony.

The crowd jostled and clamored to get a glimpse of Nico as she walked up the temple steps. Nico could not have looked more elegant as Rasia did dangerous. She wore a shroud and a blue gossamer dress that flowed like water to the distant eye.

Nico bowed as the Mythkeeper dipped her thumb in a clay-worn bowl and then spread gonda blood at the bridge of Nico's eyes. While all eyes were on Nico, Rasia gazed intently at Kai, where he finally raised his head to watch his sibling unveil her face. He was not wearing the pants from the market. Rasia had delivered them to his house earlier that morning while he had his interview. Why wasn't he wearing the pants? The whole point was for Rasia to take them off of him later.

The Mythkeeper announced, "We welcome the newest member of the Grankull. Introduce yourself."

Nico peeled back layers of her shroud one at a time until she stood full-faced before the crowd.

"My name is Nicolai, child of Avalai Ohan and Kenjinn Ilhani. I am the magic-born heir, of the First Rain. I am the soil of the Wingfields and the Han before my time. I am the Oasis. I am the Elderheart. I am the Ohan."

Cheers rang out through the crowd, followed by audible name-songs of 'Ohan'. Rasia rolled her eyes at the fanfare. Thanks to Nico, who had to go and pick up every straggler on her way back to the Grankull, it was the longest ceremony in years. It was the first Forging in generations where everyone had either passed or died. There were no survivors in between.

"Child of Kibari Oshield and Shamaijen Windbreaker."

Goosebumps sparked up Rasia's arms when they called her name. This was it. This was the moment she had been waiting for all of her life.

"Shall I throw you on stage?" Ysai asked.

"I'm game."

He chuckled and crouched. Rasia jumped down to the ground,

and he squeezed her shoulder. "I'm proud of you, Raj. Tah is too."

"I know," Rasia said through a watery grin.

She turned toward the temple steps. No matter how congested, the crowd parted the way for her. Thus far, she was the farthest candidate from the stage. People cheered and congratulated her as she walked through them. More than one person echoed Ysai's sentiments about Shamai-ta and how he would have wished to be there.

The Mythkeeper had changed out the bowl for one filled with thick black liquid. Rasia bowed as they smeared the dragon blood between her eyes, the first to ever receive the honor.

"The Grankull welcomes you. Introduce yourself."

Rasia turned to the crowd and unwrapped her shroud. For so long, she imagined standing on this stage smothered by Shamai-ta's absence. She imagined herself gritting through the pain of words never spoken and a hug that would never come. She imagined herself staring out at the crowd and seeing nothing but strangers.

Alone.

But she felt Shamai-ta as tangible as the sun on her skin. She felt him in the tall and proud carriage of Ysai's shoulders and in the encouraging words of his peers who remembered him. She felt his unflinching acceptance and understanding in a kulani Rasia never saw coming. Shamai-ta left little parts of himself everywhere for her to find.

The biggest part was her.

"My name is Rajiani, child of Kibari Oshield and Shamaijen Windbreaker. I am the hunter, the wind-chaser, and the horizon-seeker. I am the discoverer, the wanderer, and the adventurer. I am the mane of wild horses. I am bones thrown afield. I am a map with no end. I am two-blades and dragon-sail. I am swiftness and movement. I am the dark waters of the dragon's coast, a Graveyard of bones, and the today of Yestermorrow. I am Rasia of the Dragonfire."

Cheers roared throughout the Grankull. Thunderous applause

vibrated from every crevice. Rasia lifted her face to the faint lights in the sky, at that sea of stars peeking through the sunset.

"Tah, I did it."

The Mythkeeper dipped the pen in the black blood of the dragon and handed it to Rasia. She signed the first symbol of her name. She squinted at the paper. Then she unabashedly turned and flowed through the motions to the crowd's confusion and Kiba-ta's mortification. She remembered the symbol that stumped her and wrote the rest. With confidence, Rasia signed her names.

She flipped the page to the next entry, then stepped back in line with the other kids. She lined up beside Kelin who glanced up and down at her clothes. "Nice outfit."

Rasia glanced up and down at Kelin's magnificent dress of heron feathers. He had made quite the entry. "Same to you."

Neema walked onto the stage next.

Then Zephyr.

Then Azan.

Then-

Rasia searched the crowd for Kai and couldn't find him where he had been standing before. She wondered if he had moved closer to the steps in preparation for his turn. In her focus to find him, she had almost missed the Councilor's parting words: "Thank you to everyone for attending the Naming Ceremony. Please convene in three drums at the Tail for a feast and celebration in honor of our new faces to the Grankull."

The fuck?

"Wait," Rasia stepped out of line. "What about Kai?"

CHAPTER TWENTY-SEVEN

—

"Name the parts of a windship."

"Huh?" Kai asked, confused as to how the interviewer's request related to his Forging story. He had been careful in choosing his words, and he hoped that the plot holes paved over for Nico's decisions hadn't been discovered. The interviewer, the council member elected from the belly of market street, gave no hint of expression or emotion.

Despite the non sequitur, Kai attempted to answer.

"The hull, the ropes, the . . ." he paused, frowning, and tried to remember. Rasia never really taught him the name of things. He said slowly, unsure, "the black hook thingy?"

"Do you think me a fool to believe a story so preposterous?" the interviewer asked. "If you can't name the parts of a windship, how am I to believe you can steer one? Not only that, but to steer one so well as to evade a dragon?"

Kai's stomach dropped. This wasn't about jih's story. This was about *his* story.

"I knew something didn't add up right while reading Nicolai's interview. You're not capable of killing a dragon. You couldn't have been truly there, and you all are telling one big lie to cover it up because your jih believes she can cheat the system. She's so like her parents—foolishly believing themselves higher than the power of the Elder. For your jih to blatantly lie, and involve so many others in that lie, so that the Grankull's greatest shame can become one of us? I will not have it. Now, tell me the truth."

"It is the truth," Kai insisted. "I hunted a dragon with Rasia. I steered the windship."

The interviewer picked up their cup of tea and sipped at it, waiting. The scritch-scratch of the scribe recording the interview in the corner of the room had stopped.

Kai gritted his teeth as all his hopes and dreams slipped through his fingers. When he finally gained control over his magic, he had promised himself he wouldn't be defined by it, but he bit out a story the Councilor could more readily believe, betraying himself so easily, "I used my magic to help steer the windship."

"You mean the magic the Council has tried to get out of you for the past five years? How convenient. Where is this magic now? Show me then."

Worry gnawed at Kai's stomach. He hadn't attempted any magic since returning to the Grankull. He hadn't had the need to. He inhaled and focused on channeling his willpower, but the interviewer scowled at him as if his existence deeply offended her, and he found it difficult to concentrate. They had scowled like that too when the Council had him pinned to the floor and whipped him bloody. Phantom fire burned up his back, and his flesh cracked in his ears.

Panic and anxiety choked him as he willed the bone curtains to shake, sand to sweep from the floor, the tea to spill hot over the interviewer's lap, *something*.

"Do you think this a joke? You can't fool me. I know how your magic works."

"You don't!"

Kai's neck snapped at the force of the teacup slamming across his face. He scrambled to wipe away the worst of the burning tea, and his hands scalded. His shroud had shielded him from a permanent facial injury. Even the scribe had jumped, but had done nothing to help.

"You will watch your tone," the Councilor snapped. "You are

only alive by the grace of the Council. You owe every moment of your wretched life to us. Now, tell me the truth or everyone involved in this lie will go down with you. No one will show their face tonight. Not even your jih."

Kai squeezed his eyes shut, shaking. He should have known. He should have tempered his expectations, battered back his hopes, stuffed his dreams deep down never to see the light of day. Maybe then he wouldn't have to feel the pain of everything crumbling around him. Because how could he possibly ruin the lives of so many kids for the truth? If they stripped Nico of her face, how would he and jih survive the coming year without rations for them both? It was a death sentence.

"If I—If I tell the truth, then Nico-ji and Rasia and the others won't get in trouble for lying?" he asked, needing to confirm.

The Councilor's eyes drilled into his chest. "*If* you tell the truth."

Kai thought of Rasia—about her certainty if you fought for something hard enough, wanted it badly enough, that you had the power to make it come true. How in Rasia's world, life boiled down to grit and determination and not birth and circumstances.

Life wasn't fair. And it wasn't fair to Kai most of all.

He straightened and studied this face who despised him, who had already made up their mind about his story before he ever walked into the room. No amount of magic, or words, or grit and fucking determination would ever change their mind.

"You're right. I never managed to leave the oasis. I never joined Rasia at all . . ." Kai gave them the story that they wanted to hear—the story where he would only ever be the runt of the Grankull.

The world fogged at the edges of Kai's periphery as he fought to place one foot in front of the other. Like moving through water. Like drowning. It was only a matter of time before his strength failed him. His surroundings flickered and shifted, and a jolt shot through his left foot when he hit the familiar step in front of his home.

"Watch out, tah! The dragon is coming!"

Rae roared. Soft and chubby hands imitated claws. The budchild jumped off the serving table, flying. Booming laughter and eyes crinkled at the corners tucked shoulders under Rae and gave the child wings. Rae glided through the air on Kenji's back.

An ugly poison of jealousy slithered up Kai's veins, then bitter fear, then hot fury, then all of it over again, in a never-ending spiral that reeled Kai dizzy in a torrent of his own emotions. All his life, he had been a shadow watching, existing on the edges, tiptoeing boundaries, and never daring to cross the line. It felt an eternity standing in that doorway, watching Kenji and jih play.

It was Nico, coming through with a basket of freshly plucked clothes, who noticed him.

"Kai? You didn't . . ." she paused, then glanced at her tah rolling on the floor, sailing a toy windship away from Rae's stomping feet. Kenji looked up at Nico's entry. Rae hopped atop the ship, shouting in glee, made all the louder in the sudden quiet of the room. Rae clutched the reclaimed windship to their chest, eyes wide, shriveling in uncertainty at the sudden tension. Nico asked, "How was your interview?"

Kai opened his mouth to respond, but the only air he could force from his lips was a creaking dying gasp.

Kenji said, jaw locked and eyes intense. "I heard you killed a dragon."

This was it. This was supposed to be the moment Kai had waited his entire life for—the moment when he could finally face Kenji and not feel like a fucking disappointment. Blood pounded in his head. He feared if he moved, he'd faint.

Nico glanced between Kai and her tah, understanding the momentousness of the occasion but unable to fully comprehend

Kai's non-response.

"Here," she said, approaching Kai and throwing an arm around his shoulder. "Rasia delivered a pair of pants for you earlier this morning. I've put them on your bed. How about we make sure they fit for the ceremony?"

Nico got him out of there. She took him all the way to his room where the new pants Rasia had commissioned for him lay on his bed. His first pair of pants tailored specifically for him.

Kai's world had just imploded, the ground itself come undone, and it was unfair that for everyone else, the rupture of his being was barely a vibration underfoot. He wished to force sound from his throat and give the destruction voice. He waited for the eruption of sobs, or downpour of tears, but it all sat on his chest and strangled his lungs. In the end, his world shattered in silence.

"Kai?" Nico's voice floated around his ears. He blacked out, he thought, for he didn't remember her coming to stand in front of him. She shook him about the shoulders. He wondered if she could see all the anger and all the fury unable to heat hot enough to boil showing on his face. She saw *something*, for she grew more and more concerned. "Kai, what's wrong? What happened?"

He didn't want her to worry. He didn't want to ruin her world too. So, he forced himself to face her. He forced all the destruction, all the upended tectonic plates, all the dust and debris back down into the far reaches of his being. He gave her a blank slate.

"It's nothing."

Nico jolted back. "This isn't nothing."

He licked his lips and lingered over the sour taste of the lie falling out of them. "I've been thinking about Ava-ta."

The worry smoothed from her face and she softened. "Me too. She would have wanted to be here today. She's proud of you. I know it."

Jih didn't know a thing.

"There are still a few drums until the Naming Ceremony. Get some rest. I'm sure you didn't get much last night, considering you didn't come home," she said, trying to lighten the air. She squeezed his shoulder. "I'll scold you about that later, but for right now, try on those pants."

He forced a nod, and Nico left him to the silence of his cacophonous thoughts.

He sat alone in his room. The emotions deflated out of him, and in that moment, he didn't feel much, other than exhaustion. He was so tired of beating himself against obstacles and never gaining a vibration. He felt ragged and worn and heavy. He had pains in his bones that ached, and wounds in his lungs that bled. He didn't know if he had the strength for tomorrow much less another year. Would his life always be adversity and closed doors and an uphill battle? Is the top of this impossible mountain even worth it?

Oddly enough, he had been here before. He had asked these questions of himself before. This wasn't the first time Kai's world had been completely torn asunder, and ironically this ravaged state of being felt far safer than the hopefulness that twisted him up since his return from the Forging.

This despair almost felt... comfortable and familiar the longer he stewed in it. He laughed hollowly as he dragged the pants into his hands. Then he tore them. Because it didn't matter. Nothing mattered anymore.

CHAPTER TWENTY-EIGHT

I

Nico glared at that annoying piece of hair that kept springing free from her elaborate bun. Frustrated, she snatched out the dragonglass pin to start all over again. The tresses of brown fell down her back as the drums rolled through the Grankull. Oh no. How long had she been doing her hair?!

She scrambled into Ava-ta's old naming dress. She carefully shuffled into the delicate blue gossamer silk. She reached behind her to tie the strings that tightened diagonally up the back. She tried contorting, bending, and twisting, but couldn't get a grip on the cord. Why would anyone make a dress this way?!

"Kai!" Nico called for help but didn't hear a reply. "Tah!"

She pressed the loose fabric to her chest and marched down the hall. She skidded to a stop at the sight of the entire lounging room turned into a windship course. Kenji-ta always had the imagination to match a child's, but she couldn't believe they had gotten so caught up to be completely unaware of the time.

"Didn't you hear the drum?" Nico cried out in alarm. "What are you doing? You should be getting ready."

"We've got time," Kenji-ta said smirking, right before stumbling and slipping down a slide of pillows.

"No, we don't. We need to be there early!"

"The temple is right across the courtyard."

"Get dressed!"

"Okay, okay. I'm on it." Kenji-ta said, laughing at her. He pulled Rae out from under a mound of pillows, threw them over his shoulder, and rushed with them down the hallway. Nico shook her head. She was glad this was one of Kenji-ta's good days. Then she paused at that sudden mental acknowledgment. Kenji-ta had both good and bad days, and she was honestly never sure which she was going to get.

"Why aren't *you* dressed?" she said in further alarm when she entered Kai's room. He sat on his bed, the same as she had left him a drum ago, holding his pants in his hands.

Kai lifted them, with almost a helpless note that reminded her of Rae. "They're torn."

"Torn?" Nico marched in. She grabbed at the pants and her dress fell to her waist.

"Do you need help?"

"*Please.*"

Kai tightened the ties of her dress while she inspected the pants. She didn't remember seeing the rip when Rasia had delivered them, but she had been so busy getting everyone else's clothes washed on time to inspect them too closely. What sort of bootleg tailor did Rasia pay for? This sort of rip was going to need more than quick needlework.

"Okay," she said, taking a breath. "I'll ask Kenji-ta. Maybe he'll have something that might fit."

"I'll wear my caftan."

Nico swiveled her head over her shoulder. "You can't wear your caftan. It's your Naming Ceremony. I know you don't want to ask him, but we don't have a lot of options."

"NICO!" Came a shout down the hall. "I CAN'T FIND RAE'S ORORO!"

"IT'S ON THEIR BED!"

"IT'S NOT HERE!"

Nico slapped her hands to her face. Kai tied off the strings with a hasty bow, right before she rushed down the hall to help Kenji-ta dress Rae. She would deal with Kai later. She swore if

Kenji-ta wasn't in some sort of mood, then Kai was. It drove her crazy how much the two were so alike sometimes.

She stomped into Rae's room and dragged her hands down her face at the missing articles of clothing. She just took them off the line. Where were they?

Kenji-ta crawled out from under the bed. "I've looked all over the room. They're not here."

"They have to be somewhere." Nico closed her eyes and focused on re-tracing her steps. Roof—Kai came back from his interview—Kai's room—oh, wait. Nico turned on her heels, ran through the halls, slid through the door, and glared at the set of clothing on *her* bed. She snatched them up, crossed to the next room, and threw them at Kenji's face.

"Kai's pants are torn. I'm borrowing your clothes to put something on him," she said, not asking permission. She rounded the inner chamber towards tah's room and thrust open Kenji-ta's large armoire. She pulled out clothes she thought might fit Kai if she found some extra pins. She tossed them over her arm and then froze in horror when she passed a dragon glass mirror.

Ack! Her hair still wasn't done!

She groaned but didn't have time to do anything about it right now. She ran around the inner chamber, through the maze, and all the way to Kai.

He was wearing the blasted caftan!

"Take that off!" Nico demanded and shoved all the articles of clothes into his arms. "Try them on. One of them has to fit."

"NICO!"

She groaned, and without waiting for a response from Kai, circled back out of the door. She rushed back through the maze. This was utterly ridiculous. After the Naming Ceremony, she was revisiting the whole conversation about Kai moving closer to everyone else's bedrooms. It shouldn't take five vibrations to go from Nico's bedroom to Kai's.

"HAVE YOU SEEN MY SHIRT—THE GOLD ONE?"

Halfway through the maze, she immediately spun back on her heels. She rushed into Kai's room, snatched the gold shirt out of his arms, and ran back the way she came. She tossed tah his shirt and finally made it back to her room to do something with her hair.

She looked at her reflection in dismay. She had already sweated through the silk. At least that could be solved with magic. Nico extracted the moisture from the armpit stains. She freshened up and shook the wrinkles from her dress. Then she meticulously began to pick up her hair back into the careful bun. She gathered it in both hands, and twisted it, while she held a pin in her mouth.

The next drum rolled. Nico coiled it atop her head and thrust in the pin. She was out of time. She pushed Ava-ta's bangles up her biceps and ran out of her bedroom. She slid into tah's room just as Kenji-ta combed a hand through his hair, which tousled down, laying perfectly and effortlessly in place. Ugh.

Rae kicked their legs atop the bed. Kenji-ta glanced at her with a reassuring smile. He wore his most formal *ororo*, a traditional formal garment with multiple pieces—including an embroidered skirt, a transparent blouse, and a hand-painted silk jacket. Golden dragons danced along the silk. Newer styles of dress were currently in fashion, but in Nico's opinion, none could truly rival the ororo's all-sided elegance.

"Ready," tah declared.

"Great. Let's go." She rushed them toward the front of the house. Kai met them in the serving room—*and he was still wearing that old and tattered caftan*. But Nico was tired, and she didn't have time to argue.

"You're wearing that?" Kenji-ta asked, with an obvious tone of judgment and disapproval. Kai froze, echoing the shock of everyone in the room that tah had actually spoken to him.

"He can wear what he wants," Nico said sharply. She shoved Rae into Kai's arms and shoved them out of the front door. She twirled back around and planted her hands on her hips. When Kenji-ta had come home from the kulls, she barely had time to address the gonda in the room before Kai came stumbling back home from his interview. Nowadays, it felt as if she didn't have time for anything, but she had learned the hard way that some conversations never had a good time. "The pants he planned on wearing tore. I pulled some of your clothes as options, but do you really blame him for not wanting to wear them? Kai killed a dragon so he could prove he had something to contribute to this family. Can you at least give him a chance?"

"It was only a question," Kenji-ta grumbled.

A question that Kai would no doubt pick apart and be all sensitive about. Nico had seen Kai obsess over Kenji's casual gestures, or glances, or mumbled curses until it ruined Kai's entire day.

"*Will you try?*" Nico demanded.

"Fine." Kenji shrugged. "Why should what I say matter anyway?"

She swore. He was not this obtuse. If anything, he was as perceptive as Kai most of the time, but she was tired of fighting this mental block that he refused to relinquish. She mentally logged it as a work-in-progress.

"Okay," Nico pointed at him. "And no alcohol tonight. You need to watch Rae."

"One? I've got to toast to my Nico-po finally earning her face."

"*One*," she hissed. She turned on her heels and motioned him to follow. Kai and Rae had only gotten as far as the veranda, eavesdropping, obviously. She wrangled them all toward the direction of the temple. She swore, managing an entire wingfield was easier than herding her own family.

Kai walked on one side. Kenji-ta, with Rae in his arms, walked on the other side. Nico subtly tried to maneuver them in a way that looked, if you squinted, like they were walking together as an actual family unit.

They made it pretty close to the temple steps. Most of the Forging kids were already there, dressed in either their best pants, dresses, or ororos. The Naming Ceremony was about self-expression more than anything else, and this year's ceremony flaunted a range of styles among the Forging candidates. Nico felt a little self-conscious in Ava-ta's old dress, even though Jilah had told her more than once it looked stunning on her. Nico had hand-woven the embellishments into the plunging neckline herself.

"See?" Kenji chirped, once they staked out their spot among the other candidates and their families. "We're right on time. Everyone is always late to these things. You had nothing to worry about."

She glared at him. Then a loose strand of hair popped out before her eyes.

He chuckled. "You're so much like your tah. Here, turn around."

She turned with a pout. Kenji dropped Rae to their feet and unpinned her hair. With sure hands, he gathered up all the weight of her hair and brushed back the coarse loose strands. Nico missed this. Ava-ta was always too busy and never had the time to sit down and pay much attention to Nico unless it involved some sort of training or studying. It was Kenji-ta who used to do her hair as a child.

Kenji looped it around, twisting and braiding until it sat immaculate at the center of her head with the bright dragonglass pin catching the sun. Nico glanced over at Kai, brows raised, to ask for his opinion. Tah was rusty after all. Kai nodded, approvingly.

"Thank you," she said.

Then Kenji pulled her into a sudden hug. Nico could feel all the pride, pain, and years of nurture in that grip. If she closed her eyes, she almost felt like that little girl again, watered and nourished by giants. But she wasn't so little anymore, and she pulled out of his embrace.

Most of the actual ceremony was a blur. She tried hard to root herself in the moment, to stand there and bask in the cheers and the pride. But honestly, she was sort of tired, and wanted to get it all over with. When they said her name, she walked up the steps, showed her face to the Grankull, and signed her name to the book.

She stood in line with the rest of the new faces as the Mythkeeper called more names.

Then her eyes caught Kai's, and she was suddenly drawn to the wide-eyed guilt of them. 'I'm sorry,' he seemed to mouth and started to back away into the crowd.

What hadn't he told her now?

Nico should have known it was going to be one of those days.

CHAPTER TWENTY-NINE

O

"Wait." Rasia stepped out of line. "What about Kai?"

The Councilor blinked at Rasia with an expression as blank as when Zephyr had first introduced his names in a different language. The Councilor squinted at her. "Who?"

"*Kai*. First-born of Avalai Ohan. Once known as the runt of the Grankull. Gold-fucking-eyes. He was on my kull when we took out the dragon. You forgot to call him to the stage."

The entire crowd moved in waves, heads turning, bodies shifting to find him. A sudden circle blossomed out to reveal Kai at the center of everyone's stares—farther away from the stage than he had been before. He turned to lock eyes with Rasia, wide-eyed and trapped.

He was not wearing the pants.

"I interviewed him," the Councilor of the Belly said, creaking from their position. "There were inconsistencies in his story. Several council members reviewed the situation and determined that there were several lies fabricated on his behalf. Some on this stage are fortunate that the Council has deemed to accept those with successful hunts, despite the plethora of lies from those involved."

The Belly Councilor glared at Rasia, accusingly, even though she was pretty sure she had done nothing to deserve it this time around. The only lies Rasia had told were to cover Nico's ass, but the rest—the important parts—were truth. That should have been enough for Kai as well. Did someone not have their story straight?

The Mythkeeper turned to her colleague. "What? You didn't report this to me."

"The child is related to you. You have a conflict of interest. You could not be trusted to oversee this particular case."

"Cheat!" Someone yelled from the crowd. "Banish him!" "Kill him!"

Those who had cheered Rasia's name just moments ago, flipped cruel and angry. Someone in the crowd shoved Kai so hard that he stumbled to his knees. When he pulled back onto his hands, someone kicked him in the face. Blood drenched the front of his shroud. The crowd surged on him like a pack of lean Desert dogs.

Rasia raced down the temple steps to stop the bloodbath. She lost sight of him when they dragged him under their hateful fists. She yelled at people to stop and unsheathed her blades, ready to carve a bloody path if she needed to.

"Rasia, move," Nico said from behind her.

Rasia side-stepped as a deluge of water cascaded down the steps. It flooded over the crowd, parting persons, until the river reached out and swept over Kai's position. The water receded to reveal Kai crouched and drenched on the ground.

Ysai squeezed out of the congestion of bodies, breathing heavily from literally shoving his way through, and hooked an arm under Kai. Ysai carried him through the parted damp pathway of the crowd. Rasia released a breath when they reached the steps of the temple and made it out of reach of the angry mob.

She met them on the steps. Kai was wet and bloody, but thankfully fucking breathing. He refused to meet her eye, and instead elected to huddle in his shroud and hide.

It all made sense now. He had been attempting to run away earlier. He never dressed with the intention of getting on this stage. He *knew* what was going to happen. They would have words about this later. But right now, someone was going to pay for this.

"Belly Councilor," Nico said, her anger carefully constrained by measured tones. "Kai-ji passed his Forging fair. Four witnesses were there when the dragon was slain. Are you implying that all of these witnesses are unreliable?"

In front of the entire Grankull, the Belly Councilor accused, "I am implying that you used your influence as heir to convince them all into an elaborate lie. Do you think us fools? Do you think any of us truly believe that wretched spawn could slay a dragon? Of steering a windship? Look at him! Fucking pathetic. You, nor Avalai Ohan, are above our rules or traditions."

"Cull! Cull! Cull! Cull!" the crowd chanted.

"This is horseshit," Rasia snapped. She faced the Council. Most strikingly, Kiba-ta stood among them, sneering in satisfaction at the whole situation, as if proven right.

"I taught him how to steer a windship!" she declared. "I taught him how to hunt a dragon! Kai succeeded in his hunt fair, and you'd all know that if you knew how to do your fucking jobs!"

"The Council has convened on this matter, and it is final," the Belly Councilor said. "His candidacy has been revoked. The ceremony is over. Now, step back in line."

Rasia quaked at the force of her anger. Kai had slayed a dragon and they didn't believe him? What more could he have possibly done?

"Step back in line, Rasia Dragonfire," her tah threatened this time. "Refuse and be stripped of all the names you have just earned."

Rasia tightened her grip on her blades. A hand wrapped around her wrist. She looked down at Kai's weak grip, up into the bruising around his left eye, and his blood-stained shroud.

"Don't let them take your face away, too. Please, it doesn't matter. Stop."

Her eyes narrowed at him, pissed. He had known this would happen, probably ever since his interview this morning, and never said a word to her. She turned back toward the Council, of them all waiting for her next move. But most of all, she hated the hollow-boned kids in line who had shown their faces, while Kai bowed on his fucking knees in a bloody shroud.

At that moment, she didn't give a shit about all of the kids Nico had rescued. She didn't give a shit about anyone.

Rasia swatted off Kai's hand, and took a step forward, then another, rising on the heat of her anger. This was all Nico's fault. *Again*. Rasia lied for her, and for what? So Kai could pay the price? None of those trifling pitiful cowards standing in their fear and silence deserve to show their faces when Kai could not. If he would not have his face, *then no one would*.

"You want the truth?" Rasia yelled out, then circled with it. "YOU ALL WANT THE FUCKING TRU-?!"

She grunted as her head hit the temple steps. Kai had charged head-first into her gut and threw her off her feet. He stumbled atop her awkwardly, quickly adjusting his hands to avoid illegally touching her. She hissed at the caution. He stared down at her harsh and unyielding. "Rasia, *don't*."

"Then you should have told me," she said nastily, before using both hands to throw him off of her. The crowd *cheered*. The crowd's bloodthirst turned her anger into a living thing, and it refused to die until the entire world burned around her. She'd show them the truth. She'd show them Kai wasn't the monster here.

She was.

"We are all liars! It's true. We lied for Nico, to protect Nico, to save Nico. Not everyone on this stage earned their hunt, and I refuse to watch the Grankull celebrate their cowardice. I refuse to watch the Grankull award those who do not deserve it and deny a face to those who do! There are liars and cowards among you, and they have fooled you all!"

Rasia pointed them all out. One by one. They gasped, and cried, and froze solid. But she didn't care.

"None of them deserve their faces."

CHAPTER THIRTY

o

Rasia crossed her arms and sneered at the barrage of shouts, screams, and tears the other candidates flung in her direction. After her accusations, the Council decided to convene inside the temple to re-analyze everyone's stories. She wondered if the Council could hear all the desperation from where they had trapped the first candidate in the interview room. The tall temple dome of the reading chamber fueled the rising volume of all the shouts and screams, but none burned as hot as the fury in her own bones. Good. Let them be angry. Let them wail. Let them burn.

"You should have been named a selfish fucking kulo!" Nico screamed at her. Even perfect little Nico was cursing now.

The scribes, who had been waiting to prepare the candidates for purification, swarmed in to hush everyone quiet. Jilah tempered Nico's anger with a gentle warning, "This is a sacred place. We cannot raise our voices. *And they might overhear you.*"

Nico sucked in a breath and swished her dress as she turned away. Suri stepped in, one of the few who had kept her cool, and took Nico aside. Jilah looked from Nico to Rasia and asked fearfully, "Is it true?"

"Rasia," Nico said, who had seemingly reformed herself back together. "You've got to recant. You've got to tell them you lied.

That you were angry about Kai."

"No."

Nico's eye twitched. "We'll do something to help Kai. I promise you that, but you can't condemn all of these kids. You don't need to involve everyone else."

"I don't care."

The humidity in the air thickened, cloying. Rasia tightened her hands around the empty grip of her swords. Weapons weren't allowed in the temple, and she had been forced to hand them over to Ysai at the doors. She tightened her hands into fists instead, and the humid air gathered sweat on her forehead. A crowd tightened around Rasia and Nico, awaiting the inevitable confrontation.

The tension burst when Kai emerged from the crowd, snatched Rasia's hand, and pulled her away. She allowed herself to be led around the large antechamber to the opposite end, empty of everyone else. She had briefly lost sight of him between the shuffling to get inside the temple and everyone rushing to confront her. Someone cleaned him up. Got him a new shroud. Zephyr, she guessed, judging by his absence at Nico's side.

Kai dropped her hand and stared at the floor, shoulders hunched all contrite and shit. He waited for her to move first.

"You knew," she accused. "Since your interview. Since this morning. Why didn't you find me and say something? Why didn't you tell me?"

"Because it wouldn't have mattered."

"It would have mattered if I went and slit that vulture's throat!" The scribes hushed her. She whirled, and the room moved so fast she didn't care whom she directed the words, "FUCK YOU!"

"Rasia," Kai surged forward and clasped her about the shoulders. "If you had killed a Councilor, how would that have made anything better? We'd be in a worse situation than we are now. No. You are going to go in there, and stand before the Council, and tell them you made a mistake."

"Fuck that. Fuck you. I'm telling the truth."

"For what? For revenge? These kids have nothing to do with

what happened to me."

"They have everything to do with it! Nico and her nauseating compassion ruined you! She should have left those kids for the scavengers. Everything that I am doing, I am doing for you!"

"You're doing it for *you*! You're doing what you always do when you're angry—lashing out at everybody around you. But it won't change a thing. The truth isn't going to change their opinion of me. All the truth is going to do is ruin the lives of the eighteen people Nico tried to save. My life isn't worth eighteen."

"You are worth thousands."

"If that's true, then I am every bit the monster everyone claims me to be. But I refuse that narrative. I've lived without rations for a year before. I can do it again."

"This isn't comparable, Kai. The entire Grankull is calling for your blood. That mob almost tore you apart. You have so much more to lose. They cheated. You didn't. Those kids don't deserve their faces. They don't deserve to say their names."

"*They could have easily been me.* I failed once before. The only reason I am "deserving," is because I met you. You taught me how to survive and protect myself. You taught me how to steer a windship. You believed in me, so that I could believe in myself. Maybe they need someone to believe in them too."

"You're wrong," Rasia spat, disgusted that he would compare himself with those boneless cowards. "You are the only one willing to sacrifice everything for eighteen people not brave enough to step forward and tell the truth. Maybe I taught you some shit, but you deserve to show your face because of who you are. At the beginning of the Forging, I asked everyone if they wanted to slay a dragon. You were the only one to say yes."

"Rasia," Kai said softly. "You're the only person to have ever asked. You gave me a chance when others would have dismissed me. But you looked at me and gave me a choice. If this strength is something that has always been in me, then you gave me the opportunity to prove it. Perhaps all they need is the opportunity to show us who they are too. They didn't get that chance during the Forging. It was stolen from them by scavengers. All I'm asking is for you to stand before the Council and give these kids another chance, like you gave me."

"No," she seethed out, shaking. "It's not *fair*."

"The world isn't fair! It's not fucking fair, Rasia! Sometimes you've got to let it mow you down and move on!"

"NO! We fight this. We tell them the truth and we make them believe you. Show them your magic."

"I've tried. It's not working."

"Then what if we could get them to see you on a windship? Or . . . lead a gonda to the Grankull and you fight one off? Something can always be done!"

"Not when the cost is this high. Sometimes, you surrender."

"*No.*" Why couldn't he understand? "I'm not giving up. I'm fighting this. I'll tear this whole Grankull apart. They can't do this to you. You slay a dragon, you earn your face, and you say your names. That's how it's supposed to work. That is how it's supposed to fucking work! You've earned your face! You've earned it!"

Kai softened. He stepped forward and gently pressed his shrouded forehead to hers. She bristled at the scratch of linen against her skin, and he tightened her hands in his. "I'm not giving up, Rasia. I'll redo the Forging next year, and if they don't believe me, I'll do it again and again until they do. I promise you that this isn't the end. We fail today, but we try again tomorrow. Please, I know it's not an easy thing to do—to let them win, to choose not to fight—but sometimes a hunt takes seasons, not days."

Rasia screamed at him or at least she tried, but the scream tore her throat and instead, ripped out battering sobs. She felt upside down, free-falling through a world she thought she knew the truth of. But it was all a *lie*.

Kai carried her into one of the reading nooks. He closed the gossamer curtain, and their bodies tinted a soft blue. She lay against him, tears spent and still angry. He had positioned himself atop the reading cushions as a barrier. She didn't know if he was protecting her from the world, or the world from her.

"I hate this place," she whispered between them. "I hate this fucking place."

She wanted to take a torch and burn it all to the ground. She wanted to put an axe to the bones. She wanted to slaughter everyone in that mob who dared put a hand on Kai. She wanted to destroy it all. But he held on tight, refusing to let her go. This was impossible. All she knew how to do was fight. How could he possibly ask her not to?

"I'm so angry at you," he said, with his head burrowed into her shoulder.

"Same," Rasia grumbled. She wiped at her tears, and then unwound his shroud to scan his face. The ground had torn his caftan and scratched his skin. He had bruises changing colors on his face. She wondered at the wounds she couldn't see. "Are you alright?"

"Zephyr helped clean me up. I think my nose is broken, but I've had worse."

"What were you doing out there? Why did you come?"

"I couldn't think of a good enough excuse to tell Nico, and I wanted to go. I wanted to be there, for you and Nico, even if I couldn't have the same. I tried getting out, but I hadn't expected the crowd."

"You could have died."

"It was worth it to see you up there, so triumphant." He pulled up on his elbow and scanned his golden eyes down her body. He brushed a curious thumb over her belly button piercing. "You're very beautiful today."

Those words sounded completely different from Kai than when Jilah had said them earlier. She blushed under his hand. Temporarily distracted from all the anger and the wreckage she had wrought, she pulled forward and kissed him, soft and careful.

Heavy doors swung open. Rasia leaned over Kai, to peek through the curtains. The first candidate the Council had called to interview emerged through the doors in tears. Kai reapplied his shroud, and they pulled from the nook and drew over to the commotion.

"I'm sorry," the candidate whispered, some girl Rasia didn't know the name of and didn't care to know. She shook like a frightened hare caught in a trap. "I'm so sorry."

"Loryn, what happened?" Nico asked.

"I—I—I told the truth," she said. She looked up at Kai where he had stopped at Rasia's shoulder. "She's right. He deserves his face. I'm sorry."

Rasia found herself deeply pleased by this turn of events. No point recanting her accusations now. She didn't know who the fuck this kid was, but she would remember her name. At least one of these cowards had some bones.

"It's alright. It's okay," Nico soothed. "I understand."

Loryn covered her face with her hands, looking more guilty and ashamed. Faris wrapped an arm around her shoulder, and others crowded around to give her comfort. Rasia rolled her eyes at the dramatics and flinched through every one of Loryn's stuttering words. "Nico, they want to see you next."

Nico looked at them, no doubt feeling the weight of her stupid decisions. Then she turned toward the bone doors that needed four scribes to pull them open.

"Wait," Rasia said. Everyone turned to Rasia, surprised by the interruption. Kai sent her a questioning tilt of his head, but she marched forward on a mission. Nico and Rasia stood, staring each other down.

"Kiba-ta took out the hit on you. She admitted it this morning. She thinks you're weak and stupid and dumb. Do with this information as you will."

What was one more person thrown to the fire?

Nico contemplated Rasia, who certainly hadn't offered the information out of any act of kindness. "You don't feel a bit of remorse for what you've done, do you?"

"I don't."

Their stances mirrored the ones from earlier, before Kai had interrupted them. They both stood ready for a fight. "Thank you for the information, but this isn't over between us."

"It never is, is it?"

CHAPTER THIRTY-ONE

/

Nico stepped before the eight elected members of the Council. They'd replaced the soft cushions and rugs of the interview room with the sharp edges of tall-backed chairs that formed a semi-circle around the interviewee. Someone had closed the bone curtains, which smothered the light from the oil lamps. The interview lacked the intimidating expanse of the Council room in the administration building of the Neck, which meant the Councilors sat squeezed next to one another like crows on a dead branch. Per tradition, they saved space to include the empty chair. It sat there, mocking Nico, signifying the position that had been empty since Ava-ta's burning.

She searched their faces for any hint of their thoughts. The elderly Belly Councilor, Neema's granta, sat hunched over their ottoman like a vulture lying in wait. The Ribs Councilor, whom Rasia had confirmed tried to kill Nico, sat spear-sharp and alert. If Rasia was always in motion, then her tah was always ready for it.

The Claws Councilor, a retired kull hunter and Faris' granta, hunched heavy and tired under deep brows. Dulcae, the Wings Councilor and Nico's mentor, asked questions with her eyes. The face of the Neck Councilor, Suri's tah, betrayed nothing. The brash Hindlegs Councilor found the proceedings more amusing than anything else. The slight Pelvis Councilor didn't find anything amusing. Nico's tajih, the Heart Councilor and Mythkeeper, looked grim.

"Nicolai Ohan," the Mythkeeper began, "You have lied to us all, and furthermore engineered the lies of all those involved in the Forging. We are disappointed in you. You may be magicborn, but even you aren't more powerful than our traditions."

"I did what I thought was right," Nico said. "I am the Ohan, am I not? Is it not my job to protect everyone?"

"Your job is to protect the Grankull," said the Belly Councilor, "and those kids you saved are not yet a part of it."

"You have dared to take food from our families and give it to those who do not deserve and have not earned it," the Neck Councilor argued. "Many of us question whether you truly have the Grankull's best interests in mind."

"You are no better than Avalai Ohan, flagrantly abusing your power."

"You lied. You are supposed to be our leader. How can you possibly lead us now?"

One after another, they berated and lectured and voiced their disappointment. Nico hoped for a pause, but when an opening refused to present itself, she jumped in face-first. She refused to be silenced and drowned out by their voices.

"You criticize me for abusing our ideals and traditions when for so long the Forging itself has become a corrupt institution," she projected her voice to argue. "Half the people on this very Council have paid money to alter the bones so that their children can be on more successful kulls. How is that fair? Do those who "earn" their hunts truly do it because of their own merits or because of their wealth? Is the Grankull truly giving its children a fair chance? I made the decision that I did, not out of naivete, but because I had four dead gonda, and Rasia aimed to take down the dragon preying on our food supply. The decision wasn't made in a vacuum. The Grankull could spare eighteen lives because of what a few accomplished during their Forging. Shouldn't that be celebrated?"

Tajih mourned, "You have made good points, but the truth still stands. They did not earn their hunt."

"They weren't given a fair chance to earn it in the first place. Hunting kulls aren't allowed to hunt during Forging season to prevent undue interference. Would you not agree that concessions need to be made due to the special circumstances of this Forging season?"

"Special circumstances? What sort of special circumstances could possibly explain this flagrant disgrace?"

"Special circumstances like the fact scavengers were hired to assassinate me," Nico proclaimed, then pointedly looked at the Claws Councilor. "Your children, and your grandchildren, never had a fair chance. Children of the Grankull died because scavengers hunted me throughout this year's Forging, all to prevent me from coming to power and having a vote."

"Those are serious allegations."

"You are the Ohan," the Neck councilor said. "Scavengers might have targeted you naturally. What evidence do you have? What witnesses? And why didn't you bring this to us sooner?"

Nico studied them, every one of their faces. Kibari Oshield didn't act alone. She couldn't have. Not with the sort of promises made to the scavengers. There was more than one person in this room who wanted her dead.

"Because the hit on my face was hired by one of you, and I can only assume that this scheme to deny Kai-ji is part of a larger plot. How am I to trust any of you, when you've made it clear you want to stab me in the back? In fact, Rasia witnessed a confession from her own parent just this morning. How am I supposed to say something, when the Sentry Han, who provides protection for my family, wants me dead?" she accused.

The Ribs Councilor remained unmoved by the sudden scrutiny of her colleagues. She only tensed, tighter and tighter for the aim. "I am the Sentry Han. I protect the Grankull. You dare throw this accusation at my feet, when your only witness is the child I threw out of my house this very morning for claiming the runt of the Grankull as her kulani?" Those words sent a shockwave of disgust through the Council. "Rasia is talented, but she also has a feral imagination. Everyone on the Council is aware of her . . . eccentrics. You have no basis for your claim."

Sensing she was losing ground, Nico shifted. She might not be able to prove that the Council hired the hit, but she could at least prove the hit had happened.

"We lied," she said. "I didn't go to the oasis, and gather a bunch of kulls, and hunt down a bunch of gonda. The truth is a lot more complicated. It is a far messier story. I implore you to re-interview all of the kids. Learn the truth of how scavengers attacked Faris' kull in the middle of their hunt, how they rounded our children and squeezed them all into windship hatches without water and food, and how many died in the transport. Learn how scavengers tortured Neema to learn my face, and how by the time those captured had been saved, they were too weak to earn their hunt by the Forging's end. Learn the 'details' of the scavenger's deal with the Grankull, which had been overheard by several participants. Perhaps it was my kull who killed all the gonda, but it pales in comparison to the strength of those kids in that room out there. Learn the truth of what your actions have incurred, and how we triumphed regardless."

Nico turned on her own accord and slammed through the doors. She walked hallways, lined from top to bottom by rows of myths and histories. The scribes standing at the bone doors pulled them open for her, and she stepped into the main antechamber. She looked at them, at Faris and Loryn, at the kids she first met at the oasis, and the dehydrated kids she had picked up afterward. They were all relying on her to somehow save them. They didn't deserve this. They deserved better. They deserved to tell their stories, undiluted by fear, shame, and guilt. No more lies.

"Tell them the truth," Nico told them. "All of it."

CHAPTER THIRTY-TWO

O

Rasia strode into the room where the Council summoned her to interview. The Council had formed a half-circle around the interviewee and changed the décor, but she hardly found it intimidating. Off to the side, the Council had employed an army of scribes. They sat with the recorded pages of the original interview, ready to tell the Council of any deviation.

Most everyone had been re-interviewed already, and Rasia figured her interview would go much the same way. She thought she knew what to expect, but got caught completely off guard when Kiba-ta asked, "Did you engage in underage sexual relations during your Forging?"

Immediately, Rasia's thoughts whirled. None of the kids Nico rescued knew about her and Kai's Forging. Neither Zephyr, Nico, nor Suri would have said anything because they wouldn't have wanted to get Kai in trouble. Neither could it have been Azan because he also engaged in his own illicit affairs.

Kiba-ta leaned forward, as if they were in a room alone, and only tah's scrutiny mattered. "Furthermore, did you not only engage in underage sexual relations, but did you also become impregnated outside of the Grankull's approval?"

Rasia's eyes narrowed. Like two warships they stared each other down. She licked her lips and laughed. "A baseless accusation.

Obviously, someone is peeved at me for exposing the lies of this year's Forging. What proof do they have? You could check me over right now. You're not a granta just yet."

"What happened to your hair?"

"I cut it."

"Why?"

"You've been telling me for years that I should. Kept calling it a ragged nest, if I remember correctly."

"Hair loss is a common symptom of poisoning. The accusation against you also stated that you culled the seed after consuming gonda venom."

"So . . . I hypothetically culled a seed after I poisoned myself, which was before or after I was almost killed by a group of scavengers that you hypothetically hired to kill the Ohan? I guess that does sound rather . . . believable."

"You're diverting attention from the issue at hand here."

"You mean the fact that you hired a hit on the Ohan, of which you admitted to me this morning in your office? *You're* diverting attention from the issue at hand here. I would have had that dragon home sooner if scavengers hadn't gotten involved due to your interference."

"How many times have you engaged in underage sexual activity?" tah demanded, not taking Rasia's bait to change the topic. "How many times have you recklessly disregarded the Grankull's rules? You accuse others of not earning their faces, but what have you done to earn such pleasures of the flesh? You have also laid claim to that of which you have not yet earned."

Rasia tried to think of a way out of tah's trap laid so finely with barbed words, but she was a step too slow. Tah straightened and chided her. "Your actions were stupid and selfish. The Grankull's food supply is limited. We must be responsible and considerate of each other, even if that means sacrificing self-interests for public health. The rules are in place for a reason."

"If the Grankull really gave a shit about public health, they'd give kids gonom before the Forging," Rasia snapped, unable to stop herself from voicing an old grievance. "Kids are by themselves for the first time without parents. Of course, they're going to fuck around. Everyone knows they fuck around."

"*That's the test.* One of the main purposes of the Forging is to determine who is responsible enough to become an adult, and we don't know if you are. Tell us the truth. What really happened during your Forging? Did the runt's jih whore him out to you in exchange for helping him pass?"

And there it was, tah's master brushstroke to discredit Nico, Rasia, and Kai all in one pointedly sharp sentence.

"Don't," Rasia snapped at Kiba-ta, honestly tired of all of the games. She couldn't give a shit about politics. "You want to drag my character and ruin me in front of the Council? Fine. You want to minimize my accomplishment with unproven accusations? Fine. But don't you dare disrespect Kai's name. I don't give a shit about any of those other kids. This is about Kai. He wasn't a bystander, an observer, or hiding in the fucking windship hatch. He was a windeka and a vital part of my team. I realize now that you're looking for any reason to discredit him, to justify decisions you've already made. This farce of an interview isn't about the truth at all."

Timar was right. The Grankull was a lie. In order to win, Rasia had to find a way to weave a better story. She glanced at each of the Council members. She didn't believe in fate, but most in the Grankull did, and she did not hesitate to use it to her advantage. "If Kai is nothing more than a whore, if he's nothing more than the runt of the Grankull, then why did the Yestermorrow Lake give him back to me? Why did the Lake not sentence him to death as it did for so many others?"

"There's only one witness to your tale. The Yestermorrow Lake could very well be a fabrication as well."

"How it is fair for you to pick and choose what you want to believe?" she shoved up her pants leg. She lifted her hip and showed them the vertical scar on her thigh. "This is where Kai exacted the blood price for Zephyr's tah." She pointed to another scar further along that. "This is where the Han of the Crimson scavengers ordered an arrow shot at me." She lifted her chestplate higher to her ribs. "This is where I broke them, twice." She lifted her left leg and showed the scar there. "This is where the railing of my windship scratched me when I carried Kai out of the Lake. Fuck all of you. Scars don't lie."

"That's enough. You are dismissed."

Rasia let go of her pants. She glared at them, then turned to Kiba-ta and said, "You're wrong. He is my kulani, and if you have any doubt, I've already written his name in the book."

Rasia watched with satisfaction as her tah's face shifted from confusion to horror. Tah snapped, lunging from her chair, and snatched Rasia off her feet by the sharp edge of the carapace breastplate. Several of the Council members stood in alarm. Tah hissed out, "You lie."

"I tell nothing but the truth."

Kiba-ta snapped at the scribes in the corner, who had all frozen to watch the scene. It was Jilah who moved to the Book of Names and flipped through the pages. She stared for a long time at Rasia's name page, then looked up at the Council. "He is her kulani, as it is written."

Kiba-ta snatched her knife from under her belt, and several Council members moved to stop her from spilling blood within the temple walls. Rasia twisted free and scrambled back from her tah's rage and eyed the knife held aloft in Kiba-ta's hand. "I thought weapons were forbidden in the temple? Or are you the only one allowed to vagrantly disregard the Grankull rules?"

"I disown you! You are no child of mine!"

Rasia turned on her heels, slammed the doors closed behind her, and slumped against them. It was a good thing she dropped that bomb in the temple, 'cause Kiba-ta was definitely about to kill her. She had been careful not to outright admit to anything during her interview and thought that maybe she had won that round.

With a deep breath, she shoved herself off the door and stormed through the larger bone doors she had to wait impatiently for the scribes to open. It was annoying. The temple usually kept the doors open, but the Council didn't want any of the candidates (Rasia) trying to eavesdrop. She marched past the curious onlookers and straight toward Neema's stupid intolerable face.

She punched Neema in that stupid intolerable face, jumped on top of her, and punched her some more. Zephyr grabbed Rasia about the waist to pull her away. Nico yelled at her, but Rasia couldn't care less as she fought Zephyr and sought to pound Neema's face into grubworm mash.

Zephyr, Azan, and Faris dragged her off.

"I'm going to kill you!" Rasia snapped. "You told them about Kai and me. You fucking snitch!"

"*I'm the snitch*?!" Neema crawled to her feet, with a streak of blood running down her nose. She looked not only at Rasia but the entire room. "We were supposed to tell the truth, right? Of course, I told them about you and Kai fucking around. Why are you the only ones who get to disregard the rules? How is it fair for you to earn your face when you have broken the rules, too? Why not air out all of the dirty laundry?"

"Neema, what did you do?" Nico asked.

"Why should I have to lie about my Forging to protect your jih? I told them he slayed that dragon, but I told them all the rest, too. I am not lying for any of you anymore."

"How the fuck did you even know about the culling?" Rasia demanded. "You weren't there for that part."

Neema shrugged, haughtily, "Azan told me."

Rasia threw her hands up and turned to Azan, who skipped over and hid behind Suri. "Hey," he said, "that was a long time ago when we were hunting the dragon. I was just catching her up on everything that happened."

"Rasia," Kai placed a hand on her shoulder. "It's happened. It's done."

"This is a shit show."

"A shit show you started," Nico snapped.

"Excuse me? This was all your lie."

Kai grabbed Rasia by the arm and physically separated her from the others. She pulled away to pace around the antechamber while Kai leaned against one of the banisters. "They know about you and me?" he asked.

"I didn't confirm anything. They only have theories so far, and Neema didn't actually witness anything. It was all hearsay," she said. "If only Neema said something and no one else, it's likely they'll have no choice but to drop it. But I don't know. I got the sense that . . . they don't care. They care about the lying, but they don't care about you."

The doors opened. One of the scribes stepped into the room and read off a list of names. "The Council want these persons to start their purification. If you would please follow me to the baths. For the rest, the Council is still deliberating your fates."

The names the scribes had called were all the kids who had completed their Forging before Nico arrived back to the Grankull. They had nothing to do with this mess. They followed the scribes deeper into the temple.

The rest of them waited and waited. They never called Kai to interview him. When it became obvious that they never planned to, Rasia jumped to her feet, unable to sit around any longer.

She needed to *do* something.

Rasia paced up and down the temple hallway waiting for Kiba-ta. It was a last-ditch effort but perhaps tah had calmed down enough to realize she was powerless to separate Kai and Rasia, or . . . more likely, Kiba-ta would agree to meet with her for the chance to wring her neck out of view of the Council. She didn't expect much from the clandestine meeting, but she refused to sit around waiting on someone to decide her fate for her. Even if Jilah failed to slip the message to Kiba-ta, or if tah refused to meet, at least Rasia tried.

She smirked at the sound of that unmistakable no-nonsense gait that scattered sentries and cleared hallways. It increased in volume around the corner. Kiba-ta stepped into the intersection, with her arms crossed, unimpressed.

"Rajiani Dragonfire," tah said coldly. To hear Kiba-ta address her with such detachment and formality, hurt Rasia more than expected. She was tempted to shoot back with a 'Kiba-ta' or 'tah,' but she knew further irritation wasn't going to get her what she wanted. And it felt fitting to be acknowledged as an adult, as equals.

"Kibari Oshield," Rasia said in turn and didn't waste time with the niceties. Her tah, never one for small talk, would appreciate that. "I *could* ruin you."

Rasia knew so much. She had the names of so many contacts, locations of smuggling stashes, and knew so many secrets.

"You dare threaten your entire family, all because you refuse to take responsibility for your own actions during the Forging? You've not only violated the taboo of touch, but you also dared to get yourself seeded. You deserve to be sentenced for your carelessness. It is a shame that you will not."

"I won't?" she asked, surprised. She didn't think her gambit had worked. Guess she didn't need to go through all this trouble of blackmailing her tah . . . ex-tah, whatever.

"You slayed a dragon," Kiba-ta gritted out the words, distastefully, "and you did so during your Forging season while leading a kull of barely inexperienced fighters. You are too valuable for the Grankull to waste, and some bought into your little Lake of Yestermorrow story. I voted to see your face burned off, but the numbers were against me."

"Oh," she said. Now it made sense why she and her kull hadn't gotten in trouble when the Council initially thought her to be lying. They wanted Rasia's skills. They wanted Zephyr's money, and Neema's art, and Azan's family name. Some on the Council might even want Nico for all the benefit she brought to the wingfields. Some on the Council wanted their children and grandchildren to pass. But they didn't want Kai.

Surely, they couldn't use the crime of seeding against him anymore, considering that sort of crime involved two. If they weren't going to charge Rasia, then they couldn't charge Kai either. "What about Kai? He passed his Forging. He earned his face."

"Not according to the vote."

"He completed his hunt fair!" she said, frustrated. "You know the true stories now. How is Kai any different than Shamai-ta? Tah came from nothing, but he broke all the Forging records to earn his face. They believed tah. How is this any different?"

"Kulani might have once been a tent kid, but your kulani is a curse on the Grankull. Life is a decision made by the balance that governs us. It is decided by the water, the harvest, and the hunt. Not by some child who thinks herself above the rules or the Ohan who is supposed to enforce them. Death marked that child in the womb. It belonged to Death and should have returned to Death, the same as Death marked your own seed. My only relief is that you had the strength to do what needed to be done. Perhaps your choices won't cost you your face, but there are always consequences for cheating the bones. When Death comes for him, and you're all alone—remember, you did this to yourself."

Rasia tightened her hands into fists. She gnashed, "You plan on killing my kulani like you killed your own?"

She stumbled back at Kiba-ta's charge. Her back hit the hexagonal shelves, and scrolls rained down overhead. One of them hit Kiba-ta in the shoulder. Kiba-ta didn't flinch, but simply swatted away the unfurling papyrus.

"You've been harboring that grudge for years, but it is past time you wiped your face clean. I might have delivered him to the Hunter, but I did not kill him. Your kulani's tah did that. It was Availai Ohan who took him away from us."

The air suddenly grew too hot. The familiar weight on Rasia's chest increased. She stumbled and fell against the shelves. "No . . ." she said, confused. Shamai-ta had died because his kulani had stabbed him in the heart when he failed to wake up after a piece of debris hit him on the head. That was the story. She couldn't change her mind and rewrite the story now. "You're lying. It's your fault. He could have come back, but you never gave him the chance. He would have come back to me, I know it, and it's all your fault that he didn't."

"He was gone, Raj-po! *He was gone.* The healers confirmed it. The scribes confirmed it. The kulls confirmed it. You were the only one who refused to accept reality. It was breaking you to watch him suffer. He wouldn't have wanted that. It was the hardest thing I've ever done, but I put him out of his misery, for *you.*"

Rasia pressed her hands to her eyes. No. Tah had to be wrong. But she began remembering the conversations with the healers she had blocked out. She began remembering both Ysai and Kiba-ta's concerned glances over her shoulder. She didn't remember eating. She didn't remember sleeping. She didn't remember much of anything. Of course not, her world had just ended for the first time.

Kiba-ta kneeled and placed a hand on Rasia's cheek. "He was gone."

It was too much. How much more would Rasia learn to be a lie? Whether they be the Council's lies, Kiba-ta's lies, or her own? Her rage hissed in her ears. It cracked, and she drowned up to her neck with sorrow, loss, and grief.

Kiba-ta remembered herself and took a step back to regain her composure. She stood there in the hallway in the armor she never took off.

Rasia wiped at her eyes. She hated herself for showing weakness to the person who demanded all of her strength. She sniffed, confused. "But what did the Ohan have anything to do with it? Why would she want to kill tah?"

"Because I killed her."

Rasia stared. It took a moment to process those words. "*Why?*"

"To settle a debt."

"For what? For what happened to Ysai-ji? But Ysai-ji was fine." Rasia stared at her tah, uncomprehending. She reached up to one of the hexagonal slats and pulled herself to her feet. "He wasn't one of those kids who had died. There was no debt to settle, nor was it your blood price to exact. You murdered her, and she killed Shamai-ta in turn. You did this. It is still your fault!"

"That bloodline is a scourge," Kiba-ta snapped. "I did it to protect us. I did it for your jih, and I did it for you."

"No," Rasia whispered, finally understanding. "You did it for *you*. You thought you could get away with it, but you fucked up. You destroyed your kulani, but I will not let you destroy mine. You touch a hair on his head, and I'll expose everything. I'll tell all of your secrets, even this one."

"If that's the war you want to wage," Kiba-ta said. "If you are truly willing to destroy everything—me, you, your jih, your tajihs and cousins, the merchants, the sentries, and all the far-flung corners. What are you willing to pay to win?"

"*Everything*," Rasia promised. "You harm my kulani and I'll burn it all down. Everything that you want to protect, I will see it destroyed."

Kiba-ta gave an infuriating chiding expression, as if Rasia was just having a temper tantrum. Disowned or not, no paper could ever wipe away their complicated relationship. Kiba-ta sneered, "You're not as invincible as you think you are."

Rasia knew that now. She had come to terms with the fact that Shamai-ta wasn't either. Death hunted everyone.

"Nor are you."

Rasia returned to the main antechamber. The nervous energy had begun to wear on those waiting. Some had fallen asleep in the reading cubbies, and others were bowed in whispered discussions. But many more were like Nico, quiet and contemplating how to move forward if the Council decided the worst. Kai and Nico sat beside each other, leaning against the Elder statue at the center. Rasia strode across the room to dive face-first into Kai's arms.

"Are you okay? What happened?" he asked.

Rasia mumbled into his chest. He drew back until she had enough room to say, "I talked with Kibari Oshield. The Council is not going to charge us for messing around during the Forging, but they have voted to refuse you your face."

It cut to see Kai nod to himself, resigned, with never any hope this would go any other way. Beside them, Nico bit her lip and glanced around at the obvious ears on their conversation.

"What about the rest of them?" Nico asked. "Has the Council decided?"

"The fuck do I care? I didn't ask."

Sweat fell from Rasia's face, and it burned her skin. The pain actually felt somewhat comforting, but it broke when Kai glared at Nico over Rasia's shoulder. He said diplomatically, "Okay. Thank you for the information."

"*No*," Rasia said. She jumped back onto her feet and waved her hands to get his attention. "You don't understand. The Council doesn't matter right now. You are in danger. Kibari Oshield threatened to kill you. We need to leave, *now*." She reached down to pull at his arms, and he was so off-guard that he easily rolled onto his feet. "The windship is in impound, but with the sentries pulled away for the namepour we should be able to break it out."

"Whoa, wait, Rasia. Slow down."

Rasia managed to get him three strides closer to the door before Kai dropped his weight and dug in his heels. She released him, frustrated.

"What happened to the windship?" he asked. "And you want to leave the Grankull? What about everything here?"

"Kibari Oshield disowned me and impounded the windship this morning. Look, that's not important right now. I don't know what she is planning, but I know she wants you dead."

Kai didn't react with the same urgency and concern she needed from him. He shrugged his shoulders. "Everyone wants me dead."

"Everyone is not Kibari Oshield. You don't know her like I do. She's not a group of scavengers, or a dragon, or the Yestermorrow Lake. She has more power, more money, and more skill than you could ever imagine. But she still has her limitations. The Desert is the one thing I know better than her. It is the one place I can keep you safe. We need to break my windship out of impound and get the fuck out of here."

"Rasia, I'm sorry Kibari Oshield confiscated your windship. I'm sorry she disowned you, but if we break out the windship, the punishment for that sort of violation is banishment. We won't ever be able to come back."

Rasia blinked at him. "Yeah. We can stay out in the Desert forever. Just you and me. It'll be fine." He didn't seem convinced. "*Kai*, she killed your tah. I don't know how but she said that she did. If she can kill Avalai Ohan with all her magic, what chance do you have?"

Kai frowned. "That's not true. I killed my tah."

"Are you sure?" she asked. "Sometimes we don't remember those moments right. What do you remember?" He hunched into his crossed arms, and she said quickly, "I bet if you think on it, the details don't add up. If Kiba-ta says she killed your tah, she did . . . Have you ever talked to anyone about it?"

He gave a brief shake of his head. She stepped forward and pressed her hands to his shrouded cheeks. "Hey. If you don't want to talk about it, that's okay. Just consider that the possibility is there and that we need to get the fuck out of here."

Kai's jaw solidified into that stubborn tic, the same as right before he decided to face a skinko or a dragon. "I'm not leaving."

"You slayed a fucking dragon! You have done everything you possibly could and they still deny you your face. What do you have to stay for?"

"I am not leaving jih to fight this on her own, and I refuse to leave in the middle of the mess that you have made on my behalf. No matter what the Council decides, Nico will still be a target. My family is still in danger. I'm not abandoning them."

"Have you considered that leaving is protecting them? Nico can't protect you. She can barely protect these kids."

"You're wrong. I am the bigger target, thus staying makes them safer."

"It makes you a liability. You owe this place nothing."

"It doesn't matter." Kai took hold of her wrists, eyes burrowing into hers as he boldly stood his ground. "You're scared of Kibari Oshield. You're scared you can't protect me here, but I'm not afraid. I'm not leaving."

Ugh. Why did Kai have to be so stupidly brave all the time? Rasia surged forward, to shove his face into hers, then just as quickly shoved him away to finish her pacing. She needed to consider their options.

Kibari Oshield was the one fight Rasia didn't know if she could win. Despite her earlier threats, she knew a war between them would be costly on both sides. At least if they made a tactical retreat into the Desert, it forced Kibari into Rasia's territory. This fight would be far harder in the Grankull where Kibari had all the respect, all the power, all the connections, and all the sentries in her pocket.

Rasia followed a stray thought and looked at Nico. She remembered the overwhelming force Nico could bear if sufficiently motivated. She skipped over. "Hey, Nico. Want to kill my former parent?"

"Fuck you, Rasia."

"I was being serious."

"I am not an indiscriminate killer."

"See. That very attitude is the reason why we're here! If they feared you, they would never have dared to touch Kai in the first place. No one fucked with him when Avalai Ohan was alive."

Nico pulled up from her feet to glare at Rasia, and in that glare, she could see all the ways in which Nico wished to see her killed. A lightning strike. A flood. The classic hands around the throat. "You're lucky we're in the temple," Nico threatened.

"She killed your tah," Rasia said, hoping that would at least get a reaction out of Nico. "You're owed a bloodprice."

To Rasia's surprise, she nodded. "I know."

"You know?" Kai asked.

"I've only learned about it recently and I couldn't talk about it, but now that you know, I think that I can," Nico said. "Rasia is right. While you were knocked out after the dragon's attack, Kibari Oshield dropped a rock on tah's head—the way you found her."

Kai's mouth dropped open as he struggled to process the truth: Ava-ta's death wasn't his fault.

"Great. Let's kill her," Rasia chirped.

"What do you expect me to do? Storm into the interview room and drown her before the entire Council in the middle of the temple? Demand a blood price for a claim I have no evidence for? That would solve nothing."

"It would eliminate an enemy."

"That is not how this game is played."

"The game is fucking rigged! They are never going to give Kai his face! Fuck playing the game. In a game you can't win, you upturn the entire fucking board!"

"And how many innocent people would get hurt?"

"You are a boneless coward!"

"Rasia, that's enough," Kai said, and wrapped an arm around her waist. She didn't fight when he dragged her away. He asked, "Could you please stay away from Nico for a while? You two together are only making things worse."

"It was a very valid idea."

"*Rasia.*"

"Fine." She pressed her face against the ivory wall. "All this waiting is making me crazy. If we're not going to run, and we're not going to fight, what do we *do*?"

"We do nothing."

Rasia slid down the wall and stuffed her face into her arms when she flopped flat onto the tiled floors. She couldn't change the Council's opinions. She couldn't convince Kai to run. She felt trapped, stuck in a snare, waiting for the Hunter to come around and collect her. She had never done anything this hard in her entire life.

Doing nothing sucked.

CHAPTER THIRTY-THREE

1

The wait was the most difficult part of the night. Nico would rather answer a hundred questions than swim in this quiet and watch the panic seep like a poison through everyone's faces. Despite her own turbulent thoughts, she tried her best effort to maintain her composure for everyone in the room, which had become easier once Kai had distracted Rasia's attention with one of those hand-slapping childhood games. Finally, after what seemed a lifetime, a scribe stepped through the bone doors.

"They want to see Nico."

Time to face the dragon. She entered the interview room once again and stood before the Council's judgment.

"We have heard many stories and many versions of those stories," the Mythkeeper said. "But the one truth that the Council agrees on is that there has been interference in this year's Forging. There has been no evidence to definitively prove the perpetrator, but the wide-reaching consequences of the assassination hit against you are indeed severe. In light of this violation, the Council has determined there were unfair circumstances and thus those named," tajih listed off the eighteen, "have been allowed to retain their faces. In addition, not enough evidence has been presented to press additional charges against Rajiani Dragonfire. She has also passed her Forging."

Nico closed her eyes in relief. She asked, hoping Rasia's information had been incorrect. "What about Kai?"

"His is a different circumstance."

"A different circumstance? His Forging was as disrupted as the others. Not only that, but despite it all, he succeeded. There are four witnesses to his hunt, and, without Kai and his magic, none of them would have made it back to the Grankull on time."

"Magic," the Belly Councilor said. "That child doesn't have a magical bone in his body. We've spent years trying to beat it out of him. He is as worthless as the day Avalai Ohan expended him from her womb."

"What she is trying to say," tajih said sharply, "is that, unfortunately, too many doubted his story. According to the rules, if there is any doubt to the legitimacy of a candidate's story, then they are to fail."

"How does that make any sense? You pass the others but not Kai? If there is interference, then all should pass."

Tajih stared at Nico with wide meaningful eyes, and Nico understood that none of it mattered. This was about more than Kai. It was politics. "This is the first time we've had to judge such unprecedented events. After tonight, everyone's story will be publicly published, and the Grankull can decide the truth for themselves."

"Lastly," the Belly Councilor announced. "There is still the matter of you to address. As punishment for your lies and for involving others in your deception, the Council has determined that you will be stripped of the title of Ohan, which abdicates your right to a seat on this Council. The sole heir remaining will be the young child Raevin."

No.

Nico died for that title. She bled for that title. She spent her entire life training for it. Without the title of Ohan, she would have no control or power in how the Grankull was to be run. How could she make good on her promises now?

"But I have successfully bonded with the Elder. I am the dragon's heart," she argued.

"Yet you proved that you cannot be trusted to guide the Grankull," the Belly Councilor said. "You lied, and many are concerned that you are not ready. You chased after your jih during half of your Forging without any regard to your responsibilities to the Grankull. You are lucky that you are the Heart, for that is the only reason you aren't being marched to the gallows for your deceits. You are not the Ohan this Grankull needs. Even Avalai Ohan knew how to make the hard choices."

"Until she didn't," Nico said bitterly. Because in the end, that was all it had ever been about—control. How and in what ways was it possible to control someone of great power, especially when they don't make the decisions you want of them? That was what Kai's birth had truly been about, the reawakening of the Grankull's fear of its own magicborn and the terrifying consequences of when you piss them off. The Council had long wanted this—to kick the magicborn out of politics—to strip them of their voice.

And Nico gave them the perfect excuse to do it. It was Ava-ta's worst nightmare. She understood it on some level. She'd read the bloody histories of magicborn at war. She'd seen the memories through their eyes. Persons of great power have often abused their positions, but the Council at times was no better. There needed to be a balance. For all the Council's proclamations that they served the Grankull, they too could be influenced by power, self-interests, and corruption.

"You are dismissed."

Nico's hands tightened into fists. The room suddenly went eerily silent as a fog thickened. Their mouths dried, and she could feel every pore gather sweat at their foreheads. Afraid of her. She sucked in deep, the magic readied in her lungs, and then she exhaled a calm stoic breath. She turned on her heels, and the fog rolled in her wake.

She could feel the choked faintness of tears approaching, but she refused to cry. If abandoning her title meant she saved eighteen lives, then it was worth it.

Without waiting for the scribes to pull open the door, Nico

released her pent-up magic and shoved the bones open with a jet of water that flooded the floors. She stepped into the antechamber where they all awaited their sentencing. She looked at them, at their hopeful, hesitant, and hopeless faces. She smiled because this was a victory, and she would not let it be anything less.

"The Council declared that due to interference during the Forging, you all will retain your faces." Cheers rang out throughout the room. Many cried. They hugged her, and she couldn't help but be proud of their joy.

Nico walked through the crowd of kids to where Kai and Rasia made their way toward her. Kai asked the question with his eyes. Rasia spat it out. "But not Kai?"

Now the tears were getting harder to hold. She shook her head. "I'm sorry."

"This is horseshit." Rasia kicked at the holy statue of the Great Elder and then stormed toward the doors protecting the Council. In one smooth motion, Kai caught her about the waist and reeled her solidly against his chest.

"We take the loss," Kai said. "Don't do anything stupid, *please*. You cannot afford to lose your face, too. I can't get a job. I don't have rations. I *need* you." She responded less to his words, and more to the plea in his voice. The fight left her as she stuffed her head into his shoulder and choked him tight about the waist.

Nico looked to the door, the one the Council might come out at any moment.

"My face for eighteen isn't a high price to pay. In the end, we were lucky. It could have been worse," Kai said. Rasia made a squawking indignant sound into his shoulder, but it didn't distract him from the expression that crossed Nico's face. He braced himself. "How worse?"

"They stripped me of my title. I am Ohan no longer."

Rasia popped her head up. "They can do that?"

It was then that Nico broke down crying. Kai stepped forward and quickly wrapped her up in his other arm. She cried unashamedly into his shoulder, which was stupid. Because it wasn't as if her life was in danger like Kai's was, but her bones felt crushed. He pressed his cheek against her forehead and tightened his arms around both Nico and Rasia into an all-encompassing hug.

"I'm so proud of you," Kai said, steadfast. "No matter what happens, you saved eighteen lives today. You gave these kids a second chance. No matter what, in the end, you did it. You became the Ohan you always promised you would be."

CHAPTER THIRTY-FOUR

O

Rasia soaked in the heated purification bath. The purification rooms were narrow private spaces located in the back of the temple. Jilah, who had arranged to be Rasia's attendant scribe, had filled the bath with goat's milk, honey, and lavender. Typically, you soaked for drums after the Naming Ceremony to meditate on your transition to adulthood, and then emerged a newly purified adult to be celebrated at the namepour. As it stood, they had a little less than a drum before the celebrations, not that Rasia cared much for celebrating anyways.

"I hadn't meant for Nico to lose her title."

"You're not sorry for it," Kai said, from where he sat atop the ottoman beside the purification bath. He wasn't supposed to be here, but Jilah had helpfully smuggled him in through the secret hallways.

Rasia amended and said a little more sincerely, ". . . I'm sorry how losing her title makes things more difficult for you."

"You promised that you would treat people better. You promised not to diminish anyone. You broke that. You almost ruined those kids' lives."

"I told you that I would *try*. If I had an ounce of Nico's power, the Council would all be dead right now. I'd have seen them all drowned."

"I'd fear for the world if that were true. Not everyone on the Council voted to refuse me my face. Would you punish everyone for the actions of a few? It is what it is, Rasia. This curse follows me always," he paused, and sighed out, "Have you considered, maybe, denouncing me?"

The water splashed around her. "The fuck?"

"Kibari Oshield kicked you out of the house and took your windship because of me. She disowned you because of me. And now, I have no face and no rations to my name. You would have a lot more room to maneuver if we . . . broke up. Maybe Kibari Oshield wouldn't care about me anymore."

Rasia laughed at how utterly logical the suggestion was, and how even if she had the choice, she would never give Kiba-ta the satisfaction. "I can't."

"It doesn't have to be the truth. We play the game, at least for a year, to make it through."

"No, I truly mean I can't. During the Naming Ceremony, when I signed my name, I also signed yours."

His face went slack in shock. For the first time that night, not during the ceremony, not in the antechamber, but *now* his emotions exploded. He snapped up from the ottoman. "What the fuck, Rasia?! *What is wrong with you*?! We never really had the chance to talk about it. This is a decision we should have made together!"

"Oh, now you want to decide shit together?"

"You've tied yourself to me for the rest of your life!"

She stood and splashed milky water across the floor. "If you had fucking told me this morning that they were doubting your story, then maybe I would have reconsidered! I had no reason to believe we weren't earning our faces and signing our names to each other by the end of tomorrow. I figured what difference would it make if I did it now? I had to prove to tah that you weren't some brief flame. I was protecting you."

Kai stared at her, aghast. "You signed my name just to spite your tah? You did this for her! You didn't do this for me. If you had, you'd have known I wanted us to wait. But you can't wait for anything in your fucking life!" He collapsed back onto the ottoman with his hands on his head. Then he sobbed, watery. "I don't want to be a fucking anchor to you. I'm only going to weigh you down, and now there is nothing you can do to escape it."

She sat naked on the edge of the bath. The milky droplets ran down her skin. "It's done. You're my kulani."

"What does that even mean? Can you have an underaged kulani?" he asked. She didn't know the implications either. She looked up when Jilah returned to the room with an armful of towels. Jilah stared, wide-eyed, having caught part of the conversation.

"Have you ever heard of an underaged kulani pair?" Rasia asked Jilah. As a scribe, she would know the histories and laws better than anyone.

Jilah pursed her lips and walked over with the folded linen towels. She grabbed Rasia's arm and began wiping her dry. "A couple of hundred years ago, there was an Ohan who had the magicborn ability to see into the future. He had a vision of his future kulani. At the time, she was only five years till, but he didn't want to wait. The Council argued he couldn't claim her as his kulani because she wasn't yet a member of the Grankull, but the Ohan argued a kulani transcended even that of the Grankull, that a person's kulani could be a child, from the Tents, or even a scavenger."

"Or a foreigner," Kai said. "That was the basis of Kenjinn Ilhani's argument when he defended Zephyr's tah to the Council."

"Exactly," Jilah said. "Your kulani is the one name you choose, and the Grankull has always historically bowed to that precedent. Joson Ohan used this loophole to sign his kulani's name. When he did so, the Council established at the time that he had all rights to his kulani as if she were of age, but they also set in place limitations for fear of future abuse. Kulani must sign their names to most application forms, but that application is void if one is underage, so that means no applying for children or individual housing. Further, to protect the child's agency, the Grankull deemed that when she did finally come of age, she would be given a right to choose herself. She could choose to carry or refuse the Ohan's name. If she refused, then the Ohan forfeited all rights to her."

"What did she choose?" Rasia asked curiously.

"Joson Ohan treated that child like the Han of his life. She never wanted for anything and took his name without hesitation when the time came. The situation has the potential to invite abuse, but it happens so rarely. No one really wants all that responsibility just to see under someone's shroud. Also, most triarchs would riot and contest the claim." Jilah looked between Rasia and Kai. "I assume it would be the same for you. If Kai ever comes of age, he'll have a choice. But for now, you've claimed him as your responsibility. He's part of your household now, and that also means he's no longer part of Nico-shi's household. He can't touch his jihs without it being illegal. He can't touch anyone but you."

Kai stood to his feet and turned away from Rasia. The wind howled a fierce shriek outside. They could hear the bone curtain rattling from here.

"Kai, I didn't know that's how it would work. I didn't know we both wouldn't be of age."

"Of course, you didn't, because you don't think! You took me away from my family without my consent. You took me away from Rae. The rules regarding budchildren might be looser, but do you really think they're going to give me a break? No! They'll only critique and judge me more harshly. How can I possibly forgive you for this? I'm going home."

"You shouldn't be out there by yourself."

"I'll ask Ysai-ji!" Kai snapped and stormed out of the room. Ysai had been waiting on the Temple steps for them since this whole mess started. Apparently, several concerned family members have been camped out on the steps waiting to hear the fates of their children. Rasia had heard their cheers through the temple doors when Nico relayed the Council's decision.

"You should go after him," Jilah told her.

"And do what?" she asked. "He's going to be mad at me no

matter what I do. No. I am going to the namepour, I am going to have a fucking drink, and then I'm going to figure out how to kill my damn tah."

"Some might consider denying your kulani a face as enough grounds to demand a blood price."

"You don't demand a blood price from someone you can't beat," Rasia scoffed. "Kibari Oshield once told me that if I ever raised a sword to her, I better be ready to fight for my life. We've always had our disagreements, but I've never outright challenged her. There are too many variables needed to win."

"Poison?" Jilah suggested.

Jilah and Rasia glanced at each other, with a sudden shared understanding. Rasia licked at the sweat above her lip, gathered from the steam of the bath. It was an option. Together, they formulated and devised different plans of action.

Rasia had once thought that Aurum would be the greatest hunt of her life. How wrong she had been.

There were always greater dragons to slay.

CHAPTER THIRTY-FIVE

I

Nico lay in the purification bath, and for once, took the time to think about nothing. She traced her eyes along the brush strokes of the colorful dragon mural overhead and yielded to the hands of the scribe washing her. She dripped into the milk bath and dispersed around the lavender petals. The smell of honey absorbed into her skin. Scented oils softened her shoulders. She released all her grief, and all her anger, and let it drip, drip from her.

"Nicolai Oasis, it's time."

She surfaced and emerged from the bath an adult, and yet naked and stripped of the title she had rightfully earned. She glanced down at the scribe scrubbing her dry. No doubt the scribes have been gossiping about this mess all day long. They, more than anyone, could give her insight into the Grankull's current mindset.

"What do you think of all this?" she asked. "What do you think of the Council's decision?"

From his knees, the scribe looked at her and wrestled with his silence.

"The truth," she asked. "You don't have to fear any harm from me."

"I think the Council was right in regard to your jih," the scribe said, shrugging his shoulders. "If there is any doubt, you fail. That's the rule. And who can believe that the runt of the Grankull learned to steer a windship, survived the Lake of Yestermorrow, went up against scavengers, *and* slayed a Dragon? It's more than a little unbelievable. It's like some mythic tale, edited over so much it's more fiction than fact."

No doubt many others would share the same opinion. Nico feared this could happen. She had begged Kai to focus on a gonda, but he got caught up in Rasia's wind and flew too high. *No*. That was giving Rasia too much credit. In the end, Kai had been the architect of his own triumphant downfall. Jih had always been prideful. But at the same time, how did she dare ask Kai to shrink himself to better fit the Grankull's narrow view of who he should be?

No one should have to be less to be enough.

When Shamai Windbreaker, a former tent kid, had broken all the Grankull's records to bring back a Forging kill within the span of two days—there had been precedent. Tent kids have passed the Forging before. No one could deny their ingenuity and determination to survive. The Grankull had a good harvest and hunts for several years, so relations with the Tents weren't as tense as they are now. That year, a Council member had a kulani who had been a former tent kid. All the bones had landed right.

Change didn't happen in a vacuum. The Grankull hadn't been ready for Kai, but Nico would have a year to make it ready. She would make sure this did not happen again.

"Thank you for your honesty," she said. "And what about me? What do you think of me?"

"You lied," the scribe said simply. "But I've been a scribe for several years, and I have overseen several Forging accounts. I know we lose kids to scavengers but never to this extent. I am hesitant to outright believe the Council would do such a horrific thing, but some of the stories don't add up. We lost a lot of kids this year. If it's true, I understand why you did what you did. You've got good bones, and I don't reckon you'll take this lying down. Stripping you of your title must feel like a shroud thrown at your feet. But I'm a scribe. I've read our histories. I know where this will lead. The Grankull never benefits when the Council and Ohan go to war."

"You think I should do nothing?"

"People always get crushed when giants go to battle."

"But this isn't the promise of the Grankull. We're taught that we're all in this together. We're taught that you earn your face, and that once you do, you're as equal to the person next to you. We're taught that if you contribute, you'll always eat. Where is the Grankull promised in our myths and stories?"

"You grow up," the scribe shrugged, "and learn they're just stories."

"That's it then? I'm supposed to settle for a broken dream? I'm supposed to settle for a Grankull who cheats their children, who values some over others, and refuses stories deemed impossible because of prejudices and too small imaginations? We live in the middle of the Desert under the dead bones of a dragon. We continually toil and create life out of nothing. Why is it so hard to look at the runt of the Grankull and believe he could one day become the best of us?"

The scribe said, "I just want to eat."

"We all do."

The night wind whispered shivers across Nico's bare skin. The scribe had stripped her of her silk dress, bathed her, purified her, and sent her to join the others on the temple steps as naked as the day she came into the world. Many complained of the cold, but the scribes assured everyone they'd get the warmth of drink and flesh on their bones soon enough. The bitter taste of gonom clung to the back of Nico's throat.

Per tradition, the scribes lined them up by the number of their names. Another scribe had interrupted Nico's purification bath to tell her that apparently, now that the truth was on record, the Mythkeeper determined that Nico was eligible for more names. She couldn't honestly remember what she had agreed on, but it had placed her behind Rasia in line.

"Where's Kai?" Nico asked once she settled in line. The temple lanterns illuminated the scars on Rasia's skin. The three long claw-like monstrosities drew the eye the most, inviting you to trace the curve of them from shoulder blade to hip. Rasia tilted her head over her shoulder with a sneer, to lock eyes with Nico.

"Ysai-ji took him home."

Then Rasia very explicitly cut her eyes down Nico's body, head to toe. She snorted, unimpressed, and turned back around. Nico had the urge to push Rasia down the steps. She never thought she could contain so much complicated hatred for one person.

She searched for somewhere else to plant her eyes, and gradually, her vision lost focus as she stared down at her feet. It was weird. To wear nothing when you've worn a shroud your entire life. But Nico expected that. The thought that soon she would have to face the entire Grankull without her birthright numbed her. It weighed heavily on her chest. She had made so many people so many promises, and now she had to look them all in the eye and tell them she had failed.

This was supposed to be a moment of triumph and celebration. Not long ago, she had been a child watching the procession, amazed by how beautiful everyone looked in their bare skin and at how proudly they carried themselves finally freed from their shrouds.

She didn't feel very free.

"Are you alright?"

She turned to Zephyr, who had been placed behind her. Usually, she would have noticed him. With the bath oils, his darker skin gleamed a brilliant sheen of copper in the torchlight. Usually, she would have been trying her hardest not to stare at his nudity. But she was really struggling to focus on anything.

Before she could answer, the procession started with a drumroll. The Council walked ahead first. Rasia raced forward, ignoring the signal. She kept a brutal pace, not meant for the others to follow, but prowled in the Councilor's footsteps. While Rasia drifted away, Nico quickly shifted and paved the way toward the namepour for the others behind her.

People spilled out of their homes once the procession began. Many had been out on the streets since the Naming Ceremony and had been gossiping and reveling in the drama of the past few drums. The Grankull converged at the Tail. Shimmering lights speckled the area as if a messenger had jumped up and borrowed stars from the sky. Contracted musicians added a rousing chorus to the drums.

The Council led the new faces to a table that looped onto itself with space at the center. They were led to sit inside the circle, to face outward toward the crowd. Families gathered in groups atop embroidered quilts. Some of the smaller families climbed atop the tail vertebra. Children jostled each other to get the high seats. Nico found where Kenji-ta had seated himself with Rae and his jih's family. It always amazed Nico the breadth and size of the Elder, that all the Grankull could gather in the loop of their Tail.

Tajih sat directly behind Nico and whispered between them. "I'm sorry. They out voted me at every turn."

"There's nothing you could have done."

"You don't understand. There's something you should know—" The cheers of the crowd drowned out tajih's voice as the Councilor of the Neck stood. To Nico's right, Rasia glowered, studying Kibari Oshield like prey.

Chosen to speak for the Council, Suri's tah, addressed the gathered crowd.

"We owe all of you an explanation for what occurred earlier today. As many of you are aware, there were accusations that some had been lying about their Forging. The Council has investigated these stories further and has concluded that to protect her sibling, the Ohan heir lied to us all. The first-named of Avalai Ohan did not slay a dragon and because of the heir's deceits, the Council stripped her of her title and responsibilities as Ohan. She has earned her hunt, she has earned her face, but she has not earned the responsibility to guide us to the next horizon."

Shouting, booing, confusion, and disappointment swept through the crowd.

"*What?*" Rasia snapped. Nico pressed a hand down on Rasia's leg, afraid of what she might do.

It all made sense now.

Kai was the scapegoat. The Council didn't mention the eighteen, or the assassination attempt, or the interference—not when there was an easier story to tell. In one fell swoop, the Council succeeded in turning everyone against Nico and her family.

"But let us not forget that tonight is a celebration," the Neck Councilor continued. "Thus begins the time to celebrate first hunts and new-faces. Let's celebrate those who have shed the skins of childhood and emerged among us as adults. Let us fill our bellies with the offered bounties. Let us welcome them and learn their names."

The confusion, anger, and disappointment quickly dissipated once the scribes and volunteer children ushered out the food. When they sat a plate before her, Nico couldn't stomach the smell, not when she knew this grand feast had been cooked atop the rations of those who didn't survive the Forging, and ultimately, atop the gonda and dragon Kai had slain.

"Fuck this shit," Rasia snapped, and flung the plate over to spill most of the contents. Several people in her vicinity gasped. A scribe rushed over to save it. Nico didn't agree with Rasia's actions, but she understood the sentiment.

Unable to stomach the injustice, she scanned through the crowd, then frowned, and skipped back to where Kenji-ta had sat moments before. Rae sat on their cousin's lap.

A boulder of dread dropped in the pit of her stomach. She stared out at the crowd, where hundreds and hundreds of people waited to swarm her with questions. It could take her forever to navigate her way out. She could use her magic, but how would the Council further twist that against her? No doubt they would judge her for trying to flee.

Nico made a decision.

"Rasia Dragonfire," she squeezed the flesh of Rasia's thigh hard, demanding her attention. *"Kai is in danger."*

Rasia glanced over at Kibari Oshield, in the wrong direction. "Yeah, no shit. That's what I've been trying to tell you."

"No. *Kenjinn Ilhani.*" Rasia might be a little shit and an asshole, but at the end of the day, Nico trusted no one else more with Kai's life. "You're faster."

Rasia searched Nico's eyes, and then she exploded into movement. She stepped onto the table and vaulted over it in a burst of power, movement, and breasts. She sprinted off faster than most messengers who run for a living. She ran over people, jumped over heads, and slipped through openings. She didn't give a fuck to anyone in her way.

When Nico moved to follow, a hand clasped onto her shoulder. She flinched under the stranger's touch. She turned, ready to berate the stranger for their audacity, and remembered that people were free to touch her now. She faced Kibari Oshield's harsh stare, who glanced over at the messy plate the scribe had put back together, and the space Rasia had vacated.

"Is there something I need to be aware of?" the Rib Councilor asked. "We don't need any more disruptions."

Nico was tempted to turn into a puddle right under the Councilor's hand and evaporate, but she didn't want to reveal to the Councilor how much her power had grown.

"Everything is fine," she gritted her teeth. She would have to think of another way to escape, maybe employ her friends for help with a distraction.

The Rib Councilor's grip tightened on her shoulder. "Good. I hope you aspire to be a better role model for the Grankull in the future."

She forced herself to smile at this person who killed her tah, who tried to kill her, and who had stripped her of her title. The Councilor was a snake, waiting to strike.

"Thank you for your concern," she said, smoothly. Kibari Oshield was not the most pressing problem right now. She had to somehow extricate herself from the feast without causing a commotion. Nico desperately hoped that Rasia reached Kai before it was too late.

CHAPTER THIRTY-SIX

—

"Thank you for taking me home," Kai told Ysai. All they had to do was walk across the temple gardens to get to Kai's house, but after the Naming ceremony, even he knew to exert a higher level of caution.

"It's nothing," Ysai said as he leaned against the entranceway. "It's fucked up, what they did to you. You completed your hunt. You earned your face."

Kai shrugged. He was over it now. He had been over it since the interview. People hating him was nothing new. He blamed himself for thinking a dead dragon could possibly make a difference. Currently, all the heat suffocating his chest was aimed in Rasia's direction—at her cruelty, her indifference, her anger, her pride, and at how massively much she cares.

"I know Rasia doesn't make it easy at times," Ysai said. "Believe you me, I know how frustrating and infuriating she can be. But I do think she's trying her best in the messy ways she knows how. I pause to think if I had been on those steps, and the Council had denied Jilah her face. What would I have done?" His entire stance sharpened, and he shook his head. "But it's easier to see the roads from the spine. I know Kiba-ta is trying her best in the messy ways she knows how, too. They are so similar. They've always butted heads, and tah . . . she bends less without her kulani. She's so determined to protect us from the world that it pushes us away. If Rasia and tah both had a little more patience and a little more grace to give each other, maybe things would be different. I don't know." Ysai looked around the dark and quiet house. "Are you sure you're going to be okay here all by yourself?"

No sentry was on duty today, as everyone had the holiday off, but Kai wasn't too worried about intruders right now. For an entire civilization constrained to rations, when there was a pouring, all petty squabbles were set aside for another day. "I doubt anyone is going to bother thinking of me once the food starts flowing."

"True," he conceded. "I'll see you, Kailjnn."

Ysai left for the celebrations, and Kai entered his home. He unwound his shroud and left it to hang off his shoulders. It was a relief to finally be on his own. He took the time to exist in the quiet, to process, and to breathe. When the quiet became too suffocating, he sat in the serving room and placed his fingers on the strings of his namesake. He filled the silence with the melody of his favorite song, haunting and beautiful in equal measure.

Heavy footsteps charged toward the house.

He missed a note.

Irrationally, he scrambled for his shroud and frantically wrapped it around his face. The ilhan clanged against the floor, and Kenji's shadow filled the doorway.

"That's kulani's song," Kenji growled, and his face twisted into the angry snarling monster of Kai's nightmares. "I should have ended you a long time ago. Nico-po lost her title because of you. You have been a curse on this family ever since you were born, and I'm finally going to end it."

Kenji snatched up the ilhan.

"That's mine!" Kai shouted, then swallowed the words when the ilhan swung towards him. His body reacted, and he crouched into a defensive position before truly conscious of what was happening. The wood cracked with a twang and splintered across his shoulder. The ilhan came down a second time on his back and then the broken instrument was tossed to the ground. He watched the scattered pieces skid across the hard adobe floor, some straying under the serving table and others going as far as the kitchen.

Finally, the world on the outside looked as wrecked as he was on the inside.

His shroud and hair pulled tight, then Kenji's fist collided with the side of Kai's head. Everything flashed in ringing agony. Light spun in his eyes. Vertigo tossed him. Another sharp pain in the back of his head. Then he couldn't breathe.

Kenji pinned him to the wall by his throat and reached for the dagger at his belt, and Kai slackened in surrender, waiting for the inevitable and all the pain to finally end.

Then out of the darkness came Rasia.

She charged in, vaulted off the serving table, and leaped up to wrap her thighs and forearm around Kenji's neck. The movement altered the angle of the dagger. Instead of a quick stab to the heart, it caught against the bone of Kai's ribs and glanced burning down his stomach.

Kenji dropped Kai and pulled at Rasia's thigh from where she choked him. He locked a hand around Rasia's legs, then dropped back, and slammed her into the table.

The mudbrick slab cracked. Rasia's hold slackened, and Kenji twisted himself out, flipping his hair as he bounced back onto his feet. He unsheathed his sword to attack—

—and froze.

Kenji asked, confused, "Rasia-po?"

Rasia rolled to her feet, past Kenji, and positioned herself between Kenji and Kai. Behind her back, she urged Kai to hand over the dagger currently sitting halfway in his stomach. He bit down as he slid the blade out.

"Touch him again," she threatened, "and I'll kill you."

Kenji looked outright baffled. Meanwhile, Rasia kept wiggling her fingers at Kai, annoyed, but he was frozen in indecision. Kenji wasn't going to hurt Rasia, but Rasia would hurt Kenji, and he didn't want that.

"What are you doing here?" Kenji demanded.

"I'm trying to stop you from killing my kulani."

Kenji processed that information with a hard huff of his nostrils, then sneered at Kai in utter disgust. "How dare you. What lies have you told her?"

Kenji lunged toward him. Rasia snatched the dagger from his frozen hands. When Kenji moved to knock Rasia out of the way, she stabbed the dagger into his forearm. And Kai watched, frozen, unable to force himself to move. It was his worst nightmare. He never wanted this and now, fuck, great, he was having another episode—a panic attack. Utterly and pathetically useless.

Kenji barely flinched at Rasia's attack and used his charging momentum to upend her and shove her aside. She evaded underneath, rolling back against Kai to prevent Kenji from decapitating him with his sword. Kai fell against the floor under her weight. Rasia remained on top of him, shielding him.

"Turn away Kenji-shi. I don't want to kill you, but I will."

"You know I don't want to hurt you, but it's time I finally end this family's curse. I was soft once. I'm not going to make the same mistake again."

Rasia stood, defiantly, with no weapon and no clothes. "Then you're going to have to go through me."

Kenji sheathed his sword. He unhitched it from his waist and placed it atop the decorative cabinet shelf.

"Don't think you'll need it?" she taunted.

"Don't want to accidentally kill you." Without hesitation or even a movement in warning, Kenji went low and charged. He grabbed Rasia around the waist and threw her to the floor. She countered out of the hold, then he countered her right back into it. He twisted the dagger out of her hand, slammed her to the ground, and wrapped his grip around her arm.

Realizing what Kenji intended, Kai finally unstuck. He pushed himself off the wall and threw himself forward, and then, batted down like a bug, dropped back to the floor a moment later.

Kenji looped Rasia's arm out of the socket with an audible pop. Kai winced where he lay against the floor at the sound of her sharp cry.

Kai's hair was yanked from its roots, then his vision went black as Kenji slammed his face into the dusty flooring. Blood gushed from his nose. Then again with a ringing whine in his ears. He lamented the fact he was about to get his brains smashed out on the serving room floor. Kenji lifted his face up for a third time, then a sharp crack followed.

Kai dropped unceremoniously. He glanced over at the sight of the oven peel Rasia wielded, cracked from where it bounced off Kenji's head. She discarded the broken peel and took advantage of Kenji's brief disorientation. She held the dagger aloft in her one good arm.

"Rasia," Kai coughed on his own blood. "Rasia, no."

He crawled forward to stop her over the bloody sprawl of his loose shroud. He flailed into her.

"What the fuck?"

The momentum of the crash landed them both awkwardly on the cracked pieces of the serving table. Rasia yelped when she was dragged out from under Kai and thrown aside into the kitchen. Kenji picked up the dagger Rasia had dropped. The dragonsteel gleamed like sharp teeth overhead. Kai hid his face in his hands.

Then suddenly, a wave burst through the room, taking Kenji off of his feet and swallowing him under a powerful current. Nico stormed into the house. She glanced over at Kai, then turned back to Kenji with a snarl. She released the wave, and the water stilled to a stagnant pool that rose to Kai's knees.

Kenji sputtered as he splashed to his feet.

"*Get out*," Nico demanded.

"That thing doesn't deserve your mercy," Kenji said. "Not after all that you have lost because of him. If it wasn't for his lies-"

"I LIED! It was me! I lied, and it was Kai who took the fall for it. You could have talked to me, you could have asked me what had happened, but instead, your hatred has overpowered all sense, and I will not stand for this behavior any longer. I am tired of you treating him like shit because you are too prideful to see clearly. Kai has always and will always be the best parts of you. And until you realize that, until you get your head out of your ass, you are no longer welcome in this house!"

Kenji opened his mouth to argue.

"GET OUT!" Nico demanded. Rolling thunder punctuated her words.

Kenji stared at Nico for several moments before he waded out of the house. She watched him go with a hard look that reminded Kai eerily of Ava-ta. Then the rain stopped, and the water drained through the cracks into the earth.

Nico looked at Kai with a wince, and then turned to Rasia. "Thank you for making it on time."

"I almost didn't," Rasia snarled. She stomped over to Kai and lifted his robe to inspect the injury at his waist. "Any vibration later, and that dagger would have gone right through your heart. You got lucky. At least one of us gives a shit whether you're alive. You sure didn't help any."

"Your arm," Kai said.

It was still out of socket, creating an unsettling curve to her shoulder. Rasia sneered at him for pointing it out.

"Here," Nico offered. Rasia clenched her jaw under Nico's touch, and Kai flinched at the ensuing pop that came afterward. Rasia rolled her shoulder, and Nico stepped back, frowning. "I'll go get our medical supplies."

While Nico left for the kitchen, Rasia none too gently tore at the bottom of Kai's robe for bandages. Might as well. It was ruined now. She dampened it in the puddles Nico's magic had left behind and used it to get a better look at Kai's stomach wound. It burned and bled profusely down his waist.

Nico brought over the tub of supplies they kept in the kitchen. She looked him over, and suddenly seemed overwhelmed. "I don't know if this is enough. Perhaps I should go get Suri."

"No," Rasia hissed, with all the steam and heat of a dragon defending its territory. She snapped out, "Shouldn't you be getting back?"

Nico's eyes narrowed and her teeth ground down on her initial reaction. It was a testament to the seriousness of the situation that Nico didn't forcibly try to supplant herself over Kai's welfare. Even she recognized Rasia wasn't in the best of moods.

Rasia clicked her tongue at Nico's non-answer, then whipped around to clean at the blood, but there was so much. "Think you can walk all the way to the bath?"

Kai grunted in answer, which practically meant maybe. Both Nico and Rasia held him up on either side and helped him limp his way through the maze.

In the dragon scale mirror of the bath, Kai winced at the sight of his bruised and swollen face. He could barely see out of his left eye without blinking pus down his cheek. His nose had been broken by that mob. Every drag of breath burned through his throat. A cut streaked ragged across his arm, his waist was on fire, and he was light-headed from all the blood loss.

But he was alive, and that was something.

They sat him down on the first stair of the bath. He bowed his head, dazed, and blacked out for a few vibrations as Nico and Rasia worked in a tense silence to stitch and bandage him up. He refocused when Rasia pushed a gourd to his lips. Automatically, he drank down the water. He found it painful to swallow.

Rasia sat back on her haunches and studied the blooming bruises and the swelling beginning to seal one of his eyes closed. Her brows scrunched into a frown, as if collecting all the pages of a story she didn't like. She tracked Nico's movements as Nico cleared the basket of soiled linens. The moment Nico returned; Rasia pounced.

"You knew."

Nico stopped. Kai felt faint, either from the blood loss, or the inevitable direction of this conversation.

"Kenji," Rasia said, for the first time dropping the familiar address, "has done this before."

"Yes," Nico admitted. She sounded so very small from the jih that he knew. "It was about a year ago. Kenji-ta had been drunk, and I almost didn't make it in time. But it was just that one time, and I thought . . . I thought . . . But tah had hurt Kai that night before the Forging and threatened to kick him out. I feared that after everything that happened tonight... I hoped I was wrong."

"Boneless," Rasia sneered.

"Don't you dare insert yourself into a situation you barely know anything about," Nico argued. "There is nothing I could have done until I became an adult and assumed the role of triarch. And tah was drunk. He promised he would stop drinking."

"He wasn't fucking drunk tonight."

"I threw him out! What more do you want, Rasia?"

"I WANT HIM DEAD!"

"You want everyone dead! How many bodies will it take until you're satisfied?"

"*All of them.*"

"Enough." Kai bit out and struggled to gain his footing. He leaned against one of the carved pillars and trembled at the pain which erupted from the movement.

Rasia turned on him, in fight-mode, looking for any action or excuse to give her a reason to attack. He swallowed when her gaze narrowed, looking at him with new information. She studied his bandaged torso and the scars she trailed her fingers over a hundred times before.

"Why do you protect him? What are you hiding? Nico doesn't know shit, does she?" Rasia rushed forward like an incoming windship about to ram him over. She pushed her forehead against his own and quietly demanded, "How many times has he hurt you? How many scars are because of him?"

Rocks sat on Kai's chest.

"Kai?" Nico asked, her voice over Rasia's shoulder, confused and watery.

Rasia stepped back, giving Kai some air to breathe, but it was too much space because now there was room for Nico to fill in the rest with dawning realization. He wrapped his arms around his chest, in a pathetic attempt to continue hiding from her. Before, her attention had been focused on making sure he didn't die from the blood loss, but now she was forming her own interpretations of the scars.

He didn't want either of them to find out this way.

"The truth, Kai," Rasia snapped out, furious. "We deserve the truth."

Kai couldn't say it. For the life of him, he couldn't say it. He didn't know why it mattered so much to protect the person who had just tried to kill him. In the end, he didn't have to speak the words.

Nico translated his silence.

"He won't ever touch you again. I promise you that," she said. "We'll discuss how we're going to handle Kenji at another time, when you're not so weak and barely conscious. For now, you should rest, and I should be getting back."

"That's it?" Rasia snarled.

Nico ignored her. "Tomorrow, I am finally able to submit the paperwork to become the triarch of the family. Tah's alcoholism is known, but with the situation that occurred today, the process might be messy, but I will camp out at the administration building every day until it is done. What do you want me to do? Do you want me to banish him from the family line? Do you want him branded? Do you want him dead?"

Kai shook his head.

"Then I respect your wishes," Nico said and nodded calmly to Rasia, "I'll send someone by with food."

Rasia crossed her arms and added, "And alcohol. Lots of alcohol."

"Will do," Nico promised and left. Kai stared after her, surprised the conversation was that easy. Or maybe they both were extremely tired and would deal with this mess another day.

Rasia, on the other hand, looked unsatisfied by the whole affair. She plopped onto the edge of the bath and sneered at the streaks of blood that painted the water. He sat beside her, where she hung her head. They sat there for a while. Her stillness worried him.

"Are you okay?" he tentatively ventured to ask.

"*No*, I'm not fucking okay. You almost died. *Again*. Any vibration later and it would have been over. Add that on top of every other shitty thing that happened today. And . . . and, you didn't fight back! You refused to hand me the dagger! You refused to let me kill him! What the fuck?"

"He is Nico and Rae's tah."

"He stabbed you!"

"It doesn't matter."

"Of course it matters!" Rasia yelled at him, and then hopped up and paced around the bath, until she swung back around to face him. But he had no response. She screamed at his silence. "I am tired of you keeping shit from me! I would have never promised to help you with Kenji-shi if I knew he was beating you. I can't protect us if I don't know who our enemies are."

"I've told you. Everyone wants me dead. You can't kill everyone."

"I can sure as fuck try."

"What does it matter?" he asked. "If I never met you, you wouldn't have given a shit. No one gave a shit. No one gave a shit when a mob of strangers I'd never spoken to my entire life stabbed me in the stomach and left me for dead in an alleyway. No one gave a shit when the Council beat me half-to-death. Who gives a fucking shit if the person whose life I ruined hits me from time to time? It doesn't matter."

"I GIVE A SHIT!" she screamed at him. "You are mine now!"

"Rasia, where are you going?"

"To get my blades and armor and finish what I started."

"No. NO." Kai scrambled to his feet. He limped after Rasia as she charged into the hallway. "Rasia, stop. Listen to me. Nico already threw him out of the house. That's enough."

Rasia screamed in frustration when she hit a dead end of the maze. She turned on her heels and branded a pointed finger in his direction. "It will never be enough. As long as he's alive, he is a threat to you."

"Stop."

She shoved past him. She circled back down the wrong corridor. She was walking too fast. Kai caught his breath at the beginning of a hallway where he knew she would find another dead end. After several vibrations, she charged back toward him.

"Rasia," Kai said, as she approached. "Please. I know what it is like to live with one parent's death on my hands. Regardless of whether your tah was involved, that doesn't change the fact that Ava-ta died protecting me. I can't . . . I can't live with myself if another death was because of me. He's the only parent Nico and Rae have left. The Grankull is a big place. I will avoid him like I've been doing my entire life. He doesn't have to die. Please."

She marched right past him. He didn't know what else to say, and he was out of breath and exhausted. He collapsed to the floor. Rasia marched back toward him, and demanded, "How the fuck do I get out of here?"

He looked at her, defiant.

She threw her hands up. "This is stupid. How can you possibly protect someone who hurts you?"

"You've hurt me," Kai spat out. "You've punched me in the face. You pushed me into the Yestermorrow Lake, by accident sure, but I almost died. Just the other night, you slapped me. Twice."

Rasia halted. "That's not the same."

"Isn't it? He usually doesn't mean it. Most of the time, he's drunk. He drinks to forget that his kulani is gone. Then he remembers and gets angry, and I'm the one who took her away. I ruined his life." Kai combed at his hair. "Everyone I've ever known has hurt me in some way—tah, Nico, you, even Rae. It's me, Rasia. Something is wrong with me."

She collapsed down beside him. She stared at the colorful tapestry hanging across from them on the wall. She said softly, "There's nothing wrong with you."

Chimes rang through the house. They stared at each other as those chimes continued to ring. Rasia said, flat, emotionless, "It's probably the food Nico promised to send over."

"I'm not hungry."

"Come on, Kai."

"Promise me. Promise that you won't go after him, on Shamaijen Windbreaker's name."

Rasia glared hard in return and broke with an aggrieved sigh. She shoved back against the wall. "Fuck, whatever. I promise. On Shamai-ta's name."

He narrowed his eyes at her.

"On my tah's name, Kai."

He didn't have a choice but to trust her word. If she didn't mean it now, she didn't mean it later. He pushed to his feet and she followed him through the maze. They approached the kitchen, carefully, in case it wasn't the person whom Nico sent over. Rasia peeked ahead, then gave the kull signal for all-clear. He came around the corner into the kitchen and found plates of food and a whole casket of alcohol, as Nico promised.

Kai examined the plates and turned to find Rasia absent from the kitchen. He found her standing in the serving room in the middle of the wreckage. She stared at the namesake she had given him, now broken, cracked, and bloody on the floor. Her fists tightened. Her visage hardened into that same betrayed expression before she had condemned the faces of eighteen people.

His stomach dropped.

"You promised. On your tah's name."

"Tah is dead."

The moon from the window bathed her face in shadows. Her curves became as dangerous as the curves of her khopesh. Her feet crunched over the broken splinters of the ilhan. Then Rasia prowled naked into the dark.

CHAPTER THIRTY-SEVEN

I

Nico's world was broken.

The cracks had always been there, but it was all crumbling apart now. All this time, she had been living under the same roof as Kenji-ta thinking that he was getting better, at least in some ways. But while she had been smiling and laughing with him, behind her back, he had been beating Kai. The time Nico witnessed hadn't been the exception, it was just the one she walked in on. She was a fool.

Maybe the Council was right. She didn't deserve the title of Ohan. She couldn't protect her own family, much less the Grankull. She could barely protect herself.

And she was so unbelievably tired. She was tired of always being on the defensive. She was tired of being so many steps behind. She was tired of being the bigger person. She was tired of Kai's lies and his silence. She was tired of Rasia's cruelty and her selfishness. She was tired of her own weakness and helplessness. She was fucking tired.

The bonfires from the feast created a mirage glow in the distance. Nico stared and stared and stared, wondering what would happen if she dared to never break the illusion. She wasn't the Ohan anymore. She no longer owed anyone her time or her feelings. Or her pain. The disappointment of all those who have supported her stalked the flames, lying in wait for her to dance into their claws and tear her apart.

She could . . . stop trying. She could finally just be Nicolai and live her life without so many titles on her shoulders.

But if Nico didn't keep trying, who would? If Nico didn't keep fighting, who would fight the messy battles and take the unfair blows? If she gave up, if no one offered resistance, who would stop the Council from doing whatever they please? Who else but Nico could stand before dragonfire?

She pushed herself forward.

She was done bearing witness to her jih's suffering. She was done making excuses for those in power. She was done with it all. There was no room to be tired. She hadn't the time. When they finally managed to assassinate her, she would sleep atop her funeral pyre.

She approached the crackling fires that thrummed under the musician's croon. A dancer leapt across the rippled space, shaping the words of song into limb and muscle. Even as the singer released the notes in a high soprano, Nico heard the song in Kenji-ta's deep tenor—the way he used to sing back when his fingers first composed the words. She hated how she heard every song in his voice.

When the Desert falls to time
And channels are washed by rain
I'll have left behind my legend
So you'll never forget my name

The dancer balanced on the lingering chords. He stumbled, but gracefully moved through his hesitation and bowed to Nico's sudden presence at the center of the Tail.

The musicians, singer, and dancer, all looked at her in confusion. The Council and the new-faces sitting at the round table looked at her in confusion. The entire Grankull, scattered among the sand and atop the Tail, all looked at her in confusion. No one had ever interrupted the performances before.

Nico claimed the stage. The Naming Ceremony had blurred

past her, but now she was present and clear-headed. The cold pricked her naked skin, and the wind tossed her unpinned hair. She projected her voice out into the ether.

"I owe all of you an apology. You expected me to lead you. You expected me to protect you. You expected me to feed you. And I have failed. Regardless of the details or the circumstances, I have failed in my responsibility to you and your families. I am sorry, and I hope you can forgive me. But know that I have made you promises, and I will keep them. There is work ahead, and I am not done. For those who dream, I dream with you. For those denied a fair chance, I will fight for you. For those crushed by rampant corruption, I will toil for you. For those who are hungry, I will hunt for you. I, Nicolai Dragonshield, hereby declare my campaign to run for the Council Seat of the Wings! When I sit on that Council, you will know that I am not there because of my bloodline, or because of my magic, but because I have earned your trust! I will not fail you again!"

One person in that dark void clapped. It rippled throughout the crowd and flooded into a wave of cheers. Her pregnant mentor, the current Councilor of the Wings stood in support.

She didn't miss the darkened stares of some of the other Council members, but they could do little to stop her. They wouldn't dare knife her in the middle of the entire Grankull. As if they could if they tried.

She signaled to one of the scribes holding a pitcher of alcohol. Understanding her intent, the scribe poured her a drink and handed her an overflowing cup. During a lapse in the cheers, she raised the cup high. One by one, cups joined hers. Nico roared with the kull's toast, "DRINK DEEP, DRINK WELL, FOR TOMORROW THE HUNT BEGINS ANEW!"

CHAPTER THIRTY-EIGHT

0

Rasia charged the figure walking the edge of the training fields. In her rage, she carved ruts in the sand and approached with all the subtlety of a rampaging gonda. She howled his name. Kenji-shi no doubt heard her coming, but for whatever reason, he didn't turn around to meet her blades. Her khopesh sliced through the air and froze at his hunched back.

"Fight me!" she demanded in frustration.

Kenji-shi lowered a clay flask and angled around to squint at her. "I'm not going to fight you."

"*Are you drunk*?"

"Trying to get there."

The flask shattered when Rasia sliced dragonsteel through the clay. Anticipating a reaction, she spun on her heels only to find Kenji-shi staring dumbly at that broken flask in his hand. She froze her khopesh at his neck, having forced herself to stop from killing him, *again*. She screamed in frustration.

He just stood there, even though his sword was *right there* at his waist.

"Do you want to die?!" she demanded.

Kenji-shi shrugged.

"Fight me!" she stomped her feet, stamping her boots into the sand. Still nothing. "Fight me, you stupid boneless limp dick kulo!"

That elicited a reaction. Shocked by Rasia's coarse language, he crossed his arms and had the audacity to demand as if she was five-years till, "Five laps."

"You're not my tah!"

"Ten laps."

"AHHHHH!!!!!!" She dropped her blades and went sprinting around the training field. It was the same stupid training field Shamai-ta forced her to run whenever he claimed she needed more constructive outlets for her anger. It was the same training field Shamai-ta used to train his kull. The same one where she'd go to fetch him for dinner when his sparring matches with Kenji-shi ran too late.

Kenji-shi had sat down atop the hill by the time Rasia finished her laps. She marched up to him darkly.

"Feeling better?" he asked.

"I . . . yeah," she said. Her words punctuated heaving breaths. She snatched up her khopesh and pointed them at him. She thought that with her armor and her blades, she could face him with better footing—if anything, the ground felt worse than when she confronted him naked in his serving room. She squeezed her eyes shut, and . . . and . . . she pressed her forearm to her face to stop the sudden tears.

"Do you want to talk about it?" Kenji-shi asked.

"I . . ." In that moment, she didn't see that angry rage-filled person who had slammed her into a table. That person was a stranger. She saw Kenji-shi, who had always been so utterly patient and kind to her, and no matter what, was always willing to listen. The anger deflated out of her. ". . . yeah."

She trudged over. She dropped down beside him and overlooked the training field that contained the sweat of so many memories. She wrapped her arms around her knees and mumbled, sarcastically, "Tah disowned me. My windship is in impound. The Grankull betrayed my kulani. His stupid tah wants him dead. Everything sucks."

"Rasia—," he paused. Then he looked at her, soft and sad and proud. "I guess it's Rasia Dragonfire now."

"*No*," she hissed. The address cut a literal wound to the gut, hitting harder than when he popped her arm from her shoulder socket. Kiba-ta would never again address her with familiarity. Because Kiba-ta was the triarch of the family, most likely all her tajihs and cousins would follow suit. She couldn't bear the formality, not tonight. "You've known me since my birthpour. Don't start with that horseshit. You'll always be Kenji-shi to me, even if I do chop off your head. That doesn't make us any less family."

"Rasia-po," he said, still careful and unsure. 'Poh' was an address that adults used with the children of their clan. Kenji-shi had always called Rasia by it due to his close relationship with Shamai-ta. Only parents continued to use that address with their adult children, but the familiar felt good to Rasia in that moment. "Listen, whatever that little shit convinced you of—"

"No, *you* listen," she snapped, swiveling and stabbing her forefinger into Kenji-shi's chest. "When I was little, you always told my favorite stories. Now, it's my turn to tell you one. And on the names of Shamaijen Kibakulani-Shiphull-Scorpionpath-Hunter Han-Dragonsbane-Dragonslayer-Heartgiver-Windbreaker, you will stay quiet until I am done."

He raised a brow, and after a moment, gave a nod for her to continue. Kenji-shi *knew* her. He had always been family until they both sort of drifted apart after tah's death. But surely, the person who had been a member of her birthing kull, who had raised her far more than any of her tajihs, who had mourned Shamai-ta as much as she had, would know she wouldn't lie about something like this.

It was the third time that day Rasia told the story of her Forging, but this time she didn't curate her words. She told him about everything: from the windship training to the sex to the assassins. She told him about the scavengers and about Timar. She told him about the dragon, smiling, because finally she had an audience who could truly appreciate the strategy of her hunt. Then she told him of everything that came after—of the farce of the re-interviews to the Council's lies. She told him everything she could think of, except for Kai's magic. Kai could tell that story himself.

"So," she said punctuating the end of her tale. "I've had a very fucking shitty night. And I don't want to kill you Kenji-shi, but I will, and now you know why. You deserve to at least know why. Whatever your relationship with Kai, that does not change the fact that despite what the Council says, kulani has earned his face. He earned his hunt. You had no right to lay a hand on him, and I demand a blood price."

Kenji-shi was measured in his silence. The wind blew, and he automatically moved to shield her from the sudden dust. It reminded her of that day long ago, watching the kulls race each other at drills, when life had been fun, easy, and simple, before Shamai-ta had died.

Kenji-shi withdrew his sword and cut a straight line, up from his palm to his forearm, parallel to a scar from a former blood price he paid a long time ago. He mopped the blood with his shroud and then handed over the bloody cloth.

Rasia clutched at that cloth, a bloody item symbolizing that sometimes words could accomplish more than rage and violence. "Promise me, on Shamai-ta's name, that you will never harm him again. If you ever do, the next blood price won't be another cut on your arm."

He let that arm bleed. It dripped a line of blood on the sand as he stared out at the training field. "Shamai-kull and I used to joke how we were fated to be friends. We often imagined how our children could be a kulani-pair. The laugh we got when you and Nico-po came out hating each other. I never thought . . ." he sucked in a breath. "The joke's on me . . . I'll never harm your kulani ever again. I promise, on Shamai Windbreaker's names." Then he smiled. "Rasia-po, he'd be so proud of you."

She tackled a great hug about his waist. He wrapped her tightly in her arms. She couldn't force the Grankull to believe her, or demand Kiba-ta change her mind, or bring Shamai-ta back to life, but she could always depend on Kenji-shi to listen. After a long night of lies and betrayals, finally, something that felt like a win.

CHAPTER THIRTY-NINE

I

Nico's declaration and toast had preemptively marked the end of the planned performances. No one could sit still anymore. They surged from their places to start the touring—the more informal phase of the namepour. The musicians picked up their instruments and plucked their strings a fast-tempo. Drums played a rolling beat through Nico's chest. The new-faces rushed from their seats, where they had previously been confined to the table, to share toasts with their family members and friends.

Dulcae Han approached Nico first. The way Nico had announced her intentions to run for the Council could be considered disrespectful, and she found herself relieved when her mentor gave her a soft and proud smile, then wrapped her up in a long hug, as if waiting a lifetime to give it to her.

"When they out-voted me to strip you of your title, I knew it wouldn't stop you. You've become such a beautiful young adult." Dulcae lifted her cup. Nico did the same, and they both performatively placed the edge to their lips. Nico suspected she had a long night of toasts ahead of her, and this was the first time she tasted alcohol. She needed to be careful and pace herself.

Dulcae leaned in and warned. "This will make some powerful people on the Council angry. Be careful."

Nico nodded in acknowledgment. Her mentor moved on, as

waves of people crashed at Nico's shores and hugged her. She smiled, names easily coming to her lips, and engaged them with enthusiasm. Even though only those who lived in the Wings could vote for her, she asked after everyone's concerns and needs. No one asked her about Kai. All thoughts of him had been forgotten in the flurry of excitement for her upcoming campaign.

Eventually, faces and toasts blurred before her. Her throat ached with all the talking, and the alcohol made her dizzy. The crowd of people had carried her far away from the center where she had started. The scribes picked up and cleaned the tables. At the flash of red hair, Nico rushed over to Jilah and asked if she could smuggle plates out to Kai and Rasia.

Once she completed that task, she surveyed her surroundings. She spotted Azan getting drunk with his gaggle of jihs. Zephyr looked trapped in a circle of admirers, and Neema batted her eyelids at any famous name she could find. Nico was pleased to see several people approach Kelin for a toast. They didn't see him as a tent kid. They didn't know his family background. They saw his face and learned his name and toasted him in congratulation like all the others they'd made their rounds of. Suri was, surprisingly, among them.

Suri shared quick words with Kelin before toasting and then walking away to join her siblings. Nico walked over to Kelin's side and stared curiously after Suri. He seemed to mirror her same expression.

"What was that about?" she asked.

"She apologized. For the Forging and how she'd treated me." Kelin took a drink from his goblet without a toast to prompt him. They were great gulps, unconcerned with getting drunk off of the Grankull's wine. "They treat me as if I'm one of them."

"Because you are."

This acceptance was why it was so hard for the Grankull to allow Kai his face. If they did, they would have to welcome him. Many have not forgotten his birth of bloodshed and curses. But Kelin had no history. He had no family name. He could make himself into anything.

"I don't know if I ever will be," Kelin said, watching the masses. From where they stood, the shadows of dancers flickered and twisted in the bonfire flames. Nico keenly felt the pounding of the drums through her feet and the pluck of an ilhan vibrate through her goblet. It was magical, but it existed on the outside, and couldn't warm the deep chill of her bones. She understood.

"It's possible to be both," she thought about the words, then amended them. "It's *okay* to be both. I think we need more people who walk the borders. The Grankull isn't perfect by any means, but there are good people on this side too."

Kelin's eyes strayed to Azan, how a jih jumped atop Azan's back, and they tumbled to the ground with the sound of guffawing laughter. Azan's tahs shook their heads at the antics and broke up the fight with pointed words. It was okay to care about people on both sides.

"A toast?" Nico offered. Their goblets clicked together, and they took a drink. "Are you staying long?"

"Long enough. I'm bound soon for the Tent parties." For those who looked close enough, 'volunteer' children in shrouds sometimes vanished with plates of food and jugs of alcohol off past the Tail. On Naming night, the Tents had their own sort of feast and their own ways of celebrating their own.

"Nicolai Councilor has a ring to it," Kelin said, amused. "Very impressed by the dramatics."

"I needed them to see me: not my tahs, or my title, or my magic. If I win a Council seat on the vote of the people, none can say I didn't earn it. It would be a title the Council can't strip away from me. I know the Council won't play fair but," she glanced at Kelin. "We don't play fair either."

He smirked in the firelight.

"What you've got in mind, Nico-kull?"

CHAPTER FORTY

—

Kai startled out of sleep at the sound of the windchimes, then the corded bells rang throughout the house. He tensed and reached for his dagger, waiting. But if someone had come to assassinate him, surely, they wouldn't have announced their arrival. He pulled from his bed and crept through the hallways. He tip-toed past the kitchen and carefully picked his way through the serving room. He grabbed his shroud from the hook.

A shadow stood in the doorway. Kai lit one of the oil lamps and shone a light on Rasia's face. A step outside the house, she went to one knee and held out a bloody strip of cloth. He looked down at the bloody thing with rising fury. He told her he didn't want Kenji dead, and now she was offering his blood like some sort of trophy?

She said quickly, "Kenji-shi is still alive. He gave the blood price willingly."

His anger dropped off a cliff. He blinked at her, perplexed. There was no world where Kenji granted Kai a willing blood price. "Was the death at least quick?"

She frowned. "No, Kai. He's alive. I told him the story of our Forging, and he believes you. He believes everything about the Lake, and the scavengers, and the dragon. Then he gave the blood price over willingly. He promised to never raise a hand to you again. You're safe, at least from him."

Kai accepted the bloodied shroud. He recognized Nico's stitching on it. All his life, he had feared Kenji at the front door. It felt odd to have that weight off of his chest. He almost didn't believe it. But this was Kenji's bloodied shroud, and Rasia wouldn't lie about something like this.

She rose back to her feet. She stood outside the doorway, uncertain of her welcome. "There will come a day when you get to choose someone else, but you're it for me. I don't want to lose you."

He squinted at her. He had been terrified to discover the destruction she might have wrought in the night. He should probably be less forgiving, but her actions spoke louder than words. He sighed. "Have you eaten?"

"Oh." She paused. "No."

He motioned her inside. He fired up the clay charcoal stove and heated the leftovers from the namepour. Once the food warmed, he returned to the serving room. Rasia ate her dinner atop the crooked adobe slab of their former table.

"I was thinking of talking to Nico tomorrow," she said. "About the possibility of joining houses, so you can touch your jihs without getting in trouble for it."

"There's only one triarch in a household. Nico isn't going to give that up."

"I know." It meant Nico would be Rasia's head of household, requiring Nico's signature to sign off on even the simplest of paperwork. Rasia's clan symbol would change. "I'm not Nico's biggest fan, but the least I can do is to make this right."

"You and Nico living under one roof are going to be a nightmare."

"This place seems big enough."

Kai doubted it, but he appreciated her optimism. Things were going to have to change if they were to somehow make this work. He told her after she finished eating, "Come. Follow."

He led her down the maze, through the secret door, into the inner chamber of bedrooms. He entered a darkened room and lit the oil lamp. It hadn't been dusted in a while, but it was far larger than Kai's small storage closet. He looked at Rasia, and said, "This is *our* room."

A smile touched the corner of her lips. All the hopes and dreams he had envisioned lay in tattered ruins, but at least he could give her this. She skipped inside and looked through all the furniture. He stripped the dusty sheets and replaced them with fresh ones. Latticed windows peeked out at the garden.

"This used to be my room," he told her. "A long time ago."

"Why did you move?"

He sat down on the replaced sheets and frowned at the memories. "I touched one of his ilhans and broke it. It was an expensive one, made of dragon-gut strings. That was the first time he beat me. Nico was too young to remember, but after that, Ava-ta moved me out of the inner chamber. Thought it would be safer. Said I could pick any room I wanted, and I chose the storage closet."

"*Why?*"

Kai shrugged. "Because I was small. And it fit me."

Rasia grew visibly upset. "Is that why breaking the ilhan woke you up from the Lake? Because you were *terrified?*"

He hadn't considered she would piece those events together. The broken ilhan had been the very first memory he remembered from his childhood.

"Kai, I . . ." Rasia's fists clenched, then unclenched. He came up behind her and pried open her fists to hold hands. Her voice broke and she turned her head into his shoulder. "I'm sorry. For everything. I'm sorry for not listening to you. I'm sorry for those kids. I'm sorry for not treating you better. I swear, I'll be better. I refuse to be another one of your scars. I refuse to be another person who hurts you. I refuse to make you small."

"I made myself small. I did that to myself." He pressed his head atop hers. At times he was so angry at her, and at other times, she was the air he breathed. He knew he had not been perfect either, but he'd try. He'd try so damn hard for her.

"I'll do better, too," he promised. "I'll hold my temper better, too. I'll say things better, too. I know I should share things with you, but sometimes it's hard. My life is shit, and I don't always like talking about it because I would much rather be here with you, in the bright spots."

"There is nothing bright about today. I don't understand. Why aren't you angry? How is it not eating you up from the inside?"

"Because I've been here before. I've failed my Forging before. I might not have my face. I might not have my names. But I have you, and that's a lot more than I had a year ago. Honestly, this day isn't the worst I've ever had."

"It's mine," Rasia said, tired. He could feel her exhaustion in the weight she leaned against him. He held her up. "Other than the day Shamai-ta died, this is my worst. It wasn't supposed to be this way. Tonight was supposed to be the best night of our lives. We were supposed to show our faces and try out for the kulls together. We were supposed to be unstoppable. They took our life away from us."

"Life is sometimes unexpected." He gathered her face in his hands and wiped at her tears. "Sometimes someone who once snatched off your shroud in the middle of the market jumps out of a bush and offers you the ride of a lifetime. Good or bad, all we can do is curve."

Kai had been curving all his life. But he admitted that he was scared—scared of the fact that terrible days might be all he had to offer her, that the life he had to give could never be enough space for either of them. Rasia deserved nothing less than everything he had to give, but what if that everything amounted to nothing more than these four walls?

He had promised to take care of her tonight, but he could barely see her through his bruised face. He couldn't give her the epic night of her dreams or preserve that rosy worldview from the day before. He couldn't even lie to her and tell her everything would be okay. But he gave her what he could.

Kai scooped her up in his arms and brought her to bed.

Their bed.

CHAPTER FORTY-ONE

I

The music changed. Dances slowed. Families picked up sleepy children and carried them home. The elders shuffled away, while the new-faces, the revelers, and the dawn long-haulers stayed. All remnants of the feast: the tables, the dishware, and the food had been cleared and replaced with jugs of alcohol rotating through the crowd. This was the moment her tahs would bring Nico home, and even though she'd never witnessed the darkest part of the night, she knew what would happened next.

The bodika.

Most people said that the bodika was truly the moment they felt a part of the Grankull. It was an experience that connected and looped you into the webbing of adulthood.

Touches lingered. Dancers moved closer. Eyes began to circle Nico with hunger and heat. Already, some were growing bold enough to approach her. The handsome ones. The beautiful. The most accomplished. Those proud and arrogant enough to hope She would choose them first.

Across the field, she locked eyes with Suri's dark ones. She dismissed the more experienced and the politically connected and stopped before the face she had once thought her best friend.

Everyone deserved a second chance.

Nico pressed her mouth to Suri's lips, and for the first time in her life, allowed herself to really want. She kissed the pretty mounds of Suri's breasts, kissed the slim dimple at her hips, and kissed her to the ground. Suri's delicate limbs opened, and Nico consumed her.

A touch to Nico's hip. Larger. Rougher. She turned to find a handsome face searching for permission. She kissed him in answer. Suri rose, flushed against her, to press Nico between the two bodies. They both doted on her. One by one, bodies joined together, blossoming into a flower made of flesh and writhing limbs.

Nico lost herself in the sweat, the saliva, and the drip between legs. She was connected to everyone all at once. She felt their pleasure flood through her. Moans and breathy groans tensed through her muscles. Her body tightened at the rising sensation, higher and higher, until she overflowed.

A thick fog burst from her lungs.

She shivered, pulsing and throbbing, as she lay in a screen of white. She couldn't see anything through the magic-dense fog, except for the fact that the partners she began with, weren't the partners she ended with. The lack of visibility did little to deter the mood. If anything, the groping turned more ethereal and carnal.

Nico slipped away into the dark.

Nico wobbled a little. It had hurt more than she had anticipated. During the health exam, the healers had warned her to prepare herself in the days leading up to the event, but she had been so busy she had forgotten. She probably should have been drunker as well, but she couldn't afford to completely compromise her defenses. When she reached the Tail, she forced the pain away to some distant shore where she used to place broken bones and bruises under Ava-ta's tutelage.

Kelin and Zephyr waited under torchlight at the border of the Tents. The moment they spotted her, they burst out laughing.

"What? What's wrong?" she asked.

"The always immaculate Nicolai looks utterly and obviously *fucked*," Kelin teased. "Never thought I'd see the day. Is the bodika all that they say it is?" He had left before it started, nor had he cared much to stay.

"It was certainly interesting," she said of the drunken orgy. She had enjoyed it, or at least what she had experienced during the short time she was there. She had enjoyed how every touch and sensation had been amplified by her magic. She had also enjoyed the connection. It served as a reminder that the Grankull was more than just an institution. At its core, it was a group of people with very human desires to lose themselves in something greater. She had been a raindrop in an ocean, and she craved to be submerged again. She had no idea what that meant for her kinks and sexual preferences, but she'd muse on it some other time.

"No one saw you leave?" Zephyr confirmed.

"No. I made sure they didn't," she said. She washed through her hair and between her legs. It was a quick rinse, but it would have to do for now. She still had a long night ahead of her.

Zephyr handed her some clothes. It was a simple caftan and shroud, the typical uniform of a kuller up to no good in the Tents. They left once she was dressed and ready.

The Tents overflowed with a rowdy pouring. Zephyr and Kelin led the way through the sounds of music and boisterous songs. The banished, the forgotten, and the outcast feasted on deftly stolen plates and pilfered alcohol. As she walked past, Nico filled bowls set out for the rain.

At the very center of the festivities, a tent had been erected only for this night. Zephyr parted the tent flaps. Nico stepped inside and greeted the sight of four individuals glaring at each other from a circle of chairs. They looked a vibration away from drawing their weapons.

The Jackal, the Vulture, the Heron, and the Scorpion.

The Jackal analyzed her behind the spectacle of his glasses. The Vulture, whom rumor had it no one had ever seen their face, sat in a black shroud that shielded everything but deep eyes. The Heron, elected as representative for this meeting, wore a feathered veil to cover their face so effectively that Nico couldn't identify this Heron among those she had met. Then there was the Scorpion Han, Zara-shi.

It was the first time all four Tent Hans had gathered in one location. The infamous gang leaders all had some sort of blood feud, vendetta, or overlapping business interests with the rest that could rip everything apart. It was a momentous occasion in the history of the Tents.

Zara-shi had stood when Nico entered the tent. Even though she had known Nico since she was a budchild, Zara-shi addressed her with seriousness and gravitas. "We, the Tent Hans, demand to know why you have called us all here tonight?"

Nico sat in the empty chair prepared for her, rounding the sharp edges of the square into a circle. Zephyr and Kelin stood at each of her shoulders.

"As you all know, the Grankull was a tie vote away from another purge. The dragon is dead, but one bad year, or one poor hunting season, and that's all the justification they will need to try again. The threat of the purge will never be gone, and I refuse to allow the fates of my family, of which I consider some of you, to remain in the hands of this current Council. If we fail to stop them, our lives and the lives of those protected by our campfires are at risk. They might have stripped me of my title, but I am a dragon at heart, and I will not be intimidated. I have declared my intention to run for the Council seat of the Wings, but one seat won't be enough. We need to do whatever it takes to flip the whole damn thing. I have called you all here tonight to talk of war."

Zara-shi's smile stretched the scars on her face.

"Welcome to our fire, Ohan."

CHAPTER FORTY-TWO

O

Rasia either woke really early in the morning, or she never slept at all. She didn't know. She lay listening to the wheezing underneath her. She had her hand sprawled atop Kai's chest, to make sure it kept rising. Back in her old bedroom at the top of the spire, first drum rolled through the Grankull like thunder, but this far down it sounded like a distant storm due to blow over somewhere else. Nine times. It drummed nine times throughout the day telling people what to do and when to do it. Ever since Shamai-ta died, the drums had begun rolling headaches through her head. Now, they pounded worse than nightmares.

"Did you sleep?" Kai shifted and peeked his eyes through the black and blue bruises. He struggled to open his left eye all of the way. The bruises that squeezed around his windpipe had deepened in the night, speckling his neck over the slight scars the scavenger choker had left behind. Kai had a lot of scars when Rasia met his body for the first time, but they've only seemed to have multiplied since. She hadn't thought they were a warning of things to come but she looked at him now, and understood without a doubt, that he'd die with a lot more yet. The truth of that revelation, one of which he'd known far longer than her, reflected in his one good squinty eye.

Many considered the Desert cruel, but at least she was fair.

The Desert often killed the unprepared and the foolish. But here, the Grankull dared to pick and choose and eat away at flesh until there was nothing left but bones.

"I don't know," she answered. She turned away, overwhelmed, and sat up to face the latticed wall that looked out to the garden at the center of the home. The inner chamber, as Kai called it, existed like a diamond with the garden in the middle. Sunbirds and warblers flitted among the flowering boughs and evory bird-baths, squawking endlessly.

"How do you do it?" she asked. "How do you wake up every day to the Grankull's drum? How do you get out of bed, and exist in this . . . litter box of shit?"

"Sometimes, I don't," he confessed. He curled around and pressed his face to Rasia's thigh. Unconsciously, she combed her hand through his hair, and she paused at a dried bloody mat on his scalp. "And then sometimes, Rae is hungry, and someone's got to make breakfast."

She understood that sort of motivation. Sometimes, there was a pair of gonda vibrating down on you and there was nothing to do but to do.

"Where is the little grubworm?"

"Probably at tajih's place. But I've got to clean the serving room before anyone can pick them up." His voice twisted dark as he said, "The last thing we need is Rae hurting themselves and the Council decrying neglect of their only heir. I fear they might use Rae's new title to justify taking them away."

"Hmm," she said, thinking on it. She wanted nothing more than to scoop Kai onto the windship and sail as far away as possible, but that wasn't an option. She had learned the hard way that despite carrying his name, he didn't belong to her, not wholly. Parts of him belonged to Nico, and Rae, and possibly even his shit of a tah. Parts of him belonged to his stubbornness, his pride, and an empathy for people he shared with Nico. Kai was not breaking and running. Which meant there was only one thing to do: you face the gonda.

"Come on, then. Let's get to it," she said, gently pushing at him and stretching to her feet. Her eyes burned a little in exhaustion, but she'd be fine if she kept moving. She glanced down at Kai who hadn't moved a vibration, still blinking owlishly at her. "We should change your bandages first."

He offered out a lazy arm, and he winced when she pulled at him. She placed a hand on his back to support him through the struggle of sitting up. She grabbed the frayed edges of his sleep robe, and carefully rolled it up and off him. The rest of him didn't look much better than his face. His stitches had held through the night where Kenji-shi had ripped a knife halfway up his side. It'll no doubt form a crossroads with the older one on his stomach. New bruises from the kicks and punches of the angry mob revealed injuries she hadn't seen yesterday. There were also burns on his arms. She had no idea where those came from.

She pursed her lips. "Maybe you should rest today."

"There's too much to do."

It was funny, how she used to think Kai the weakest, most easily breakable person she had ever met.

How wrong she was.

She checked the stitches, redressed the bandages, and cleaned the bloody mats from his hair. There were scars, new and old, she hadn't noticed before along his scalp.

"This place is going to kill you." The words fell from her lips, unthinking. He stiffened under her fingers.

"It hasn't managed to, yet."

"Because it underestimates you." She slammed the bloody linens to the ground. "Kiba-ta will underestimate you too, at first, but then she won't. We should be halfway to the saltpans by now."

"No. We know from the Forging that Kibari Oshield's reach extends all the way to the scavengers. We'll be hunted for the rest of our lives. At least here, we have support. We have Ysai-ji and Nico-ji."

She scoffed at that. "Your jih has lost her title, and Ysai-ji will be transferred to a new post soon enough. Then you'll have a ready and willing assassin right at your fucking door."

"You underestimate Nico-ji."

"She's not capable of protecting you."

"Before you revealed the truth yesterday, any of the kids could have accidentally gotten their story wrong. Exposure was always a risk. Jih got us through last night losing only my face and her title, but she still saved those kids. It could have easily gone the other way. Very few formulate and win arguments against the Council. She's formidable, in a different way than you are, but it would be a mistake to abandon that. Out in the Desert, we'll be on our own, but a kull is stronger together."

"You're willing to bet your life on that?"

"Yes."

Rasia tossed a dismissive hand as she turned on her heels. She reached down to put on the armor she had stripped off last night. She didn't trust Kai's safety to anyone but her own dragonsteel. Armed and ready to fight anything that might come their way, she moved toward the door.

He caught her by the wrist. He tugged at her, and Rasia stood, resistant, unmoving. He came behind her to wrap his arms about her waist and set his head on her shoulders. He kissed two words onto her neck, "Trust me."

Despite the armor, the hidden knives, and her dual-blades—she felt exposed, vulnerable, legs stretched wide-open, with Kai hovering above her asking permission to take the lead. She had learned to trust him with her body, but outside of sex, she was the one who drove forward with the decisions, with he often the one following after her.

But there was no Han in a kulani, Shamai-ta had told her once. After all, it was the kulls who assign themselves clear-cut roles that struggle the most. When shit hits the hull, you've got to know how to switch.

Rasia nodded, conceding. She wove her hand in his, and they walked down the hall together.

They found the serving room as much a mess as they had left it. Before she could decide on where to start, the windchime bells rang throughout the house. Kai stilled, and Rasia unsheathed her swords. It could be Ysai, arriving at his post early before second drum, but she didn't want to take any chances.

She stalked toward the shroud room, almost itching to find someone whose head she could chop off. She sneered, disappointed, to find Kenji-shi at the door. He glanced at her blades. "Expecting trouble?"

"Depends on you."

"I came to grab some clothes."

"Yeah. Sure. Whatever," she said, and bitterly sheathed her swords. She returned to the serving room and blinked to find Kai gone. Kenji-shi continued to the back of the house, and Kai peeked his head out of the kitchen a vibration later with a shroud wrapped around his face.

He had his shroud on, too, last night. Too much had been going on for it to properly click in her head, but it finally did that morning. Kai wore his shroud when Kenji-shi was in the house. No one should have to wear a shroud in their own house.

Rasia immediately regretted inviting Kenji-shi in without asking Kai first. "I can kick him back out."

He shrugged. "What is he doing here?"

"Said he came to pick up some clothes. You should talk to him. Make him see what he did to you."

She drew forward to reach for his shroud. Kai scrambled back into the doorframe, clutching at the linen, an instinctive reaction, if any. Rasia's hand stilled in the air.

He was scared.

Of Kenji.

And there was no blood price or dragon in the world that could mend that.

Her hand dropped. Kai grew conscious of what he had done and bowed his head in shame. His hands shook removing the shroud, until she stilled them. Then she adjusted the hastily thrown on linen to better cover his face. The shroud, to Rasia, had always been a cage. She understood now that for Kai, it was a shield.

His eyes searched hers, questioning.

"You should talk to him," she said. "When you're ready. I certainly would have a difficult time forgiving the things he's done, but he is a person that can . . . curve." She kissed him atop the shroud. "And so can I."

CHAPTER FORTY-THREE

1

"That was . . . less than what I expected," Nico admitted mournfully. The meeting with the Tent Hans had lasted for drums, going so long that the sun pushed at the horizon, and yet, barely any decisions had been made or plans established.

Walking next to her, Zephyr smiled, amused. "No one killed each other. It went better than expected. It's going to take time, Nico-kull, to put aside greed and old grievances."

"I'm concerned about the Jackal Han. He's . . . psychotic and cruel."

"We'll keep our faces clean," he promised. "They all have their eccentricities, but they also understand if we don't do anything, the Grankull will wipe us all out. The Jackal was a kid during the last purge. He was there. He, more than anyone, knows how important this is."

"I hope I'm doing the right thing." So many Ohans thought they were doing the right thing, only for their actions to lead to disaster. She had a whole host of memories she could access in the Heart Chamber, and she would need them all to navigate this political situation.

When they passed the checkpoint and reached the border between the Grankull and the Tents, it took Zephyr a moment to mentally traverse it. He stepped over the border as if a physical line marked the sand. As they walked through the streets of the Grankull, Nico couldn't help but look over her shoulder at Zephyr, pleased by his presence. So many times, she had to leave him behind. His nearness raised the hairs on her arms as they walked.

"This is nice," he admitted. "To be able to walk you home, instead of saying goodbye at the border. I've always had to wait until you came to me. Now, I don't have to be afraid I'll never see you again."

"I was always coming back."

"You are the magicborn heir with all of the friends. I never really understood why you kept risking the Tents to come see me and the family, especially after Kenji-shi stopped."

"You've always allowed me to be myself," she said.

Out of all her friends, out of all her admirers and followers, Zephyr had always understood her the most. They'd both been raised between two worlds, but most of all, they have seen the worst of both and still wanted to save it.

They walked together through the Grankull streets. They passed several people unconscious on the road and curled against buildings, who couldn't quite make it all the way from the namepour. The sentries would come through and sweep them home soon.

The back of her hand tapped the back of his. She flushed at the public touch, which held completely new meaning now that they were adults. Luckily, Zephyr didn't notice as he was too busy studying the Grankull in the morning light.

"I didn't really get the chance to take in all the sights when I came earlier," he said and paused a moment to stare at the tall spires of the Heart Temple. She took him through the temple gardens where the flowers curled awake. They strolled past the jasmines and chrysanthemums, and the roses and anemones. Green cyperus fanned shade over the ponds and blue lotuses. The persea trees rustled greetings from the wind. Zephyr marveled at the rainbows blossoming along their path. "I didn't think all this color could exist in the Desert."

"You haven't seen anything yet. I'd like to show you the wingfields and the orchards of the lakejaw. But in my opinion, the wingfields are the best place in the entire Grankull."

"I look forward to it," he said, smiling, which deepened his dimples into wells. A yellow poinciana framed his mighty shoulders like the flowers at the border of murals. One of the pronged layered flowers floated into his hair. She had always imagined showing him the beauty of the Grankull when they came of age, but now that they were here, none of these flowers compared to the tones of his skin or the color of his eyes.

"Kiss me," Nico said.

He thumbed her chin like the fragile petals of a flower. Her heart thrummed fast and rapid like a hummingbird as he leaned forward. Nico met him halfway, and their meeting was sweet, full of softness and care. They kissed under the poinciana.

She brushed the flower out of his hair after they separated. "Thank you. For standing with me and supporting me last night."

"Always."

She offered her hand, and he didn't hesitate to take it. They walked hand-in-hand through the rest of the garden. She guided him toward the veranda of her house. She flicked her hand and casually watered the sage and lavender in clay pots on the shelves as they passed. Zephyr paused at the doorway. He took a curious peek inside the shroud room.

"You're free to come inside."

"Shouldn't I have a bottle of alcohol or something?" he asked. He stepped inside the shroud room and noticed the shoes in the wall cubbies. He slipped off his to join hers.

"You can bring some next time," she said. Most often, guests were entertained outside on the veranda. The inside of the house belonged to the domain of the family. In the coming days, Zephyr would recognize how rare of an opportunity this was.

She closed the palm wood door behind him. They were swallowed in darkness but for the peeks of light through the cracks. Their bodies pressed close in the small room, and she licked her lips where the taste of him still lingered.

She grabbed his hand and led him through the open doorway into the serving room. An embarrassed flush crossed her cheeks at the sight of the wreckage that greeted her. The broken clay table lay in pieces. The cracked peel hung by a splinter. Kai's broken ilhan lay shattered.

"Is he okay?"

"Yeah. Rasia got here in time." She tilted her head to focus on Kai's location. She was surprised to sense him in his old bedroom in the inner chamber, with Rasia. She had been trying to convince him to move back there for years.

"I could help you clean this up."

"It's not your mess to clean," she said. "Come. There's something I've always wanted to show you."

Nico led Zephyr through the maze, past the lounging rooms, and into the library. Walls of scrolls surrounded a low wooden desk atop an intricate textile carpet.

"These are all the scrolls and writings the Temple deemed too controversial to add to the public library," she said, and she brushed her hand over the documents. She remembered reading one and racing across the Grankull into the Tents to tell Zephyr of all her new discoveries. This was where it all began, where she began to think she could make a difference. "I'm going to change the world. I'm going to build it with enough space for you, Kai, the Tents, and even the scavengers. Everyone deserves to eat."

Zephyr gave her a smile so proud it imbued her with the strength to keep going. He asked, "Then what are we waiting for?"

They got to work.

They pulled blank scrolls and maps from the slat shelves. Zephyr plotted out a tangle of relationships between the Tent Hans, archiving everything he knew. Nico spread a map of the Wings across the low table. She wrote the names of families above their homes, identified the empty ones, the names of those she didn't know, and those she needed to talk to in the coming days.

"I doubt the Council is going to let you run unopposed. Do you have an idea who they might run against you?" he asked.

She rattled a few potential names in her head but paused at the sudden soft smile on his face. He reached out and wiped his thumb across an ink stain on her cheek. "I love you."

She tilted her head, unfamiliar with the foreign word. "Love? What is that?"

He bit the inside of his cheek and said after a moment of consideration. "Here, it's more of an action instead of a word, more of a thing to do than something to say. It's stronger than a flame, but less than a kulani."

Nico thought she understood. She smiled and nodded. "I love you too, Zephyr."

÷

Nico woke to the awareness of something wrong. She swatted at a scroll stuck to her cheek. She looked around the library where she and Zephyr had apparently fallen asleep. She didn't think that it was Zephyr's rumbling snores that had set off her alarms. She focused on her magic, and on the bodies of those in the house. It took her an embarrassingly long time to figure out the abnormal, because as of yesterday, it would have been normal otherwise.

Kenji-ta was in the house.

Nico stomped out of the library and toward her parent's room. She found Kenji-ta sitting on his knees atop the hand-woven rug, curtained by soft amber light, almost swallowed by the grand vastness of the Ohan's bedroom. He held an empty bag clutched in his hands and stared out vacantly, tracing memories along the arches and mosaics. Her tah posed annoyingly beautiful like some intricately carved evory statue, stuck in stillness and never moving forward. But what caught her attention the most was the fresh wound sliced down his inner arm leaking a narrow slit of blood into a bandage, a direct parallel to the older blood price he had worn all of her life.

"You paid a blood price?" she demanded.

The question jolted tah into awareness. He blinked at her, registered her words, and then looked down at the blood price in question. "Rasia-po talked to me last night. Seemed the least of what I owed."

"*Rasia?*" Nico spat. "It took Rasia for you to finally listen?! I've been telling you the truth for years!"

"I thought you were as blinded as kulani and-"

"And you were wrong! I kicked you out of this house, and you aren't welcome anymore! Get out!"

"I know," Kenji-ta said. "I came for some clothes."

"You could have borrowed them from your twin." Not identical. Tajih was slighter than tah, but close enough. Nico knew Kenji-ta well enough to know he was here for something more. She also knew him well enough to know that he might not know why he was here. He did that more often: wandered aimlessly until someone gave him purpose. She used to think being patient with him was best, but she didn't care to wait around for him to get his bearings anymore.

"Pack," Nico spat out. "Then I want you out."

Resigned, he began grabbing his clothes. He stuffed his bag with several outfits and loinclothes from the laundry baskets. He opened the armoire, handles of smoothed dragon-glass, to reveal her parent's finest clothes: the hand-stitched, beaded, high-thread count, brightly dyed fabric for events and pourings. Ava-ta didn't often like dressing up, but she took joy in flaunting her kulani to the Grankull when the occasion presented itself. Sometimes, it seemed tah had spent too much time being admired that he didn't know how to be anything but a memorial to her memory. Kenji-ta flinched at the sight of the clothes and closed the dresser doors. He reached for the half-empty bag, filled with the few meager outfits he had chosen, and crossed it diagonally around his shoulders.

Nico vaulted over and flung the doors of the armoire wide. She snatched at all his finest shirts and threw them at tah her in anger. It hurt, to know how he used to fill these walls with joy, laughter, and light, but it was something Kai had never known, and Rae given a pale imitation.

"You will never be the parent we deserve until you finally let go of Ava-ta's ghosts! These are just things. They are not pieces of her. You are so careful to leave everything intact, so careful to honor her memory, that you've completely disregarded her true legacy. Ava-ta gave her life because she believed in Kai. The best way to honor her was to do the same, and yet you dare put your hands on him! By harming him, you are the one who treated her death as meaningless, and I will never forgive you for it!"

"I'm sorry." He bowed his head, all pathetic and mournful, but she refused to pity him.

"That's not enough! Not anymore."

"I'll do right this time. I'll make it up to you, I promise. I'll be the parent that you deserve."

"*No*! I demand that you be the parent that all your children deserve! Blowing in once a season is not enough. You used to sing me to sleep, and now it is Kai who sings to Rae lullabies. You used to comfort me when I got hurt, and now Rae runs to Kai for help. You knew how I liked my food cooked, but now you can't get Rae to eat their vegetables. I wish Rae could know you for the tah you used to be, but it is Kai who has had to step into your absence. You have condemned him as worthless for too long while he raises *your* child. You have failed all of us!"

"Tell me what to do," he pleaded.

"You look Kai in the face and apologize for the terror and abuse you have inflicted on him for all of these years. You retire from the kulls and be here for your ten year-till child who has thus far been raised by their siblings. You will—*never*—touch another bottle of alcohol again. And then maybe, I'll consider forgiving you. But I can't give you purpose Kenji-ta. You've got to find that yourself. Ava-ta would never, even in a world without her, ever want you to stop singing. It's time to burn your muse and move on."

"Okay." He nodded. "Okay."

"And with all of that said, I am not the one who determines if you come home. That will be Kai. Only he determines when you return, because this is his home too, and as long as he feels unsafe in your presence, you are unwelcomed here." She glared at the piles of clothes she had tossed to the ground. "I suggest you take all of it."

Water stains spread along the walls as she stormed from the room. Turning a corner, she took a moment to calm and thin the fog wafting through the hallways. She hadn't expected to deal with her tah first thing in the morning, and it still hurt, after all this time, to confront his shadows. He would never be who he used to be.

She returned to the library to make sure Zephyr didn't get himself lost in the maze. She found him awake, peering sleepily at the papers and lazily organizing them into stacks. He looked up when she entered. "Are you okay?"

"It's nothing." He obviously didn't buy it. He moved the papers aside and cleared a space for her to collapse down at the table. "Kenji-ta is here. He's packing his clothes. But you know what's crazy? You'd think I'd be angry at him for what he's done to Kai, and I am, I am so *pissed*, but I am also furious that after everything, after all of these years, he finally listens to *Rasia*! I try to be the bigger person, but I despise her. *So much*."

"Sometimes, it takes hearing from someone outside a situation to see it differently," he said, slow and considering. "Rasia does have a way of tossing the shroud around."

She huffed and rubbed at her forehead.

"I wish I had the time to be angry, but I don't. I need her," Nico spat out sourly. "I need to tell her my plans, and I need her to tear them apart and rip them up and show me the weak spots and what I'm missing. She sees things that I don't, and that's what I need the most right now. If I learned anything from last night with the Tent Hans, is that you don't need to like someone to be allies."

"As long as we keep our face clean," he agreed. "A ship goes nowhere if the oars are steering different directions."

Nico didn't really want to think about Rasia right now. She'd deal with that wildfire later. She brushed back the frayed strands of her hair, the ones that popped up if she didn't brush her hair back tightly enough. She was sweaty, sticky, and musty, and what she really wanted right now was to be fresh and clean.

She glanced at Zephyr, considering. "Join me in the bath?"

"You have a bath?"

Amazement shrouded his face when she showed him the Ohan's personal bath. He had been all over the world, but it was the bones of the Grankull that seemed to amaze him the most. He jumped when the mural shifted with magic, analyzed the construction of the tiles, and studied how the pumps drew water directly from the underground cisterns.

Nico slipped off the shift she had been wearing since the tents. Zephyr undressed, and she didn't look away this time. He was as solid and vast as Suri was narrow and thin. He was coiled chest hair, muscled thighs, and gentle hands.

"I want you," she declared. "But do you mind if we make this fast? I've got things to do."

He only smiled at her, endlessly amused. Those dimples really could melt anyone. "No problem."

He hefted her up in his arms. She wrapped her long legs about his waist, and he carried her into the water. A weight had shifted the scales. There was a balance that hadn't existed before. So many times, she had to leave him at the border, but now he could come and go as he pleased through her life. No more waiting on her. No more did all the power rest in her hands. He could choose, and so could she. Nico didn't know if she'd ultimately choose him in the end, but she had plenty of years to figure it out.

She kissed him once more again.

CHAPTER FORTY-FOUR

I

The smell of bread wafted through the hallways. Nico heard laughter around the corner and peeked her head into the kitchen. Black from previous cook fires stained the brick around the clay oven bulging from the kitchen wall. Rounds of flatcakes cooled atop the counter. She watched as Kai used the broken peel to slide a clay pot to the open edge of the oven and stirred at the millet porridge. He looked over his shoulder at Rasia checking out his ass, and then at the half-sliced melon she leaned on.

"How is it you can take down a gonda faster than you chop a melon?"

"I keep getting distracted!" she threw her hands up laughing.

"Get over here and carry this," he whipped a linen towel at her legs, before tossing it over at her.

"You're so bossy when you're cooking." She winked as she caught the towel and threw it over her shoulder.

Kai held his side as he stepped back. She rubbed a hand over his shroud, before bending over toward the oven. Nico didn't know if Kai wore his shroud because Kenji-ta was in the house or because he wanted to hide the extent of his injuries, but she could clearly see a teasing playfulness crinkled at the corner of his eyes. Sometimes, Nico hated Rasia. And sometimes, Rasia could put an expression on Kai's face Nico hadn't seen in years.

Rasia genuinely made him happy.

Rasia wiggled her hips as she leaned forward, then hefted the pot up and placed it atop the counter. Kai wrapped arms around her, and she blatantly smelled at the frond-smoke on his skin. She asked, "You know what stirring porridge sounds like?"

"I can't think of anything in particular," he hummed, and pushed her against the counter. He drummed his fingers up her thighs and then reached to the counter above for the honey jar. She laughed against his skin, and before he could pull away, locked her legs around his waist. She smiled mischievously, and Kai narrowed his eyes before leaning forward and diving away from her angled lips to drag an open mouth down her chest, belly, and then, popped free under her legs and spun effortlessly to mix the honey into the porridge.

"You're such a fucking tease."

He stirred the porridge slowly with a knowing smirk. Then he tilted his head, acknowledging Nico at the door. "Breakfast is almost ready."

Rasia glanced over, and a wicked grin spread across her face at the sight of Zephyr coming up behind Nico in the doorway. Rasia started a slow clap. "Look who finally got some dick!"

Nico's face heated at the embarrassment and shot back, "Look who can finally get some legally."

Rasia smiled cheekily. "Well pointed, Nico-ji."

Nico narrowed her eyes. Rasia might be in a courtship with Kai, but that did not give Rasia the audacity to address her as a sibling. "Absolutely not."

Rasia glanced over at Kai, who had immediately dropped what he was doing. "Are you going to tell her, or am I?"

"*You couldn't wait?*" he hissed at her.

"What would have been a better time? Over breakfast? When she overhears everyone talking about it all over the Grankull?"

"What are you talking about?" Nico demanded. What now? What else could Rasia have possibly done?

"Chop that melon," Kai said, pointing at Rasia before grabbing Nico by the hand, and pulling her past Zephyr into the maze of hallways. Nico quickly overtook him and had to slow while Kai limped through his injuries.

From the kitchen, they overheard Rasia ask Zephyr, "If her magic is water is she always wet down there?"

"Shut up, Rasia," Zephyr said immediately.

"Does it magic when *she* orgasms?"

"Do *you* want to fuck her?"

"Eww. No. Out of curiosity though . . ."

Kai dropped his head in his hands as they walked further out of earshot. He dragged his hands down his face and flung himself against the wall. Whatever he had to say, Nico wasn't going to like it. She squinted at him as he struggled to spit out whatever was the scandal. She knew Rasia had been disowned, and it wasn't a coincidence Kai moved back to his old room.

"You asked her to move in?" she asked, guessing at it.

If anything, his face grew paler. She tried to keep her cool. She reminded herself that it was a good thing Kai was telling her the truth and not keeping secrets. She promised, "Whatever it is. I am listening. I can handle it."

He stared out at her with owlish eyes, then he said in a rapid rush, "Yesterday, when Rasia signed her name in the Book of Names, she also signed mine."

"WHAT?!" A dry thunder boomed over the Grankull. She couldn't get any words out. Who signed someone else's name during the Naming Ceremony? *Who did that?!*

"Did you two plan this?" she asked, horrified.

"Of course not! This was all Rasia."

"So what? She's your kulani now? And there's nothing you can do about it? Absolutely not! There must be some sort of precedence we can use to fight this."

"I've already talked with Jilah-shi about it. Apparently, I can choose to sign someone else when I come of age, but I'm it for Rasia. It's done. Kulani is the only name we get to choose—and you know how historically binding that is. Even the Council can't do anything about it. Also . . . that move-in thing, too."

She shook her head. She doesn't understand how one person

can be so absolutely insane. This meant Nico was stuck with Rasia—*stuck* with her. *Forever.*

"How are you okay with this?" Nico demanded. "How can you possibly forgive her after everything she has done?"

Kai seemed to know this question was coming, for he had an answer already thought out. "No one should be defined by their worst day, and yesterday was tough for everyone. Her actions stole something from you, and I understand if that's difficult to forgive. But on normal days, she slays dragons, and on her best, she lets them live. She's not perfect. She's an asshole. Most of the time she doesn't mean it, and sometimes she does. Yesterday, something was stolen from her, too. She's hurting, too. I would like your blessing for her to stay."

Here Nico was forgiving Rasia again. If you forgave someone too many times, did that mean you condone their actions or even worse, perpetuate them? Where was the line between forgiveness and her principles? She closed her eyes and knew she had to chunk this hatred out of her, if not for Rasia, but for herself.

"She can stay."

"Thank you." Kai fled back toward the kitchen. Nico remained there, pensive, against the wall.

"Shamai-kull would wring her neck."

Nico looked up at where Kenji-ta leaned against the corner of the hallway.

"You heard everything?" she asked.

"I heard the thunder and came running. Thought you were in trouble." Tah rubbed at his neck where the strap of his bag dug into his shoulder. Guilt wore into the lines of his face. He was yet another person where the lines of forgiveness and principles blurred.

No one should be defined by their worst day. What did it mean when you add up all the good and the bad? What did that equal?

She stared at the far wall with a question she never had the courage to ask her tah before. They'd never acknowledged it, none of her tahs, but she faced it every day in a dragon glass mirror.

"After Kai was born, you and Ava-ta separated. How did you forgive her when you learned she was seeded with me?"

The silence in the hallway felt suffocating. Her tah stared at that scar of an older blood price.

"I didn't know you knew that," he finally said. "I guess we ultimately forgave each other for you. Logically, I understood why kulani did it. She needed an heir and hoped it would shift the Council's attention from . . . *Kai*," he said, stumbling over the name. "And I was . . . unavailable. But I was angry about it for a long time when I learned what she did. It hurt to know you wouldn't be my seed, but I was her kulani, and you were my child all the same. Kids don't remember much when they're young, so you wouldn't remember how difficult those years of reconciliation had been. All you know are the good parts. After we both decided to make it work, it had been a difficult, challenging, and long road to walk, but it had been worth it in the end. We came out stronger for it. And I'll do it all again, walk that road all over again until you forgive me. You have always been the best days of my life."

She squeezed her eyes shut. She could not imagine who she'd be without Kenji-ta. She might not look like him, but she had his bones all the same.

Nico needed to expel all this messy guilt and hatred to breathe again. But unlike Rasia, which had been akin to chucking her feelings out with the dirty bath water, this felt like a carving. A slicing of malignant growth from her organs. Sometimes forgiveness was easy, and sometimes it was a long, winding road. Sometimes it was a journey of years to reach one moment in time.

"I forgive you," Nico croaked out. "But I don't trust you. You've got to earn that back."

He nodded. He stepped aside and then paused. "You look like you have your hands full here. Rae is at jih's place? I could watch them if you are too busy today."

With all that was going on, she knew she needed to take him up on the offer. "Okay."

He approached her, and after a moment of consideration, leaned down to place a kiss to her forehead. "I understand I missed a pretty good speech last night. Proud of you, butterfly."

Her throat swelled at the endearment. She watched him disappear down the hall to the roof exit.

She took a moment to gather herself and then returned to the kitchen where Zephyr shared her previously traumatized expression. Apparently, Rasia had told him about the signing while Nico and Kai were in the hallway. There was nothing to be done for it now, especially if Kai didn't want to fight it.

When she walked into the serving room, she found the chaos from the previous night had all been cleared away. Ysai sat cross-legged on the floor, almost comically bent over, as he rewove a broken basket. Kai squeezed past her from the kitchen to usher plates of food outside to the veranda.

"You cleaned all this up?" she asked.

"Both Rasia and Ysai-ji honestly," Kai said. "Rasia didn't want me popping my stitches, so I did the easy stuff. They moved the broken pieces of the serving table to the side of the house and brought down the table from the roof. I hope you don't mind. I wanted to clean up the room before we picked up Rae."

Nico grabbed the extra guest mats from the serving room credenza. "It was a good idea. I wished you had waited for me to help."

"You were occupied." He shrugged and then stepped out of the house.

Nico glanced at Ysai, who, even sitting down, looked of a height. "You know, this isn't in your job description. You don't have to do this."

"I know," He chirped. She followed the effortless weave of his fingers, amazed by their dexterity. "I don't mind. I like fixing things. Something a lot of people don't know about Shamai-ta is that he was really good with his hands. He enjoyed building things—like the windship and other smaller projects around the house. I got the touch of it from him," he paused, "Rasia got all the ingenuity *and* lack of manners. She tells me she's staying here now, but if you ever get tired of her, feel free to throw her in my direction."

"I most certainly will."

Those siblings couldn't be any more different from one another. She shook her head as she joined Kai outside. She and Kai cleaned and set up the veranda table. It'd be the first time they'd eaten outside since Ava-ta's death. She watched as he maneuvered awkwardly to avoid aggravating his injuries. "Are you okay?"

"Yeah. Most of the damage is to my face. It's not pretty, but I'll recover."

The sight of a distant figure came down the road. Very few people rounded the pathway around the temple unless specifically coming to visit them. Suri gradually came into view with a bottle of date wine in her hands. Nico walked out to meet her.

"Suri," then Nico corrected herself. They weren't children anymore. You couldn't go around speaking an adult's name without an address if not intimately acquainted. "Suriya Longbow," she greeted.

"You disappeared last night," Suri said, then her gaze shifted over Nico's shoulder at Zephyr and Ysai talking as they stepped out the front doorway.

"I needed a diversion," she said, unapologetic.

"Whatever you're planning, I want to help," Suri said. "You were right. The Council is corrupt, and so is my tah. She did it. She and Kibari Oshield tried to kill you even knowing it could risk the Forging of the other children. She admitted she had placed me on your team to waylay suspicion. She wanted me to come over this morning and spy on what you were up to. I told her to politely shove her scalpel up her ass." Her eyes widened, scared. "I think I'm disowned."

Without reservation, Nico wrapped her arms around Suri and gathered her up in a hug. Suri immediately broke into hiccupping sobs. "I want to be better than her. I want to be better than my family. Maybe I can't help you change the world, but I can at least change myself. I hope that's enough."

"Suri-kull," Nico said. "The world changes one person at a time. You are always enough."

⁖

Suri pulled her shroud from around her neck and wrapped it around the bottle of date wine she carried. She shuffled toward Zephyr and held out the bottle of alcohol to him. "I am sorry, Zephyrus Dragonblood."

"Thank you, Suriya Longbow." Zephyr accepted the apology token, then smiled, and handed it to Nico. She laughed at the belated guest gift. She didn't hesitate to pop it open and pour it into everyone's morning tea.

Sitting between Kai's legs, Rasia emptied her cup all in one go. Two more figures approached from down the road, and Rasia didn't hesitate to refill both her cup and two extras.

"Oi-yo!" Rasia greeted them, waving them over as if she were the host and this was her house. Nico used to think Rasia had no manners and then revised her assumptions because no one could be that dense all the time. Rasia had to know she was being a little shit—but as Rasia rolled to her feet to grab more mats from inside the house, Nico took a deep breath and let it be.

"Where's the pouring?" Kelin called out as he and Azan approached.

Judging by their clothes, they looked like they had come from the same place, probably having met up later last night. Azan handed Nico a bottle of alcohol and nudged Kelin in turn.

"Oh right." Kelin handed over the bottle he carried.

Nico's brows shot up when he plopped the heavy gourd into her arms. She could smell the strong tent brew through the plug. This one might be better saved for a later time. Azan posted against the trellis and Kelin sat down to swipe food off the nearest plate, which was Kai's.

"You touch his food and I'll cut your intestines out to get it back," Rasia threatened.

Kelin wisely withdrew his hand.

Loryn, Faris, and a few of the other kids came soon after, all presenting Nico with gifts of gratitude. Many hadn't planned to stay, but the crowd began striking up conversations and they drank the morning wine that Nico freely passed around. They gathered comfortably on the soft mats and sprawling table of the veranda. The swinging bench creaked under their weight. They expressed their thanks, chatted about the namepour, and volunteered to help her in her political endeavors. A few drums ago, she had faced the darkness of the Grankull alone, but now she was surrounded by friends.

Kai, Nico, and Rasia finished breakfast while the rest passed around the plentiful bottles of alcohol. Once everyone had settled comfortably and was warmed with drink, she stood. Their conversations quieted, except for Rasia, who was turned around speaking with Azan in an engaged discussion about all the details of last night's bodika. She unheeded the sudden quiet. "A fog? Where did a fucking fog come from? Could you tell who you were fucking? What if it was one of your jihs?"

"By the Elder, I didn't fuck my jihs!"

"*But how do you know?*"

Azan opened his mouth to argue, then scrunched his face in a horrified pause. She collapsed in laughter at his uncertainty. Finally realizing all the attention was on them, Azan dropped his head into his hands. Nico certainly hoped her fog didn't have such unintended consequences. Rasia raised her brow at all of them and then drank her tea with fake stoicism. "Y'all nasty."

Kai gave Rasia a long-suffering look of exasperation and squeezed her thigh. "I believe Nico has something she wants to say."

Rasia snorted and gave Nico an impatient expression for her to spit it out already. She drank an entire cup of wine and cleared her throat of the sting as she looked them all over.

"Many of you came here to thank me for standing up for you, but I wanted you all to know that it was your strength and determination that got you here today. The names you have earned are yours. Many of you may feel as if you don't deserve your faces, but you do, no matter what *anyone* says," Nico looked pointedly at Rasia, who looked pointedly back, with no less the amount of disdain from last night. "And while we all may harbor some resentment towards Rasia Dragonfire, ultimately, the corrupt members of the Council are the ones who disrespected your right to a fair Forging."

"Last night during the namepour, I announced my intentions to run for the Councilor Seat of the Wings. They can take my title away from me, but they can't take away my fight. I am going to change the Council from the inside out if I must. I refuse to allow them to interfere in another Forging or allow them to deny anyone's rightful face ever again. But it's going to require more than one seat. We need a complete revolution, which means I need people willing to run on behalf of their neighborhoods. Most of you are too young and inexperienced to seriously run for a seat but talk to your family members. Convince them of the importance of taking a stand. I appreciate all of your support."

"Stop," Rasia interrupted. "Let me get this straight. You declared war on the entire Council, which makes Kai an even bigger target than he already is?" she turned to Kai. "See what the fuck I'm talking about? She's the problem. You're in more danger now."

"And I've taken steps to make sure he's protected," Nico countered. "Last night, I also entered an alliance with the Tent Hans. As part of the alliance, they've agreed to protect my family."

"Oi-yo." Kelin smirked and raised his hand.

"I can protect you," Ysai said, a little hurt.

"Ysaijen Unbowed, I am grateful for all that you've done so far, but they've already put a price on my head. This job is way more than what you signed up for, nor do you have much of a choice. Kibari Oshield might reassign your position, and you're but one person. Nor do I entirely trust the night guard not to be bought out. This family needs more protection."

Kai's eyes narrowed, scrutinizing. "What else does this alliance with the Tent Hans involve? What do they get in return?"

"A seat at the table. They want one of their own in power," Nico answered, speaking directly to Kai. "This is a risk, and I know it will affect our family greatly. You'll become even more of a target, and you'll have to sacrifice even more for me, but I promise you that things will change for the better. I have often been criticized for not having a plan, for being nothing but pretty words and hollow hopes." The plan she and Zephyr had hatched in the early morning seemed fogged by a dream now, but it was one she needed to till into reality. She scanned all of their faces, and she was reminded of that moment at the oasis when she helped the kids retrieve their supplies and how they were willing to follow her to the end of the world if she asked. Now, she was asking.

"I want all of you to know that I do not ask you to follow me blindly, and that I have a vision for the Grankull and our future. The cold hard truth we face today is that there is not enough fertile land to grow enough food for the population, which in turn makes us more vulnerable whenever a hunting season is unsuccessful. The Grankull have often responded with mechanisms of population control, with good intentions, but these systems have become so corrupted that we deny people basic human decency. We turn the other way when lives are lost. We value each other less. We climb over one another to survive. Therefore, we have two choices before us: we eat ourselves from the inside out or we change. People might argue different visions for that change, but this is what I propose: we take the Graveyard."

Rasia burst out laughing. "Really? You don't think Ohans haven't thought of that before?"

Ysai gentled Rasia's words, "Ohans have tried to take the Graveyard and have failed before. Not because they weren't strong enough to conquer it, but because it's practically impossible to keep. No one can eke out a sustainable living in the crossroads of the dragon's coast, the spider mines, and the gonda breeding grounds—it's enough for scavengers, but not enough for the entire Grankull."

Nico smiled and clarified, "Which is why I say again—*we take the Graveyard*—and we bring it to us. With a little engineering and my magic, it should be possible to move the Graveyard here, bone by bone if we must. It's a huge project. It might take years, and most certainly all the scavengers, the Tents, and the Grankull working together, but if it succeeds, there will be enough for us all. The magic in those bones changes the soil. We could have wingfields stretching from here to the saltpans. It was you, Rasia-*ji*, who gave me the initial idea. You said it yourself: With enough water, the bones float."

It took Nico almost sixteen years, but she finally, for once, managed to render Rasia speechless. The gears churned in Rasia's head—thinking of ways to contradict herself, but in the end, she had nothing.

"You really think the scavengers are going to want to work with us?" Faris asked, uncertain, and no doubt burned by his previous interaction.

"We're all starving. What choice do we have? It's either kill each other or work together. The scavengers don't have the technology to succeed alone." Nico looked at all their faces, at the faces of the kids from the Tents, the kids from all the different neighborhoods of the Grankull, and Rasia's own brand of special. Lastly, she looked at Kai, and promised, "This is how we survive. We throw no one overboard. We build a bigger ship, together."

CHAPTER FORTY-FIVE

I

"Your plan sounds solid and all, but have you forgotten about Kibari Oshield?" Rasia criticized after most of the kids had dispersed. Only the core group remained as they lounged under the veranda. "Did you include her in your plans? She still very much wants to kill Kai, and she's not going to stop until he's dead. Have you sent your little tent assassins after her?"

"First off, my alliance with the Tents does not involve murder," Nico said. Over in the corner, Kelin winked at Rasia, immediately contradicting her words. The option wasn't off the table, but Nico knew she was the thin line between the Tents and the Grankull. She had to be careful not to start a battle that could lose them the war. "We know Kibari Oshield is corrupt. There must be dirt on her. Certainly, we can blackmail her to convince her to step down from her position."

"She needs to die," Rasia declared. Beside her, Ysai agreed reluctantly.

From their brief interactions, Nico knew Kibari was not someone to underestimate. She had a reputation for being unerringly composed and deadly with a spear. In addition, the Sentry Han had killed her tah. If both Rasia and Ysai believed death to be their only recourse, Nico needed to take this threat seriously.

"Okay," she said. "What do you think her next step would be?"

Rasia and Ysai turned to each other and exchanged a wordless conversation, and then Rasia tilted her head and squinted at Nico in consideration. "I'd target you, because you're the biggest threat, but considering you've already dodged scavengers and tent assassins, I wouldn't come at you head-on a second time. No, I'd go for easier targets—like Kai or the kid. If it was up to Kiba-ta, she would target Kai, considering she'd get the added bonus of fucking me over too, but Kiba-ta isn't acting alone. As a group, the Council will probably choose Rae. You should probably go pick them up."

"Kenji-ta agreed to watch them for the day. They're safe," Nico said. Kenji-ta's hunting record might not be what it used to, but he was still considered one of the Grankull's best windekas to ever sail. He had a reputation that could bring the tight-knit hunting community to his defense. They always stuck up for their own. Even Kibari wouldn't dare.

"Besides, the Council can't kill Rae now," she said. "They're the only heir."

"The Council doesn't need to kill them to control you."

Shouts of alarm alerted Nico to the sight of someone racing toward them down the road. A streak of red hair streamed behind the runner. Ysai surged to his feet, hopped over the veranda railing, and caught Jilah as she collapsed into his arms. She gulped for breaths and searched through faces until her eyes caught wide and frantic on Nico's.

"A hikull of sentries are at tah's house. The Council is trying to take Rae away."

"Rasia," Kai snapped. Rasia bolted before Nico had time to process the words. Once it sunk in that yes—the Council had the audacity to threaten her youngest sibling—she jetted off into the air. Tajih's house wasn't too far away, as it was located on the other side of the Heart, the neighborhood that housed most of the scribes. She surfed over the gardens and the Heart Temple. At this height, she could see the gathered crowd. She splashed down at the center of the circle at the same time Rasia came to a skidding stop beside her. The suddenness of their arrival did not disrupt the tense standoff between Kenjinn Ilhani and Kibari Oshield.

"I fucking swear, you harm my child and one of us is not walking away alive," Kenji-ta threatened. Nico joined tah's side and minded the rhythm of her breaths, in case she needed to call forth her magic.

Rasia clicked her tongue and strolled to the center. Behind her back, Rasia flashed Kenji and Nico the kull signal to 'wait.'

"Wow, Kiba," Rasia said, alarming everyone with her lack of address. "I didn't know part of a sentry's job description included kidnapping kids."

"Disrespect my name one more time and I'll cut your tongue out," Kibari said, soft, in dangerous warning. As the Han of the sentries, she couldn't let such blatant disrespect stand, especially in front of her subordinates.

Rasia smirked, knowing, and taunted both syllables. *"Ki-ba."*

Kibari's spear spun and slid between grips as she dipped into a fighting stance. The sentries, who have all been at the end of her spear at one point or another during a training session, backed out of the way. Rasia reached to her back and unsheathed the wicked curves of her twin khopesh. The white dragonsteel of both weapons glinted off sunlight and drew a crowd of onlookers.

"I'm surprised you haven't fled for the Desert by now," Kibari said.

"I'm not scared of you."

Kibari attacked, and her spear echoed against Rasia's crossed khopesh. Rasia uncrossed, to trap the polearm in the curves, but Kibari flipped the blunt end of her spear forward. Rasia diverted the attack by switching her grip. Dragonsteel screeched along the polearm.

Kibari was good. Rasia was fast.

Kibari pushed forward with both hands, using the spear as a horizontal bar to knock Rasia in the face, but Rasia brought her khopesh up in time to defend. She buckled under the power of the attack and fell to one knee. Kibari lifted her leather boot to kick. Rasia lifted hers. Their right feet slammed against each other in mid-air. They both pushed. Locked together in a match of equal strength.

A stampede of footsteps burst through the crowd. Those Nico had left behind at the house finally caught up to bolster their numbers. They stood at her back, except for one.

Ysai struck with the speed of a cobra.

Kibari evaded his spear thrust, then backed up further to swat away Rasia's quick strikes. Ysai threw an arm across Rasia's path, and backed them up, breaking off the attack.

Kibari's eyes narrowed at the newcomers and slammed the end of her spear to the ground. She addressed Ysai, "You dare to raise a weapon to your Han?"

"It is my job to protect the magicborn."

"The Council has ordered us to retrieve young Raevin due to concerns of neglect."

"I haven't witnessed any such neglect," Ysai argued.

Kai dove through a hole in the crowd. He folded over his knees when he came to a stop, breathing heavily at the run. Kelin, secretly assigned by Nico to watch over Kai, came jogging up behind him. The gathered crowd immediately shifted their attention to Kai's entry. They shouted and yelled. A clear chant roared and rolled through the streets, "Cull the runt! Cull the runt! Cull the runt!"

Rasia yanked Kai behind her. Nico stared horrified at the crowd. None of the venom or hatred had been watered down but only seemed to have festered overnight. Amid the overwhelming noise, Rae broke away from tah's legs. Kai scooped Rae off the ground and stepped closer to Nico.

"You should have stayed in the house," she whispered at him.

"I won't let them have Rae," he said.

The Sentry Han raised a fist in the air and silenced the crowd. She raised her voice to announce, "Now that Raevin is the sole heir, it is of the utmost importance they are well-cared for. The Council has decided it is unacceptable they should remain in the care of a professed liar, a drunkard, and . . ." Kibari took a dramatic pause to sneer at Kai, "the runt. Hand them over. They are no longer your responsibility."

"Kibari-kull," Kenji-ta growled out. "I will not let you take my child away from their family."

"And yet your kulani didn't care about taking children away from their families now, did she? And really, Kenji-*kull*? You are barely involved in the child's upbringing. When you're not out with the kulls, you're at the bottom of a bottle. The entire Grankull knows you're a drunkard. Can you honestly claim you're what's best for the child? Besides, it is my understanding that the runt isn't even family anymore."

Kai's eyes widened and he attempted to place Rae back on the ground, but Rae clung to him with stubborn refusal.

"That paperwork will be fixed soon," Nico said.

The Sentry Han motioned her army of sentries forward. Rasia tensed to spring. Kai clutched Rae tighter.

Thunder cracked the sky and bowed everyone under the weight of the bellowing noise. The Sentry Han stood unflinching. Nico boldly stepped forward and placed herself as a shield in front of her family. They had enough numbers. She might be able to avoid a fight. "Turn away, Kibari Oshield. The Council's claims are unfounded, and I will not be intimidated. If the Council has a problem with me, I welcome any competitor you think can run against me for the Wing-seat, but you will not drag my family into your petty politics. Dare take a child away from this family, and I will not hesitate to destroy you."

"Really?" Kibari asked. She turned toward the rattled crowd. "Is this truly the person you want to represent you on the Council? Who would threaten violence over the Council's reasonable concerns? Or is she no better than Avalai Ohan?"

Kiba's words twisted Nico into a trap. If she harmed anyone unjustifiably, she would lose the people's support, or she could let the Council take her younger jih as leverage. She had to make a choice, one Kiba would win either way. Her eyes narrowed and then turned to address the crowd.

"I am not Avalai Ohan, but are there any among you who would allow a child to be taken from your arms? Wouldn't any of you do whatever it took to protect your family? Especially as triarch? I will destroy anyone who harms Rae, or *Kai*. Tell your neighbors. Tell your friends. I am not weak like my tah. You come after my children; I won't come after yours." Nico turned to Kibari. "I'll come after you."

The intimidation tamed the crowd, but Nico saw that dangerous sharp calculation in Kibari's eyes. She was going to test Nico. She was going to send in the sentries. Force Nico to make a mistake.

Kai suddenly parted from the others, carrying Rae on his hip.

"What are you doing?"

He ignored her. He sat on the ground and placed Rae cross-legged across from him and used the ends of his shroud to wipe the tears from Rae's eyes.

"Hey grubworm," he said lowly, causing much of the confused crowd to lean forward in order to hear. "They might be a little scary, but all they want to do is play with us. Let's show them how to play."

Rae sniffled and nodded.

Kai tapped his hands on the ground and created the familiar beat of an old lullaby. Then he and Rae chanted together the kah. Letter by letter. The entire crowd quieted in stunned awe. Most children didn't know the kah until their first year of school and some others never learned.

"And how do you spell your name?"

Rae exclaimed each letter. "R-A-E!"

Some of the crowd clapped in response to Rae's enthusiasm. Nico didn't miss Kai's clever look when he glanced at Kibari. He had outwitted her. In one fell stroke, he completely cut the knees off the Council's claims and saved her from having to defend the family. Proud, she scooped up Rae and hugged them into her arms. Together, Kai and Nico stood before the Sentry Han in defiance.

"Rae also knows how to write their name, they eat three meals a day, do their chores, and can recite the entirety of the origin story," she declared. "Rae has been raised just fine."

The sentries looked to their Han in uncertainty, most of them won over by the display. Without her sentries, Kibari had lost control of the situation. She stood, hand tightening around her spear, eyes pierced on Kai, lips curled into a snarl.

With the crowd and the sentries wavering, Nico knew this to be the best time to retreat. Kenji-ta must have sensed this too, for he came forward to place a supportive hand on her shoulder as they began a collective withdrawal. Kai gave Kibari one final bold stare before turning toward the others. Rasia sprinted forward, shouting, "KAI!"

Nico swiveled, in search of the threat and found Kibari's cold calculating exterior rupture with rage. A spear loosed from her hand.

Aimed for Kai's turned back.

Nico inhaled.

A beat too slow.

Kenji-ta, already in motion, scooped Kai off his feet and yanked him away from the spear that whizzed past to pierce the ground with vibrating force. Kai dangled, stunned, from Kenji-ta's arm.

It took everyone a moment to process the fact that Kibari Oshield, Han of the Sentries, threw a spear at a child's back. Such an action had only one response. Sometimes, arguments and words weren't enough to avoid the inevitable.

With Rae on her hip, Nico marched forward and pulled the shroud from her belt. Then she slammed it down at Kibari's feet. "I demand a blood price."

"Then take it," Kibari said.

"A moment," she said, indicating the child on her hip. "Or would you also attack me while carrying a child and unable to defend myself?"

"Prepare yourself then."

Unafraid, she turned her back on Kibari and was immediately met with a chorus of outraged voices. "Nico-kull, what are you doing?" "Are you sure about this?" "Are you crazy?" "Kibari

Oshield is undefeated!"

"Kenji-ta," Nico said calmly, cutting through all the panicked voices that enveloped her. "Go home and get my glaive. You know the one."

"Nico-po, this is a mistake. Let me fight in your place," tah said.

"No. If I am to be the triarch of this family, then this is my fight. Go get my spear, please," she requested. She could see that he was terrified, but he jogged off down the street to cut through the gardens.

"Nico," Kai said, as she deposited Rae into his arms. "This is what she wants."

"I know," she said. Kibari had placed her in a corner. She would lose all respect if she didn't respond to the blatant public attack, and now that she did, Kibari had her in the perfect position to kill her without legal consequences. She had known the moment she dropped her shroud that this wouldn't end with a cut on the arm. This was a death match. "I couldn't let that attack go unchallenged."

"You're using your magic, right?" Rasia asked.

"No, I cannot."

"You're not using your magic?!" Rasia shouted in alarm, drawing the attention of several in the crowd. No doubt the crowd would continue to grow as the news traveled the streets. High-profile blood price matches didn't occur often. Already, a few had procured reed pens and papyrus to record the event. Ugh. Scribes.

"Look," Rasia said. "I know you're trying to be honorable or whatever, but more is at stake here than your stupid morals. Seriously, kill that skink."

"I appreciate the advice, but do you have any helpful tips?" she asked.

"I . . ." Rasia narrowed her eyes in thought. "She's not the type of person to drag things out. Her first strike will be for the kill."

She nodded. She straightened when tah returned from the house to deliver her worn and reliable glaive. The same trusty one she brought with her to the Forging. The same one that taught her she could fail.

They all tried to say something more and delay the inevitable, but Nico couldn't afford to divert her attention to comfort them. She needed all her focus on surviving what was to come. She tightened her grip on the glaive and stepped into the perfect circle the crowd had created. She could smell the rose and lavender from the temple garden, so near that scattered petals had been trampled into the cobblestones. She could taste water on her tongue. It was going to rain today, one of those quick showers before the downpours hit.

Kibari Oshield had tied up her hair. Nico tightened the jute string of her ponytail.

They circled each other. There were none of the taunts or insults that were common in the stories. In fact, the noise of her surroundings faded into silence, the way the world did when she found herself submerged into a deep focus and nothing around her mattered but the task. She took a breath and held it.

Rasia had been right. Her tah didn't bother with any feints, tricks, or surprises.

Kibari went straight for the kill.

Two beats of dragonsteel.

Nico survived to the other side, deflecting the first strike and countering with one of her own. Both untouched, they continued to circle one another, looking for any weakness of stance or mistake in footing.

But Kibari was not some fresh-faced sentry new to the spear. In order to win, Nico knew she would have to force a mistake, and if she had learned anything with that spear throw, she knew Kibari was not infallible.

"I hope this blood price satisfies all the children *you* have slaughtered," Nico said nastily and thrust forward. This was for all those who hadn't survived the Forging.

With a flick of the wrist, Kibari deflected Nico's attack and the next one. Nico fought to batter her down but found no holes—only an indomitable defense. What had triggered her before?

What had broken her cool composure?

Nico flicked her eyes to Kai, and then she was the one on the defensive. Kibari had sprung at the first sign of distraction. Dragonsteel slashed through Nico's arm, and the crowd held in their breaths as she attempted a retreat, but Kibari relentlessly chased her back.

"You can't bear it can you?" she asked, ducking underneath Kibari's spear and then thrusting forward only for the attack to be sidestepped. "That Kai-ji got the better of you? I wonder how you'll feel when I am the one to make you look a fool."

Kibari scoffed, finally giving her a reaction. She leaned back and glanced at her reflection in the spear point that swiped overheard. Kibari said, "You are a naïve spoiled little child who believes the world bends to her whims."

"You don't know me," she said. "You look at me and see my tah. But I am not the one who murdered your kulani. *You did.*"

Kibari's face twisted, and she lunged forward. Kibari no doubt expected another retreat, but Nico lunged forward in turn. They scattered the lavender petals.

The crowd gasped. Warm blood dripped down Nico's forearm. The clatter of a polearm fell to the ground. Kibari Oshield had overextended—a mistake she never would have made if her body had been entirely in her control.

At the last vibration, Nico had commandeered Kibari's blood. She had used Rasia to convince everyone that she wouldn't use her magic. The gambit had worked, for Kibari had underestimated her. Kibari thought her weak and soft-hearted and unwilling to go for the kill, but Nico had people to protect.

Honor was a privilege.

Also, yeah, Rasia was right. When someone sent assassins after you twice, threatened to take away the youngest member of your family, outright attacked another, and vowed to wipe your entire bloodline from the sands . . . sometimes, you've got no choice but to kill a skink.

"We all must pay our blood prices," Nico said, and then twisted to dislodge the glaive out of Kibari's chest. The body dropped dead to the ground.

She straightened and the crowd shuffled back a step. From their point of view, they had witnessed Nico besting one of the greatest polearm users in the entire Grankull. Let them believe she did it without her magic. Let them wonder what more she was capable of. She eyed them all, both a warning and a promise to anyone who dared to mess with her family. "All hunters are hunted."

"All hunters are hunted," the crowd echoed.

Nico glanced at Rasia, who stared at the corpse of her parent, replaying the how of it all through those perceptive eyes. Then she looked at Nico with sudden understanding, and Rasia gave a brief acknowledging nod.

Out of the crowd, one of the sentries handed Nico the shroud she had thrown to the ground. She accepted it with thanks and then kneeled to dab the cloth in Kibari's blood.

Before Kai and Rae, Nico bowed to one knee and offered up bloody retribution. She whispered for Kai's ears alone, "This offering is for tah's death, but also for the trauma of the aftermath and believing her death had been your fault for almost four years. You both deserve some justice."

His eyes swirled and within their bright cores, she could see that for the first time, he was ready to believe the truth. Kai accepted the blood price.

CHAPTER FORTY-SIX

O

Rasia watched Kiba-ta burn. She stood so close to the pyre that the smoke burned her eyes and the heat stung her cheeks. A white shroud covered Kiba-ta's face, the only time her tah had worn a white shroud since her coming of age. Kiba-ta preferred to carry a red embroidered one at her waist that Shamai-ta had gifted her. It burned at her waist now, too. They burned her with her spear and her armor, and the namesakes from her kulani: necklaces, bracelets, earrings, and weapons that no others could claim. Jasmine flower bouquets decorated the pyre, representing death, bones, and the color of dragons when they die.

The burning was a public affair, but because Rasia had been disowned, she was barred from the bone internment afterward, which was a ceremony meant only for the family. Her tajihs had also threatened her from attending the deathpour and the scattering of ashes that traditionally happened atop the Spine. The sudden passing of the family's triarch had come as a shock to the entire family, a shock that most blamed Rasia for. Apparently, signing Kai's name had brought bad luck or some shit. Whatever. Fuck them all. She planned on going anyway.

She still had moments of disbelief sometimes. If someone had told Rasia that her tah would one day die in a public blood price match against *Nico*, she would have laughed until they apologized for fucking around.

The body continued to burn, and no amount of burning incense could cover up the smell. Ysai grabbed her hand in his. "Are you okay?" he asked.

Rasia felt . . . aimless. She had been gearing up for war and felt oddly bitter that the battle had been denied to her. No doubt it would have been a bloody and costly one—but oh, how glorious the clash would have been. She didn't know what to do with herself now. All the petty arguments had been cut short. All the obstacles paved over. All the vendettas burned atop a pyre.

Gone.

Dead.

Deceased.

Real life sometimes felt like a bad story—with all the best plotlines cut too soon.

She asked, "What am I supposed to do now?"

Ysai's grip tightened around her closed fist.

"We live."

"That was a fucking shitshow," Rasia spat an angry wad of spit over the edge of Kai's roof. It landed an audible brush atop the snarling vines that shaded the veranda.

"What happened at the bone internment?" Kai asked. He sat beside her on the rooftop and dutifully filled her gourd the moment she emptied it.

"It went about as well as you could expect," Ysai said and handed over his gourd for Kai to refill. Ysai drank and turned toward the orange glow of the oil lamps where a bruise bloomed on his cheek.

"Evidently, none of the family believe in the 'leave-your-weapons-at-the-temple-door,' rule," Rasia said nastily. "Tajih pulled a knife on me when I showed up, and the scribes kicked us all out of the temple before they could seal the urn. They blame that on me, too."

"Then Rasia showed up to disperse the ashes," Ysai added, "but I had to step in before they threw her off the Spine."

"I'd have liked to see them try."

Rasia stuck out her cup, and Kai refilled it with the fancy grape wine Ysai wasted a whole paycheck on. After getting kicked out of various ceremonies by their own family, Ysai and Rasia decided to have their own deathpour, of which Kai and Nico offered to host on the roof of their home. They decorated the rooftop with jasmine and burned incense for the occasion. An impressive collection of alcohol had been gathered, provided from the stores of both households: grape wine, palm wine, date wine, a particularly memorable one made from fermented camel milk, and lots of beer, which was always cheap and readily available.

Rasia barely remembered Shamai-ta's deathpour. Not because of the alcohol (usually, the family allowed the children one ceremonial drink on such an occasion), but because she had been numbed from the shock of the death, and it all had been an emotional blur.

Behind them, Nico and Jilah sat in an enclave of pillows and blankets. Although rainy season now, Nico made certain the sky remained clear. It was a cool and hauntingly beautiful night, and the stars multiplied in Rasia's vision.

She pushed hands against the pebbled rooftop, butt in the air first, and wobbled to her feet. Kai steadied her as she punched her gourd into the air and toasted, "Peace, Kiba-ta. Your kulani is waiting for you. Now you can leave us the fuck alone."

Her tah was wind now.

"Oi-yo," Ysai slurred, then lolled his head onto Kai's shoulder. Kai looked a little overwhelmed between them, caught between clenching tightly onto her pants so she didn't fall, and rubbing circles into Ysai's back. She puffed out a breath of hot air. She was not that drunk. The stars tipped overhead, and Kai decisively tugged her down into his lap.

Ysai looked at her with the same palm wood brown of Kiba-ta's eyes. "What's going to happen when Jilah and I have a kid? She's not going to be there. Tah is going to miss it."

Rasia patted his warm cheek. His skin was a tone lighter than hers, and his cheeks got an amusing flush when he drank alcohol. She told him, "We don't need her. We never needed her. I'll take care of jipoh. I'll teach them how to fight. I'll teach them how to sail a windship. Oh," she hopped up, with a bright idea. "We should go live in the Desert. You, me, and Kai."

"And Jilah."

"And Jilah!"

"What are they talking about?" Jilah murmured distantly from behind them. "I have no idea," Nico said.

"*No*," Rasia said with another sudden inspiration. She slapped at Ysai's shoulder. "We should go beyond the Desert! We should explore the world! You, me, and Kai."

"And Jilah."

"And Jilah!"

"But Rasia," Ysai pouted, "You almost died last time. Shamai-ta is gone. Kiba-ta is gone. I can't lose you, too." His voice cracked, and tears streamed ugly down his face. "Don't leave me all alone."

She patted Ysai's sticky warm cheek. "Of course, I'll never leave you. You and me and Kai *and* Jilah together *forever*."

He smiled, content. Then his face twisted, and Kai had a clay pot at the ready. They call them jasmine pots at the market because you grow flowers in them once their initial use had been realized. Ysai tossed his head in and vomited. The sound triggered a sudden nauseousness, and Rasia soon followed. Kai very helpfully produced Rasia her own pot.

She clung to the clay edges and vomited into its hollowed base, fulfilling the final requirements of a deathpour, the last part that symbolized letting go. She released the grief, the anger, and the sorrow—puking it out of her with the rest of her insides.

She rested on her cheek and stared at the banded designs at the neck of the pot, images of dragons and jasmines, then she vomited again. Might have been a little bit of anger still left.

She messily wiped her mouth when she finished, and then closed her eyes for a little while to listen to the cicadas. Kai checked on her briefly, and she bobbed her head to assure him that she was fine. Still, he kissed her on the temple and dabbed at her lips with a wet cloth, cleaning her up. She breathed in the scented smoke of the pistacia resin.

"Looks like it's time for us to go home," Jilah said.

"Nonsense," Nico said. "That's a long walk home at this time of night. I'll prepare one of the guest rooms."

A sudden clang made Rasia jump. Ysai had accidentally knocked over his pot. Jilah, Kai, and Nico all rushed over to help.

Rasia was feeling a lot better, but now she really had to pass water. While the others were busy, she made her way to the stairs. She stuck her leg into the open roof-hatch. Then she stuck in another leg. She crawled down, feet first, like a toddler testing the stairs for the first time. She made it to the bottom with a successful wobble and swayed around the corners.

She found the wet room and plopped her butt onto the limestone shelf, which had a spherical hole carved into the center. She held her head in her hands as she urinated into the litter box of sand. Kai and Nico's house had one of those fancy pumps usually found in the public bathhouses that sprayed out water and cleaned your butt for you. It was nice.

Rasia didn't remember getting off the toilet. She found herself wandering through the maze and jolted when she hit a dead-end.

She whipped around, confused, not knowing her location. She raced forward, turned a corner, and she hit another dead-end. Trapped. Her heart thudded fast. She turned and broke into another sweaty run. The walls blurred, all looking the same. Another dead end.

She screamed.

"Rasia?"

She turned toward Kai's voice coming to save her and didn't hesitate to cling to him when he reached her. She pulled him to her mouth and begged him to take her away into the clouds, but to her immense disappointment, he only carried her as far as their bed.

She stared at the ceiling, the latticed windows, and the walls. She didn't understand this continued racing of her heart, this anxious fear of an animal springing to flee building in her chest, overwhelming her like the shadow of some great storm-cloud. She always thought this feeling would leave her once Kiba-ta died. She always thought she'd finally be free.

But it was another dead-end.

CHAPTER FORTY-SEVEN

I

Nico washed the various dishes, gourds, and flasks leftover from the deathpour. She had tied up her hair and stationed the washbin on the paved stones of the smaller garden offshoot of the kitchen, the same garden where they grew their herbs and spices. She bent over the bin that she had with filled water and scrubbed at the clay dishware.

Wordlessly, Kai pulled up a stool to join her. He picked up a bowl from the stacks she had brought down from the roof.

"Rasia is in the bed?" she asked. "Where did she disappear to?"

"Found her lost in the maze. She's asleep now. I think her tah's death hit her harder than she anticipated. I also checked on Rae, they're still in bed. Ysai and Jilah?"

"Same. I've set them up in the water lotus guestroom," she said. They had so many empty rooms. According to the records, this villa had once housed the magic-born and all their extended family, but that had been before the population controls.

"How are you?" Kai asked.

"Why would I—" she paused as he raised a brow. "I'm fine. I wish there had been another way, but I did what I had to. We're safer now because of it. I still have the Flock monitoring the house, just in case, but from what I hear, Kibari Oshield's death has been a blow to the sect against us on the Council. They're now less focused on sending assassins after us and are now gathering their resources to oppose my run."

"How is the campaign?" he asked.

She hadn't had much time to prepare but she told him of all the ideas that she planned to implement. Suri had agreed to help her with the main campaign, and Zephyr offered to help with relations between the Tent Hans. Kai sat and listened as they worked. Before she knew it, she had washed and dried the last dishware. They sat for a moment and watched the fireflies flitter about the garden.

Kai wanted something. She felt the question like an incoming raincloud. She took a breath and reminded herself to keep an open mind. Don't shut him down. *Listen.*

Finally, he said, "I think Kenjinn Ilhani should move back in."

Her blood curdled with heat at the request. "*No.*"

"You said it would be my decision."

"Kai, he's hardly been out of the house for two days. What sort of lesson is that? You are still wearing the bruises he made when *he tried to kill you.*"

"He paid a blood price."

"That doesn't mean anything!" she caught the volume of her voice, rubbed at her forehead, and breathed through her meditations to calm down. "I understand he paid a blood price, but that's the bare minimum. He still has a long way to go to make amends. Don't forgive him so easily."

"Isn't that my choice to make?" he argued, "There are so many things I didn't get to say before Ava-ta died. I don't want to make that same mistake with him. We never know how much time we've got, and I can't . . . let it end unresolved. He's the only parent we've got left."

"You two can meet outside these walls if you want me to set that up for you, but he doesn't have to live here. It's too much too soon."

"I know what I can handle. Having him around is not going to break me." He bit out, "You promise you'd listen to me."

"I am *listening*, but he has such a long list of broken promises. I refuse to give him the chance to break his promises to you."

"He saved my life."

"That hardly balances all the wrong he's done. We've made far too many excuses for his behavior."

"So what? You've earned a face and now you've turned into Ava-ta? Without any time for the people that matter?"

Nico froze, stunned, at the low blow. By the look on Kai's face, he seemed to realize it belatedly as well. "I didn't mean it that way."

"Is that what you think?" she asked, lowly. "That I've turned into her?"

"No. I—I'm sorry," he said. He shook his head and turned away from her. He took a moment to choose his words carefully. "Not everyone chugs on like you do. It's easy for you, but I really think he should move back in."

Is that what he believed of her? That it was easy to keep chugging along? She *killed* someone, publicly and violently, and she'd always have that life now weighing her shoulders.

Nor was it ever easy to tell him no.

She shook her head. "Not if it's at your expense. I will not let him hurt you again."

"And I am telling you that I will be fine. When are you going to start *trusting* me?"

"When you start telling me the truth!" She yelled, on her feet. She bit down harshly and spun away from him, not realizing how much bitterness and resentment she was still holding from the Naming Ceremony. He should have told the truth about his interview, instead of leaving everyone on that stage helpless to protect him.

She crossed her arms, holding herself, while she shook with anger. She forced herself to wrangle in her emotions. She calmly relayed her decision, "I will allow supervised meetings with him outside of these walls. If those go well, then you may be allowed private meetings. *Then*, we will reconsider the decision to allow him to move back in."

"Whatever. Fuck it," he snarled and turned on his heel. Nico stumbled forward at the strength of a sudden bout of wind. His inconsistent magic was yet another problem she needed to deal with.

She hated this, being the bad person. Kai thought he was ready, but she knew he'd go running the other way the moment Kenji-ta stepped into the same room. She shook her head as she poured the dishwater into the garden. Then she scooped up the dishes and wondered if she made the wrong decision, but she had both Kai and Rae to consider. Rae also deserved some consistency. She was officially the triarch now, the paperwork approved the other morning. She had to think of the family as a whole and she thought it was a reasonable compromise. She paused when she stepped into the kitchen and found Kai frozen at the center.

He turned around to face her, fists clenched, determined. Then he said the words that cut deeper than any blade. "If we don't do something soon, we're going to lose him. He's going to kill himself."

A chill dripped down her spine. The Grankull didn't treat kindly those who gave Death an easy hunt. "No. Tah is no coward. You're wrong."

"We'll lose him because . . . *I know.*"

Nico stared at him, uncomprehending.

He licked at his lips nervously, and she set down the dishes on the counter, sensing the weight of the conversation. "At the beginning of the Forging," he said. "I tried to kill myself in the waters of the oasis. I was tired of being a burden, and I figured everyone's lives would be easier if I was gone. I hadn't planned on surviving the Forging."

She physically ached at the words. "But we had a plan."

"It was your plan."

The image of Kai blurred. Salty tears hugged her lips. For years, he claimed he didn't tell her things for fear of hurting her. She turned away from him and began putting up the dishes to give herself something to do. Slowly, quietly, he began doing the same, while glancing at her out of the corner of his eye and waiting for her reaction.

She knew he hadn't taken his first Forging or the year without rations very well, but she hadn't thought . . . she hadn't thought. How could she have missed so much? She paused and pressed her hands against the geometric tiled counter.

Kai had fought so hard to prove himself stronger than she gave him credit for. Now it was her turn. She could take a hit. She could prove herself stronger, too. She sucked in a breath and turned to face him. "Thank you for telling me. Do you still feel this way?"

"No," he said and watched her warily. He offered freely, "It's not your fault. You did all that you could. I . . . at the time, in the moment, dying had seemed the only choice I'd ever get to make." He reached up and stored the last plate. "The Grankull accepts that Death can come as a battle, or old age, or unexpected accidents . . . but in my experience, Death can also be a snare. It's hard to escape if you're not willing to fight, or if you don't know how, or if there's no one to help. It's not an easy thing to bite your leg free. The rabbit shouldn't be at fault for being caught in the hunter's snare. It's not the rabbit's fault they cannot run away. I think Kenji is caught in the same trap and needs your help. You are the only one he truly listens to. You are the one he strives to be better for. If there's any hope of him improving, it's going to be here."

"What if . . ." She picked her words carefully, "What if it's already too late? Sometimes I don't recognize who he is anymore."

"I've never known that person," Kai said, truthfully. "So maybe it's easier for me. But people change, Nico. Maybe it's time to accept who he is now."

"An abusive piece of shit?" she muttered.

"A person who has made mistakes and is trying to right those wrongs."

"*Trying* is a rather strong word, but I understand your point—that it could be harder for him to improve without facing the accountability of his actions every day. I just . . . I fear . . ." She rubbed her eyes, feeling so overwhelmed in that moment.

"They've given me a bigger field to oversee in the wingfields. I must prepare for this upcoming election. I need to find alternate candidates for the other Council seats and help build their campaign, all while making sure the Council doesn't get too bold and try to take Rae away from us again. And the assassins, lest not forget about the assassins. Those aren't entirely off the table. I barely have enough time for anything. For all my magic and how powerful I have become, I can't stretch the days any longer. I simply can't monitor him all vibrations of the day."

"*Trust me*," Kai said, again, except this time it had more weight. He had actually given some honesty in exchange for all that trust he'd been begging for. She sighed, relenting.

"You will no longer lie for him," she said. "You will no longer protect him. You will allow him to be held accountable for his actions. If he hurts you again, you will tell me immediately, understood? Promise me on Ava-ta's name."

"I promise."

"And Kai," Nico said, as he turned for the hallway. "We're not done. We also need to address your magic."

He slumped against the door frame, half-in and half-out of the kitchen, twitching to flee. "What about it?" he pouted.

She swept past him and motioned him to follow. He reluctantly followed her down the hallway into the dojo. She looked around at the reed panels that made up the walls and that were easily replaced if destroyed. She remembered all the blood and sweat she had spilled here. But Kai never had that same instruction.

"Tell me about your magic. Rasia said that you had control of it, but I've noticed a lot of outbursts lately. Before, when you've not been in control, the outbursts were small but now they are bigger. You could hurt someone."

"I know," he said, frustrated. "I thought I had it under control, but it hasn't been working right since I've been in the Grankull."

"So what? You were hoping to ignore the problem and it would go away?" she asked. He gave her a flat stare because yes, that was exactly what he had been hoping. "You've been eating, right?"

"I can't go a drum without Rasia trying to stuff something into my mouth. Yes, I've been eating. Have I been eating enough? I don't know."

She nodded and sat down cross-legged onto the mats. She patted the space across from her, urging him to sit down too. He sat down, curling his knees up under him, an almost comical sight at how gangly he was becoming. He was hitting that growth where everything was just a little out of proportion. "So, let's assume that's not the issue. When did you first notice that things had changed?"

He hunched his shoulders and explained what happened during his interview. He stumbled over some parts of it, and Nico mentally raised the name of the Belly Councilor higher on her list of those she needed to take down.

"In the records, there was once an Ohan who could no longer use their magic after a particularly brutal civil war. Sometimes . . . it's mental, Kai. During the interview, you panicked. You know the magic responds to emotions, but emotions are personal. Mine gets out of control when I get angry, but perhaps yours manifest as a block. The power and level of control you exerted in the Desert were impressive, but you were lucky to be inundated by your elements. You're in the Grankull now. It's no longer easy when all you've got is a puddle to manipulate."

Nico offered her hands, and Kai placed his hands in hers. He had given up on magic so long ago that now he was always sensitive about it. She had tried to connect with his magic before, but the connection had felt like oily clogged pores and her attempts slid right off. Now, his magic was bright and open and so full that she feared he might explode with all the energy swelling his bones. "It feels so different now. What changed?"

"I came into my magic during the Forging," he mumbled.

She snapped her eyes open. "Why didn't you start with that? Kai! That changes everything. How did it happen?"

He squeezed his eyes shut and mumbled.

"What did you say?"

He mumbled it again, only slightly louder this time but enough for her to hear the words, ". . . sex . . . first time."

She blinked at him and laughed. She couldn't imagine how painful that must have been. He covered his face with his hands in embarrassment. She had access to all the memories of previous Ohans and that certainly was a first. She snatched back his hands. "Stop that. What's done is done."

"But that's not normal," he whined. "I just . . . I'm never going to be normal, am I?"

"I think I know something that might help," she said. She focused and connected their magic. The amount of magic Kai contained truly awed her, for it was as immense as the magic in the Heart Temple. They sat across from each other, like two blazing suns.

"Don't fight me," she warned, and then began absorbing some of his magic. She was connected to the Elder Heart, and she further pulled his magic through her to join the immense store within the temple until he wasn't so bright anymore. She released him and watched as he lifted his arms in awe, staring at them.

"It doesn't hurt anymore."

She frowned. "Did it always hurt?"

"I think so," he said uncertainly. "You know when there's background noise so constant that you don't hear it anymore until it's gone? Like that. The pain is gone. But what does this mean? That I don't have to eat as much anymore?"

"I don't know, but it'll come back," she warned. "Bones attract magic, and all bones have their own natural capacity to hold a certain amount. Your capacity is extremely large, conditioned from holding so much for so long, I suspect. All the magic I sucked away will eventually return. Perhaps if we did this draining every morning it could help, but that's not a long-term solution. You will eventually need to learn how to handle your capacity, and I think that's something we can train. You've got to start meditating, learning the breathing techniques, and practicing. Rasia was also right—your body is a vessel. You need to eat right and train it as well, which can often increases your magical endurance. If you really want to control your magic, then you've got to put in the work. No more running away from it."

"Okay," he said, after a moment, and then squeezed her hands. "I think . . . I'm afraid of failing. That even after all this hard work it won't matter. I think out of everything in my life, it is my magic that has disappointed me the most, and it is terrifying to have to rely on it to do anything."

"If you do nothing, most likely it's going to get worse. But even if it all ends in disappointment, at least you tried, right?"

"Yeah," he said, suddenly mournful as he nodded to himself. "At least I tried."

Nico knew they were talking about something slightly different now, and it pained her to hear the surrender in his voice. The brave face he put on for her and Rasia was an exterior, but for a moment, she could see through the cracks of his walls and spied all his hurt, disappointment, and anger at the injustice of it all. She leaned forward and wrapped him in her arms. "I am so so so proud of you, and you should be so proud of yourself. You slayed a dragon, and even though it feels so overwhelming and daunting right now, I know that you have it in you to slay so many more. I know it's not fair that this world demands so much of you, but I want you to know that you are not alone. It is okay to ask for help. It is okay to feel defeated. It is okay to feel hurt. Despite all the adversity that you face, every day you choose not to give up, and that is the bravest and most courageous choice anyone could ever make. You have always been my hero, Kai."

He tightened his grip around her and pressed his head into her shoulder. For the first time since the interview, he wept.

CHAPTER FORTY-EIGHT

/

"Do you have a moment?" Ysai asked, catching Nico in the hallway. She had finished the morning meditations with Kai and was on her way to get ready for work, which usually took her half a drum. She didn't really have the time. But despite all that, she motioned him to follow.

They convened in the library. Zephyr and Nico had moved a reed screen from the dojo to pin with various information and names. The web of information took up an entire section of the room.

"As you know, I've been going through all the stuff I inherited from tah," he paused. "I found the records you were looking for."

Nico's eyes widened as Ysai untied a cylindrical case from his belt and pulled out the documents. She immediately cleared a space on her desk.

"At first, I couldn't figure out where they were hidden, but then I remembered both Shamai-ta and Kiba-ta were in on the scheme, and Shamai-ta was always good with his hands. I considered where he might hide something, and I found the documents in a false bottom of a display case in their bedroom. But it might not be everything you were hoping for."

She unrolled the scrolls and pinned evory paperweights at the curled corners. She shuffled through pages of transactions and sucked in a breath at the extent of the records and how far they went back. It was absolutely everything.

And nothing at all.

While the detailed accounting records implicated half of the Council in Nico's assassination attempts and other shady dealings, not one page existed with solely Kibari's name on it. All Kibari's vendors, all those who had illegally bought food from her, all the smugglers, and all who have enabled the operation were also listed. In a year when most were starving due to a food shortage and forced to do anything they could to do to survive, the list was endless.

Kibari Oshield had ensured that if she ever went down, most of the Grankull would go down with her, including both of her children.

"You're going to show these to Rasia?" she asked.

"No," he scoffed. "I don't plan to ever tell her. Rasia will gleefully sacrifice herself and everyone around her if that meant taking down the Council. Not for some self-righteous cause either, but for revenge. This is a bomb in her hands."

"It's a bomb in mine too," she said. If she published this information a day before the election, and she could win decisively, taking down the reputations of all those who opposed her. But to drench a few, she would have to rain on everyone else.

"We might win," she told herself. But she might not.

What should she choose? Certain victory and unequivocal control of the Council at everyone's expense, or court the risk of not winning and face the wrath of a Council stacked against her? Could she look people in the eyes afterward? For small infractions, most people would face fines, but the Grankull would certainly shut down any vendor shops involved. They'd banish Rasia and Ysai, too, for their heavy involvement in the smuggling.

Nico was shocked Ysai had said anything at all. "Why did you bring this to me?"

"Because you're not Rasia, and I know you'll at least think about it."

She sighed. Ava-ta would do it in a heartbeat. But sometimes the truth wasn't always right. "I'm not going to do it. It hurts too many people. Thank you for this. If anything, thank you for the closure. Now I know the names, without a shadow of a doubt, of those who want me dead."

She turned to the board she and Zephyr had been working on and rearranged the sketches of the various faces. At the top, she placed those who had contributed to the assassination attempts: the Ribs Councilor, the Belly Councilor, the Neck Councilor, the Hindlegs Councilor, and the Pelvis Councilor. In the middle were the moderates, of which she didn't have to worry about: the Claws Councilor, the Wings Councilor, and the Heart Councilor. Nico stared at the five at the top and drew an 'X' across Kibari's face.

"What are you going to do now? Are you going to destroy the records?" he asked.

"I'm not that naïve," she said. "The threat of having the information could be useful in certain circumstances."

She folded the documents back into the leather case and sealed the case closed with candle wax. Then it disappeared in a splash of water to the bottom of the Black Sea off the Dragon's Coast. None but her would be able to access it.

"I'll just have to do this the hard way," she said. *The hard way.* It was the story of Nico's life.

"I've considered your other request."

She raised her eyebrows. When she had asked Ysai if he would run for the Rib-seat to replace his tah, she hadn't thought he would consider it. He hadn't been with the sentries for very long, but the Grankull did have a weakness for nepotism. He could have a chance.

"I heard that tajih is thinking of running in Kiba-ta's place, but he was involved in a lot of tah's operations and would be just as corrupt. I think, I guess, I should probably try," he said, with a lot of hesitance.

Perfect.

Nico looked back at the board at the four other seats left to tackle. It wouldn't be easy, but she knew exactly where to start.

CHAPTER FORTY-NINE

—

Rasia had never been self-conscious about the volume of her pleasure. Her breathy moans were as loud as when they fondled each other in the windship hatch as now in the soft morning light of the lounging room. Kai figured his family would give them a wide berth but jerked in alarm when Nico came rushing in, paying not a bit of attention.

"Kai, I'm headed out—Oh."

Kai scrambled his fingers from between Rasia's legs and shoved a pillow over his erection. Rasia hadn't offered any help other than to laugh. She turned to Nico, with her night robe hanging askew and bare breasts still heaving with her laughter. She shooed. "Go away. We're busy."

"Don't you two have a bedroom? With a door?" Nico tsked and narrowed her eyes on Kai. "I'm leaving for the wingfields and have a few meetings afterward, but I'll be sure to make it back in time for dinner. I might be a little late, but I'll be here."

He nodded his head in an impatient bob.

"Be careful not to exacerbate your wounds and please, try not to get blood on the furniture," she reprimanded, before rushing out in a whirlwind of hair and silk. He blinked, confused by her words, and then looked down at where his fingers clutched onto the silk pillow to find his middle digits glossed with blood.

"Huh . . ." Rasia said, surprised by the blood herself. "I'm off schedule."

Then she shrugged and continued exactly where they had left off. Before, Kai would have been concerned if it was safe to have sex, but it had been one of several answers Ysai had freely provided without needing the question.

Rasia was on gonom now. Her deathsblood wouldn't affect the contraceptive. This was the safest time during her cycle to have sex. Kai felt confident this time around that they were protected. But Nico probably did have a point about the furniture. He raised his hips, and immediately hissed as the movement burned down his stomach, along the wound where he had been stabbed.

"Here," Rasia said, and helped pull off his robe to lay it underneath them. He dropped back down and was out of breath from just that small action. Rasia's face twisted in concern.

"I'm fine. I . . . you might have to do most of the work."

"You'll tell me if I'm hurting you?" she asked. He nodded. He wasn't exactly completely healed but they hadn't had sex since the Forging, and they both were a little impatient.

She plucked the pillow from his fingers, glanced at him with that smirk he wanted to kiss the corners of, and leading with her tongue, swallowed his dick into her mouth.

"Geez, Rasia, you'd think someone didn't have breakfast this morning."

Cold air struck his dick at the speed in which Rasia sprung up. She whipped around to glare at where Ysai had planted himself against the doorway. A chill ran down Kai's toes at the almost maniacal mischief in Ysai's eyes. Kai knew that look, but most of the time, it was Rasia wearing it.

"*Get out.*" She hissed over her shoulder.

"Hey, remember that time when you walked in on Jilah and me fucking, and you refused to leave until you'd released a series of farts into the room? Wasn't that *soo* funny?"

Horror crossed Rasia's face.

"Or that time when you hid in the closet and jumped out to scream right when we were almost finished, and I broke my foot?

Or when you caught us in the windship and stole our clothes, so we had to wait until night to walk home naked? Oh, how I have waited to exact my revenge."

"Ysai, *please*. I'm sorry. I'm so sorry. I was a little shit. I won't ever do it again. I promise. But please, go away."

He moved into the room, dramatic with each step.

"*Don't you dare.*"

A loud fart ripped through the room. Kai grunted when Rasia bolted off and chased after Ysai. Righteous laughter echoed down the hallway. Kai pressed his shroud to his nose to cover the smell, dressed, and decided to retreat.

Rasia stomped back with a huff, her robe torn and half-naked.

"Maybe we can try again later," he soothed. "I do have quite a bit of chores to do."

"No," she snapped, determined. "We cannot let him win!"

He studied the fire in her eyes and knew she wasn't going to let this go. He grabbed her hand and led her down the hallway to the large vacant training room. The perfect place considering the floors was accustomed to blood, and if they made a mess, he could simply switch out the reed mats.

He rubbed his thumb at Rasia's hips, and teased, "Your past isn't going to come exacting vengeance again, is it? Should I be more prepared?"

She laughed. "There are too many weapons in this room. Even Ysai-ji would think twice about interrupting us again. Now, on the floor so that I may claim my prize."

"Your prize might need help getting on the floor."

Rasia snorted at him, but she helped him down. She stripped him again of his robe, and he realized belatedly he had forgotten his loincloth in the lounging room. He lay, spread out across the training room floor with nothing on but the bandages. The wound burned every time his stomach clenched or he twisted his torso. Their usual positions were reversed. Rasia liked being catered to. She liked being the one worshiped, but looking up at her now, there was nothing but reverence in her eyes.

"Kulani," she said softly and she tossed off the remains of her robe. Her eyes pinned him to the floor. She stood over him like the agent of Death that she was, powerful and marvelous in the bright natural light of the room. He was ready for her to swoop down and claim him.

"No!"

Out of nowhere, Rae came running into the room to shove at Rasia. She remained unmoved and stared at the child with the indecision of someone deciding to crush a bug. After a moment of consideration, she pushed them back. Rae fell on their butt, indignant, and with tears gathering in their eyes, looked at Kai to make sure he had seen what had happened.

"*Rasia.*"

"Ignore them." She moved to straddle him, but he caught her by the hips.

He said, struggling, "I can't have sex in front of my jih."

"My tahs had sex in front of me all the time. You just need to set boundaries." She rolled her neck all the way around until her eyes landed on Rae. They flinched under her glare and flinched further when she poked them in the chest. "No sex until you earn your face."

"Because that worked really well with you," he said, with biting sarcasm.

"Hey, look who's talking."

"Rae?!" Ysai called out through the hallways, right before rounding into the sparring room. He spotted them and immediately tumbled into laughter. "I didn't do this on purpose, I swear."

"I am going to kill you," Rasia threatened.

"You would miss me." He winked and grabbed Rae under the armpits. He turned the child around and addressed Rae directly as he walked out of the room. "Let's give them some alone time. We'll come back when they're done in about . . . three vibrations."

"Kai can last a whole lot longer than that!"

Ysai guffawed down the hall. When Ysai accepted the job as sentry, Kai had not foreseen these sorts of problems. He grumbled, "Your jih is a menace."

"*Your* jih is a menace," she shot back. She blinked down at him. "Somewhere else?"

Kai agreed.

They went to the baths. This time, they got as far as one deep satisfying stroke before he looked up and found Rae glaring at them from the steps. Rasia screamed for Ysai.

Ysai came rushing in, scratching his head, and admitted, "Okay, this is getting weird. But I can't decide what is weirder—the fact Rae keeps disappearing on me, or how you sound like a dying gonda."

Rasia threw a block of soap at his head, and Ysai rushed out the bath with Rae, cackling. She dropped her chin on Kai's shoulder with a pout.

"You were a lot worse, weren't you?" he asked, knowingly.

"I regret all of my past shenanigans."

They tried the rooftop next since Rae couldn't yet climb the stairs without help, but Kai was immediately reminded that Nico had tent guards posted around the house. While Rasia was down for some exhibitionism, he was not, and they immediately retreated from the gleam of a distant eyeglass.

They chose a random closet in the maze where he stored the cleaning supplies. He was certain no one could possibly find them, and then a scream erupted from the other side of the door.

"I don't fucking believe this," Rasia said. He heard her forehead drop against the opposite wall. They had frozen awkwardly, with Rasia bent over. "Maybe if we don't do anything, they'll go away?"

The scream developed into a full-blown tantrum. He tried to ignore it and let it pass, but he didn't have it in him to let Rae get away with such bad behavior. He freed himself of Rasia, much to her annoyance. He grabbed one of the baskets on the shelves to place it in front of him and snapped open the door.

"Stop," he said in a no-nonsense voice.

Rae immediately stopped crying, then blinked and wilted, knowing they were in big trouble. They rarely had such tantrums around Kai, and he didn't appreciate the desperate measures to get his attention. The child had his full attention now. "You are supposed to be playing with Ysai. Running away from him is not nice. What is wrong?"

"I want to play with you." Rae's eyes shifted over to Rasia emerging from the closet. She stepped out naked into the hallway and fanned herself with one of the basket lids. Rae's eyes turned downright hateful looking at her. Kai wasn't used to seeing such harsh emotions on the young child, so much so, that it caught him off guard.

"You've got to learn how to share," he lectured.

"No!"

"I'm done with this," Rasia said and sneered down at Rae. "I'm out."

"Where are you going?" he asked, alarmed.

"I don't know. For a fucking run. I'm cramping too much for this shit."

"Are you going to be back for dinner?" he called out, but Rasia had already rounded the corner. He turned back to Rae, who sat on the floor triumphant and pleased. He never got the chance to tell her about Kenji coming over tonight. He desperately hoped that Rasia made it back in time for dinner.

CHAPTER FIFTY

1

"I've never seen anything like it," Zephyr marveled as he and Nico walked the wingfields between the copper plots of sorghum. "These fields are an impressive feat of construction and engineering. I understand now why you're so proud of them."

She smiled, pleased. She had pumped not only her magic, but also so much of her sweat into these fields. The temple may have been the heart of the Elder, but the lifeblood flowed here.

"Imagine these fields stretching on forever," she said. She could see the dream so clearly—the lush greenery, the rich soil, constructed aqueducts, and food plentiful enough to overflow rations.

"How was work? You looked quite busy when I arrived," he noted. They had a lunch planned, and she had told him if he arrived early, she could give him a tour, but she had only managed to show him a third of it.

"We found an infestation of aphids in the wheat fields," she said with a sigh. "We had to hose down each individual plant, which had been a massive-unplanned drain on our water supply that left me responsible for replacing it."

And then there were the endless meetings among the botanists on how to prevent the infestation from happening again—from introducing more ladybugs and lacewings to growing more pungent smelling crops like onion and garlic around the fields. Most likely she and the other botanists would decide on what to do when they met later this evening.

Finally, the lunch drum rolled through the Grankull. The following drum signaled high noon, and the next drum signaled a return to work. Lunch often lasted over an extended two-drum period, ending well after the hottest part of the day.

"You're ready?" she asked.

"As ready as I'll ever be," he said.

They joined the crowd of people breaking for lunch. Some headed toward the market to get some errands done, to their homes for lunch, or to the bathhouses. They walked toward the Belly neighborhood. Zephyr had brought the guest gifts, and they walked down the street with a gift in their hands.

The Belly Councilor glared at both Nico and Zephyr as they approached up the road, from where the Councilor sat playing mehen on the veranda of their house. The home was one of the largest dwellings in the Belly district, built with swooping arches and columns of the new geometric art style sweeping the richer areas.

Nico gave her best smile and bowed her head in acknowledgement. "Nakimin Belly Councilor. I appreciate you agreeing to meet with me."

"Nicolai Dragonshield," the Belly Councilor acknowledged and didn't bother to incline her head. They hadn't bothered to get up to greet them either, but since they were an elder, Nico let it pass without comment.

She offered the prepared guest gift, a bag of tea leaves from her garden. Neema, who was attending her granta, accepted the gift on her granta's behalf. Nico hadn't seen Neema since the namepour and judging by her expression, she hadn't wanted to be seen. Her braids were intricate and woven immaculately. During the Forging, she had worn clips of dragonglass. Now she wore expensive rubies and turquoise decorating her hair. The Belly Councilor had plenty of grandchildren. Choosing Neema to serve her today had been a calculated choice.

"I understand this is some sort of introduction?" the Belly Councilor asked.

"Yes. I have been requested to introduce you to Zephyrus Dragonblood, the child of Raiment Zara-kulani. As you are aware, Raiment-shi is only allowed to do business in the Claws district, but now that his child is of age, Zephyr-kull has been tasked with settling a few business items for him. I have been asked to make an introduction."

"Zephyrus Dragonblood," Zephyr said, introducing himself. "I appreciate you meeting with me."

Zephyr pulled back the linen from the basket he carried to display several bottles of assorted foreign wine. Neema's eyes bulged at the expense. "I thought this was the custom. I apologize if this is not the standard guest gift."

Neema's eyes narrowed at him, smelling Zephyr's horseshit, but his face stayed unbreakable. She snatched the basket away and then crouched over to show the gift to her granta.

"It is acceptable," the Belly Councilor said and waved a dismissive hand. "Join me for tea."

Neema withdrew to carry the gifts into the house and returned with a tray of tea. She cleared the table of the coiled snake board and the matching game pieces.

Nico and Zephyr sat down on the opposing cushions. Neema served the tea, first her granta, and then Zephyr, and then Nico. It was a subtle insult. The order all wrong. You always served the guests first. Then you served by the number of names.

"What is this about?" the Councilor asked. She looked at Nico, but Nico was only here for the "introduction." Nico left this part for Zephyr to handle. She picked up the hand-painted teacup to take a sip of the hibiscus tea, a light and refreshing tea often served during high noon.

"I regret to inform you that my father's clients are becoming a little disinterested in the evory trade," Zephyr began. "As most of our supply comes from your family, my father is considering diversifying his assets."

A clatter rang out when Neema stumbled with the tray. The

Belly Councilor narrowed their eyes dangerously. The evory trade made up most of the family's income.

"And how much are you planning to diversify?" the Councilor asked and took a sip of tea. Neema mumbled out an apology that her granta didn't acknowledge.

Zephyr's face flattened with so little emotion, he had turned into another person, one born of a merchant. "We have decided not to buy any of your evory this season. It's just business."

The Belly Councilor swiveled and pointed their finger at Nico. "Your tah murdered my grandchild and now you're trying to ruin my family?!"

"Excuse me," Zephyr interrupted. "Your vote for a purge is on record. Why would my family want to do business with someone who is trying to ruin them? Did you think there wouldn't be any consequences?"

"Your family would have had special protections," the Belly Councilor said. "It was the rest of the Tents we wanted to purge. The Grankull would not have risked its relationship with your tah. In fact, we were planning on strengthening it."

After everyone was dead, and Raiment didn't have a choice, Nico had no doubt.

"You further disrespect us," he said, dark and disapproving. "My father would have not taken that deal out of respect for his kulani. Zara-ta does not care for the Grankull. You think you know us, but you do not. You will learn soon though, for I am here now to ensure my family has a voice."

Nico did not doubt that the reason Zephyr didn't experience the same difficulties as Kai during the Naming Ceremony was because the Grankull wanted his father's wealth. They thought accepting him into the community would further ingratiate the Council with his father, without ever considering who Zephyr might be. The Belly Councilor now looked as if they were regretting that choice.

The Councilor snapped, "What do you want?"

"Step down as Belly Councilor," Nico said, finally joining the conversation. "Azan's tah plans to run this season, and you will make sure he runs unopposed."

The Belly Councilor spat in Nico's tea. She placed a hand on Zephyr's arm and did not let that deter her.

"Ava-ta owed you a blood price," she said. "I understand that, but she is gone now, and all blood debts are left with the dead. Therefore, your actions against me and my family have been wholly unjustified. In fact, there might be certain," she tapped a fingernail against the teacup, "cases if I ever learn about that might entitle me to a blood price. I certainly seem to be collecting quite a few recently."

"Leave my veranda."

The Belly Councilor was a stubborn old carrion, and if the decision was up to them alone, Nico doubted she would ever convince the old bird to step down, but Neema had been there to overhear and relay the news. This was a family matter, and the family might decide differently.

"Thank you for your time," she said. She and Zephyr got up. As they started away, she turned to look over her shoulder at the white-haired elder, bitter and stubborn in their old age. Then she looked at Neema, who had always glared at her with daggers. Nico said, "It is time you choose what is more important: your hatred or your future."

Hate never dies.

Perhaps someday, Neema could allow herself to let her hate go.

CHAPTER FIFTY-ONE

—

"I think Rae's magic is starting to develop," Kai told Nico later that day while they prepared dinner. He told her what happened with Rasia that morning and the tests of "hide-n-seek" they played after with Ysai. "Rae could tell me everywhere you were today and found me no matter where I hid, but not anyone else. They're becoming more sensitive to magic. It's too early, isn't it? I could always sense you and Ava-ta, but it was different with you?"

"The sensing comes at an earlier age," she agreed as they moved around each other in the kitchen. He sort of missed when they used to cook dinner together, but now she didn't have much time anymore. "But it's true that Rae is a few years earlier than me. But why so sudden? I remember it more gradually. Maybe something triggered it?"

"There's also the increase in nightmares and how clingy they've become," he said. "At first, I thought it was Rasia being in the house and having someone around they're not used to, but I don't know."

He frowned and tried to pinpoint when this all started. Then his mouth went dry at the realization. He froze and too much salt slid onto the vegetables. "How close was Rae during the Naming Ceremony? Did they see . . . when the crowd . . ."

Nico looked at him, and a stewing silence bubbled between them.

"I don't know," she said honestly. "I wasn't paying attention to where they were. I was focused on you. I can ask tah how much Rae saw."

Kai thought he remembered now a distant cry calling his name as he disappeared under the fists and feet. He pressed his face to his hands and couldn't believe he hadn't realized the problem sooner. He had been so caught up in Rasia and making sure he was there for her following her tah's death that he had missed what was going on with Rae, even though they had been trying to communicate the problem in their own childlike manner.

"Rae saw," he said, brokenly. They shouldn't have had to see that. The Naming Ceremony continued to haunt him, leaving unexpected cracks in Kai's life that sometimes showed themselves much later, lying in wait until you stumbled over them.

"We'll talk to them," she promised.

"It should probably be me," he said. His shoulders drooped as he attempted to salvage the salty vegetables. As he did so, he considered what words he might say. Rae understood that Kai and Kenji's relationship were complicated, and their interruptions into a room had sometimes saved him from physical abuse, but to have witnessed on such a wide scale how everyone hated him . . .

Nico came through and teasingly bumped him with her hip as she passed by, jostling him out of his depressing train of thought. She carried the steam-pot of couscous to the spot on the counter next to him.

He had feared how last night would change things between him and her, but he finally felt that some of the pressure had lifted. Even the weightier conversations weren't as heavy to push through as they had been before.

"Let me know how it goes," she said.

"I was also thinking," he said as he laid out the dishware. "That maybe, you should bring Kenjinn into your campaign? You need the help, and he's good with people. It'll give him something to do to keep him busy."

"That's funny," she said, amused. "I was sort of thinking the same thing. You can't be expected to shoulder most of the chores around here. I was thinking of assigning breakfast to him as his responsibility. It'll keep him from sleeping in but also give you some much needed help. Also, you have a kulani now. I understand that you two need some alone time."

He blushed as he thought of the position she had caught them in that morning. She was a lot more chill about things now that it was all sort of legal. She plated the vegetables over the couscous. He followed behind her with ladles of broth. They filled four plates.

"Is Rasia not coming to dinner?" she asked.

He hadn't seen Rasia since she ran off earlier that morning. He squinted to try and sense her, but controlling his magic was harder in the Grankull. The buildings made the wind more erratic, and sand was dusted away nightly by the sweepers. As he focused, he could sense the vast ocean of Nico's magic, but anything smaller was a lot harder to discern. He had to shift through a lot of people in the Grankull. Out in the Desert, Kai sensed Rasia as easily as the next gust of wind. He gave up with a sigh. "Can you sense where she is?"

"Try again," she encouraged. "Focus on what is there, and not what is lacking. Don't invoke magic half-expecting it to fail. Hold your confidence and know exactly what you want."

Kai pouted and with a sigh, tried again. Tracking Rasia had been so easy in the Desert that he had initially done so unconsciously. Back at the gorge, he had been so intrigued by her that he had wanted to know what she was up to every vibration of the day. He focused on the breath of her, on the way air expelled from her lungs. He focused on the sand stuck to her skin and hair. He focused on wanting her—on wanting to know where she was, and how she was doing, and if she was feeling better, and he hoped she still wasn't mad about earlier, and—oh. Rasia flared a bright light to his senses.

"She's at Ysai's place," Kai reported.

"Good job." Nico patted his arm. "Maybe she got distracted. I'm sure she would have been here if she knew how important this dinner was." Nico glanced over at him, suspiciously. "You did tell her Kenji-ta was moving back in?"

". . ."

"Kai!"

"I was seriously going to tell her but we kept getting interrupted. I didn't get the chance."

"You're telling her as soon as you're able," Nico said, brooking no argument. She handed the two completed plates over to him, while she grabbed the other two.

He moved toward the doorway and froze. He could hear Kenji and Rae in the serving room, where Kenji asked Rae about their day. The nerves and anxiety he had tried to push down all day suddenly battered him full force. Nico placed a hand on his arm, and only at her touch did he realize his shaking hands were rattling the plates. She took one from him to lessen his burden.

"Kai, if you're not ready, that's *okay*."

He clenched his eyes shut and could audibly hear the blood pounding in his ears. He licked at the salt sweat above his lip. Last night, after speaking with Nico, he had come up with all the things he would say, but at that moment he couldn't remember any of them.

Time swallowed him, and he came back to awareness panting, where he had raced with his plate all the way back to his storage closet. He placed his plate atop his curled knees and glared at the food mulishly. He chewed, embarrassed, on the salty taste.

Nico had been right. He hadn't been ready after all.

CHAPTER FIFTY-TWO

I

Kenji-ta lay sprawled across the bare floor of the library and tossed a scroll in his boredom. He had a habit of never sitting in actual chairs, often more comfortable on dirt floors. He came in a little while ago, without a word, while Nico updated her vote tally.

She studied her tah, thinking of how she liked Kai's suggestion. She asked him, "You're good with talking to people. I could use some help with my campaign, if you're interested?"

"Sure," he agreed, without much consideration, as if he had been sitting around waiting for her to give him something to do and didn't much care what it would be.

"Great. It's so difficult not only having to think of my campaign but also that of my opposition." She turned to the faces of the Council members who opposed her.

Tah pointed his scroll at her reed board. "The Hindlegs will be easy. I grew up with him, and he is still that same greedy self-serving bastard. All you need is someone competitive enough to run against him. If the Councilor thinks he'll come close to losing, he'd be willing to make a deal, and with both sides in your pocket, you win no matter who wins that seat."

"That's brilliant, but I don't know that neighborhood very well. You were raised there. Do you think you could find me a candidate that could oppose him?"

"I'll ask around."

"That would be a great help. The Tents are eyeing the Pelvis, but none of them can agree on which person to back. It's a mess. Maybe if you got a job as a musician, you could run for the Pelvis seat," she teased half-heartedly. Members of the same household couldn't hold two different seats, and Kenji-ta left that job long before she was born, but people still spoke of those legendary nights on the Pelvis stages.

"Hmm," tah said.

She wasn't sure which part of what she said had bothered him. The idea of picking up the ilhan again, or the idea of getting a new job. She chose the safer topic. "You promised you would retire from the kulls. You'll have to replace that job with something else."

"Right. Right. I know," he said and tossed that scroll back in the air.

"Have you *told* the kulls you're going to quit?"

"I'll tell them after the tryouts. They'll hate it, but it's time. They know it's time. If I don't, I'll die out there." He caught the scroll perfectly balanced on his palm. "I know that."

Nico saw it more clearly now that Kai had pointed it out—or maybe she had been too afraid to face it. At that moment, she knew with a certainty that tah had been hoping to die a hunter's death—but his kull wouldn't let him. They were good to him. They covered for him. They protected him, even when he had become a liability.

"Why didn't he come to dinner?" Tah asked, pulling them away from those emotional storm clouds in the distance. "I thought you said he agreed to let me move back in."

"What did you expect? He's been banned from family dinners with you ever since he could remember. He'll work himself up to it."

"I tried talking to him after. Walked in on him in the baths, but he just ran away." His expression soured. He tossed the scroll back up in the air and grumbled. "That kid is weird."

She squinted at him and then swatted that scroll out of the air with a jet of water. It plopped onto his face and tah blew it off with a pout. "Really?" she said. "You? Calling someone weird? Weren't you the one who burst into tears on your first kull hunt?"

He turned to look at her and held his head propped on one hand. He scratched at his leg with his toes and huffed. "Gonda are beautiful majestic creatures."

She shook her head. She always had trouble consolidating the empathetic nature people often criticized him for with the enduring hatred he had for Kai. Sometimes it was the softest people that could harden the most. She wished life was as easy as the stories. What did you do when the villain and hero are one and the same? What did you do when the resolution didn't require a fight or some grand battle? When the obstacles are just pride, mistakes, and flaws?

She cleared her throat of the growing emotional knot and changed the subject. "The school season is starting soon. Rae is of age, and I fear giving the Council another reason to criticize us if we don't send them to school. But we . . ." She bit her tongue, reminding herself she didn't need to ask permission anymore. Now it was her name on the clan seals. "I'm selling some of tah's things to pay for Rae's schooling."

A rigid vein popped in tah's jaw.

"Sell my ilhans," he suggested instead.

Her fists tightened in her lap where she sat at the desk. She tapped down on the swirling torrent in her chest. She suggested slowly, "Maybe that's a little premature? Rasia says Kai is pretty good at playing. I'm sure you can teach him a lot. Perhaps that is something you can do together."

Tah scoffed. "He can't even stay in the same room as me."

"And whose fault is that?" she snapped.

"Look Nico-po," Tah said, heaving his entire body in an exhausted sigh. "Give him all the ilhans. Whatever. I don't care. But I don't think . . ." He shook his head. "I don't think I'm ever going to play again."

She looked down and watched the pitter-patter of tears fall

onto her fists. She didn't know why those words hit her so hard, but they felt as if he had given up. A metaphorical storm hung over their heads. It rained down on every beat of their conversations. But she was done detouring every time the conversation grew too ominous. She was done avoiding the subject and running away and hoping the truth wouldn't catch her. The only way to beat a storm was to sail through it.

"Do you want to die?" she said the words out loud, the words she had been circling around for years without ever truly knowing it. But she knew better now. After her conversation with Kai, she decided to rifle through the memories stored in the Elder bones. She had only received snippets of lifetimes during the bloodrites, but the memories of all the Ohans remained in the bones whenever she needed them. She hoped the memories could give her answers, but they only gave her more questions.

She watched anger cross his face. She wondered if anyone had ever blatantly confronted him before. Suicide was often a taboo topic in the Grankull, as if talking about it invited the gaze of the Hunter's Eye.

"I know you've tried once before," she said. He couldn't hide from her anymore. At the admission, as if recognizing the futility of all that heat, his anger deflated out of his chest. He dropped back down and cradled his arms around his knees.

This wasn't the first time Kenji-ta had struggled. It also happened after Kai's birth when he had disappeared for blinks to everyone's worry. She glanced down at that scar on his arm, from what she once thought was a blood price. Tah seemed to have clawed out of that pit of darkness when she had been born. So perhaps Kai was right. Tah could come back again. Past Ohans have been ensnared within Death's trap, as Kai described it, and she had traveled their memories trying to understand.

"Jih wouldn't have told you," tah muttered. He stilled in thought, then glanced at her with a brooding consideration, just as perceptive as Kai. "Your tah knew things she shouldn't have known either."

"I can't say," she said.

"I know." He planted his chin onto his arms. "I . . . I'm sorry."

She glanced down, choking up. "You can talk to me about it. I'll listen."

"I don't know," he shrugged, with a tone as if commenting on the weather. "You don't need me anymore. You've outgrown any lessons I've got to teach, Rae prefers Kai, and Kai wants nothing to do with me. I'm wasting space, and my kulani has been waiting for me."

"I'll always need you, tah," she said. "It may seem like I've got a handle on everything, but I'm drowning here. I always need help. And Rae needs you, too. I don't think they've taken everything that's happened very well. And Kai is the one who advocated for you to return home. It might not seem like it now but give him time and he'll talk. It might take moonblinks, or seasons, but he'll talk. As long as you're trying, he'll try too."

"What if it's not enough?" he asked. "I've slayed dragons, and yet I can barely find the strength to get out of bed at times."

She thought of something Zephyr had said—how in his language they had a word for love. In the Grankull, it was an action. It was something you did. That was why she felt hurt every time tah broke his promises, and why she struggled so much with the fact he couldn't seem to *do* anymore.

But that didn't mean he loved her any less.

She got up and walked over to her tah. She placed a hand on his back, and he shifted to hug tightly around her waist. One of the strongest persons she had ever known shook and crumbled in her arms. She felt guilty for almost giving up on him. Tah was struggling. She could see that now. Perhaps she didn't know how to help, but at least now she knew he needed it.

The stories warned you of dragons, and crafty silk spiders, and gonda that vibrated the ground. They warned you of all the things you could slay, but never the things you couldn't. Never those things that required building, or healing, or the sort of grind that needed more than one story to tell.

In real life, happy endings required work.

CHAPTER FIFTY-THREE

O

"It's not fair," Rasia whined as she dropped her chin onto Ysai and Jilah's dinner table. Jilah, not taking Rasia very seriously, patted Rasia on the back as she held in a laugh. "First, we had to wait until the Naming Ceremony. And then, he was too injured. And now, everyone keeps interrupting us. I'm finally on gonom and we can't get one moment alone. It's been forever! What's the point of having a kulani if we can't have sex whenever we want? But *no*, if it's not Nico interrupting us, then it's someone else!"

Ysai scoffed. "You might be surprised to find this out Rasia, but adulthood isn't always fun sexy times. Sometimes your little jih hides in the closet while you're having sex, only to scare the shit out of you right at the end."

"It wasn't that bad."

"I broke my foot!"

She pouted and blinked up at him all innocently. "Come on, I was a child back then. I didn't know any better."

He glared at her. "That was only a few blinks ago!"

"Okay. Okay. Okay. I'm sorry. I am truly sorry for being a little shit, and now that I know better, my little shit ways are completely reformed."

Jilah gave a mock gasp. "Did you hear that? Did the great Rasia Dragonfire actually apologize?"

Ysai grinned wickedly. "You should have heard her earlier when she had Kai's dick-"

He ducked underneath the sitting mat Rasia threw at him. Jilah shook her head, amused. She began clearing the empty plates from the table and glanced down at the leftover food on Rasia's plate. She asked more seriously, "Are you okay?"

"Yeah," Rasia mumbled. She dropped from her chin to her cheek against the table. "Just cramps. Making me feel nauseous." Ysai motioned and she slid over her plate for him to eat the rest.

"It's your first deathsblood since . . . the culling," Jilah said, concerned. "Maybe you should see a healer? Don't tell them what happened obviously but . . . It's not usually this bad for you."

"I'll be fine," Rasia huffed. She peeked up at Jilah. "Where's the alcohol?"

"We're out right now."

Rasia looked at both Jilah and Ysai in horror. Alcohol was always on hand, if for nothing more than unexpected guests who might drop by.

Ysai chuckled at her misfortune and explained, "I used all my supply for the deathpour. I was going to pick some up tomorrow."

"And you really shouldn't be drinking alcohol," Jilah said. "It makes you dehydrated and can worsen your cramps."

"I don't care. I want to get drunk." With an idea, Rasia pushed herself up from the table. "I'm going to the Pelvis."

"By yourself?" Jilah asked in alarm.

She snorted. "I'll be fine."

"Absolutely not," Jilah said. She grabbed Rasia's shoulders and turned her back around. "Everyone knows your name. The moment you walk into the Pelvis, you'll be the center of everyone's attention. You barely have much patience to deal with people on a good day."

"But I haven't gone yet," Rasia complained. Ysai raised a brow, and she admitted, "legally."

The Pelvis was the party district of the Grankull, where the gambling halls, entertainment houses, and the stables were clustered in one area. It was where all the new faces and anyone without familial obligations went after work to blow off steam. Children were forbidden from entering, although Rasia had snuck in with Ysai last year but had to flee early when one of her cousins recognized her. Yes, she thought. The Pelvis could be just the distraction she needed from the twisting pain occurring right now in her own stupid pelvis.

She looked over her shoulder and pouted at Jilah. "Why don't you come with me?"

Jilah tilted her head in consideration. While Ysai was more of the homebody, Jilah often went out with her friends. She glanced over at Ysai. "We haven't had a night out together in a while."

Rasia smiled. Her work here was done. All she had to do was convince Jilah and Ysai would inevitably follow.

Ysai groaned. "I can't risk a hangover for work tomorrow."

"We could leave early," Jilah suggested, and then her eyes brightened. "And your tah's not around to criticize every little thing that we do anymore. This will be fun."

Ysai sighed. "Fine. Let's go be stupidly irresponsible adults."

Jilah and Rasia cheered. Then she turned to Rasia with a grin that could rattle most bones. "Let's get you dressed."

Jilah wrapped Rasia in a halter made of silk spider gossamer, atop a matching pair of red pants so she didn't feel self-conscious about her deathsblood all night. Jilah had chunked Rasia's wrap, and Rasia kept looking down at how her nipples were visible through the thin fabric. It was perhaps the most revealing thing she had ever worn, and she grinned about it gleefully. She wondered what Kai might think of it and remembered sourly that he was stuck at home. Nico decided that he should stay inside and keep a low-profile until the heat from the Naming Ceremony had died down. Even afterward, Rasia doubted he'd be able to come to a place like this without finding some sort of trouble.

Rasia smirked when they made it through the sentry checkpoints and entered under the wide arch of the Elder's pelvic bone. Different musical styles competed to entice the most customers. The close quarters of people drinking and dancing produced too much heat for it all to be contained within adobe walls. "Stages" were nothing more than columns and open sky. In her thigh-length silk, Jilah sashayed the way to her favorite stage. Her beaded broad collar, a namesake, reflected light as she walked.

The Evory Stage, built atop an evory floor as white as the saltpans, was one of the most infamous stages in the entire Grankull. The entry fee was expensive, the alcohol was expensive, and only the best musicians ever played on its tiles.

Ropes around the stage restricted access. Because of the rainy season, they'd stretched blue silk from column to column. Glittering windchimes danced in the wind, and the dragonglass inset into the evory sparkled. The stage felt like dancing on the night sky.

As they approached, the ticketer immediately lit up at the sight of Rasia's face. "Rajiani Dragonfire," the ticketer said with a smile and moved to allow her free access. "We've been waiting for you."

Rasia strolled in and then laughed when she turned to find Ysai and Jilah stuck in line to pay. She turned on her heel and informed the ticketer, "they're with me," before grabbing them both in each arm and skipping them past the line straight onto the most exclusive stage of the Grankull. That was the sort of power you accumulated when you had a name.

Behind her, the ticketer announced to the next passer-by, "Welcome to the Evory Stage, the favorite stage of Rasia Dragonfire!"

One point in time, she thought this was going to be her life—hunting with the kulls and in the off-season, partying and fucking every day until the sun rose. Up to the Naming Ceremony, she had imagined doing all those things with Kai at her side. Even now, she wanted to be out having fun with him.

"Rasia-kull!"

She turned at the informal shout and grinned when she spotted Azan with all his jihs, sitting at a table that encircled a fire in the middle. She raced over and slammed into Azan's hug that engulfed her in biceps. She hugged Azan back, so excited she could do that now.

"Get her a drink!" Someone demanded. She wholeheartedly agreed.

Content that Rasia and Ysai were situated, Jilah left them to greet some friends from her old Forging kull. Aden grinned up at Ysai's approach. "You're not normally out and about."

He shuffled his hand atop Rasia's head and skewed the borrowed carnelian headband. Jilah thought it looked nice with Rasia's shorter hairstyle. "Someone's got to keep her out of trouble," he said.

One of Azan's jihs leaned in wickedly. "Then you've come to the wrong place."

Azan delivered drinks to the table, and it was the good, strong stuff. Aden lifted his mug solemnly. "All hunters are hunted."

"All hunters are hunted," the table echoed, taking a respectful moment to acknowledge Rasia and Ysai's loss. Every time anyone offered their sympathies, she was reminded that Kiba-ta was gone. She sort of wished people would forget.

She blinked, having zoned out as Azan and his jihs set up a drinking game. Ysai placed a hand on hers. "Are you okay?" he asked concerned. "We can leave if you want."

"I'm fine," she said and then swallowed the alcohol all in one go.

Not once that night did she needed to buy her own drink. A crowd had gathered around her, all of them recognizing her from the Naming Ceremony. They asked her about the dragon, and if she would like to dance, and if she wanted sex, and if she was interested in any courtships. She stumbled over her words to explain that she had a kulani, but they looked at her absence of namesakes, and thought she was joking or drunk. She had even worn the necklace Kai had gifted her, but it remained empty of the names he was supposed to have received, and the reminder of that absence only made her angrier. Ysai often stepped in to verify she was off the courting market.

"Want to dance?" Azan offered, saving her from the endlessly multiplying crowd that hemmed her in on all sides. She found it increasingly difficult to breathe.

"Yes," she said in relief.

Ysai snapped out his hand and dug claws into Azan's forearm. "She has a kulani, and I expect you to respect that. You do anything untoward; I will rip off your dick to satisfy the blood price."

"And I thought Rasia-kull was the scary one."

He smiled. "Have fun."

Azan pulled her into the crowd of dancers. Couples danced around each other, swiveling and writhing their bodies like a snake slithering through the sand. She twisted her hips to the beat of the drums. The traditional dances performed at ceremonial celebrations were displays of technique and skill. But the informal dance of the pelvis was something more primal and suggestive.

Kai should have been here. She could imagine him here, awkward at first, but more and more bold in his movements with some alcohol in him. The dances often switched roles at the beat of the music, one partner the anchor, and the other rotating around to tease the other with an intoxicating gyration of hips. They say you could tell if someone was good at sex by how well they could dance. In that case, Kai had to be a good dancer, too. Maybe with all that self-consciousness stripped away.

She wished she could dance with Kai sweaty under the stars, she wished she could show him off to the doubters and disbelievers, she wished he could strut anywhere he wanted on the power of his name, and wished they could have the opportunity to patron one of the stables. Most new faces still lived with their families, and the stables provided a place for discreet trysts.

But the Grankull took that away from them. The Grankull took away their Naming night, which should have been filled with sex, drinks, and laughter—but all they got was blood and pain instead. She never got to toast her names with her family.

She never got to enjoy the bodika. And even though Rasia would have chosen Kai over anything else that night, it should not have been a choice required of them in the first place. The Grankull had taken so much away from them.

"You don't seem to be having fun anymore," Azan said.

She hadn't noticed when she stopped dancing. She looked around in frustration and suddenly hated that she had decided to come out that night. All she wanted was to have some fun, and she didn't know why that was suddenly so hard to do.

She shrugged. "I don't know."

He tilted his head thoughtfully. "Do you want another drink?"

She looked down. The heavy earthenware mug that she held had been emptied. She didn't remember doing that. "Yeah, sure."

He touched a hand to her waist and guided her out of the crowd of dancers. His hand was deliciously warm. She glanced at it, and then up at him, and asked, "Do you want to have sex?"

Azan's normally affable disposition turned rather serious as he glanced down at her necklace. "That's his namesake, right? Take it off first."

"No," she said immediately and clutched at it with her free hand.

"You're hot, but there are way too many grains of sand to get caught up in a bloodprice war. Also, your jih is terrifying, and your triarch just killed a person. I'm good."

He patted her shoulder consolingly, and she shuffled forward with an indignant huff, offended he had the nerve to turn her down. She asked, "But if I didn't have a kulani, you'd fuck me, right?"

"In a heartbeat."

That made her feel better.

"Why did you do it?" he asked after they made their way to the bar and got the bartender's attention. "Why did you sign his name?"

"I . . ." She palmed the necklace in her hands. It was warm

sometimes. She admitted, "I was afraid. That tah was right. And then, Kai and I had been arguing a lot. I thought it would fix everything. I was scared of losing him," she said, softly. She wiped at her eyes, and she shrugged. "It fixed nothing at all."

※

Rasia hiccupped and hugged the jug of wine she shared with Azan. Or it started off that way, but now she hoarded all the wine for herself. She and Azan lay across one of the hammocks at the side of the stage, in the dark corner for the flames and the drunks. A couple was making out in the hammock on her right, and on her left, some random person had coiled into sleep. The stage attendants came by the check on them from time to time. The dancers blurred and wafted in her vision, sometimes like the crackling flames of a campfire, or a rain shower of stars depending on the tempo. She had no idea where Ysai and Jilah had gone, but since they were both gone together, she could guess at what they were up to.

"It wasn't supposed to be like this," she bemoaned. "I'm supposed to be living my best life!" Here she was on the sidelines, while everyone out there was having so much fun. *It wasn't fair.*

Azan nodded his head, with one leg swinging out of the hammock.

"I'm supposed to be having the time of my life and enjoying myself! I'm telling you, never sign anyone's else. Don't do it! This kulani thing is *so hard*." She squinted and pointed at Azan. "You fuck everybody."

"I'll fuck everybody," he wholeheartedly promised.

"Don't be a stupid idiot like me writing someone's name during the Naming Ceremony. Who does that? Rasia fucking Dragonfire does that, that's who! Don't you make my mistakes. Live your life! Enjoy yourself! I'm an old fart like Ysai now, never wanting to go out and have fun anymore." She beat her forehead against the opening of the wine jug, then laid her cheek atop the jug's mouth to lean forward in horror. "I'm boring now. Even *Nico* is having more sex than me! I haven't had sex in—" She squinted and counted her fingers. She ran out of fingers. "—in forever!!!"

Azan sputtered out a laugh, but when she glared at him, he quickly fixed his expression. His eye twitched as he attempted a nod. "That must be extremely difficult."

"See! You understand. I knew you'd understand. Ah shit, I'm sorry. You could have been having fun and dancing and sexing people. Now you're stuck with me."

"I'm rather enjoying myself."

She gave a deep sigh and then heaved. She hung her head between her knees and threw up over the hammock. She hated throwing up. It always tasted nasty.

"I think it's time to take you home to your kulani," he said.

"Yeah. Prolly," she said, and then upturned the wine jug. It splashed all over her face. She hadn't realized how much was left and had accidentally bathed herself in it. Jilah was going to be so pissed about her clothes. She wiped at the shirt and was saddened at the fact she couldn't clean off the wine. And she was so sticky now.

"Here. Let me help." Azan chuckled as he helped her to her feet and wrapped an arm around her waist to stabilize her wobbly legs. She frowned and forgot the reason she was so sad, but something must have been funny, so she began laughing too.

"Don't throw up on me," he warned, before dipping an arm under her legs to carry her home. They passed other bumbling groups.

He asked softly, "Do you regret it?"

She clutched the namesake dangling from her neck. She whispered her name, and in the dark, it glowed. It pointed headward, in the direction of the guiding star. Filled with the magic her kulani had gifted her. It was the most beautiful thing she had ever owned.

"Never."

CHAPTER FORTY-FOUR

—

Water slid down Rasia's skin and dripped drops through the thin linen of Kai's night robe. He caught her slick bare hips as she crawled on top of him. Despite her recent bath, her breath smelled of alcohol. He hadn't been asleep yet, on the edge of falling into it, when she tripped into the room with an unruffled laugh. She kissed him with tipsy abandon.

"What have you been up to?" he asked, amused by her loose smile. Drunk-Rasia was a bit more temperamental and emotional than Tipsy-Rasia. All Tipsy-Rasia wanted to do was laugh and fuck and have a good time. Right now, she was in the middle of both, sobering toward the latter.

"Went out with Ysai and Jilah. Had some drinks. I missed you. Come out with us next time."

"You know I can't. It's too dangerous for me," he soothed. He did not want to be around a large crowd ever again, much less a drunken one.

"I'll protect you."

"It's fine. You go out and have fun." she pouted at him, and for a moment, a spark of clarity lit her eyes. An ember flared with hot anger and disappointments. He kissed her, demanding enough to regain her attention. "Are you feeling better?"

Nico didn't usually cramp that badly, so he hadn't really known how to appropriately take care of her. He had been worried about her.

"I'm fine," she said, leaning forward, mind on other things, "now that I've got you all to myself."

The sound of familiar feet raced down the hallway.

Rasia tensed, clenched her fists into the sheets, before slamming down beside him. He quickly hid his erection as Rae burst into the room, crawled their way into the bed, and bundled against Kai's side. Now that he suspected what was going on, he didn't have the bones to fight it this time. He wrapped Rae into the covers. Rasia's disappointment razed across his shoulders like a cold draft in the room.

He knew this wasn't the ideal situation. He knew that she expected them to be a lot more intimate now that she had moved in. He turned to meet her blunt glare.

"Rasia, I'm sorry."

She exploded, tossing up the covers. "Rae is too fucking old for this shit! And you're doing them no favors by babying them. Don't you see? Rae is a little shit who hates me and wants all your attention. But you're not their tah. They aren't your problem, but you *are* my kulani, and you should be able to give me dick when I fucking want it!"

"Are you done?" he bit out.

"No!" Rasia glared down at Rae, who flinched under Kai's protective arm. "There are worse things than monsters and the fucking dark, kid. Get over yourself."

"Rasia," Kai said evenly. "You've been drinking. Go to sleep."

She hissed at the order. She tried storming out of the bed, but her legs got caught up in the sheets. She wrestled with them, losing, until she collapsed back into the bed in defeat. Her heated breaths calmed, but Rae's grip didn't lessen. They shook in Kai's arms, terrified.

"It's okay," he soothed, rubbing a hand up their back. "Sometimes adults have temper tantrums, too."

"I heard that."

He ignored her. Having Rasia around for this conversation

probably wasn't the most comforting, but he couldn't avoid it any longer. He had to remind himself that Nico and Rasia weren't the only ones who needed to hear his words. Kai adjusted in bed and turned over to block Rasia completely from Rae's view. He gave Rae his full undivided attention. "Are you afraid of Rasia?"

Rae nodded against his chest, so fearful that she might overhear the answer.

"Why?"

He waited patiently while Rae picked at the linen of his shirt. Finally, they said, soft into his chest. "Because she hurts you."

"She's my kulani. She'll never hurt me."

"Tah hurts you. And . . . and . . ." Rae's face scrunched and gazed up at Kai so confused and uncomprehending. "Why no one like you?"

His mouth went dry. He thought he was ready for this conversation. How did he explain to a child who had only been alive for five years why the entire Grankull despised his big jih? No one should have to face such awful understanding.

No doubt Rae had always known something. It was why they didn't argue when asked to hold Kai's hand whenever they walked through the streets of the Grankull. They knew that people didn't like Kai but before, they had only ever witnessed Kenji being outright violent against him. Now . . .

His throat creaked sore and heavy. "Rae, a few days ago, did you see when the people hurt me?"

They nodded against his chest. "They hurt you when I sleep too."

Kai felt himself shutting down, and at that moment felt powerless to stop himself from withdrawing. He should have taken Nico up on her offer to explain it together. He thought he was strong enough for this. But all he wanted to do was sob. He used to be a hero in Rae's eyes. Now, what was he?

"Jijih?" They asked, but Kai had no words.

A weight pressed suddenly on Kai's arm. Rasia popped her head over him and looked at Rae intently. "Do you like dragons?"

Rae looked at Kai, then at Rasia, and nodded timidly. "The

nice ones."

"Right. In the stories, there are both nice and bad dragons." Rasia leaned forward and whispered to Rae, secretly. "Kai is a dragon."

They scrunched their face.

"People are mean to Kai because they're afraid of him. They think he's a bad dragon, but you and I know the truth. Our Kai is a good dragon. Our Kai is gentle and sweet and full of magic and power. But he can't defend himself, because if he does, people will fear him even more. He can't fight back in the ways that I can," she said, almost painfully. "That's why I'll protect him from anyone who wants to harm him. I'll keep him safe."

Rae stared at her, mistrustful, and unconvinced. "But you hurt jijih today."

"I did not."

"You did."

"Kid, I have no idea what the fuck you're talking about."

"You hurt jijih!"

Kai realized the misunderstanding. Rae didn't grow up in a household that had tahs with a healthy sex life, nor did they get out much. Compared to the rest of the kids of the Grankull, Rae was rather sheltered. Kai sighed. Looked like there were several conversations happening tonight. "Rae, she wasn't hurting me. We were having sex."

Above Kai, Rasia snorted. "Is that what this is about? Alright, look kid, Kai has a penis and I have a vagina. Or sometimes you can have two penises. Or two vaginas. There are a lot of ways to have sex. Like, a lot. But don't have sex without gonom because that means a baby, and you don't want those problems."

Kai squeezed her arm. "Thank you, Rasia, but I got it from here."

Rae blankly blinked at them both. Kai didn't think Rae was ready for or mature enough to understand the technicals right now. What they really needed was the assurance that it was safe. Kai tried to grasp an example that he thought they could understand.

"Do you know what a kulani is?"

"Tajihs are kulani."

"Right, and would Anji-taji or Juno-taji ever hurt each other?"

They shook their head.

"Rasia is my kulani too, and she would never ever hurt me either," he said. "We were trying to have sex today and that's different. It doesn't hurt. It's a sort of . . . play that only adults do. Do you understand?"

They nodded slowly. Kai raised his arm, and they didn't hesitate to dive underneath. He brushed at Rae's hair. "Sex feels good, but it's something you've got to earn. You can only do it when you're an adult. If you do it before then, the Council won't like it, and they'll try to take you away from us like they tried to take you away from us before. Understand?"

They nodded against him. Then their head quirked in thought, and Kai waited for the question. "Are you an adult? You slayed the bad dragon, but you wear a shroud outside."

Another difficult question. But one that needed an answer. The line between childhood and adulthood in the Grankull was so clear-cut, and Kai feared blurring Rae's understanding of those lines.

"A lot of people don't believe I slayed the dragon. That's why all those people were angry at me. They thought I was lying."

"Jijih never lies."

"Exactly. One day I'll show them the truth, but for now, I wear the shroud outside to protect myself. But with you, and Nico, and Rasia, I don't need it. Here, inside the house, I am an adult."

Kai had to remember that himself, too, sometimes. Despite what the Grankull believed, he was an adult. This wasn't the Forging anymore, where the underage had to lock any mention of sex into boxes of dragonsteel secrets. There was nothing to hide or be ashamed of. He'd earned his pleasure. He didn't have to stop for anyone.

"Jijih." They asked, "What are your names?"

"I . . . don't know."

"Nico has too many names. I can't remember them."

Kai smiled and reminded himself to tell that one to Nico later. "I think jijih is a fine name. Now, go to sleep. If you have more questions, we can talk tomorrow." He pulled up the covers and tucked they in more securely. He listened as they fell asleep.

"You two are disgustingly sweet."

"You go to sleep too."

Rasia snorted.

He flipped over onto his back and a cool breeze circulated into the room through the gardens. He told her, "Thank you for your help. About the dragons. It was a good example."

"I'm sorry for being an ass."

"I do get to fuck it every now and then, so you're forgiven."

She laughed, and then curled over to sleepily lay her head against his chest. He combed his fingers through her hair. The short strands were still damp from the bath.

"Do you think I'm doing a good job? With Rae?" he asked. "Sometimes I feel the Council might be right. This isn't the type of home a kid should be growing up in—always afraid someone is going to break in and assassinate your jihs at any moment."

"You have a maze in your house," she said. "You have a secret chamber and underground hatches. I don't think the magicborn have ever had the luxury of growing up without fear."

"I just . . . want Rae to be safe. Ava-ta would never—I feel as if I'm failing them both."

"Stop." She told him. "You are a good tah."

Kai's throat swelled with emotion. He tried hard not to think of himself that way. Nico reminded him all the time that Rae wasn't his responsibility. Rae didn't belong to him. One day, either Kenji was going to get his shit together, or Rae was going outgrow what Kai could provide. His name wasn't on Rae's paperwork like Nico's was now that she was triarch. He couldn't make decisions for them. He had no claim to that title, and yet it stuck hard, the way she flung it at him so unflinchingly.

"You're a dragon, Kai," Rasia yawned, sleepily, "Don't you forget it."

CHAPTER FIFTY-FIVE

/

By the time Nico made it home from another long day at work, the sun had set, and the drums had stopped beating. She slipped off her shoes in the shroud room and leaned against the serving room entryway, amused to watch Zephyr attempting to teach Rae a few words of his second language. Zephyr had recently gotten a job as a sentry and replaced the night sentry to fill that hole in their security. She was lucky to have so many people around to help and support her. She couldn't imagine going at this by herself. She was truly only as strong as her kull.

She kissed Rae on the forehead, greeted Kai and Rasia messing around in the kitchen, and then went to work in the library. Later that evening, she had plans to meet up with Suri to go knocking on voters' doors with gifts of tea and alcohol. She found that listening and forming relationships with people were always better than throwing talking points at them.

"The Belly Councilor just announced she's stepping down from the Council," Suri said as she entered the library. "The gossip is all over the market, but messengers will have it announced throughout the Grankull soon enough."

Nico looked up from the tome of laws she had been studying. The small script hurt her eyes, but she wanted to be prepared for any loopholes the Council might take advantage of. She smiled at the news. She had known it was coming. Her tent spies had informed her that the family was in an absolute panic. She stretched up from the desk and figured it was a good time to take a break.

She walked over to her board and crossed out the Belly Councilor with the clayish red mark of her reed pen. Three more names to go.

Behind her, Suri shuffled through the stacks of posters on the low table, which listed Nico's campaign promises that she planned to pass out with the gifts. Suri was a great help, but it had also created a greater fissure between Suri and her tah. As of right now, she had officially changed households and was staying at her oldest jih's place.

"You don't have to do this," Nico told her, not for the first time.

"I know," she said. "But someone needs to hold my tah accountable."

But her tah was a tough nut to crack. Nico couldn't use the records Ysai found that incriminated the Neck Councilor in the assassination attempt. She had to find some other way.

"I might have something," Suri said, uncertainly. "I was talking to my jih about the job thing."

Suri had been apprenticing as a healer her entire life, but because her tah was also Han of the Healers, her job application had been quickly rejected. The consequences were often harsh for those who supported her. Sometimes Nico felt guilty about it, but she couldn't change Suri's mind. All she could do was make sure it was all worth it in the end.

"Apparently, jih has ambitions of becoming Healer Han herself," Suri said. "She wants tah's position and promises that she will give me a job when she obtains it."

"And that's when? When your tah retires?" Nico asked. "Your tah is too entrenched in the Neck—as both the Councilor and the Healer Han. You'll be waiting half your life for that to finally happen."

Suri bit her lip. She was extremely anxious about finding a job.

She couldn't keep living off her sibling's family. "Then what do we do?" she asked.

Nico stared at that board. She wasn't going to intimidate the Neck Councilor as she had with the Belly Councilor. The Neck Councilor had held her position for years. In comparison, Neema's family was new to power, and many hadn't liked how they skewed Grankull contracts in their favor. The seat had been entrenched in Azan's family for generations, until the current Councilor came along—who had been someone new and exciting and . . .

"I have an idea," Nico gasped. "We need to give people another option. Your tah is old and represents the establishment. We need someone new. Someone who will get people excited but whom constituents in the Neck will respect." The Neck was filled with administrative types. They respected skill. They respected intelligence. They respected someone who could make bureaucracy, and therefore their jobs, more effective and efficient. "And if we find someone who can run against her, then your jih can make a play as the Healer Han at the same time. It'll divide your tah's attention and make it difficult for her to fend off attacks from both sides. But we need a candidate who truly has a chance at a successful run." She smiled. "And I know the perfect person."

Nico hiked the Neck's vertebrae steps through the rainy season drizzle to reach the rationhouse. She entered wearing a green linen draped dress. Before, she stood out as the lone speck of white. Now, she stood out for other reasons.

"Nicolai Dragonshield," the people in line greeted her with acknowledging bows of the head or clasps of the elbow. She responded with the names of those she remembered and asked for the names of those she didn't. She rarely found herself able to walk the cobblestones without someone wanting to talk to her about her campaign, the wingfields, or her relationship status. After the high-profile blood price match, many went out of their way to show her respect. Nico had longed to join the colorful breadth of adulthood, but she never thought she'd become the light that reflected rainbows. The only person who could match Nico's current popularity was Rasia, but Rasia was infamously known for being unapproachable.

A breeze through the entranceway wrapped a cool shawl around people's shoulders. Several offered to let Nico skip them, but she politely refused. She chose the longest line and yet, she reached the ration counter before many of those who had arrived before her.

She smiled as she greeted her cousin's bored face. Her cousin wore beaded earrings, a bejeweled broad collar, and the newest shade of eyeshadow that highlighted the kohl around his eyes. He was handsome, a young style icon of the Grankull, and extremely intelligent. But also, extremely lazy unless pushed otherwise.

"No," Ashe said. "I know that look. I'm not interested."

"I need someone to run against the Neck Councilor."

"Absolutely not. I already have two jobs. I don't need three. Why is everyone always volunteering me for things? Leave me alone. Let me sleep," he lamented.

His tahs often forced him to do things with a combination of threats and guilt. Jilah forced him to do things by dragging him where she wanted him to go, but Nico came with a plan. She leaned forward and clasped her hands atop the counter, careful not to displace the abacus or the scales that took up half of the space. She smiled. "I am also backing the challenger to the Pelvis Councilor, and if they come into power, they have promised to ensure that your ban from the gambling dens would be repealed."

Ashe froze. Before they banned him, he used to play multiple games at once for the challenge. He craved the mental stimulation and generally went through life painfully bored by everything.

She continued to sweeten the deal. "And I'll talk to your tah about releasing you from your commitments to the windship builders. I know you're too scared to ask him. You won't have to work three jobs."

Ashe narrowed his eyes. "How do you know this candidate of yours is going to win?"

"Aren't you the gambler? You tell me the odds."

He opened his mouth, then closed it. Then he straightened and corrected, "I am a mathematician."

"And that is exactly why you're going to win me the Neck. I'll meet you for dinner at your house to start planning your campaign." And then, she raised her voice over the other conversations in the warehouse, "You've decided to run for the Neck Councilor?!"

Immediately, his coworkers swiveled toward him.

"You're running for Neck Councilor?" "It's about time someone from the rationhouse represented the Neck." "It's good to see you wanting to do more with your talents."

It didn't take long for the entire warehouse to light on fire with the gossip. There hadn't been a challenger for the Neck seat in five years.

Ashe dropped his forehead against the counter so hard he jostled the scales. He bemoaned, "Why does this always happen to me?"

"Ashe-shi." She stroked her cousin's hair soothingly and chided, "You can't win if you're not playing the game."

CHAPTER FIFTY-SIX

—

Kai adjusted Rae's shroud, carefully tucking and pinning the loose ends, while Kenji waited by the doorway to take Rae to their first day of school. Kai checked Rae's lunch sack to make sure it was properly secured, tightened the cords of their sandals, and straightened the wrinkles from their new white robe.

He wanted to fuss some more, to linger in this moment before he gave Rae to the rest of the world, but he didn't want his nervousness and fears to further rattle Rae's own. So, Kai gave them a confident smile and told them, "You're ready."

Rae mimicked that same pursed look of Nico's, when she wondered at what Kai wasn't saying. Rae looked at Rasia who leaned against the wall of the shroud room.

"You promise?" they asked her.

"On my names," Rasia promised. "I'll protect jijih. Now, go eat sand or whatever you snot-noses do at school."

"Do not eat sand," he corrected. She chuckled behind him. Even Kenji hid a smile. He kissed Rae on their shrouded forehead. "Listen to your teacher. Be nice, and you'll make lots of friends."

As if he had outlined a mission assignment, they nodded gravely, so absent of the excitement or giddiness most kids should have for their first day of school. With a sense of helpless defeat, he watched as Rae reached for Kenji's hand and they shuffled down the road.

He wished he could be the one to drop Rae off at school, but he didn't want a snide remark or a confrontation to ruin their day, so he stayed behind in the doorway while Rae took on the world without him. Nico was already gone all drums of the day. Soon Kenji would start a new job. Rasia would join the kulls. And he would be here, on the doorstep, waiting.

"Be nice, and you'll make lots of friends," Rasia mocked. "Unless you're weird, then they'll just run away from you."

"Or put goat shit down your shroud."

She raised an eyebrow. Kai shook his head. Hopefully, Rae would have a much better time at school than he did, or at least the fourteen days he had managed to attend.

Now that Kenji had left, Kai unwrapped his shroud down to his shoulders while Rasia pressed her face against his arm. He could feel the smirk coil around his bicep. She said, "Nico-ji is off to work. Ysai-ji has the day off. And I have it on good account that Kenji-shi is staying away for the rest of the day. The whole house is empty except for you and me. Whatever should we do with ourselves all by our lonesome?"

He teased, holding himself a breath above her lips. "Shouldn't you be training for the kull tryouts?"

"I can pass the tryouts with my eyes closed."

"I don't know." He grinned wickedly. "Perhaps we should test your flexibility."

"I think," she kissed him. ". . . you'll find," they tripped over the raised foundation leading from the shroud room, ". . . my flexibility," he clutched her ass, ". . . to be more than satisfactory."

They made it as far as the serving room.

Kai ripped open her robe, and her breasts spilled out from the silk. She scrambled at his linen caftan, snatching it up past his thighs, his back, but couldn't get it off him before he was inside of her. She abandoned her previous task and wrapped arms and legs around him. His stomach twinged a little, but the wound had closed, and the stitches were out, and it was such a relief that every little movement didn't cause such agonizing pain anymore.

They'd been waiting an eternity for this moment—to be truly alone and allowed the time to finally lose themselves. To explore with leisure. To be loud without care. To fill all the cravings and finally satiate the hunger. To finally be uninterrupted.

He had forgotten how deliciously wet she felt around him. Had it really been that long ago since he'd unintentionally spilled inside of her? Such a long time since he was that inexperienced self-conscious kid from the gorge who had been pressured to have sex because he thought he'd never get another chance. Now, he was slightly more experienced, a little more confident, but that pressure hadn't changed any. His gut told him to savor her, to enjoy her as much as possible, for tomorrow wasn't promised. He never knew when it could all fall apart.

He hiked her legs over his shoulders. He had a few good memories in the serving room, but a lot of bad ones. He thrusted as if he could stamp the image of her forever into the floor, warm and perfect underneath him, better than shattered ilhans and broken adobe slabs. He printed her sweat into the foundation, creating memories for him to find and appreciate for later when the bad ones overwhelm him.

He pressed her across the serving room table, a feast for one, just for him. Her chest heaved at the pause, all succulent and ready to be consumed. He nipped at her nipple, licked at her scars, and indulged himself between her legs. He knew when Rasia was close, for her vocal curses always grew quiet, and a tension clenched her limbs.

With a tap, she turned over, communicating with that same ease of exchanging kull signals from one side of the windship to the other. He reached back and finally stripped himself of that caftan. Then he grabbed her by the hips and rode her into the table. Her encouragements cursed in his ear until they crumbled into ragged breaths. He steered her exactly where he wanted her to go. Home.

Together, they crashed to a glorious brilliant end. He slayed a dragon. He faced scavengers. He survived the Yestermorrow Lake. But his greatest pride would always be his ability to sail his kulani to a stillness.

They melted off the table and dropped against the cushions of the serving room.

They breathed, and breathed, and breathed.

Kai and Rasia fucked all day. Atop the kitchen counters, across the lounging room ottomans, and in the bath waters. Against the hallway walls. On the training room mats. Under the sycamore shade in the garden. Until Kai couldn't move or think anymore. A pleasant fog shrouded his brain. A soreness hummed through his body. The garden, where they ultimately ended, smelled fragrant of jasmine and mandrakes. A hawk hunted for the mice under the tamarisks. He closed his eyes and allowed himself to be.

"Do you want kids?"

The brain fog scattered. He studied Rasia's shaded face. She lay kicking her legs and poked at his sprouting facial hair, coming in embarrassingly fuzzy and uneven.

"Where is this coming from?"

A small part of him was terrified of the answer. They have done everything so terrifyingly fast—from flame to courtship to kulani—he didn't know what he would do if Rasia wanted a child *now*—never mind he wasn't of age for the Grankull to grant him that request.

She turned, hiding a blush, and shrugged. "You are cute with Rae, you know. It's sort of hot when you go all tah on them. And I realized, I've never asked. I know back during the culling you said some things, but that was sort of under duress. I'm not sure what you really want."

As always, they did things backward. It was certainly the type of question to ask before you decided to carry someone else's name.

He licked at his lips and stared at the sycamore branches shading the harsh midday sun. "Before, I never considered having kids a possibility. Then I forgot to pull-out, and I was terrified by the what-ifs. What would I do? Would my child be as sickly as me? Would they be broken like me? Would people judge them because of who I am? It is widely known, that I almost killed

Ava-ta in childbirth. What if the worst happened?"

Then it did.

"When you lay there dying, I'd have done anything to save you. I begged you to take the antidote, and despite all my fears and reservations, I'd have become a tah if that meant saving your life. I think back on it, and I'm as scared now as I was then. But if we were granted a second chance to do everything the right way, then despite all my fears and doubts, I'd do it, because I know my child will be okay as long as they have a little bit of you."

She smiled softly and sat her chin on his chest. "I get that."

"Do *you* want kids?"

"I've always been kind of curious about how it all works."

"We know how it works, *now*."

She swatted at him. "I mean, inside of me. I want to know what it feels like. To have a whole other person in there. They say that after your body changes forever. Not bad, but different. I want to know how it'll change me when I'm ready for that. But lately I . . ." She paused. She narrowed her eyes and said in a reluctant whisper, "I feel empty. And lately, I've been thinking, what if we do go off into the Desert, but we have no gonom, and it happens, and we keep it."

"We wouldn't ever be able to come back," he whispered. "We'd be leaving everything and everyone we've ever known behind without any support. Who's to say you can give birth on your own without a birthing kull? And we don't know how my magic will affect things. What if there are complications? Then, there is everything that comes afterward. We can't keep a newborn quiet when a gonda is charging at us. The Desert is too dangerous."

"The Grankull is too dangerous. Would you have our child spat on because of who you are? Maybe one day they'll let you have your face, but there will always be people who will hate you. I get that now, and who's to say they'll ever grant you the right to have children? You stay here, and with your medical history, they might never approve of it. We'll do fine on our own."

"They might," he said slowly. "If it's not my seed."

Rasia snapped to a sitting position. Their soft bubble had

irrevocably burst. The anger in her voice sent the birds scattering. "I want the kids I'd have with *you*. I want my kids to have your bones, and your gentleness, and your cleverness. I want them to have your strength and your courage. I don't want them of anyone else."

"Those things aren't *born*, Rasia," he said, frustrated. "You think it's easy to watch the world move on without me? I was born with the same bones as everyone else. I am clever because I've had to be. I am gentle because I've had to be. I am strong because I've had to be. I don't want that for my children. I don't want that for any child. I want them to be who they are, and not what the world has made them into. When the time comes, we are going to have to seriously consider putting someone else's name on that application. It doesn't have to be my seed. I'll raise any child you give me."

He anticipated more arguing or yelling and found himself floored when Rasia broke into tears.

"*How much more are you going to allow this place to take from you?!*" she demanded. She looked at him, wide-eyed and frantic. She shook her head. She jumped to her feet. "I've got to get out."

She raced for the latticed walls around the garden. She scratched at them, searching for the sliding door.

"Get me out. Get me the fuck out of here!" she screamed and punched at the wood. It splintered with a crack around her fist. With one last frustrated yell, she wrapped her fingers in the sun slats and climbed. Then ran away naked across the roof.

Kai moved to follow, and froze, remembering the fact that he couldn't leave. He wobbled back down to the ground and wrapped his arms around his knees. Because of his medical history, he had known he'd most likely never have biological children. The Grankull often rejected the applications of persons with known genetic issues. He had accepted his circumstances. He had never considered that Rasia might not.

His brows furrowed, and he blinked blurrily to remember that firefly flutter in Rasia's belly. He didn't let himself think about it much. It had been a dream. He didn't get to have that life, and he was a fool to imagine anything different. One day, he might have a face. One day, he might have his names. But this . . . His shoulders bowed at the knowledge he could never give Rasia this particular want.

The day had started off so perfect, but all things fall apart.

Kai sensed when Rasia snuck into the bedroom later that night. He peeked open an eye to watch her shadowed figure limp toward the dresser to change into her night robe—wait, limp? He reached for the slow-burning oil lamp on the nightstand. He grabbed the rounded handle, and careful not to spill any of the oil, hovered it over the bed to properly see.

"Is that blood?" he whispered, careful not to wake Rae sleeping snugly beside him.

"Shit," she covered her face, turning, but not before he caught the sight of a gruesome cut above her brow. She quickly tied on her robe and lunged for the bed.

"Rasia, watch out."

She did an awkward twist to avoid falling her full weight atop Rae, and then stretched out to fill all the empty spaces of the bed.

"Did you get into a fight?"

"It's nothing."

He slipped from the bed and crouched into the cupboard for the medical supplies. He had a feeling she might do something drastic, but he hadn't known what it was. He came around the bed with the oil lamp and the supplies. He snatched the covers off of her.

She crossed her arms and glared at him, as if he couldn't see the cut on her brow and the fact that she had chosen to wear her thick linen robe. Rasia's favorite was the silk translucent one. He snatched at the robe. She snatched it back, but not before he had lifted it to reveal a large bruise on her hip. He placed the lamp on the stand, grabbed her protesting hand, and inspected her bloody split knuckles. Definitely a fight, but what was she doing punching someone instead of cutting them with her sword?

"Just a couple of tent fights, that's all," she grumbled and snatched her hand away.

His attention snapped to her face. "Those are to the death."

She shrugged. "If it wasn't me, it would have been someone else."

"*Why?*"

"Because I'm not you," she snapped. "I can't sit here every day and pretend that things aren't fucked up. Every night, I dream of slitting the throat of every member on that Council, but Nico wants to do things the right way. The long way. But I need to fight, so this will have to do."

"You're killing people to make yourself feel better?"

"Ugh. Didn't think you'd get all fucking self-righteous on me."

"There's got to be a better way. I know things are hard right now. If there's anything that I can do-"

"You can't do shit," she snapped at him. "I want what our life should have been." She snatched the linen rolls out of his hand and began wrapping them around her knuckles. "It's fine. I've never lost a tent fight. I'm undefeated."

He sat down on the edge of the bed, against her propped legs, and tried to understand. "What if you get hurt, and it affects your tryouts?"

Even though he could no longer try out for the kulls, Rasia still planned to. She didn't have much of a choice. While the first vial of gonom was given out freely the night of the Naming Ceremony, she wouldn't receive a new gonom vial or rations until she was accepted into the kulls. The Grankull did this to encourage young adults to get a job, but it placed a lot of pressure on those with new faces. So far, she had been mooching off Ysai's rations.

"It won't," Rasia said.

"I don't approve."

She paused and stared at he with eyebrows raised. That cut

above her left eye sludged blood down her temple every time she blinked. "You're going to stop me?"

"No. You do whatever you want. But I don't approve."

She drank the bottle of alcohol he had brought over instead of using it to disinfect her wounds. She slammed it back against his chest when she finished it all in one swallow. "You don't understand. No one fucking understands."

"Not if you don't explain it. Help me understand, kulani."

She threw up her hands. "Tah is dead, and yet I feel so fucking suffocated. It's like . . . I'm stuck in a room with walls on all sides and there's no way out. Every day, the walls are shrinking. I feel like I'm dying, or going insane, or both. I need this. Just until the kull tryouts. Until I can get my feet back on a windship and the fuck out of here for a while."

"We can figure something else out," he said. "I can sell something to get your windship out of impound. Do you think my dagger would be enough?"

"And I can make money just the same in the Tent fights." She dabbed at the cut on her brow. "How did the grubworm's first day of school go?"

He sighed and didn't fight the change in topic. Nico had picked up Rae from school and gotten the report from their teacher. "Rae says they had fun. They liked playing with the new toys, but they refused to speak with any of the teachers or approach any of the other kids. We hope Rae will grow out of it."

"Hn," Rasia said with a sneer. "They said the same thing about me."

She paused, and her eyes narrowed in that way she did before threatening someone. Realizing she was doing it, she softened a bit, but the command was no less sharp. "Don't tell Ysai-ji."

He reluctantly nodded. She tossed the bloody linen to the floor and collapsed back into the bed. He automatically began to clean up her mess. When he crawled back under the covers, he felt scared. He didn't know what to do or how to help her. He hugged his arms around her waist, determined to care for her as long as he could.

CHAPTER FIFTY-SEVEN

I

"Those are quite interesting ideas," the Hindlegs candidate said to Nico's pitch, and then he widened his legs suggestively beneath the heated waters of the bathhouse. "But what's in it for me?"

Nico could promise a future of untold prosperity and riches, but the ambition of some was always limited to sex. Not as if the Councilor could hope for much here, with the sheer number of people enjoying the steamed baths after work. Each neighborhood had its own bathhouse, and they were undoubtedly the best places for meetings and gossip.

She lounged naked across from the Hindlegs Councilor and smiled shrewdly at the roving eyes. Kenji-ta's suggestion had worked like a charm. He had found an old friend willing to run for the Hindlegs seat, and once the competition grew serious, all she had to do was wait for the inevitable message to arrive.

"If you aren't industrious enough to see the benefits of my proposal, then perhaps this isn't a good match. I'm sure your competitor will more than appreciate my endorsement," she said. She stood up and water dripped down her skin. She might not be the Ohan, but she had the power to rip the blood from a person's veins or drown them on their own spit and bile. She had a respectable number of names, and everyone clamoring for her favor. They needed her, more than she needed them.

"Wait-" the Councilor said. Nico hiked a well-crafted indifferent eyebrow. "I believe the heat is making me a little light-headed. I meant no disrespect. Your vision for the Grankull sounds like a worthwhile endeavor. Of course, I'd like to have your endorsement."

She smiled and mentally crossed the Hindlegs Councilor off her list. She knew she had to keep her face clean with this one. Someone who was so willing to flip sides would easily do so again. She'd continue playing the two candidates against each other and maneuver the Councilor exactly into the corner she wanted him.

She waded forward, and the Hindlegs Councilor straightened with lecherous hope. He was of her tah's generation but built well and no doubt unused to rejection. He didn't have a kulani, but she had no doubt he would sign a stranger's name tomorrow if he thought that it would win him the campaign.

Steam thickened around them. The shrouded kids playing nearby disappeared within the white haze. The Councilor's eyes widened and pressed a hand to his throat. Nico gripped the tiled edge of the bath and bent over the Councilor. She whispered in his ear as he gurgled up water.

"You ever send assassins after me again, and you'll never be able to take another bath without seeing Death in the steam. It is so easy to stay in too long and get light-headed, after all. It would be a shame to accidentally drown." She patted him on his bearded cheek. "I look forward to working with you."

Nico moved toward the stairs. Behind her, she heard the Councilor cough up water from his throat. She held him pinned to the spot long after she had dried, oiled, dressed, and left the bathhouse behind.

As she exited, she locked eyes with a messenger weaving through the crowds. She retrieved the scroll the messenger had been tasked to deliver. Her stomach dropped at the contents, and a storm brewed overhead. She raced home.

Nico thundered into the lounging room, and even though she knew what to expect, nothing compared to the visceral sight of Zephyr bleeding all over the ottoman. All sound blurred as if she had been dipped underwater, and for a moment she stopped breathing.

"*Nico!*" Kai caught her attention from where he knelt beside Zephyr, applying pressure to a stomach wound with what had previously been Zephyr's shirt. The knife was still in him. She focused on the present, one step at a time: If she allowed herself to slip and imagine a future without him, she might become a useless sopping puddle, and that was no help to anyone.

She moved forward with purpose. She crouched at Zephyr's side and used her magic to dry the top layer of blood to temporarily staunch the wound.

"You sent a message for Suri?" she asked Kai.

"Ysai sent her a message at the same time he sent yours," he said. "We didn't want to pull out the knife until she got here."

She crossed over to the window and opened wide the shutters of the lounging room. "Go get the linens and needle ready for when she arrives."

He cleared Zephyr's bloody shirt away as he left the room. It was heavily pouring outside, and she honestly didn't know if that was her magic or the season. She whistled, and a drenched Flock scout appeared at the windowsill.

"Double the security," she ordered. They nodded and disappeared.

"That's a little overprotective, don't you think?" Zephyr grumbled when she returned to his side.

She breathed a little easier to realize he was conscious. She squeezed his hand and demanded, "What happened? Who did this?" The message she received had been light on the details. "Give me a name."

"My cousin," he grumbled, "came after me for revenge against tah. His parent had been the one they killed in her stead."

"That bloodprice is owed to your tah, not you. This attack on you was unlawful. We can apply for restitution. I can—"

"No," he said. "This is my family's mess. I'll handle it. I should have been more careful."

Suri finally arrived and entered the room soaked to the bone. She stripped off her shroud, worn against the rain, and moved with that intense concentration of someone expecting much work to do. She didn't hesitate to start inspecting Zephyr's wound.

Kai quickly returned to deliver the supplies and then left to join Rae and Ysai in the serving room, while Nico remained to assist Suri.

"What are you feeling?" Suri asked.

"Cold . . . burning," he said.

"Hold him down," she instructed. She twisted the blade to break the suction. He groaned, and Nico had to force him down with her magic as Suri pulled out the dagger. Nico could see his small intestines.

Sweat gathered at Zephyr's brow as Suri worked to clean the wound. He blinked feverish and unfocused. Both Suri and Nico frowned. She reached out with her magic, while at the same time, Suri leaned down to smell the wound.

"He's been poisoned," she confirmed. "We don't have time to brew an antidote. You're going to have to do it."

"Zephyr-kull," Nico said. "Listen to me. You've been poisoned. I'm going to pull it out, like I did with Rasia, okay?" She tightened his hands in hers. "Stay with me."

She didn't know if Zephyr heard her, but she couldn't afford to wait for an acknowledgement. She focused on the poison spreading from the brackish wound. The poison wasn't as pervasive as when Rasia had been poisoned. Still, it was a different type than last time—oily instead of heavy. It was slippery and hard to hold onto. She summoned magic from the Elder's stores and picked through Zephyr's blood like picking lice from hair.

She extracted the poison from the open wound. She replaced the water in her gourd with the poison to preserve it for Suri to study later.

Through a concerted effort, both she and Suri stabilized him. He lay unconscious on the ottoman, heartbeat steadied. Nico slumped back and pressed her hands to her face, shaking. That had been too close for comfort, and it was still a wait and see for any infections. Outside, the Elder bones groaned at the water flooding the streets, but she knew the heavy storm wouldn't last long.

"Thank you," she told Suri.

Suri closed her eyes, her head also reclined back against the ottoman while she held her bloody hands upright in her lap. She glanced in Nico's direction. "Are you okay?"

"Sometimes, I question why I fight for such a terrible place," she whispered. "At times like these, I wonder if it's worth it or if I'm wasting my time. How many more people are going to get hurt? How many more people are going to die for this cause? How many more sacrifices are going to be made? Can the Grankull truly be salvaged?"

The rain pelted the roof, striking hard enough to beat drums against the adobe. Zephyr's arm drooped from the ottoman, and she pressed her forehead against it.

"Sometimes, I want to give up," Suri admitted and gazed down at her hands. "I don't even like blood."

"There's got to be something better than this. There has got to be," she said, tightening her hands as if she could physically, stubbornly, hold on to hope.

Sometimes, Nico wanted to give up too. In her weakest moments, she wondered at a life where her only responsibility was herself, at a life where she didn't care about everything and everyone so damn much. But for all her stubborn faults, she didn't know how to stop trying. No matter the results of the election, she would never stop fighting for this harsh, beautiful, and complicated place. Even if it was hard sometimes.

She welded the armored cracks of her resolve, sharpened the spear-edge of her determination, and kept dragging on.

Nico checked on Zephyr the moment she came home from work several days later. She had offered him one of the empty bedrooms to stay and recover, and she admittedly preferred to have him close while he was injured and weak. They had been keeping an anxious watch on him for infection, but the danger had now passed.

"How is he?" she asked as she passed Kai in the kitchen preparing for dinner. Smelled like scorpion kebabs.

"He managed to sit up today," he said, as she dipped a finger into the bowl that he used to mix the seasoning. Had a little spice to it. She nodded her approval, and then wound through the maze to the bedrooms.

She was a little surprised to find Rasia on the bed talking with Zephyr. Rasia leaned against the lotus carved pillar of the bed frame and gesticulated her hands as she talked. "You're lucky that cousin of yours was stupid. If you're trying to kill someone, never stab them in the gut—too high rates of survival. Should have gone for the heart or the throat."

"I doubt he cared where it hit considering the blade was poisoned," Zephyr remarked. He looked like he desperately wanted to escape, while Rasia deliciously enjoyed the fact that he couldn't.

"Look at that," she teased. "We're poison buddies."

Zephyr glanced at Nico, who found herself holding in a laugh at the door. He mouthed, 'save me.' Rasia turned and rolled her eyes.

"Fine." She patted Zephyr's leg and hopped from the bed. "Protect yourself better. I'd have been pissed if you had died. It is so hard to find a good sparring partner."

"We're not sparring partners."

"Right." She winked at him. She nodded at Nico and then swiveled out of the room.

"And *I* have to live with that," Nico said, as she came in and replaced Rasia on the bed. "Becoming friends?"

"She enjoys torturing me," he grunted and crossed his arms. Despite the grumbling, she could tell he didn't mind Rasia's company, but he also didn't want to encourage her. He shrugged his shoulders and added, "But she does have good fighting insights."

"Hmm-hmm." She smirked. She looked over him and checked his bandages. "Your tah is pissed."

"I know," he groaned. He had been more than willing to take Nico up on her offer to stay over in order to avoid his tah. "I should have been paying more attention to my surroundings. She's going to ream me out for that. I should have been more careful. I knew living in the Grankull was dangerous and I knew . . ."

"It was more than that," she said.

Immediately after the incident, since Zephyr had been unconscious and couldn't tell her anything, she had gone onto the streets and pieced together what had happened from eyewitnesses. Zephyr's cousin had ambushed him on a crowded street, but the initial assault hadn't grazed or harmed him. In fact, he had evaded and avoided every attack, never going on the offensive until he had slipped on a too smooth stone and gotten a knife in the gut. Only when he had a foot of steel in him, did he finally decide to kill his cousin. The fight was all over one quick brutal move later.

"You know what happened?" he asked and blew out a breath when she nodded. "I thought I could be strong like my tah wanted me to be. I thought I could be cold-hearted, but . . . he looked like her. I didn't want to kill him. I fully knew situations like this might happen, and I . . . I don't know if I can do this."

"I know," she whispered and rearranged herself on the bed. He didn't hesitate to settle his head into her lap and she stroked her hand through his coils. "Perhaps your tah will be disappointed in you, but there is no shame in not wanting to kill your family. You deserve to feel devastated."

"She warned me," he grumbled. "She thought me strong enough to handle living in the Grankull, and I've let her down."

"You can't always be her embodiment of vengeance. Nor can you always be the voice of your family, or always the shoulder people lean on. You also need to take care of yourself," she soothed.

He scoffed and pinched her side where she was the most ticklish. "Take your own advice."

"Hey, I have a self-care day planned with Jilah-shi after this election is over. We're going to do mud-masks, braid my hair, and I'm going to go shopping and buy something for myself, for once. Then, I'm going to close my door and finally get some uninterrupted sleep." She smiled and then wondered when sleep had become something to long for.

He placed a loose lock of hair behind her ear, that same lock of hair that had escaped her bun in the middle of work today. "Let me know if you need any help with your self-care."

"I said *sleep*, Zephyr-kull."

"I could join you for the mud-masks."

"Sure." She laughed at him. After all, she certainly wasn't lacking any in her sex life. She had admittedly taken advantage of Zephyr's new role as night sentry on several occasions, and Suri had a habit of popping in whenever she thought Nico could use a break from work.

She placed a kiss on his lips, careful to keep it light and avoid crossing into the dominance territory Zephyr sometimes craved from her, and the submissive pliancy she sometimes craved from him. Didn't want him to get too worked up with his injury. "Feel free to stay as long as you need."

"I appreciate it, but . . ." He lifted off her lap with a groan, "might as well face her sooner rather later. Help me to the Tents?"

She sighed. Maybe she should have seduced him to stay if he thought himself strong enough to traverse the Grankull and face

Zara-shi, but she helped him dress since he was so determined. The shirt he had come with had been bloodied and torn beyond repair. Kai's shirts were too small, but she had found an older shirt of tah's that fit tightly around his chest.

She smirked at the comical sight. "You might as well walk to the Tents half-naked."

"The cruel luck of genetics," he said, tone flat, but Nico heard the sarcasm.

He grabbed one of the lotus pillars. She placed a hand around his waist and helped him to stand from the bed. She didn't remove her hand from his arm.

"Listen," she said. "I know you don't want me involved, but there is something that you should know. Suri analyzed the poison used on the knife and identified it as one of her tah's mixes. The Neck Councilor knows I can heal poisons from my Forging story, which means the poison was a message intended for *me*. A lot more layers are at play here, and it seems other people might be exacerbating the conflict between you and your family. It might be your family drama, but it's politics, too."

"Politics or not, you're not my triarch. You have no legal obligation to avenge me, and I'm sure they know that. It would be messy for you to get involved."

She turned and stared at the wall, all hand-painted with water and lotus flowers. It was one of the rooms they always used for when extended family came to visit because it was the most beautiful. Even the wall that looked out toward the garden was located on the colorful side of the pond. Nico stared at the pond lotuses and admitted, "I was scared to lose you."

"I know. I was scared, too," he said and grabbed her with big hands, pulsing with a fragile heart at his wrists. "If they're so willing to resort to subterfuge and threats, it means that they are scared of us too. It means that we are winning."

"But at what cost?" she asked. "They're targeting everyone around me, now. Who will it be next?"

"It won't be me," he promised. "Spend all your worry on someone else, but do not worry for me. I'll be more careful. Next time, I won't hesitate."

She frowned at that. "Who do we become when we no longer hesitate?"

"Survivors," he said easily, as if knowing that was what he should have been all along. He sounded like his tah. Nico didn't know if she agreed. And yet, hadn't she done whatever it took to win against Kibari? She certainly hadn't hesitated.

She didn't know when she had become a survivor. She didn't remember the exact moment when she began searching for assassins in the shadows, when strategies waged war in her head before breakfast, and when each day had become a battle.

She hoped for a future when all the survivors could finally walk the Grankull's streets in peace.

"It's so heavy," she whispered. Life was so damn heavy sometimes.

"Yeah." Zephyr dropped his forehead to hers and they held each other for a brief eternal moment. Sometimes, they needed this from each other too—someone to hold onto, someone to lean on and to lessen the weight to stay standing. He said her name as a promise. "We'll help each other carry it."

CHAPTER FIFTY-EIGHT

O

Rasia shifted in bed, right into Rae's cold toes. She cracked an eye open, unsurprised to find an elbow in her gut and Rae drooling onto her pillow. Somehow, they always started over on Kai's side only to drift towards the middle during the night. She tolerated it all because at least now, Rae waited to crawl into their bed until after she and Kai had sex. How the kid knew was anyone's guess, but the timing was always convenient.

She glanced over Rae's back at Kai. His bruises were almost healed. Even the gut wound had faded to a faint scar. Rasia wondered if anyone else had noticed how Kai was healing a lot faster than he should be. She first assumed it was his magic and didn't really question it, but her eyes followed where Rae's hand stretched out in sleep, to lay a hand right over Kai's stomach.

Sometimes, she wondered.

She peered out of the window. The sky was dark, but she could feel encroaching dawn in her bones. She rolled off of the bed and ambled into the bath. She scrubbed at her skin and wiped away the layers of sweat and sex from last night. The adrenaline high of the tent fights always had her craving sex after. Kai fucked her, then cleaned her wounds, like some nighttime ritual she needed in order to go to sleep.

There was a void within her, and she was not sure how to fill it. Contentment leaked through the holes. Laughter got caught in her throat. Smiles didn't hold anymore.

Maybe because she was a hunter without a hunt. It was that familiar aimlessness that came without purpose—but deeper somehow. How did one possibly live in the ravines after flying the highs of a dragon? Rasia hoped once she joined the kulls, she'd find her sense of direction again.

She counted her turns in the maze and made it to the front door of the house without incident. She walked the dark streets and reached the training fields a little before first drum. She was surprised to find she was not the first one there.

She sat down in front of Kenji-shi, and they stretched in companionable silence.

"How are you holding up?" he asked.

"I'm fine." She shrugged, knowing he was referring to Kibata. "No point holding their ashes."

"I know you struggled after Shamai-kull, and I've always regretted how I couldn't be there for you. You've seemed distant lately."

It was weird for Kenji-shi to notice, considering Rasia spent most of her time with Kai. She hadn't been pleased when Kai told her he was moving back in, but those fears were quickly eased since Kenji-shi and Kai were rarely in the same room at the same time. It was a big house, and they avoided each other pretty easily. She rolled her shoulders and in that one motion, she felt every bruise and hit she had taken in the past week.

"I wish you weren't retiring." Sort of sucked that she planned to join the kulls the same season he decided to quit.

"I'm getting older. I'm not the hunter I used to be, and I need to be here, available. I'm going to start teaching windship lessons at the school soon."

"You're abandoning me to a bunch of fools who think they know more than me."

"There are some things even you can still learn," he said. "Most of the kull Hans have already read through your Forging story. I can count on one hand the number of windekas we have employed that can sail out of the sandbowl. At the same time, it's readily apparent you struggle with people. The Hans will do right by you, I promise."

She sneered. "I'd rather have you do right by me. Teaching grubworms must be the most boring thing I have ever heard."

He chuckled. "Yes, well . . . I didn't exactly choose the hunting kulls either."

"You didn't?"

"The kulls were your tah's dream. I wanted to be a musician." He shrugged. "Sometimes you do things you don't want to do, but you do it because you have to. When kulani was pregnant, I had a choice to make. I could continue doing what I wanted—writing and performing songs for contract rations or get a more stable job that my kulani's tah approved of. I chose what was best for my family. Luckily, I had plenty of downtime to do what I enjoyed."

"But you don't sing anymore." She frowned. "You were the one who once told me, right on these sands, to grow what makes me happy. What happened to that? What happened to you?"

He stared blankly at the sand. "You meet those days where nothing makes you happy."

His words struck an odd familiar chord. She turned, bitter, at how her days have felt hollow. All she ever wanted was to be a Han of her own kull like Shamai-ta. And she did it. She managed to pull a kull together, she had led them, slayed a dragon, and kept them all alive. But managing people was not fun. It had been the most tedious and frustrating part of the whole venture. She was too good not to have her own hunting kull, but how was she supposed to deal with people without Kai? He was supposed to be here, trying out with her, and proving himself a better windeka than half of those currently in the kulls. Nothing would be the same without him. Did she even want this anymore?

The field gradually filled with aspiring participants. Most people were accustomed to going to work and getting out the door at second drum, but the kull tryouts started at first drum. It was the first test, to see if you could break from schedule, a sign of the anarchy to come out in the Desert. For years, Rasia had gotten up early with Shamai-ta to watch him conduct the tryouts. She knew the order, the speeches, and the tricks by memory.

Kenji-shi disqualified anyone who showed up late. Rasia lined up for laps, next to the other new-faces and the older ones who had failed in the previous years and were trying again. The face next to her settled into line. He looked her up and down. "I am Noam Evory-carved Swiftfoot Dunechaser. What are your names?"

She glanced at her competitor, unimpressed. "I am Rasia, the Hunter, Wind-chaser, Horizon-seeker, Discoverer, Wanderer, Adventurer," with each name, Noam's eyes widened in size. The next face in line stopped stretching to stare at her with a dropped jaw. "Mane-of-Wild-Horses, Bones-Thrown-Afield, Map-With-No-End, Two-Blades, Dragon-sail, Swiftness, Movement, Dark-Waters-of-the-Dragon's Coast, Graveyard-of-Bones, Yestermorrow, *Kai-kulani*, Dragonfire."

"It's you."

They all shuffled closer to each other to give her space, and their eyes sparkled with admiration. No one laughed at her anymore. She had wanted that sort of explicit respect and recognition all her life. So why didn't it feel enough?

She sprinted off at the first beat. The laps were laughably easy, and painfully boring as all her competitors fell further and further behind. It wasn't a challenge. She was running through the motions. These past few weeks had been nothing but going through the motions.

Rasia had dreamed of the kull tryouts all her life. She often imagined Shamai-ta standing on the sidelines, cheering her on, as she dominated every opponent. She dreamed of running laps around her competitors, sparring them all into submission, and making fools out of everyone. By the end of the day, she would have proved she was the best that ever was and ever would be. Then one day, she'd command her own kull, earn the name of Han, and not only match Shamai-ta's legacy, but exceed it.

It was everything she thought she wanted.

Once.

"Rasia Dragonfire, what are you doing?" one of the examiners yelled. She had stopped and now several of her competitors had run past her. The dry air felt harsh and inescapable.

What had the Grankull ever given her but lies and empty promises? Shamai-ta's dreams of ambition and carving out his place didn't belong to her. She didn't give a shit about the Grankull. She owed these bones nothing but her hatred and resentment. They didn't deserve the best of her. They didn't deserve her struggle or her strive. She was done squeezing herself into too small spaces. She was done hitting dead ends. She was never one to run the Grankull's circles, and she wouldn't keep running them now. Because at the end of the day, the only person who mattered, the only person she needed to make proud—was herself.

Rasia Dragonfire walked away.

CHAPTER FIFTY-NINE

—

Kai tasted the slow boiling gonda stew. Gonda meat was chewy, but it softened a bit in the boil. Almost ready. He stirred the pot and added herbs and cumin from the garden. His face dripped with sweat from the oven heat and the rising temperature of the kitchen as he cooked.

He startled at the sudden rush of feet. He dropped to the wall in defense when Nico charged into the kitchen, her hands slamming onto the doorway. The stirring spoon clattered to the floor. Nico usually did rounds with potential voters before coming straight home, and he hadn't been expecting her.

"Where is she?" she demanded.

"*Who?*" Kai stuttered as he clawed at the wall to push himself back to his feet. He picked the spoon off the floor and wiped at the droplets of burning stew that ate through the sleeve of his caftan.

"Rasia! Where is she?"

". . . at the tryouts."

She stared. "You don't know."

Before Kai could ask, the chimes rang out. Rae's high-pitched voice echoed through the adobe brick, and Kai left Nico in the kitchen to greet Rae. The kid tumbled at the border of the shroud room, wrestling off a shoe. Ysai barreled past Kai into the serving room.

"RASIA!" he called out, then whipped toward Kai. When Ysai dropped the address on Rasia's name, you knew something was wrong. Nico, on the other hand, could rarely force herself to add the familial address. "*Where is she?*"

"I-I don't know what's going on," he said as he looked at Ysai and then Nico. "Is she alright? Did something happen? Did she not pass the tryouts?"

"She didn't even try," she spat out. "It's all over the Grankull. Rasia *walked away*. Just, up and walked away in the middle of some laps. How could someone be so utterly fucking selfish! *We had a plan*. Now, what are we going to do about rations? What are we going to do about money? She was supposed to help you. You're her fucking kulani!"

Ysai stood, shaking his head, too angry to speak.

Nico ranted, "Who in their right mind walks away from a job that is all but certain? People try out for the kulls for years, and all that kulo had to do was put in the bare minimum! You deserve better than this. If she cared about you, if she truly cared, then she would have done what she needed to do! All she cares about is herself, and *you deserve better*!"

"Nico-ji, you're angry. Calm down. I'm sure she has her reasons," he said. "We'll figure something out. There are other ways of making money."

"How? These walls are practically empty, and we sold most of Ava-ta's stuff to pay for Rae's schooling. We sold off her sword. We use Kenji-ta's paycheck to supplement your rations. Should we start selling off the cookware and the wicker baskets?"

"What about Ava-ta's dagger? I still have that."

"No," Ysai said, finally speaking. "Rasia can't keep expecting you to make all the sacrifices, and yet she's the one who is always walking away. We've got to stop making excuses for her and demand some accountability."

He shuffled, and with a sigh admitted what he'd known for a while now. "She's not happy anymore."

Ysai stared at him. "That's not on you. She can't keep flitting from one distraction to the next. After Shamai-ta died, *I tried*. She would be happy for a time, but only for a while. It was never enough. She kept looking for the next big thing to distract her from her anger and her grief until it almost killed her. The only thing that can make Rasia happy is Rasia. It can't be on you, or you'll be dragged right along with her. She is the type of person who always demands everything and never settle for halves. Even then, your everything is never enough, and you're left hollowed out by the end. I learned that the hard way. The most difficult thing I have ever done was walk away from *her*."

"But I'm her kulani."

"At what cost? A kulani is a partnership. It isn't sacrificing everything until there's nothing of you left. That's just selfishness, and quite frankly, you've got it hard enough as it is. I don't care if she's unhappy. I don't care if the hunting kulls isn't what she wants to do. She signed your name. From that moment on, *your* happiness was the only thing that mattered."

Kai opened his mouth to respond, then the chimes rang out. Both Ysai and Nico spun to confront Rasia, but Rasia never rang the chimes. It wasn't her.

Kelin skidded into the serving room and relayed, "Rasia lost a tent fight."

Kai stopped breathing.

"Is she alive?" Nico asked.

"*Barely*."

Nico dropped her shoulders in relief. Kai breathed again, but it was Ysai who scared them all. His face contorted in rage, and his fists clenched, shaking. All of him shaking.

"*She promised*," he hissed out. "*She fucking promised*."

Then Ysai charged out of the door.

"I should go with him. I have some influence in the tents," Nico said quickly and reached out her hand. A bubble of water sent her spear flying into her palm. She rushed out of the door behind Kelin. Kai moved to follow, then froze in the shroud room and stared down at Rae still struggling with that shoe. He began to call for someone to wait but they had already disappeared down the street. Kai pulled at his face, frustrated. *Someone* had to stay behind to watch the kid. He hated the fact that everyone assumed it would be him. That was his kulani out there.

Something bitter sullied the air. Then he raced toward the kitchen to move the stew off the open flame. He coughed at the bellowing fumes when he opened the lid. The stew had burnt black. He cursed and leaned against the counter. He coughed, unable to shake this tar from his throat, feeling utterly helpless to do anything more than to sit and wait.

As always.

CHAPTER SIXTY

O

Rasia came to in some random tent she didn't recognize. She blinked through the swelling and stared blankly at the unfamiliar leather tarp of her surroundings. She automatically reached for her swords and her hands wrapped around air. Memories flashed back at their absence. No weapons were allowed in the tent fights. No armor either.

Her opponent had been this scrappy stick of kindling, nothing but mash fat and reed bones. She remembered his bloodshot eyes, drugged up, but alert enough to know Death had come for him in the form of Rasia's face. Should have been an easy fight. She didn't remember any underhanded trick or deception. She simply got . . . distracted.

Her gut had been telling her not to throw herself into five fights in a row, but it was either that or go home and deal with all of the shit on the other side of the Tail. At the time, walking away felt like the right thing to do. Liberating. But in hindsight, she wasn't sure anymore. All throughout the day, she found herself preoccupied by this uncomfortable stirring in her stomach that might have been guilt.

She rolled from the bare cot of worn threshing. That old familiar rib-pain haunted her as she limped through the linen curtains. Honestly, she was lucky. Fall unconscious in the Tents and more likely you'd never wake up at all or wake up to a pair of dicks in you. She passed several other smaller nooks until she reached the front room. She knew this room, and she knew the face counting his towers of bonechips at a desk scrapped from a broken windship.

The Jackal Han, a stout face squinted at her through the receptacle of his glass lenses. "You lost me money."

"And I've won you plenty of it," she said.

"That's the only reason you're still alive. Luckily for you, your fight had been *conveniently* interrupted." The Jackal dropped his gaze in warning. "Your life is owed to me now."

She eyed the bodyguards at the entrance tightening their fists on their weapons. She scoffed at the intimidation. "I don't owe you any fucking money. I don't owe you any fucking favors. I don't owe you my fucking life. You're so used to controlling people, you mistakenly think everyone can be controlled."

"You think you're untouchable on the other side of the Tail? Your tah isn't here to protect you anymore, and I don't care if you are a Flock legacy, they can't protect you either. You owe me a life. It doesn't have to be yours. I understand you have a kulani now."

She laughed madly and pointed at him as if she had her sword in hand. "I'd be careful the next thing that falls from your mouth. I am the wrong fucking one. And I am not in the mood."

The Jackal Han said, teeth gleaming, "I could easily have had you drugged while you were unconscious and made my money selling out your cunt. But I didn't. You're not just another dirty tent flap. I consider you a valued business relationship."

"Then you should have killed me. We all make mistakes. Got to cut your losses somewhere. See you tomorrow for the next match and fuck that skinny sack of bones who ruined my record. Now, I'm leaving."

"I'm altering our terms from 60-40 to 80-20!"

"Whatever."

A gust almost blew her over, brought in by the force of the body charging into the tents. The bodyguards reacted too slowly.

Shouting erupted outside. The braid of Ysai's hair whipped as he jumped atop the Jackal Han and proceeded to punch the shit out of him—and kept punching, and punching.

"I fucking told you last time to *never* talk to her again."

The bodyguards finally got their wits about them and rushed forward. She casually put out a leg and tripped one. The other reached Ysai, who whipped up, grabbed the balance scales from the Jackal's desk, and stabbed it into the bodyguard's neck. It was funny how people thought Rasia had the worst temper of the family.

"Enough!" Nico stormed into the tent. "Remember the alliance!"

A wave of water physically washed Ysai away from the bloody Jackal. Rasia doubted anyone had gotten a hit on the Jackal in years. It was such a humbling experience; she certainly would know.

"Ohan," the Jackal Han said as jovially as he could with a broken face. He spat out a bloody tooth and clutched at his chest. "You saved me!"

Nico's face dropped, and everything about her expression said she really wish she hadn't, but she didn't have much of a choice. The Jackal's Han death could descend the Tents into a war scrambling over his territory and business. Not helpful when you're trying to unite the Tents against the Grankull.

Ysai spat at the Jackal Han, then grabbed Rasia roughly by the arm and dragged her out of the Tents. They left Nico behind to clean up Rasia's mess. She glanced at the corpses outside. Armed reinforcements arrived and froze at the look of murder on Ysai's face. They wisely backed away.

She snatched her arm out of his grip when they made it to the border. He stopped in the middle of the empty Tail, quiet of any ceremonies or games.

"You promised."

"It was just for a few days."

"*You promised.*" He walked away, and then back to Rasia. "I thought this was different. Is Kai just another distraction?

Because if so, you need to leave before you hurt him."

Her face scrunched at the accusation. "Of course, he isn't."

"Then what the fuck are you doing?! You could have irreparably injured yourself. You could have gotten yourself trapped in a spiral of debt that most people never get out of. You could have died today, like you almost died the last time I had to save you, and the last time. All you ever consider is yourself and never the people you could leave behind. You have a kulani, and you chose that. You chose him. What would he do if something were to happen to you?"

"I reckon he'll sit in that house not doing much of anything," she said bitterly. "He knew."

"Did he know you were going to walk away from the tryouts?"

"The Grankull is fucking horseshit! From the day of the Naming, we are only allowed a limited amount of gonom and rations until we find a job. It's fucked up. The only options we have are to either support the Grankull or die. Why should I get a job, and support it, and put in the work, when it can't even give my kulani his fair due?! I'm supposed to just accept that?! *No!* It doesn't get to set the rules, change them when it's beneficial, and expect me to fall in line. Perhaps you work and scrape in the system—but that's not me. It'll never be me!"

"You think I wanted to work as a sentry every day under Kiba-ta?! No! But I did it because it was a good paycheck, and I didn't want to be gone every hunting season to abandon my kulani alone with tah. Do you think I was happy living with Kiba-ta? Happy watching my housing application get denied again and again? Happy to watch Kiba-ta treat Jilah like some dirty sex tool I found in an alleyway? You don't think I didn't feel trapped?! That I didn't want to run the fuck away?! Guess what, Rasia? Life isn't easy, and you can't always cut it down with a sword. It would have taken me three years to save the money for the bribe you gave me for the house, but I would have borne those three years because I have a responsibility to my family. And you have a responsibility to yours. Eat the shit, Rasia."

"*No.* Some crooked Tent Han doesn't get to dictate my life, nor does the Grankull. I am Rasia Dragonfire. I slayed a ta-fucking dragon!"

"When are you done using that line as an excuse?!" he asked. He shook his head, disappointed. "Kiba-ta was right. You weren't ready."

The one comfort I have is the certainty that your attention never lasts for long. You'll get bored. You'll throw him away, like you do with everything else.

"Take that back," she demanded.

"I lied to you, Raj-ji. I walked away from you not because of kulani. I wish I had never worded it the way I did for you to throw all your blame on her, but the truth is, I couldn't do it anymore. I couldn't watch you beat yourself bloody against walls anymore. After the forest, when that shadowcat almost sliced you in half, I realized then it was never going to end. You were never going to settle down like Kiba-ta hoped. You were going to die, and I couldn't do anything to stop it."

"We all die."

"That's what you want? For Kai to watch you die in his arms? To burn bright and fast like a shooting star? No one can build a life on that. When Shamai-ta taught us how to survive in the Desert, it wasn't about the next big hunt. He brought us out there to show us the sunrise. To watch the skinkos dance, and the palms bend, and the water shine. Life isn't one hunt to the next. Where is your sunrise, Rasia? Until you figure that out, you're not ready."

"You don't understand. Only Shamai-ta ever understood."

"You're seeing mirages! You think tah would approve of your tent fights? You think he would approve of you signing the name of someone you've only known for a season? And then abandoning them by walking away from a job? If there was anything Shamai-ta valued more than anything else—it was family!"

There was no arguing with Ysai, she could see that now. He had a retort for everything. So, she turned on her heels and stomped off, knowing she had left him disappointed behind her.

Her thoughts were a whirlwind, an uncomfortable spiral, when she was so typically certain of her path and the direction she needed to go. She had stood at this crossroads a lot these past few days.

She could break into the impound right now, steal her windship, and *leave*.

Or she could slit every council member's throat while they slept, and *then* leave.

Or she could go home where Kai was no doubt waiting for her, sitting there all sad and alone. He'd bandage up her hurt and pains. He'd fill up her with sex. He'd hold her as she slept. Then he'd wake up, heart-racing, sweaty in the middle of the night from a nightmare she couldn't save him from. If she reached out too fast, he'd flee. If she reached out too slow, he'd retreat. She'd feel useless and powerless and trapped in a cage of two. She'd lie awake.

And know tah was right.

She wasn't ready for this shit.

Kai sat at the serving table, poised in stillness like morning dew, hanging in suspension and waiting to finally fall. Rae was curled in his lap, limbs all splayed out like a gonda, rocked to sleep. He looked up at Rasia when she shuffled inside, and his face was wide open and thankful to see her. He knew that every time she walked out that front door, there'd be a chance of her never coming back. But she did. These bones are dead, but the Heart beats here.

"Are you hungry? The stew is burnt, but it's still edible."

She gave a broken smile and dragged herself to the table. He got up, made her a bowl, and then left to put Rae to bed. She brushed blood from her eyes and glared at the gonda stew. It was disgusting, but she swallowed it down.

After dinner, Kai cleaned her wounds, bandaged her up, and wiped the blood from her skin. They had sex, soft and slow and gentle and everything she needed in that moment. Tears trailed down her face as she held him.

"I'm sorry," she whispered.

"I'm proud of you for trying, but if you don't want to be part of the kulls anymore, then that's fine." He shrugged. "You shouldn't have to do something you don't want to do."

His easy acceptance washed over her like a balm. She unwound, not knowing how tense she had been until he wrapped an arm around her waist. "Say that to Ysai-ji, or your jih."

"We still have options. We can sell Ava-ta's dagger. It'll be enough to get the windship out of impound and pay a few blinks of the renting space. You can go out hunting. It'll bring in food and money until you find a job that you actually want. With Kiba-ta gone, you can even go back to the smuggling business. Or find other options."

"But it's your tah's dagger," she mumbled.

"And it's just as good as any other. The windship will give us far more options than the dagger ever will. And maybe," he said slowly, "I'll go with you."

She snapped up in bed. "Yeah?"

"Yeah. A couple of days can't hurt. Rae is at school all day now, I'm not . . . I'm not their tah, not really, and I've got to give Rae's actual tah the space and opportunity to be there. And I'm . . . I'm worried about you. I think having the windship back will be good for you."

She pounced on him, already charting their path in her head, excited—relieved. She knew she made the right choice.

Rasia stretched, loose and content. A sliver of sun warmed her skin as she sprawled across the whole bed, taking up the warmth Kai had occupied before leaving to bathe Rae. She smiled at the thought of sailing the Desert again with Kai at her side.

In the corner of her eye, he had left his dagger for her on the nightstand. She rolled over to study the delicate designs on the hilt. If she started now, she could probably sell it and get the windship out of impound by morning. She'd also need to go to the market for a few extra supplies and equipment.

She flipped out of bed and got dressed. She strapped on her wrap and tossed on her clothes. Then she opened the drawer to the nightstand. All the items rolled from the force she used to snatch open the drawer. A long oblong object studded against the inside wall, the one Ysai had gifted her as a late Naming gift. She shuffled through the rest of the random objects—pushing aside the sex tool, her baubled namesake, and random piercings. Rasia snatched up the small vial.

Her stomach bottomed out. All her fantasies and all her dreams crashed down around her, hitting heavy like a warship atop her head.

She flashed back to the moment yesterday morning—no, the morning before that—when she drank the rest of the gonom and didn't give it any concern because she had been so certain she was passing the tryouts.

She would have to get a job to acquire more gonom or acquire some illegally but that meant selling the dagger with not enough left over to get the windship out of impound. Or she could use the money for the windship, leave for the Desert, and risk the sword of unprotected sex hanging over her head.

If the worse happened, could Rasia bear another culling? Physically . . . emotionally . . . mentally . . . *no*. She refused to go through that again. She'd never be able to let go of another one, damn all the consequences. Then they would be on the run, and Kai would be severed from his family again.

Or she could ignore it all and hope for the best and pretend at the carefree life she always wanted to have.

The empty vial shattered in pieces against the wall.
Fuck.

CHAPTER SIXTY-ONE

—

Kai plucked clean clothes off the laundry line. He folded the linens and dropped them into the wicker basket. Sometimes, he could briefly sense the Tent guards Nico had posted around the house in case of trouble. He felt their eyes on him sometimes, when he was on the roof or out on the veranda. Rasia snuck up on them for fun.

Finished, he hefted the basket and turned to spy Rasia coming down the road. He frowned. She didn't seem anywhere as excited as she had been last night. He set down the clothes and climbed the ladder from the roof to the veranda, to meet her at the doorway. She trudged down the road with a handful of parchment squeezed in her fist.

"What's wrong? Could you not get enough money for the dagger?" he asked.

"I got the job."

He blinked blankly as she shoved past him. Confused, he chased her into the house. "What job?"

"With the hunting kulls."

"I don't understand. Why would you do that?"

"Because I fucking had to."

"No, you didn't."

She threw up her hands. "It's like I can't fucking win."

"I didn't ask you to do this."

"Well, I did it, and it is what it is, so either you can be angry, or you can help me with all of this stupid paperwork." She slammed the papers down onto the serving room table and stared at the parchment in preparation for battle.

"I'll go get a pen," he said, using it as an excuse to gather his thoughts. Rasia still surprised him at times, but he was utterly flabbergasted. He made the long circle around and paused in his bedroom to stare at the dagger still lying atop his nightstand. He hadn't noticed it was still there.

By the time he returned with a reed pen from the library, Rasia's look of determination had since turned into a panicked fluster. "I can't figure out some of the words."

He joined her and glanced over the various applications. "How did you get this? The kull tryouts ended yesterday."

"I talked with the Claws Councilor. He used to be the Hunting Han for my tah. He pulled some strings." Her shoulders slackened and the stars dimmed from her eyes. She snatched up the pen and started wildly signing her name to papers she couldn't read.

He placed his hand down, slamming the table on accident. "You don't have to do this."

He would rather do anything than see this defeated look on her face. She stared at his hand for a long time, until she finally bit out, "I'm out of fucking gonom, and this place doesn't give you any other choice. So, I need to finish this application and hurry to get it to the administration office because you fucking came in me twice last night."

His stomach dropped. "I didn't know you were out."

"I know. I forgot. I fucking forgot. No matter how much Nico controls the Council, or the fact I carry your name, there is no saving either of us from an unapproved pregnancy. It's a fucking death sentence." Her hold tightened angrily around the pen. "And I almost didn't survive the last culling. I can't do that again. I did what I had to."

"You did it again," he bit out. "You made a decision for the both of us, *again*. We should have talked about this. We could have sold the dagger to buy gonom off the black market."

"Then the windship would still be stuck in impound and we'd be right back where we started. A blink's wages with the kulls, and I can get both gonom and the windship out. I'm trying to do the right thing. *I'm trying.*" She looked small, and tired, and no amount of scavengers or dragons could put that caged expression on her face.

He jolted to his feet and turned away from her, stuffing his hands under his armpits. He searched for some way out, some way even Rasia couldn't find, but he felt just as hopeless. This was the worst thing that could have happened.

"Besides," she said, "this was always the initial plan. I do the kull thing for a year, Nico cleans up the Council to make sure you pass the next Forging, and after, we'll have more options to regroup and decide from there. I can tough it out for a year. I can eat shit when I've got to."

"But you shouldn't have to!" he snapped, then caught his temper and rubbed at his chest.

She crossed her arms and raised a brow. In a mocking tone, she asked, "And what are you going to do about it? What the fuck can you do about it? You can't even get angry. You've given that up, too, just like everything else. So, fold. Like you always do."

"Anger solves nothing. It has never made any difference."

She only nodded, as if expecting that response. "Ysai is right," she mumbled. "You've sacrificed too damn much. It's my turn."

"Since when do you care about other people's opinions?" he asked. "I don't care what Nico-ji or Ysai-ji think. This is our relationship, and they are not a part of it. I want nothing more than for you to be happy."

"And what about your happiness, Kai?"

"You make me happy." She scoffed, and he rushed over, to his knees, and picked up her hands. "The world didn't have color before you, kulani. I lived my entire life in routines, but at your side, every unpredictable day is a joy. Every day with you feels like flying."

"Stop."

"If I could, right now, I'd write your name in the book and carry it for the rest of my life. I want to wake up every day next to your smile, I want to hear your laughter every day, I want to know all the things that evoke your wonder and gift it to you as a namesake." He placed his hand atop the application papers. "We can still rip this up. We'll find another way. There are always other options."

She placed a soft hand atop his, and said, heartbroken, "But there aren't. Not good ones, anyway."

He turned his back on her, bitter and angry and frustrated. They'd beaten the Yestermorrow Lake. They'd outsmarted scavengers. They'd slayed a dragon. Certainly, they could figure a way out of this. He didn't understand. Why had Rasia given up?

Behind him, he heard her shuffling through the papers.

"At what cost is being with me too much?" he whispered. "At the cost of who you are? This isn't you. You shrink for no one. Sometimes, I wish you'd never met me."

Rasia slammed down the pen, and they sat like that—Kai's back turned and Rasia glaring at a piece of paper with words she didn't understand.

"I—" "You—," they said simultaneously.

"Kai," she finally said. "You think I don't want those things, too? You think I don't want to see you smile or laugh every day? A year isn't that long. I can suck it up."

"It'll turn you bitter."

"I'm already bitter," she said. "We need the money. We need the rations. We need the gonom. This is the only option that gets us all three. We need to *survive*, Kai. That, right now, is more important than what either of us wants. So," she wiped at her eyes. "Get over here and help me with this damn paperwork."

He grumpily swiveled over. He glanced over the various sheets of parchment scattered across the table, including applications for rations, gonom, and housing. He pulled them closer and read through the tight script.

She asked, "There's no point filling out the housing application because then I would have to register as a separate household, and we don't want to do that because we want to stay with Nico-ji. Correct?"

"That's correct," he said. She filled out the blanks on the ration sheet. He pointed out, "You're an adult now. Your pronoun has changed. The symbol is different when you're writing it, too."

"Right." She crossed out the mistake. They worked on the paperwork together. He went through every tedious clause to make sure she understood everything she put her name to.

The front door opened. Nico's eyes swept over them both as she came through, and she immediately recognized the paperwork. Both Kai and Rasia glanced at each other and silently agreed to keep some things to themselves. Nico was going to absolutely explode in the face of another pregnancy scare.

"You got a job?"

"Don't look so surprised," Rasia said, sharply.

"Nico-ji, we need your signature on these documents," Kai interrupted diplomatically.

Nico brushed a strand of hair behind her ear and crouched to scan through the completed applications. "You've looked over these?"

Rasia fumed while he held onto her thigh. "We've gone through them together."

Nico nodded and signed the remaining blank lines. She straightened and lingered. Odd, as she usually headed straight for the bath. Kai glanced at her quizzically.

"I spoke with Kenji-ta a little today. He was wondering if you two could do tea out on the veranda? Something really informal? I told him I'd talk to you about it."

He frowned at her. "Why?"

"Because he wants to get to know you."

Kai didn't know how to feel about that. So far, Kenji seemed to be keeping his promises—cooking breakfast every morning, taking Rae to school, helping Nico with her campaign, and generally leaving Kai alone. That was good enough for him.

"If you want me to say no, I'll say no."

Cheek propped on one hand, Rasia scanned his profile. She

said hot, like an accusation, "I never thought Kenji-shi, of all people, would be the one thing that reduce you to a coward."

"I didn't think I'd see the day you'd become one," he said, just as hot and bitter. She stiffened, and he regretted the words the moment they came out of his mouth.

She snatched up the papers and clutched them to her chest. She snarled, "I've slayed dragons. I've survived the deadlands, and the northern forests, and the Lake of Yestermorrow. But this is the hardest thing I have ever done. I could have run away, but I stayed. *I stayed*."

"You didn't have to," he whispered, head bowed. He shrugged. "It's okay. I'm used to being left behind."

"Fuck you. I am going to drop this off with the administration building before it closes. I am joining the hunting kulls, and doing the stupid drills, and taking whatever orders because we are a kull, and a kull leaves no one behind."

She turned on her heels and stormed out the door, while the guilt only settled deeper in his gut.

Everyone had been trying to force Rasia into one strict definition of how to live. But she wasn't the type of person to go to work, in the same job, day after day, until the day she died. The kulls were usually an answer for those who craved less structure, but Rasia needed more. She needed adventure and momentum. He thought of her cherished maps, of the etched wonders and inked passions, and all the empty edges on all sides.

A kulani was supposed to be a partnership, but what did Kai ever have to give?

CHAPTER SIXTY-TWO

—

If Rasia refused to fight any longer, then Kai would do so for her. The moment tajih stepped through the door, he unfurled from the ottoman under the windowed view of the temple gardens and organized his presentation atop the Mythkeeper's famously gold desk. He had been waiting all morning for her to come into work.

"What is going on?" tajih asked, concerned. "Are you in trouble? Have you been at the temple all night?"

"What?" He looked down at himself and realized he wore his night robe. He had been obsessively thinking about Rasia's predicament and searching for a solution, and he might have woken up in the middle of the night with an idea that wouldn't leave him. He had taken the underground tunnels from the house to the temple to do some late-night research. Might as well, since Rasia had been staying at Ysai's house since the argument.

"Yes, I mean . . . listen," he said and pulled out her tall-backed chair for her to sit. She eyed him and then walked over to sit down and imperiously looked over all the scrolls he had gathered for her to study.

"A few centuries ago, before much of the Grankull had navigated beyond the mesas, there used to be a contingent of scribes that explored and charted the Desert." He cited his references: recorded accounts, personal entries, and old sketches.

"I know," tajih said, patiently.

"Well, yes, I know that you know, but I pulled everything you could use to convince the Council. They do not know."

"Convince the Council of what?"

He asked for her patience. She crossed her arms and conceded. "Okay, so, most of the missions ended when we reached the Dragon's Coast, primarily because the other directions became too treacherous and too dangerous to continue exploring. No one made it far into the deadlands or past the northern forests, even though throughout the years, missions were sent to try again. Our need for more food sources always forced us to try again, but that all changed with Zephyr-kull's father. He made it through the northern forests, and yet there's no record of how he accomplished this. Thus, I can only assume that the Council knows how to get through the northern forests but doesn't want anyone else to know."

He stopped in his presentation and looked to his tajih for confirmation. She reluctantly nodded. "It was a decision of a Council before me, but yes, they swore Raiment Foreigner to silence as a condition for allowing him to trade here."

"Why?"

"For many reasons, and some I'm inclined to agree with. One of our biggest concerns was the fact that the outside world has no magic. It is believed to have died out."

"Impossible," he said. "Magic doesn't die. They just don't know where it is."

"But if that is what they believe, what do you think would happen if the outside world were to hear of the sort of things that Nico-po could do?"

"That's it, isn't it?" he asked. "The Grankull has been searching for years for other sources of food, and it just gives up, even knowing all that Raiment Zara-kulani brings in every year? Ava-ta silenced him. She was the one who made this decision."

"With a majority vote of the Council, but yes, she did greatly influence that vote," tajih revealed. "She only wanted to protect you."

"It's too late for that," he said. "Raiment Zara-kulani has become rich off our evory. It is valued in other parts of the world in sums the Grankull can barely comprehend. That sort of greed will bring outsiders here whether we want them or not. If there is a way, other people will find it, and we need to be prepared for when they come."

"What are you suggesting?"

"We need to know what is out there. We can't keep our heads in the sand. You have the full authority to bring back those scribes of old if you wanted to, and I can think of no better candidate than Rasia Dragonfire. Look," he said quickly before she responded. "Here are her maps."

He spread them all out on the desk, including the large one that engulfed the gold surface and hung off the edges.

"This map is just pictures."

"Look," he insisted. He rolled out the official Grankull map to compare. "Truly look at them. There are places and markers on Rasia's maps that don't exist on any map here in the temple, and they are more accurate regarding distance, too. She did all of this without any of the standard cartographer tools. Her writing might not be perfect, but all she needs is a little practice. She is brilliant. All she needs is the chance to prove it."

Tajih stared at him and said softly, "You really care about her, don't you?"

He raised his shoulders to his ears. "She was always going to leave," he said achingly. "Sooner or later. Is the Grankull so willing to let the greatest asset of this generation walk away? If there is not a job here to fit her, then it should build her one that does."

"Okay," she said, convinced. "Creating this job is within my authority, but I can't lift the secrecy ban regarding the forests. That must go through the Council." He splayed his hands meaningfully over all the information he had gathered for her to present her case. "I get it. Thank you for doing my job for me, but why not wait until after the voting season? By then, most likely your jih will be in power and this will be easier."

"But, by then, Zephyr-kull's father would have already left for the year, and it would be far safer for her to leave with him. She could submit an eyewitness account of how he gets through the forests as one of her first tasks."

"Alright. I'll present it in the next Council meeting," tajih promised. "But don't get your hopes up. Politics are always unpredictable during the voting season."

"I know. Thank you," he said. He knew the chances were slim, but he would never forgive himself if he didn't try.

"I don't need help," Nico said as she boiled water for the tea. She glanced over at Kai, judging him as he fussed over cleaning their saucers. "Why don't you go out there and sit with him?"

Nico finally managed to wheedle him into agreeing to an informal tea out on the veranda. There was a full moon tonight, so people had the day off from work. Most people spent the day doing errands or spent the time with family and flames. He could hear Rae laughing outside from the kitchen. Kai wouldn't know what to do with himself. He didn't have anything to say.

"You don't have to say anything," Nico said and poured the boiling water over the tea leaves. "No pressure. You can take things as slow as you want."

He wished Rasia were here to shield him from all the awkwardness, but she was out in the Desert with the hunting kulls practicing drills. Maybe she wouldn't be so pissed at him by the time she returned home. Maybe he'd have the chance to earn her forgiveness before the true hunting season began, when he wouldn't see her in several blinks of the Hunter's eye.

Nico lifted the tea tray. He snatched off the bowl of prepared sliced peaches and jujubes, just to have some excuse as to why he was helping (not hiding) in the kitchen. She shook her head at him, and he trailed after her outside to the veranda. Rae held their hand over their eyes and jumped on count, showing Kenji the newest game they had learned in school. Kenji looked up with those laugh-lines at the corner of his eyes, and Kai could see the concentrated effort to pretend this was all normal. Unconsciously, his hand went up to his shroud and nervously adjusted it around his face.

"Kailjnn," Kenji acknowledged.

Kai gave a quick nod, then wobbled down to the low veranda table. Nico set down the tea tray, and Rae ran over to stick their fingers all over the peach slices.

"Now that you've been at it for some time, do you prefer teaching little ones or the new-faces?" Nico asked, charging forward with the conversation and proving true that no one required Kai to provide any input. He'd wanted this his entire life, to finally be a part of the family, to belong, and in the end, he couldn't bring himself to breathe a sound.

"They both have their challenges," Kenji laughed.

"Honestly, I didn't think the school prepared me very well for the Forging," she said. "There's so much knowledge I found lacking, and what about those families that can't afford school? They are literally thrown out into the Desert without an oar to turn. If everyone has a job, then the expectation is that everyone should be able to afford school, but when food is scarce, that is simply not how it works. People are forced to choose how to allocate their resources. They are forced to favor one child or none at all. School should be free."

"I ended up alright," Kenji said, thoughtfully. "Sometimes I do wish I had gotten the chance to go to school growing up, but Anji-ji was undeniably brilliant with numbers. It was hard putting him through school, but we did it. And now he single-handedly designs the Grankull's windship fleet."

"You don't talk about your family much," she said. "I can recite the names of Ava-ta's bloodlines, but I barely know anything about yours."

Kenji lounged back in the cushions, settling in, and took a sip of tea. Surrounded by the pottery and the lush vines sprawling around the pergola posts, he looked like an artist's perfect subject. "My ancestors bred and trained horses."

A stone dropped in Kai's stomach. Everyone knew what happened to the horses.

"Oh," she said.

"Yep. The family was pretty poor afterward, but tah was always prideful about that legacy. It would have been great if he cared less about that and more about his gambling debts. Got him killed in the end, so it was just me, Anji-ji, and your granta. I wish you could have known her. She was a tough little thing with fingers that could work a loom the speed of a hummingbird. You were too young when Death came for her."

"Putting Anji-ji through school all worked out in the end though. Jih suggested to your granta that I play at one of his pourings, right here on this veranda. The musicians had their equipment set up under those trees, and kulani sat right where you're sitting right now. I still remember that moment when she looked at me. After dinner, she asked if I wanted to dance."

Nico smiled, knowing this part of the story. "And you told her no. No one had ever told Ava-ta no before. After that, you were invited to every pouring afterward, and the real dance began."

"Yep."

Nico smiled and looked out from the veranda. "I would like to do that—host a big pouring like old times. Maybe as a celebration once the election ends?"

"That would be nice," he agreed. "Any update on the campaigns?"

"My competitor for the Wing-seat can hardly drum up enough support to compete against me. The Hindlegs Councilor is in my pocket. My candidate for the Belly Councilor is running unopposed. Ashe-shi is doing surprisingly well, but Ysai-kull is having a tough time against his tajih, and the campaign for the Pelvis seat is getting really messy. They've recently sent assassins after each other. I have a meeting scheduled with the Pelvis Councilor today."

Kai zoned out as they talked of politics. It was all Nico talked about nowadays, and he was already well-versed in the current political situation and how hard it was to usurp established seats. He leaned over and cleaned the stickiness from Rae's cheeks and eventually was pulled over to the swing bench. He sat Rae in his lap and pushed them into the air.

"Jijih," Rae whispered, in that loud childish voice, "It's okay. Tah knows you're a good dragon, now."

"Yeah?" he smiled and hugged Rae in his lap. They swung on the bench, then stopped at the sight of someone approaching down the road.

"Fair winds," tajih greeted and smiled even further to see them all gathered.

"Ji-lani! Join us," Kenji greeted, waving her over. He leaned on the leaves twined over the railing. "Does jijih need me to come rescue him again? If he keeps getting pulled out of meetings, they're going to catch on."

"Wait, what are you two doing?" Tajih raised her hands. "I don't want to know. I'm here to speak with Kai-po regarding his request last week."

He slammed his feet to the ground to stop the swing. His heart pounded in his chest. He asked, hoping, "You heard from the Council?"

"I didn't know the Council was meeting," Nico said, frowning.

"It was an emergency meeting." Tajih cracked a pleased smile and said to him, "The Council said yes."

He jumped to his feet and then scrambled to grab Rae before they fell.

"Said yes to what? What's going on?" Nico asked.

"The Council has agreed to offer Rasia Dragonfire the position of scribe," tajih explained, "like the scribes of old who charted the Desert. They agreed to lift the secrecy ban and fund an expedition for Rasia Dragonfire to join Raiment the Foreigner on his travels. It was Kai-po's idea."

"And they agreed to everything?" he asked. "To the gonom and the money?"

"Yes, it is an official job. It'll follow the same rules as the hunting kulls."

"Wow," Nico looked between him and tajih. "That is an amazing opportunity for her."

"You're partly responsible," tajih said. "The Council has become increasingly concerned about your campaign. They hope that this new position shows that the Council can be progressive. The Council just voted. It's approved. I talked to Raiment Foreigner this morning, and they've agreed to cut his trade taxes if he allows Rasia Dragonfire to officially submit to the public record an account of his passage through the northern forests and beyond."

"Where is Rasia Dragonfire?" tajih asked. "I'd like to see the expression on her face."

"She is outside the Grankull right now. She's with the kulls running drills," he answered.

"But Raiment Foreigner is due to leave in two days. She needs to be here. She needs to be back on time."

"She will. I'll make sure of it," he promised.

"Okay. Get her here," tajih insisted, nodding, and then left in the direction of the temple.

He couldn't stop smiling. He did it. He found Rasia a way out. Then his mind crunched the numbers. He needed to leave *now*. He turned to Nico. "I need you to sell Ava-ta's dagger at the market. I need you to get Rasia's windship out of the impound. I've got to go get her or she's not going to make it back in time."

"No point in doing all that. I've got a few webs I can pull. I can get you a ship," Kenji said, and shrugged.

He froze. He said, hollow over the words, "I didn't ask for your help."

"Seems to me you need it. The impound office is closed today." Kenji stood and stretched from the table.

His jaw tightened. It hurt to physically creak the word from his mouth. "*Fine.*"

Kenji finished off his tea and set off down the road. Kai glared at his retreating figure.

Nico hunched, introspective, staring at the tea leaves like bones tossed in the sand. She asked softly, "You're going with her, right? If that's what you want to do, I'll be supportive of you. Tah is around to take care of Rae. Things are going well with the campaign, and I'm fairly sure I'll have the votes when the time comes. You've been doing well with the meditations and at containing any large outbursts. It'll be good for you to do something for yourself. Out there in the world, you won't have to look over your shoulder anymore. I admit, it's scary to think of you out in the unknown, but I feel better knowing you and Rasia will be together. I question Rasia's dumb decisions sometimes, but I don't question that she'll protect you with every fiber of her being." She leaned forward. "Kai, I can change the Council, and you can earn your face, but the fact of the matter is, you'll never be safe here."

Kai hadn't really thought beyond the fact that Rasia would be potentially leaving. Now it was real, and he had a choice to make. His brain tentatively tried to consider the possibilities, but his bones felt interred to the spot.

"It's not forever. You can leave with Zephyr's father and return with his caravan within the year to make it back in time for the next Forging. Zephyr did it. By then, everything will be different, I promise. This is perfect. You finally have a chance to truly experience life. Go live, Kai."

CHAPTER SIXTY-THREE

—

"You two be careful," Nico said, as she stood at the doorway with Rae on her hip. It was an odd reversal of their roles as she pulled Kai forward and kissed him on his shrouded forehead. She told him softly. "You don't have to go. Kenji-ta knows the kulls' schedules. He can find her on his own."

"She's my kulani," he said. He tightened his hands around the strap of his packed bags. His water gourd hit heavily against his thigh. Behind him, Kenji leaned one arm against the pergola pillars, not at all pretending he wasn't listening in on their conversation. "*He* doesn't have to go."

"The windship is loaned from his friend. He's got to make sure it's returned."

That familiar whine whenever he was in Kenji's presence wound tight around his thoughts. He didn't want to be stuck alone on a windship with Kenji, but he was also aware of the dipping angle of the sun. It was getting late.

"I'll be back," he promised and kissed his siblings, then turned for the road and froze. The dirt path grew five times in size, stretching endlessly away. His heart sped so loud it pumped through his ears. He hadn't stepped outside since Rae had almost been kidnapped. Then, he had been so concerned for his jih that he didn't have time to think about being afraid.

He tried to breathe through the choking panic. The fear was all in his head, even though it tightened his joints like a physical illness. It was in his head. It had been weeks since the Naming. It was the middle of the day. He'd be fine. He'd be fine. He'd be fine.

"Are you ready?" Kenji asked, concerned.

"I'm fine," Kai bit out. He dragged one foot forward, as heavy as if dragging behind a windship anchor. He slayed a dragon. He should be able to walk down a fucking street.

He glared at the ground and fought for each step, and felt nauseated by the exertion. Kenji hovered beside him as they walked, while maintaining a hesitant distance. The streets were crowded by those off work today, and even though he carried his head down to hide his eyes, he couldn't help the paranoia that eyes were on him. What happened if Kenji became embarrassed to be seen with Kai? What happened if Kai looked up to find himself suddenly alone, abandoned, and surrounded?

He remembered the angry mob, the crunch of going down, and the terror of thinking he was going to get kicked to death right in front of Nico and Rasia, and how that would completely ruin their Naming Ceremony.

Someone brushed against him, shoving him back, and the world blanked. He crouched, frozen, in the middle of the crowd—drawing even more attention to himself. Donkeys brayed. Overladen carts creaked to a halt. People shouted at him. An arm wrapped around his waist and hauled him up, and carried all seventeen years of him down the street.

White hot fury shattered the fog in Kai's ears with a pop. He snarled, pushed Kenji off of him, and found his own feet again. *"Don't touch me."*

"The carts almost trampled you."

He would rather have been trampled than hauled down the street like a budchild tired of walking. What was worse, his legs almost gave out when they reached the hull of the loaned windship. He dragged himself up the stairs and collapsed atop the deck in sheer exhaustion.

"I'll get the windship prepared to sail. Why don't you rest for a while?" Kenji said, a little stilted, stepping over him.

Kai clawed his shroud over his eyes.

Fuck.

How weak and pathetic could he possibly be?

÷

"I know you've been avoiding me, and I wanted to give you the space that you needed. I'm sorry if you weren't ready for this," Kenji said from the steer of the windship.

Honestly, Kai would rather be pushed off the ship by kids who hated him than trapped on a windship alone with Kenji. He watched the Grankull fade into the distance with numbness and was tempted to jump over the railing. Instead, he tightened his grip. It was a quiet and tense journey, and he found himself wired for every vibration of it. His eyes followed Kenji with an intensity that drained him of energy. He didn't know what to do with himself other than to stay out of the way lest he mess up again.

He jerked up and focused on the horizon. He sensed a large mass out in the Desert, moving quickly. "There's a sandstorm headed toward us. We need to find shelter."

"It's not sandstorm season."

"If we don't find shelter now, by the time it's on us, it'll be too late. We'll have lost this windship."

"Kid, I've been doing this a long time-"

"I'm not a fucking kid!" he snapped. He could endure not showing his face, could endure wearing white, and the lack of address around his name, but this was where he drew the line. "I am the Han of this expedition. You're the one who volunteered to come, but this is my kulani at stake, and I am the most qualified here to make decisions on her behalf. Make the detour."

Kenji's eyes narrowed at the command. Kai tensed and gripped his hand around the hilt of his dagger. He faced Kenji, ready for a fight he had never won.

Then Kenji shifted the steer, and the windship turned. Kai tripped over his feet and caught his shaking hands on the railing. He stubbornly turned away, hoping Kenji hadn't seen him stumble.

A couple of vibrations later, the air thickened with sand. Kenji put on his shroud as the visibility worsened and guided the windship into a slant entrance of a large redstone formation.

Once Kenji brought the ship to a stop, they scrambled to protect the ship. They dismantled the lines. Kenji dropped to the ground, Kai threw the ropes over, and they staked the ship on its side. They wrapped the tough dragon-wing sail around the hull like a protective cocoon and tucked it away from the worst of the wind.

A large scorpion carapace, dusted and covered in sand, leaned beside the entrance. They retreated inside, with the storm gaining power and battering at their heels.

Kenji moved the carapace to cover the entrance, but it stuck on a rock in the path. Kai kicked at the nuisance, dislodging it, and the make-shift door popped closed, swallowing all light and plunging the entire cave into darkness.

Fire erupted from a torch fastened to the wall. Then, a whip of sound and a dagger embedded beside his face. Kai looked up slightly, where the dagger still vibrated in the rock, pinning a snake to the wall.

"Grab that. We might as well eat dinner while we're waiting out the storm." Kenji lit more torches along the wall as he traveled deeper into the cave.

Kai took a breath, then grabbed the dagger and snake. He pocketed the dagger, just in case, and followed the trail of torches deeper inside. The narrow pathway led to a surprisingly comfortable room filled with bedrolls and supplies. Kenji lit a small campfire. The smoke winded upward toward a ceiling that stretched so tall, small cracks of light shone through.

"I'm sorry," Kenji said. "For not initially listening to you. You were right. You saved our lives."

He tossed the dead snake at Kenji's feet in answer. Then he walked away, feeling trapped and claustrophobic in the small space. Without much to do, he took stock of the space and ruffled through the supplies that the kulls had left in storage. In the corner, dusty and leaning against the wall, was yet another of Kenji's ilhans.

The storm outside increased in volume and howled against the rock. He couldn't believe his shit luck. He tried to take control of the storm, but despite all the meditations and training he had with Nico, the storm stubbornly refused to obey. Which meant they were stuck here for however long the storm lasted.

When dinner was ready, he grabbed his snake skewer and took it to a corner. He sat with his back away from Kenji. He unwrapped his shroud, forced the food into his belly, and then curled into one of the bedrolls. He hoped that by the time he woke up, the storm would be gone.

It wasn't.

"Why won't it break?" he asked himself, frustrated, as he listened to the storm raging outside.

"Not like any storm I've seen in a while," Kenji answered from where he lazily tuned the ilhan on the other side of the cave. "The last time I experience a storm like this was the day you were born. Worst day of my fucking life."

Horrified realization dawned on him.

"I am the storm."

He jumped to his feet and raced through the cave. He slammed into the scorpion carapace shielding the entrance and pushed at it, trying to open it and get outside. This was all his fault. Rasia might miss the deadline because he couldn't keep his shit together.

"Stop."

Kenji roughly grabbed Kai's shoulder and slammed back into the tough hide. His head bounced off it surprised, and on instinct, he braced for the incoming blow. When it didn't come, he peeked his eyes open at Kenji, staring at him, with sharp haunted eyes.

"You go out there, you die."

"Why do you care anyway?"

Kenji blew hot air from his nostrils, then dropped Kai to his feet. Kenji indicated the small crack in the door that Kai had made. He could probably squeeze through. "Go then. I'm not stopping you. But you'll never make it to Rasia-po. You didn't grab any water or food. I'm sure you'll survive just fine walking through the Desert. By all means, go."

Kai stared crazed at Kenji, who was so certain he knew everything.

"This is all your fault," he accused. "If you hadn't come, this wouldn't have been a problem. I'd have reached kulani by now. This is all your fucking fault."

All Kai needed to do was get far enough away, far enough from Kenji's stupid face, and the storm would disappear.

He slipped through the crack and ran out into the storm. He pushed through the whipping winds and sands. He could barely see two feet in front of him. He forced one foot in front of the other, but the storm never lessened. If anything, it increased.

Kai stopped in the middle of the storm of his own making that he was powerless to control. His breaths came in rapid beats as the storm swirled and thickened dangerously around him. His brain wracked, scraped, and pounded against his skull. He closed his eyes, fell to his knees, and willed it all to stop.

Why did something always have to go wrong? Why couldn't it ever be easy for him? He had been so close. *So close.* He pounded fists atop the sand and buckled. His breath came faster and faster until the scream-yell-shout he'd been holding onto for years exploded out of him. All his fury and rage stormed around him. The incessant whining that trailed him since the Grankull finally burst.

Anger had no purpose, until it consumed you.

CHAPTER SIXTY-FOUR

—

In the calm eye of a sandstorm, Kai stood stuck in place. A wall of impassable sand whirled around him. He finally understood. As Nico once told him, sometimes magic was mental. His panic and fear manifested as a block, but his anger and rage stormed. He couldn't push it aside and ignore it any longer. If he wanted to go forward, he had to go back. He had to stop running away.

He turned around, and a curtain of sand parted a path for him to follow. He spotted a mound buried by sand in the distance. His eyes widened in realization and raced to where Kenji had collapsed, battered by the storm. Kenji must have come out to rescue him. If he didn't do something, Kenji would die out here and then he would never get the chance to say all the things he had been too afraid to say.

He tapped down on his panic and tightened his grip around his fear. He focused on his breathing and channeling his will. The storm continued to swirl, but he took hold of a minuscule part of it. He grabbed Kenji by the arms, and the sand underneath him moved his weight in the direction Kai wanted him to go.

Kai managed to return to the cave and closed the carapace door. He watched Kenji breathe beside the still burning campfire. Adrenaline shook through his limbs. The lingering panic beat in his ears. He rested atop a thin bedroll and listened to his heartbeat slow.

"You're like Nico-po and kulani?" Kenji rasped from where he lay. "When Nico-po is upset, she rains. Kulani grew thorns. You storm." He groaned from where he sat up. He reached for his gourd and took a deep swallow of water. Then he asked, "We're not going to make it of here until we deal with our shit, hmm?"

Kai squeezed his eyes shut. Knowing he couldn't run away anymore didn't make it any easier. He didn't know where to begin. The words jumbled a mess in his head and buzzed in his ears. He didn't know which right thing to say that would fix this swirling cyclone ripping him apart from the inside out. The indecision left him paralyzed. But time was ticking down, and Rasia had only two days to return to the Grankull. If he failed, he would never forgive himself.

He forced the words up and out of his throat, "I don't know where to start."

"I'm sorry," Kenji began for them both. "I am sorry for what I've done to you. I am sorry for rejecting you. I am sorry for ignoring you. I am sorry for abusing you. I know no number of apologies will change what I did, nor do I deserve your forgiveness. You want nothing to do with me, but if there is anything I can do to provide you peace, I will do all that I can. I know that I scare you, and this can't be easy-"

"You don't scare me," Kai corrected. Kenji's brows raised, dubious of the claim. "I'm not scared," he announced, again. "I'm . . . I feel—out of control. I feel out of control around you, and I hate it. That's why I avoid you. That's why I hate being around you. I'm scared . . ." he bit down on the word, harshly, and kept himself from saying the rest.

I'm scared you'll think I'm a monster—that I'll mess this up—that I'll scare you off—that I'll ruin everything that could ever be. In the end, it'd be safer never to try at all.

Kai turned away. He stared at the shadows of flame dancing on the wall. The silence weighed heavy and suffocating, but he couldn't articulate any of the words stuck in his throat.

"Kulani and I cheated the bones," Kenji said softly. "Your

granta hated me. He hated that I came from a poor family out in the Hindlegs. He hated my art and didn't value it as essential to the Grankull or respectable enough for his lineage. When I asked to formally court his child, he refused me as her suitor. He threatened to kill me if we dared sign our names to one another. But kulani and I kept seeing each other anyway. We were dumb and determined to be together. We had a plan. Despite being unable to carry each other's names, or unable to apply for a child, we decided to have one anyway."

That caught Kai's attention. "You two didn't get in trouble?"

Kenji huffed out a twisted laugh. "Your granta beat the shit out of me. Broke my fucking fingers so I couldn't play the ilhan for a whole season. After kulani and I had our signing ceremony, your granta pulled some strings to get the baby approved, all to save face—of which, was exactly what kulani had been hoping for. We were together. We were happy. We had a baby on the way. We thought it was our happy ending . . . but there are always consequences for cheating the bones."

"Because I came along," he said, knowingly. Kenji turned silent and vacant as he often did when the subject came up, or Nico accidentally said something in conversation, or in Kai's general presence. Except this time, Kai refused to let Kenji dwell on his memories. He demanded, "I want to hear the rest. I want to hear it from you."

All Kai's life, he had gotten snippets of the story from other people. Never from Ava-ta. Never from the face who seeded him and disowned him out of the womb. He had always been too afraid to ask, but he had a right to it. It was just as much a part of Kai's story, too.

Kenji blinked at him, and at the cave, and remembered the present. "I . . . you know when you have a nightmare, and when you wake out of it, you remember the worst parts in startling clarity but all the other parts in between are . . . a blur, mixed up, sometimes flashes of things . . . I don't remember all of that day, so I might not be able to answer all of your questions. I've forgotten some things. I forgot that there were twins until Rasia-po recounted your Forging. Even years later, there are details, some triggers, that I'm still remembering. I remember . . . ." He closed his eyes and huffed out hoarsely. "I remember you—this little heartbeat in lani's belly—I . . . fuck."

Kenji walked to the other side of the cave. Kai hunched over his knees and waited, while he gathered himself.

"I'm sorry," he apologized, then returned. He had replaced his previous emotions with something a lot more bitter. Kenji rubbed at that old scar on his left arm, adjacent to the blood price he had paid on his right. Nico had always assumed the left scar was an old blood price, but Kai knew scars. It was too long, and too deep. "You must think the worst of me. Forgive me. This isn't a story I'm used to telling."

He cleared his throat and tried again. "It was a rough pregnancy. About the four-blink mark, kulani's health rapidly declined. It was nothing like when lani was pregnant with Rae. That was easy. You and your twin were hard. It got so bad the healers considered culling the pregnancy early, but she insisted on having you. She barely slept. And then came the pain. I sat up with her during those nights when she'd refuse to alert her tah or the healer that something was wrong. I watched her give everything she had in keeping you both alive that there was almost nothing of her left. She was on bedrest for the last three blinks. That was also when the rumors started. Most people were smart enough to figure out we didn't do things on the right timetable. Many said the Elder was cursing her for the unapproved pregnancy. Then came the birth, and it was all a fucking nightmare."

"It happened in the middle of a sandstorm like this one. It took drums for the birthing kull to get through the storm while Ava screamed in my arms from the contractions, all while fighting your fucking granta who wanted to cut you out and be done with it. The healers were too late for your twin, and I held them, in my arms, gone, dead out of the womb. And I . . . I had forgotten that. I had forgotten them, as if they never existed." He shook his head, eyes strained by the images only he could see. Kai's shoulders hunched, unable to stop himself from flashing back to the terror of that night with Rasia and the gonda venom. He had also lost a dream very traumatically and it had been *awful*. He didn't judge Kenji's difficulties in remembering, or the choices he had made. "If those healers hadn't arrived in time, neither you nor Iani would have made it. Then you came out, and they put you in my arms. You were this bloody small twisted thing, and I knew right then and there that I had to let you go."

"But Iani couldn't. She sacrificed so much to bring you into the world. She refused to give up on you. But you wouldn't cry. You wouldn't latch. You were in pain and Iani refused to see it. So that night when she went to sleep, I held you in my arms and said goodbye. Or at least I tried. I should have been the one to end it. I should have been strong enough. But no matter how hard I tried, I couldn't. Instead, I handed you over to the Council and hoped they could make the impartial decision."

"Then kulani woke up, found out what I had done, took six of the Council's children hostage, and killed four of them by the time the Council gave you back. I think back so often on that moment when I had you in my arms, and all the pain and suffering I could have saved on everyone's part if only I had been strong enough to do what was expected of me."

"I don't know. I wish the answers were easy, but I should have culled you then. I should have been strong enough, but I wasn't, and you're still here. You're still here, and as I should have taken responsibility for your death, I should have also taken responsibility for your living. It's too many years too late, but I want to do better. I want to do right by you. Tell me how to do right by you."

Kenji's eyes pleaded for some sort of direction. Fear stilled Kai's words because what if what Kai wanted was too much? Would it scare him away?

He continued, uncomfortable. "I'm willing to be anyone you need—be it a stranger or a friend. I've taken steps to rectify some of the wrongs I have done. I fixed and submitted the paperwork to the Grankull. Legally, now at least, I'm your parent. Regardless of how you choose the parameters of our relationship, I'm your tah, and I'll never forsake that role again."

"What?" Kai scowled, springing to his feet, snarling. "I didn't fucking ask you to do that! Why the fuck did you do that!?"

Kenji looked helpless and confused. "I thought it was the right thing to do."

"Fuck you," he snapped out, "You don't get to—I don't—Fuck." He swiveled around and pressed his shroud to his eyes.

"Then what do you expect of me?" Kenji asked, with that familiar tone of anger. "I'm trying, I'm fucking trying, but you keep giving me mixed signals. You're angry that I've fixed the paperwork, you avoid every room that I enter, every attempt at a conversation is met with silence, you claim you're not scared of me, and yet we're stuck here, in a storm of your own making. *What do you want?*"

"I WANT EVERYTHING!" Kai exploded. "I want everything that Nico and Rae got to have. I want stupid fucking nicknames. I want inside jokes. I want stories. I want a song. I want to sit at the serving table. I want sword lessons, and windship lessons, and lessons on how to play the ilhan. I want a fucking hug. I want to be more than an obligation or a responsibility or your fucking guilt. I want you to want me. I want you to want me for me, and not the bump I used to be in Ava-ta's stomach, or the baby that should have died. I want you to want me for the person I've fought so hard to become. Want me for everything that I am now. *See me!*"

Kenji stared at him stunned, and Kai turned, holding himself, afraid. He had ruined everything. He didn't mean for it all to come falling out so fast that he couldn't control his words. It was stupid. It was all so stupid.

He tensed when Kenji crouched in front of him. Kenji reached forward, slowly, giving Kai plenty of time to stop him. But he didn't. He didn't have the wherewithal to breathe at that moment. Kenji grabbed the frayed ends of Kai's shroud and then slowly unwound it.

The shroud slipped past his ear, past his cheeks, and chin, and fell to the ground. Kenji looked at Kai's face for the first time since his birth and Kai announced to the only person who ever mattered, "I am the child of Avalai Ohan and Kenjinn Ilhani. My kulani is Rasia Dragonfire, and I am the windeka of our kull. I am jijih. I am a friend. I am brave. I am smart. I storm. I endure. I persevere. I slay dragons."

"I see you, Kailjnn Dragonblood. I finally see you." Kenji embraced him.

Tah smelled of sweat, and smokefire, and the crisp clean air of the Desert. Kenji-ta felt so solid, like Kai always imagined he would, and more real and messy and painful than the Yestermorrow Lake could ever conjure.

The storm finally settled.

CHAPTER SIXTY-FIVE

I

"Thank you for meeting with me," Nico said, from where she sat in the Pelvis Councilor's office. The Pelvis Councilor managed one of the largest stages of the Pelvis, but his office, as many of the stage managers, was located in the upper levels of the gambling houses. The Councilor's campaign competitor worked directly across the hall. "The Tents sent me to offer you a deal."

The Pelvis Councilor scoffed from where they stood before the latticed window of their office. Windowpanes of dragonglass muffled the music and the battering rain from outside, insulating the two in a bubble of silence.

She sipped at the provided tea (after of course checking for poisons). She noted the expensive palm wood desk, the fresh flowers, and a brightly painted chest in the corner of the room with gold accents. Stage managers received a percentage of the bonechips of everyone who visited their stage. That wealth was present everywhere in the office.

As they leaned against the window, she could see the Councilor's breasts through their sheer linen tunic, and their tight skirt highlighted their broad frame. The Pelvis Councilor was of the fourth sex, both male and female, a person said to be born with a dragon's shapeshifting spirit. They were so revered and respected that, traditionally, many attained the title of Mythkeeper. Nico knew from the beginning that this would be a hard seat to overturn, but the Pelvis was the only territory where the Tents had someone positioned high enough to have a chance at winning. The Tents desperately wanted this seat.

"I have a deal for you," the Pelvis Councilor said, before Nico could lay out the terms of her own deal. "You have thrown your support against my competitor, but perhaps I can change your mind."

She took a sip of tea. "I have hard evidence that you tried to have me killed."

They glanced at her, trying to determine her bluff. After all, if she truly had hard evidence, why hadn't she revealed it? Or was it a ploy for them to accidentally say something and incriminate themselves? She could see both those thoughts run through their head.

But Nico wasn't here to point fingers. She was here to stop a war. She rattled off the number of bonechips the Pelvis Councilor paid to have her killed. Their eyes widened. "You could have everyone destroyed."

"But I have not," she said simply.

After a moment, they glided away from the window. They sat down at the desk, across from Nico to treat her as an equal and not as the ignorant child how the Councilor had first received her.

"I'm an opportunist," they said. "I have no animosity against you or your family. I read the winds and made a bet on what I thought had been a winning throw. It seems we've all underestimated you. Let's talk frankly. You are going to win your seat. You've killed the Ribs Councilor in a highly public blood price match, the Belly Councilor has retired, the Neck Councilor is losing to your young mathematician, and I suspect you've already got that greedy Hindlegs Councilor in your pocket. The winds are shifting, and this time, I'd like to choose the right side. Give me your support, and I will gladly vote for any initiative you put forth, even a vote to reinstate your title as Ohan."

She narrowed her eyes at them. She hadn't expected the

frankness, nor had she yet pinpointed the source of the Councilor's motivation—power, ambition, money—people always wanted something.

"I appreciate the offer, but the title of Ohan isn't given. It is earned," she said.

"You are much harder to pin down than your tah. She was much more predictable. I can't figure out what you want."

"I want to stop this war," she said. "You might have tried to have me killed, but I don't relish seeing someone dead simply because they were on the wrong side. You've recently sent assassins after your campaign opponent."

"Those rats have caused fights on my stage four nights in a row. They are losing me money," they said.

"This situation risks spiraling out of control." She leaned forward. "The Tents want this seat, and they will stop at nothing to get it. The deal they want to offer you is this: end your campaign and abdicate your seat, and in exchange, they promise not to kill you."

"So, this is a threat," they said.

"This isn't about losing a Council seat, anymore. This is about losing your life. If I leave this office without the express consent that you are willing to fold in the middle of the election, you won't live past tomorrow," she told them. "You still manage one of the largest stages in the Pelvis. You are still a very successful businessperson. Give up the seat."

The Pelvis Councilor stood and glared out the window. They oversaw their domain with a stubborn expression. Ah. That's why they were so intent on fighting this. This was about pride.

"You aren't used to people threatening you," she said slowly. "But all the Tent Hans have come together for this one goal. They don't care who you are. They only see you as an obstacle."

"Why me?" they spat. "Why target me? There are other Councilors who are dirtier than I am."

Nico picked up a metal weight. She placed it on one side of the gold scale atop the Councilor's desk.

"You have everything," she said as she stacked two weights

atop of one another. Empty, the other side of the scale began to rise. "But if the Grankull is to ever be truly equal, then those with everything will have to sacrifice something." She took off one of the weights and placed it on the other side. The scale balanced—one weight on each side.

"My goal is to create such an abundance of resources that both sides remain equal while having more than they had before." She added more weights, and now two balanced on both sides. "This is an opportunity for you as well. If my plan works, our food supply will drastically increase. An increase in food supply means an increase in population. An increase in population means you make more money. Sacrifice isn't always forever. Sometimes, a sacrifice now is a long-term gain."

"How do I know this candidate of theirs won't take all the contracts? What if they change the Pelvis beyond recognition? I built this empire. I kept the scavengers out of this place, so our youth would have a safe place to be."

"Don't everyone deserve a safe place to be?" she asked. "The Tents see this seat as their safeguard to prevent future purges. I will ensure the Pelvis remains fair. I will ensure the Pelvis remains safe. Trust me," she said. "I didn't have to ask you to meet with me. I could have stayed out of it, but when I heard the Tents had gotten tired of your obstinance and were planning to have you assassinated, I went out of my way to speak with you. Even knowing you paid to have me killed." She stood and joined the Councilor at the window. A sharp rain battered against the glass, one not of her making. "Sometimes people choose the wrong side, but it's never too late to choose the right one."

"Or I die," the Pelvis Councilor said.

"At least it's a choice. That's far more than you gave me."

Together, they watched the rain. They watched couples walk hand-in-hand, friends laughing in the streets, and the cheers and cahoots of people blowing off steam after a long day at work. The Pelvis, for all its debauchery and escapism, was the one neighborhood that brought the others together.

"I hadn't considered the consequences of what might happen," they murmured. "Your tah brought a lot of death and hurt to the Grankull, and I made the decision based on what others said about you. It wasn't my intention for all those kids to be caught in the crossfires, and now I must live with their blood on my hands. I thought . . . that somehow, I'd get the chance to redeem what I had done. That is what this seat means to me—a chance to make things right again."

"Sometimes, the world demands of us redemption in ways we don't expect." She placed a hand on their arm. "I can't speak for the others, or for those who are gone, but I can speak on behalf of the hurt you have caused me. I forgive you."

"I appreciate that," they whispered, voice strained against the window. After a moment, the Councilor's rain speckled reflection conceded. "You have a deal."

CHAPTER SIXTY-SIX

—

Kai struggled with a particular knot. The Forging hadn't been that long ago, but he had been preoccupied with so much, that the version of himself who could navigate a windship without thought felt like a distant time. He had forgotten some of the more intricate knots Rasia had shown him. He struggled with one knot in particular and panicked every time the rope slipped through his fingers.

His hands trembled. The foreboding sense that everything depended on this one knot grew heavier with each passing moment—that if he didn't get it right, his tentative relationship with Kenji would fall apart. He had named himself a windeka, and now Kai couldn't even prove it.

"Sometimes a good way to get over the nerves is to narrate the steps. It helps you from forgetting things." Kenji said, coming over to help even though he hadn't asked. Kai flinched, then dropped his useless hands. Kenji picked up the loose strands of ropes and sang a quick ditty, "Curve the lines around the pole, under the legs, and through the hole."

It was the first time Kai had heard him sing in years, and it caught him by surprise. "Rasia didn't teach me that."

She most certainly would have if she had known it.

"It's something I made up once I started teaching the kulls.

You'd be surprised how easily people remember the dirty songs," Kenji huffed, and he quickly undid the knot and handed it back over to Kai.

"And you're teaching this to school children?"

He laughed. "I've had to modify it. They like the bunny version. I can't get through one class without being asked to sing it."

Kai smiled to know that in some form Kenji was singing again. Kai narrated the steps of the song. Overhand and through. The rope pulled tight and knotted with ease. He shook his head in exasperation. He should have remembered how to do that.

Kenji leaned against the railing, noticeably making an effort to be near Kai than at a distance like before. "Most new faces make a fool of themselves when they get in front of me on a windship. I'm used to the nerves. It's okay. This isn't a test. I'm not going to think any less of you because you can't do a shift knot."

. . . a shift knot? Once again, Kai was reminded how his education had been as tossed together as Rasia's windship.

"How about you take the steer this time around?" Kenji suggested.

"You trust me to do that?" he asked. He wasn't sure he trusted himself.

"No better way to shake off the dust." Kenji clapped him on the shoulder. "Why don't you finish up? I'm going to grab some supplies from the kull stash."

Kai stood there for a moment and basked in the warmth of the touch through his shoulder. He felt lighter since he released all the tension and pent-up emotions twisting him up for so long, but a lot was still weighing the air between them. Nervousness churned in his gut at times.

He paused between knots. During the whole conversation, Kenji had referred to Kai using the adult pronoun. Even Nico was careful about using it in public. He found it difficult to wipe away his smile.

Kenji returned rather conveniently after Kai finished his preparations, and he realized Kenji had left him alone intentionally, giving him space to work.

Kenji sat down the extra supplies and most noticeably the ilhan against the inner railing. He visibly did a scan of Kai's work. Kai made sure to check all of the ropes, pulled up the anchor, and adjusted the sails.

Kenji nodded. "Alright, let's go."

He bit the inside of his cheek to stop the stupid smile tugging at Kenji's approval. He grabbed the steer and pressed down slowly to get the feel of the ship's drag. Rasia's windship snapped much quicker. They sailed out from the redstone formation without further storms.

He maintained a steady course. The longer he sailed, the more confident he became, and the more he remembered the familiar rhythms. He increased their speed and zipped around sand dunes. Once certain Kai wasn't going to send them headlong into a crash, Kenji climbed the scout's nest to keep a lookout.

After a while, Kai almost forgot he was up there until he dropped down and signed to stop for high noon. Kai gradually slowed the ship and parked under the shade of a large rock plateau located alongside a strip of cracked shrubbery.

"You're good," Kenji complimented with a nod. "Rasia-po certainly wasn't wrong about that. You could be great; she wasn't wrong about that either. You have a few holes in your knowledge, but that certainly isn't your fault. Not even I could get Rasia-po to sit long enough to listen to the details."

Kai rubbed at his chest, at the warmth that spread there, and searched to put a name on the emotions welling up inside of him. It was . . . different now. The intensity and tension from before transformed into an almost bumbling awkwardness. Kenji was better at moving through the awkwardness than Kai, certainly, but it felt like two unfamiliar musicians trying to figure out how to create music together.

They ate the lunches Nico had packed for them while sitting on opposite sides of the windship. They sat closer to the bow, so when Kenji stretched out his legs, their feet almost touched. Kai stared at the proximity. He never imagined this. He never imagined such a balm slathering cool on the aches. He wished he had on his shroud to hide all of these silly childish emotions from his face.

"I'll take the next shift at steer so you're rested," Kenji said. "The storm put us behind a bit, so we might need to sail through the night."

It was true that they lost a lot of time to the sandstorm, and they would have to sail through the night to reach the gorge in time.

Except for one thing.

"Rasia isn't at the gorge anymore. She's headed back in our direction toward the Grankull," he said. "My kulani is coming to me."

CHAPTER SIXTY-SEVEN

O

Rasia peered through the spyglass at the unfamiliar ship approaching off the horizon.

"Hey," Aden snatched the spyglass out of her hands. "That's mine."

"I didn't tell you to come with me," she grumbled.

It had to be some sort of punishment that she got stuck on straight-laced Aden's kull, along with the rest of the bumbling gourds: Azan, Faris, and that older male she met at the tryouts, Noam. Thick-headed. The lot of them.

At least Aden was smart enough to know that if he tried to stop her from doing what she had to do—stealing a windship in the middle of the night to return to the Grankull to check on her kulani—she would have kicked his ass. Aden decided to wake the rest of the kull and accompany her instead, covering for her when she never asked for the help.

"This is better than being stuck back at the gorge sweeping sand and doing drills," Azan said from the steer.

"We could get in trouble for this," Faris mumbled.

"Who are we to forego the call of adventure?" Noam asked. He leaned into Rasia's periphery with a wide grin and winked. She rolled her eyes. She was in no mood to humor Noam's flirtatious advances.

"We're not here for fun," Aden criticized them all, and then said after observing through the spyglass. "It's a Grankull ship. Looks like it's hailing us. Slow our speed."

"Maintain speed," Rasia immediately countered. "It could be scavengers. They could have stolen a ship, and now they're leading us into a trap." She turned to Azan, currently steering the ship. "Don't listen to him."

Azan looked between Rasia and his older jih undecided.

"*I'm* the Han," Aden said, in exasperation, for the hundredth time since they placed Rasia on his kull.

"Could it really be scavengers?" Faris asked as he tightened his fist on the hilt of his scimitar.

"What was that?" Aden said. "Did any of you see that flash of light?"

"You sure you aren't just miraging?" Noam asked as he squinted into the distance.

Wait.

Rasia snatched the spyglass from Aden as the opposing ship came further into view. The sun reflected a flash in the area of the opposing ship's steer. Rasia knew that brilliant light up-close and personal.

"It's Kai," she said to herself, in relief. Thank Elder. She feared him dead in some ditch after that crazy out of season sandstorm. She might be mad at him, *still*, and bitter about the whole situation, *still*, but she wouldn't hesitate if her kulani needed her. Also, she was about ready to pull out her hair, what little of it she had, if she had to sail the same boring arc maneuver one more time. She didn't care if she discovered Kai had stubbed his toe, she'd jump at any excuse to leave. Kulani in distress was usually a forgivable offense.

With that storm though, she had feared the worst.

"Slow down," she ordered. Aden threw up his hands when Azan actually slowed down this time. He threw his younger jih a sour face, before snatching the spyglass back from Rasia.

"You keep doing that and I'll break your fingers," she warned.

"No, you won't," Aden said, dismissively. Then he moved the

spyglass up and down.

"Are you checking out my kulani?"

"No," he said quickly, then nervously admitted, "I'm checking out your kulani's tah."

"What?" she snatched back the spyglass. The windship had come closer in view for her to spot Kenji-shi at the railing, pointing a spyglass right back at them. If Kai was out here looking for her in the middle of the Desert, with Kenji-shi no less, something had to be going on. Kai looked fine, but her thoughts swirled in all sorts of distressing directions.

She side-eyed Aden. "He's going to overshoot."

"You've got to let him learn." He turned to Azan, "Slow it down. Go easy."

Azan went too slow, then too fast, and as she predicted, Azan overshot. She backed up to the other end of the ship, and as the tip of Kai's ship broke the bow, she sprinted forward at full speed. She vaulted off the railing and rolled to a landing on the strange and unfamiliar windship deck. She surged to her feet, unsheathed her swords, and demanded, "Who do I need to kill?"

Unexpectedly, Kai's face broke into a wild satisfied smile. She hadn't seen a smile that wide since they'd killed the dragon. Maybe he was out here because he was super horny and missed her fire pussy? She would be down for that. Wait, no, she was still mad at him.

"I found you a job."

She blinked and played the words over again in her head. She was certain she misheard. "Say that again."

"I got you a job as a scribe."

Rasia must still be stuck in the endless nightmare she had been living these past few days. Long mast-banging nights of sharing watch with Aden who did nothing but rant his mortification at the fact his younger jih was blatantly fucking his way through the entire hunting kull. Or long days of menial chores with some other kull member who wanted to fuck her but couldn't seem to ask without demeaning and belittling Kai in the process. Getting in trouble for punching someone in the face, again. Getting in trouble for striking a hunting Han in the tits, again. Getting in trouble for eliminating the word runt from everyone's vocabulary, over and over and over again.

Always getting in trouble.

Sure, she could add this atop the already horrifying nightmare of her life. She laughed at the absurdity and the outrageousness of whatever the fuck was happening. "Stop shitting me."

"I'm serious. I showed your maps to tajih. The Council decided to offer you a job to accompany Zephyr's tah out of the Grankull. They agreed to fully fund an expedition to map out the lands beyond the Desert. But we've got to get you back before Zephyr's tah sets out with his caravan."

The Grankull would never. But then again, Kiba-ta was dead. And Kai sure as fuck wasn't out here for nothing. Perhaps the sandstorm had been some sort of signal to get her attention?

"It's true, kulani. It's really true."

Air swelled in her lungs. Then Rasia laughed from her bellows, which danced into shrieking excitement. Giddiness fluttered down her arms. Elation sparked off her skin. She raced across the deck, and at the end of her sprint, tackled Kai to the ground. She squeezed his face and felt that toss through her stomach when sailing full speed with a gonda behind her. "This is it. This is exactly what I saw in the Yestermorrow Lake. We're going to conquer the world together."

"Lani," Kai said, face soft and sweet. "We need to go."

"Shit, you're right." She leap-frogged to her feet. She turned back toward her short-lived kull. Aden and the others raised their hands in goodbye. Maybe they weren't so bad after all, but they could never have been enough. She was finally out of here.

Rasia slammed her hand down on the steer.

Luckily, Kai was already on the ground, but Kenji-shi caught his grip on the railing as the windship sped forward. The hull creaked at the force.

"Whoa, easy. I promised a friend I'd get this thing back in one piece," Kenji-shi said, plastered to the railing.

Rasia slowed down, *slightly*.

For all the immense size and breadth of the Desert, she had been crushed by it. You couldn't re-discover something new. You couldn't re-learn the same information. You couldn't re-experience a first time again. Drills and mundane hunts couldn't fill the corrosive hole of aching boredom or stem the slow torture of living life unchallenged.

The Desert, in all its vastness, was too small for Rasia Dragonfire.

CHAPTER SIXTY-EIGHT

O

Rasia aimed for the horizon line as if she could break it. The hull of this piece of junk creaked at the effort, but this baby was solid. It would make it. Soon, the shadowed hunch of the Grankull gnawed out of the sands and crawled toward them.

Kai placed a hand on hers and gently pressed down on the steer until the windship came to a complete stop.

They were only a few vibrations out of the Grankull, but it was the middle of the night, and surely what business she had could wait until morning. She immediately understood his intentions. She moved her hand to an entirely different steer and pawed at the empty space where Kai evaded her grasp.

"Rasia . . . that's not why we stopped." He looked over his shoulder, at Kenji-shi. "Do you mind taking a walk?"

Kenji-shi nodded, grabbed his ilhan, and climbed down the stairs. She looked between Kai and Kenji-shi because now was an even more perfect time to celebrate and snatch off each other's clothes. She watched warily as Kai stepped back, almost to the other side of the railing.

Rasia frowned, confused at where this was going. Whatever he had to say, it became more obvious it was something she wasn't going to like. His face was shrouded with so much guilt and apology, with so much weight, it yanked her head out of the clouds. She knew the words before they left his mouth.

"I'm not going with you."

"*No.*" She shook her head and stumbled back. She clutched at a sudden stitch in her side and demanded, "Why the fuck not? You can't walk the streets of the Grankull for fear someone is going to hurt you. That's no fucking life. We have the opportunity to explore the world!"

"I don't need the world. That is your dream. Not mine."

"We can come back for the Forging. We can come back to earn your face. You wouldn't miss a thing."

"It's about more than the Forging. *I* want more. I want to someday try out for the kulls. I want to be a windeka. But you . . . you can't stay. No. The Grankull built windships because it ate all the horses, and I will not watch this place consume you, too. There's not a lot I can give you, but I can give you this. Eventually, you'd have tried to leave the Desert on your own, and either you'd succeed or get yourself killed. This way, it's safe. I didn't want to face it but . . . I've always known that the Grankull would never be enough for you."

"It's not enough for you! You don't belong here either!" she yelled, frustrated. "You are so much bigger than this place. You will always be bigger than this place, and if you don't get out now, you won't grow any bigger than their cage."

"I'm staying."

"Fuck you, Kai! I signed your name! I joined the hunting kulls for you! I'm here, trying, because of you!"

"I never asked you to!"

"You promised! Remember? You promised never to leave me."

"I know," he said, all sorrowful. "I thought it was a promise I could keep, but that was before we returned to the Grankull. I'm sorry."

"*Sorry?* What about all the things you said just a few days ago?" she demanded. "I thought you wanted to wake up to me every day, and hear me laugh, and all that other stuff? And yet, you're choosing the Grankull over me? *Horseshit.*" It frustrated Rasia to no end—this twisted broken logic he used sometimes. "Nothing is stopping you from coming with me. There are no more excuses to hide behind. Nico can take care of herself. Rae will be fine. Kiba-ta is dead. The Grankull spat you out and disregarded you, then it hurt you, and betrayed you. You don't owe it anything anymore."

"*I owe myself!*" he yelled. "If I leave now, I might never come back. It'll feel like giving up, and I'll always be afraid. If I leave, everything that I have gone through, everything that I have struggled for would be meaningless. You have your names. You have your face. I have nothing."

"YOU HAVE ME!" she screamed at him. "I hate to fucking break it to you lani, but not all stories have a fucking point. Sometimes you sail a dead end and all the obstacles and all the shit mean nothing. How do you expect your story to end? Born the underdog, struggle all your life, and then finally, you earn your name and the happy perfect ending? Wake the fuck up! The truth was right in our faces on Naming night. No matter how many names you earn, you will always mean nothing to them. Life isn't a story with neat little conclusions. Sometimes it's dead fucking ends, and you've got to turn around and find another way. You want it all to mean something, you want everything you have suffered to have a point, but it won't! Because the Grankull don't give a shit about you! And it never will!"

Rasia watched the stubbornness set in his jaw, and at that moment, she knew she lost him. They were the same in that way. Tell them they couldn't do something, and they'd stop at nothing to prove you wrong. The realization cracked a hollow void into her chest.

"I've survived this far," he said, determined. "I can make it. You think I'm not strong enough?"

"You're the strongest person I know," she said. She tiptoed her words, carefully. "You'll succeed, I do not doubt that, but there's no happiness at the bottom. Not anything real. You're drowning all over again in the Yestermorrow Lake, sinking after what you think you want, weighed down by your stubbornness and your pride. I'm trying to save you."

He spat out bitter, "I never asked to be saved."

She honestly didn't know if he was referring to now or the first time in that Lake. She never knew what to do with this Kai—this moodiness thick and viscous like mud. She felt him sludging from her fingers, and she grew angry at the helplessness of it all. In her bones, she knew he was making the wrong decision.

"Maybe," he said softly, "one day I'll have a face you'll be proud of, and I'll be the partner you deserve."

Rasia charged forward and slammed her hands on either side of the railing, trapping him against her. He met her unflinchingly.

"All I want is you," she declared, and saw the conflict in his eyes. The 'you' that he was now wasn't enough for Kai. He never thought he was enough. His insecurities had always created cracks between them. "I want you to have your names. I want you to have your face. I want that for you, but if your bones are all that I'll get to have, I'll take them gladly. All I want is to be together."

"No." He shook his head. "I can't. I can't go with you."

Heat boiled in her chest. Her grip squeaked tight against the railing. She remembered the first time he told her that word. It still burned, even now. She whispered, throat thick, "You didn't have nightmares when it was you and me in the Desert, but in the Grankull, you have them every night. You don't have to choose that. We could be free. Walk away, *please*."

Kai closed his eyes. Her attention hyperfocused on the way his gold eyelashes, almost white at the roots of them, slumbered on his skin. She wished they had more time. She wished they had met sooner or never met at all. She could barely breathe through this twisting agony.

"Rasia." No one would ever say her name like he does, the way he lingered over each syllable with respect, admiration, and care. He opened his eyes, irises bright and swirling, and the light of her life. "This is my dragon. I can no more walk away than you could from yours."

"But it's not real."

"It's real to me."

She broke into a pace around the deck. Chest hot. Fingers

trembling. She caught herself against the railing, tilting down to glare at the thousands of sand-grains underneath her. She scratched at tears. Then she screamed.

He promised. He had promised. He was never supposed to leave her. She was never supposed to be alone anymore. Why do they all leave her, in the end?

She spat out, bitterly. "Drown in your lake, Kai. But I'm getting out."

Then she jumped the railing.

She dashed across the sand dunes, gaining speed and momentum. She ran, and ran, and ran. Till her legs gave out, and she folded over, clutching at this wrenching torment in her chest. She heaved, gut churning as emotions crisscrossed dark, sticky, and messy like silk spider webs. She had never known a pain like this, a shattering weight that left no physical wounds.

How dare he hurt her like this? How dare he abandon her to choke on the dreams of what could have been? How was it possible for potential and possibilities to wound deeper than dragonsteel? It *hurt*, the pain wrenched and tore at the beating organ in her chest.

She couldn't even muster up the energy to be angry. She had been angry so much over the past blink that she had emptied out all her rage, finally scraping the bottom of it. She had no more anger left to expend. She pressed her cheek against the sand, numbed and weighed down by her grief and mourning and tears.

And the worst part—the horribly terrible worst part—was knowing that Kai wouldn't be the person she had fallen for if he had chosen to walk away. She would respect less that person who gave up. But what did that mean? Were they always headed toward branching paths? Had this relationship always been a dead end, and she too afraid of being alone to have seen it?

The sun dawned on her face, brilliant gold and orange hues that painted a new day. She had to get back to the Grankull or the ship would leave without her. So she picked herself up. Brushed off the sand. Wiped off the tears. Shook out her disappointment.

Rasia had things to do.

CHAPTER SIXTY-NINE

—

Kai stared at that inky blackness Rasia had disappeared off into. Movement caught the corner of his eye, when Kenji returned from his imposed stroll and climbed up the windship steps. He assessed the emptiness of the deck and didn't need much but the shadowed outlines of the ship to piece the story together. Kai pushed himself off the railing and threw himself toward the steer. His hand tightened around the bone grip, with shoulders hunched against the impending judgment.

"You're making a mistake."

He glared at the face who had the gall to talk to him about mistakes. Kenji raised his hands, and his next words were slow and deliberate. "From the perspective of someone who has outlived their kulani, I think you're making a mistake. You'll come back to this moment and regret it for the rest of your life."

"Then I'll fucking regret it. I'm staying." His grip tightened around the steer, and he stared at it harshly. "Rasia thinks it's so stupid that I care what the Grankull thinks, but I want them to see my face and know tah didn't die for nothing. I want to officially succeed in my Forging. I want to try out for the kulls. I want to be a windeka. I want to no longer be a curse. I want . . . I don't want to be afraid anymore." He shook his head. "Rasia and I are sailing two different paths."

Kenji was quiet for a moment, considering his response. "Your tah cared for you, but she wasn't perfect either, and although I was wrong about most things . . . kulani's fight against the Grankull wasn't always about you, sometimes it was about her pride and her ego and her entitlement. With Rasia-po, you could be happy. But this road here? This road toward the adoration and acceptance of the Grandkull—it's long and it's hard and leads only to bitterness and disillusionment. Remember, you're the one at the steer, and you can always change direction."

Kai finally looked up to face his tah and said derisively, "You could never understand."

"I was born out the shit-end of the Grankull. I fucking understand everything. I come from a family where we only had enough for one to make it, and it wasn't me. I never thought I'd live long enough to reach my Forging, much less show my face, but I got lucky—because I happened to have some talent and met the right people. But so many kids I ran the streets with didn't survive. You can spend your whole life fighting for just a brick of dignity and respect and still die faceless. Somehow, I made it. I got out. I climbed that mountain, but guess what? You get to the top and all there is another fucking mountain. This shit doesn't end. It's just one nightmare after another, and I-" He dropped his head and sucked in a breath. "The only thing that matters are those standing beside you. The rest means nothing. Don't make my mistakes."

"I am not you," he hissed out. He glared at his tah, bare-faced, unwavering. He had lived his entire life in Kenji's shadow. "I will not crumble as you have. I will not fold. I will not surrender. I will *always* get back up. I have endured your anger and your blows. I have slayed the dragon you couldn't. I have always been, and will always be, stronger than you."

He frowned when his declaration didn't have the intended reaction, for Kenji threw his head back with a strained cutting laugh. Kenji shook his head and said, "It's like looking in a fucking dragonglass mirror. Yeah, I practically said the same thing to my tah back in the day. You are as stubborn and as hard-headed as

I ever was. This fight you have chosen is never-ending. It will always be a struggle."

"Struggle is all I know."

"You deserve peace." Kenji sighed and raised his eyes to the stars. He tilted his head in a pained expression and admitted, in a haunting tenor. "I'm cursed too, in a different way. It's considered a weakness . . . so you don't talk about it. You keep quiet, even when it's loud in your ears. I know what happened to you yesterday on that street. I know what it is like to freeze. I know what it is like to drown on air. Like you, I have seen Death's face."

On some subconscious level, Kai had known. He had always known. They always had a kinship he could never explain. He asked, softly. "Is it my face?"

"No," Kenji said. "It happened way before you. Before you were ever conceived."

Kenji turned his face into the wind, and his grip turned pale around the windship railing. Kai saw the weight. In that moment, his anger and self-righteousness blew away. What was the point of fighting a person already lost?

He crossed the deck and leaned against the railing at Kenji's shoulder. He gazed at the stars and said more gently, "I, more than anyone, know you aren't perfect. You don't have to hide anything from me. I won't tell Nico-ji."

Kenji's grip on the railing grew paler. "A lot of people assume Shamai-kull and I met during the Forging, but we weren't on the same Forging team. We met before, out in the Tents, and there's only one reason why a kid in need of money crosses the border. I'm not ashamed of it. Most don't talk about it, but many on my edge of the Hindlegs did it. I reckon Nico-po has guessed at it, but what she doesn't know is all that came before."

"I . . . only Anji-ji knows. Tah used to sell me to pay some of his debts when I was younger. I think he grew ashamed of it, and of me, what he made me do. Started justifying it by calling me a whore, that I was born to it, and as if to prove it he'd . . . sometimes he'd . . ."

Kai wound tight at the haunted blankness in Kenji's eyes—a blankness he had seen first-hand in the eyes of the no-faces at the scavenger camp. He almost retched at the thought, horrified, and dared to somehow wrestle that horror into words. A triarch was supposed to protect the family. He never considered the worst that could happen with an abusive one. "Your tah raped you."

"Until the day his kulani stabbed a needle through his eye. For all the sacrifices we'd made because of his gambling, the debts got worse and worse, and she had grown tired of it. His death was a relief, but when tah died, his debts didn't. We were still expected to pay, and we knew our best hope was a good job with a good salary. That part was up to jih, but we still had to pay for his schooling and the debts we owed. So, I went into the Tents and did the only thing I thought I'd ever be good for."

"I got lucky. I met Shamai-kull who looked out for me. I met Heron who taught me how to play the ilhan. And I got good at it, and I started getting contracts for ceremonies and pourings before I ever had a face. You begin to think you could be somebody. You begin to think you could be more than the dumb-twin, more than the one everyone wrote off. I passed my Forging, I earned my face, and I thought I made it—that I left all the monsters behind under the bed."

"Then," he snapped his fingers, "you have a panic attack in the middle of the fucking bodika. The monsters don't go away. They aren't a dragon in a story you can slay and are suddenly free of. No. It's a fucking fight every single day. When you become an adult, you're suddenly thrust into a society that sexualizes you at every turn. I knew how to go through the motions to make money, but it was never an act of pleasure for me, and I envied those who took that for granted. As an adult, you're expected to enjoy sex, or else something is wrong with you. I kept freezing. I kept leaving partners unsatisfied, and I became so afraid of being labeled a skink, I stopped altogether."

"That day, when I first met kulani, I told her no because I was *afraid*. And then, when we did get together, her fucking tah spoke to me like I was a pile of donkey shit in the middle of the road.

And of course, he investigated my family history and found out I used to whore myself, and that was it. I'd never be good enough for his bloodline. I'd never be anything other than a tent whore. But I was determined to prove him wrong. I joined Shamai-kull in the hunting kulls, and we slayed a dragon. A fucking dragon, and it still didn't matter." He shook his head. "No matter what you do, sometimes it will never be enough. So, lani and I said fuck it and we had you anyway. You know the rest. You know how that turned out. And when they placed you in my arms, I knew at that moment, tah was right. I wasn't good enough. You embodied everything wrong and broken about me. And I hated it. I hated myself. I hated you. I know better now that it wasn't some physical inferiority on my part, but the awful truth is that the twins came from *me*, from *my* bloodline. That's what messed the magic up, right? Too much of it? It's still all my fucking fault."

Kenji took a deep breath, eyes sallow, and continued, dark and bitter. "And in the end, I became no better than my fucking piece of shit tah."

Then he crumbled and wept, hard sobs that Kai could do nothing to ease, except to give witness to. Their experiences weren't identical. He had never experienced such sexual abuse, but he related to so many of the same emotions.

The bitterness. The anger. The inadequacy. The helplessness. The fear. The self-doubt.

It was like looking in a dragonglass mirror.

He had feared Kenji most of his life, but Kai had also admired him. It unsettled Kai to hear such insecurities. He wondered at his own words, said such a short while ago—was Kai truly stronger? If not . . . if not . . . was Kenji right? Was Kai falling into cycles he'd never escape from? Was he doomed to become the person standing before him? Or was Kai being unfair? The world could crush even the strongest of bones.

Even Rasia, at times.

Kai loosened the shroud he had tied around his waist and offered it, tentatively touching Kenji's shoulder to get his attention. He stared at the shroud, surprised, and then reached for it to wipe his face.

"None of this—none of what I've told you is an excuse for my actions and what I've done to you, but I understand, better than anyone, this path you have chosen." He looked Kai straight in the eyes. "I'm nothing but a piece of shit. I'm sorry I'm not strong enough for you. I'm sorry I can't get my fucking shit together. I'm a mess. And I'm trying. *I'm trying*. But Kai, I am not worth staying for."

Kai stared down at the bumpy grooves of the deck, uncomfortable at the outright accusation.

"This is your chance to get out," Kenji said. "If I can't do anything else for you as your tah, the least I can do is show you my monsters and convince you all this pain is not worth it."

But it was, Kai thought, because they were here together. For so long, they'd been drowning, right next to each other, alone. Fighting a fight that no one else understood. For so long, all Kai had ever wanted was to reach out and hold each other up.

"I'm staying," he said—unshaken, resolved, determined. He was unconvinced that leaving would solve all his problems. He had run from them for too long, and if he must face monsters every day, whether they be of his or the Grankull's making, then so be it. He reached out a hand, like the hand Rasia had reached out to him not that long ago with the offer of a lifetime.

"This is the fight I have chosen," Kai said. "The choice you need to make is whether you'll help me fight it. I truly believe there are better peaks ahead. I believe the good days are worth the climb. There will be falls, and setbacks, and bad fucking days. It might all seem insurmountable, but it can be endured together. You and I are survivors. Will you slay dragons with me?"

A difficult expression crossed Kenji's face—then appeared a tired bruised smile, one that was both bitter and proud, both resigned and renewed, both broken and stitched back together.

"Okay, Kailjnn. Okay."

Kai stuck his legs between the windship's railing and watched the wind shift dunes of sand. Rasia was out there somewhere, and he didn't want to turn back until she had either returned to the ship, or he sensed she had returned to the Grankull.

"I'm sick," Kenji said suddenly, beside him, legs also stuck through the railing. Kenji looked nervously over at Kai at the admission and then turned back toward the Desert. "I can't explain it, and it's happened once before, after you were born. Anji-ji wants me to go to the healers because he remembers what I tried to do last time, but I'm so afraid the healers will deem me unfit for work. That's less money, and fewer rations, and I can't put anything more on Nico-po. The hunting kulls . . . they covered for me. They kept my secret even when I barely had the energy to do anything. As a hunter, your relationship with Death changes. There is a certain . . . recognition of those who have been death-touched. The hunting kulls understood. They took care of their own."

"But this new job terrifies me. What if I mess up? I can barely keep track of the drums on a good day. The only thing getting me out of bed is the fear of disappointing Nico-po but . . . I don't have the energy for the things I once did. It's harder without the alcohol. She believes it's so easy to move on, and I want to for her, but it's hard. Something is wrong with me."

Kai recognized the courage it took for Kenji to admit this. He tapped his fingers along the poles. "What about an apprentice?" he suggested. "Most jobs allow them. You've taken on one before. An apprentice could help to keep you accountable and on track."

Kenji stared at Kai, and Kai's eyes widened at the unspoken question.

"Oh."

"I didn't want to ask because I thought you were leaving with

Rasia-po. I didn't want it to change your mind. But I need the help, and I don't know if anyone else will understand. But I also feel that I don't deserve to ask for your help. It should be the other way around. I should be the one making amends but . . . I can't afford to lose this job."

"The family got to eat," Kai said, knowingly.

He nodded.

Kai looked down at his hands and sucked in a breath. "The story of my Forging that Rasia told you, I might never be that person again. Jih and I are working on my magic, but the reality is that I might never be that powerful again. I might . . . never be completely healthy on such limited Grankull rations, and I've come to terms with that. I'll try. I'll certainly try. But someone else might be better able to help you." He mumbled, more self-consciously. "I'll never be as strong or as capable as Nico-ji."

He looked up when Kenji placed a hand on his shoulder. "I demanded unfair expectations of you when you were born. Sick or not, you're still mine. It's certainly not fair that I can hide my illness, while everyone knows yours. You don't have a choice but to walk with your face. You're far braver than I ever could be, and I'll never again doubt the strength of your bones. Think on my offer and let me know."

He nodded.

Kenji turned back to stare out toward the Desert. "You think Rasia is coming back?"

"She still hasn't come this way. I want to make sure she gets home."

"You really care for her."

"She's the hunter's cloak to my elderfire," Kai paused, "if you don't mind me borrowing your words."

Kenji huffed a soft smile and motioned over to the ilhan leaning against the railing. "That is yours to borrow as well, at least until you make your own. All musicians worth their strings make their own instruments. Though they're not usually namesakes. I am sorry I broke yours. Rasia-po says you play pretty well."

"Rasia has a big mouth," Kai grumbled, without much heat.

He looked over at the ilhan and reminded himself of the promise he made to stop running away. He slapped his hands on the deck and walked over to grab it. He sat back against the railing and placed it between his legs. "You've already tuned it?" he asked. The instrument was notoriously hard to tune, and Kai couldn't get it right.

Kenji nodded and pressed his cheek to the railing as Kai placed the instrument between his legs. His sudden burst of confidence faltered. It was a little nerve-wracking to have Kenji watching him, whose Last Name was literally Ilhani. He glanced over at Kenji. "I can't sing. I don't have your voice."

"Between you and me, I don't either. Very much out of practice."

He curled his forefingers around the pegs and laid his thumb on the strings. Confidence failing him, he asked, "How do you write songs? How do you create something out of nothing?"

He found that his fingers always went back to the familiar chords, unable to veer off from well-known lanes.

"I don't," Kenji answered. He flung himself back and sprawled across the deck. "I hear the songs in my head long before I put them to strings. I hear melodies in the rain and beats from the dragonsail. I've created chords to the way Shamai-kull stalks a hunt and I've harmonized to the vibrations of gonda in the sand. I listen, and the Desert plays her songs for me. But it's quiet now. I haven't heard anything in a long time."

"Were you and Shamai-shi truly a thing?" he asked curiously. He doubted it now, after hearing Kenji's backstory.

Kenji huffed. "Why do people always assume that? Adults can be platonic friends without the sex, you know. He was like a jih to me. It was us against the Grankull for so long. Then the whole courtship dance began, and everything got complicated. I remember the day he laid eyes on Kiba-kull, declared right then and there she was his kulani, and spent the next three years chasing after her. After we slayed a dragon, he saved his portion of the heart and gifted it to her when we got back. She shrugged her shoulders and said, these exact words, 'You'll do.'"

"I was so jealous of him sometimes. Everything always seemed to work out for him, but there was no doubt he was the greatest friend anyone could have ever asked for. He was always there when I needed him, and now he's gone, and I'm still here." Kenji shook his head and said with such disbelief, "I'm still here."

"How did you two meet?"

Kenji's eyes brightened, and Kai leaned over the ilhan as he launched into their hilarious first meeting. He reminisced, "I had never met someone with so much ambition and cunning. He was the one who wanted the world. I just wanted to sing my songs."

Kai smiled soft, bittersweet. "I get that."

He looked down at the ilhan, grabbed a stranglehold around his courage, and began to play. He missed a few notes in his nervousness, but he tried the opening again and flowed easily into the rest.

He faltered when he noticed how Kenji had sat up, frowning and withdrawn. Kai stumbled over his fingers and ended the song abruptly. Kenji shrugged his shoulder. "Yeah, I deserve that."

"I didn't play it to punish you. It's my favorite song."

Kenji gave him an odd disbelieving look. "*Why?* I composed that song a few days after you were born. It's dark as fuck. I get asked to play it at deathpours."

"Doesn't change the fact that it's the most beautiful thing you've ever composed," he said. "It taught me that sometimes you've got to wade through all the darkness to experience that last note of hope at the end. That last note would be meaningless without everything that comes before it."

Kenji harrumphed. Then he rolled his head and offered his hand. Kai's eyes widened, and, with tentative hope, handed over the ilhan. Kenji glared at the instrument as if it would come alive to bite him, and then with all the caution of approaching an unknown animal, he carefully familiarized his fingers with the gut-strings. And then without any warning, the Desert swelled with music.

Kenji continued from the exact spot of the song that Kai had left off. He didn't just play the song. Kenji-ta painted grief across the moon and seasoned heartbreak on his stars. He wove new experiences into the old tapestry, creating a constellation of sound Kai had both heard and never heard before. He serenaded the Hunter's Cloak as if Death was his sole audience. There was no chorus, no chords that repeated, just a breathless symphony of notes that painted a transcendent mural of an imperfect life.

The final effervescent note marked not an end, but a beginning.

A sunrise.

CHAPTER SEVENTY

O

"You wanted to see me?" Rasia asked as she poked her head into the Mythkeeper's office. The office hadn't changed much since the days the Mythkeeper used to lecture her about her absences from school.

The Mythkeeper sighed in relief. "You made it. I was concerned you wouldn't be here in time."

"I feel hurt you doubted me so," Rasia teased as she swept in and took a seat on the Mythkeeper's desk to lean a look at the documents she was working on. The Mythkeeper quickly shooed her off the desk, and she skipped back to one of the seats.

"Congratulations, you're hired as a scribe."

"Yay," she said in faux-excitement.

The Mythkeeper shook her head at her dramatics. "As you know, this isn't a typical scribe position. I've modeled it after the hunting kulls. While you are out of the Grankull, your family will still receive a paycheck on your behalf. But for right now, I've approved a monetary advance for you to buy equipment and supplies. I advise you to go check in with Raiment Foreigner about the things you might need for the journey."

The Mythkeeper handed over a large pouch of money. "That's enough for three blinks of a scribe's salary. After the initial three blinks, your salary will then be paid out to your family."

"What about gonom?" she asked.

"You will receive an upfront year supply of gonom as is your due, but first, you have quite a bit of paperwork to fill out before you can receive the gonom from the administration office." The Mythkeeper tapped the tower of paperwork she had been snooping on. She groaned at the size.

"Quite frankly, this position is tentative—it's an experiment. We hope it can strengthen and rebuild the relations that the Grankull broke with Raiment Foreigner, and we hope it can provide us with information and more options in the event of another bad year. You don't necessarily have to come back to the Grankull and physically report in, but if you're sending reports and maps back to me, that's sufficient. I don't want you to worry about the Council, or if they'll eventually consider this job unnecessary. I think this is important, and I will fight for it as long as you submit the work."

"I will."

"Good. How about we work on the paperwork together? You won't be here to correct any mistakes."

"Thank Elder," she said in relief. They tackled the stack of paperwork. After it was all said and done, she stood with an armful of paperwork to file.

"Also," the Mythkeeper said as she reached the door. "Please, do work on your handwriting."

Rasia laughed. Then she smiled and said, sincerely, "You're one of the few people who have always believed in me. Thank you."

For once, the Mythkeeper's face was not tinged with exhaustion or exasperation, but with unabashed pride.

"Go conquer the world, Rasia Dragonfire."

Rasia neared the private renting spaces where Raiment's windbarge was located. Every merchant knew the exact day of Raiment's departures, often getting bulk orders prepared and calendared for the large pay day when he returned.

The crew directed her to the Han's quarters, and she passed the preparations with mounting excitement. By tomorrow morning, she'd be leaving the Grankull behind. She peeked her head into Raiment Zara-kulani's office. "Hello?"

"Ah, it's you. Glad you could make it," Raiment said, jumping up from his chair and whisking her into the office. He wore his hair styled in waist-length dreads that were decorated with expensive evory beads. It was funny how short he was compared to Zephyr, which meant he was her height. Sort of nice not to have to look up.

Her eyes flicked to a painting of people in large furs playing amidst a white blanketed landscape, then to a painting of wooden windships sailing atop water, and another of a busy city protected behind giant walls.

"The Mythkeeper wanted me to stop by and ask what I'll need for the journey?" she asked.

"Honestly?" he answered, "Bones of dragonsteel, but I hear from Zephyr-po you've got plenty of those. I run the largest trading business through the four main empires—a dangerous way to make a living for sure, as all lands are beset with their own manner of behemoths. This job requires a person of a certain fearlessness. And after that dragon business? I can't think of anyone better the Grankull could have nominated for the job. I'm glad to have you along for the ride."

"I'm glad to be along."

"We'll set off first thing at dawn tomorrow. First, we'll sail the windship to the forest, where we'll maneuver through to meet up with my brother and some wagons and horses on the other side."

"Horses?"

"Aye. Now, that forest isn't for the faint of heart. I've lost a lot of people who couldn't keep their heads about them. The behemoths that reside in that forest are-"

"I know." Rasia stood and pulled up her shirt to show him the scar. "Gave me this one. I know how dangerous the shadowcats are, but I don't understand. How do you get a whole ship past those things? You can tell me now, right? I'll learn the secret in a few days."

He smiled and leaned forward with a whisper, "Dragon shit."

"Huh?"

"The smell of dragon shit repulses them. It's disgusting, but rub it all over your skin and they won't bother you."

Rasia couldn't believe she didn't think of that. Most creatures fled at the scent of a dragon. Now that she knew, she could probably get through the forest by herself, but it would be best to go with Zephyr's tah. She didn't know what other 'behemoths' awaited her on the other side.

"One day I'm going to have to tell you the story of how I found that out. After we make it through the forests and meet my brother, we'll take the wares to my base of operations."

"So . . . we're going to your warehouse and coming back? What about those places in the paintings?" she asked. "Are we going to see those?"

"Ah, we'll be going through the countries of Fjaren and Alohver, but I'm afraid the Alohverian capital and the Fjaren canals are out of our way. But I have plenty of trade routes and merchants that go through those economic centers. You're more than free to do whatever you like or go anywhere you want once we arrive at my warehouse."

"Good," she said. "I don't want to come back. I hate this place."

Lines wrinkled at his eyes. "You can certainly send back any documents through me—but, if you're looking for somewhere perfect, I'm afraid that place doesn't exist. There are always the poor, always those who have less and those who have more. There are always systems to keep people in power."

"No, I—that's not what I'm looking for. I—" She could never really put into words or explain this pull that tugged insistently at her chest. "How can anyone possibly sit still when there's the unknown over the horizon? I'm not looking for a place to be but somewhere to go."

Raiment melted into a warm understanding smile. "Ah, an adventurer after my own heart. We're a rare few indeed. Well, my dear wind child, all roads lead to my warehouse. Once we're there, the whole world is yours."

CHAPTER SEVENTY-ONE

O

Rasia ran all her errands. She made all her preparations. She paid all her debts. She sharpened all her weapons and packed all her things. Then she dressed in her best pants and the red gleaming chestplate from her Naming Ceremony. She tied the namesake around her neck. She combed the short curly tufts of her hair. She bathed in fancy oils, tinted her lips with Jilah's pigment powder, and lined her eyes black with kohl.

She had one last thing left to do.

That last conversation on some stranger's windship wasn't how this ended for Rasia and Kai. At the very least, he owed her some dick.

She walked down the roads of the Grankull and heads turned. A distracted messenger stumbled, and whispers erupted in her wake. They echoed her name. She wondered how many of them had read her Forging story. All she wanted her entire life was glory. She wanted a name people would read for the rest of time. But now all she cared about was one person, and how he'd remember her. She didn't have much time left, and she'd use what remained to etch her legend into his skin.

Zephyr sat at the sentry post of the veranda. "They're ready."

Rasia troubled the chimes. The door creaked open, partway, to reveal a sliver of Kai's face peeking through the crack. His eyes widened and scanned her outfit. "You don't have to do this."

She didn't bother with all the trouble of organizing the whole event through Ysai and ultimately Nico, not to go through with it.

"It's my last night in the Grankull. We might never get this chance again. Now, open the door, you damn romantic and officially introduce me to your family."

Kai slammed the door closed in her face. She blinked, caught off-guard, before the door creaked open again. Her breath caught in her throat. A smile touched her face as she glanced over him.

He wore the pants.

The gonda waistband clenched perfectly around his waist and ankles. The pants were dyed a sand-shift, the color of predators and camouflage, and refuted the bright white of the shrouded. The sheer gold shirt fitted him perfectly, too. The gold shimmer caught in the oil-light, mimicking the illumination of his eyes. His scars showed through the spider silk, crisscrossed and jagged. He wore his hair pulled up, away from his face to display the sculpt of his jaw and cheekbones, and all the handsome features his tahs had gifted him. It was the outfit he would have worn to the Naming Ceremony. It was what he would wear if allowed to step out on the street and be himself—this brilliant unashamed creature of magic and gold.

"Wow."

They stood, staring at each other. Rasia actually jumped when Zephyr scoffed. She glared at him, still always interrupting them, but also grateful because they didn't have much time, and she couldn't afford to waste it by standing around. She shoved the wrapped package of her rations and bottle of date wine into Kai's arms.

He stepped back and invited her inside with much gravitas and seriousness. "You are welcome into my home."

His family waited for Rasia in the lounging room—Nico, Kenji-shi, and little Rae in Kenji-shi's lap. Rasia really tried to keep a straight face when Kai dipped his head in a bow and kept his eyes on the ground. "Nicolai Triarch, I'd like to introduce my courtship, Rajiani Dragonfire."

Nico rose a brow in Rasia's direction. She rolled her eyes and then diverted them. When Ysai had introduced Jilah to Kiba-ta, Jilah almost fell by how deep she had bowed to the floor. Tah had not been impressed. Rasia gave a dramatic flourishing bow. "It is an honor to be invited to your table."

"Well met, Rajiani Dragonfire," Nico said, completing one of several of the ritualistic traditions of the Introduction Dinner. Rasia found it all boring and hopelessly stiff, but Kai stood between them, fiddling his fingers nervously because it mattered to him. He continued the introduction by repeating the same greetings for Rae and Kenji.

"Dinner should be finished soon," he said and then left to cook the rations Rasia brought to dinner. Kenji-shi poured a tray of tea, already set up, and then left to join Kai in the kitchen. Rasia still worried sometimes about Kai and Kenji-shi in such close quarters, but the kitchen was Kai's domain, and he was more comfortable in that space than any other.

Rasia and Nico sat together, in the lounging room, drinking tea.

Weird.

"So . . ." she said as she lounged back against the fluffy pillows. "I assume we skip the whole interview and veiled threats part of the night, huh?"

Nico raised an eyebrow. She had gotten all dressed up too, in a pastel multi-hued dress that reminded Rasia of rainbows after a heavy rain. The top layer shimmered diaphanous when Nico shifted into the sunlight. Her hair was twisted into a large bun that sat atop the center of her head. Dragonglass embellished her earlobes, wrists, and the corners of her eyes like dewdrops. All very pretty and impressive, but Rasia had seen Nico late at night half-awake on the toilet with a glare that threatened Death. Nothing got more intimidating than that.

Rasia swatted at one of the potted plants and lifted the evory cup. "You didn't have to bring out the fancy dishware for little old me," she teased. For Jilah, tah hadn't bothered to change out the calabash.

"They are borrowed from tajih for the occasion. We sold ours a long time ago," Nico said flatly, before taking a sip of the tea and then placing it ever so delicately back atop the saucer. "I do admit, this idea was brilliant. We can use the dinner to convince Kai to change his mind. I've begun organizing our talking points. If we both lay out our arguments, certainly we'll get him to see reason."

Rasia straightened, because of course, they would never be on the same page. According to Ysai, everyone had tried to sway Kai from his decision, but he was adamant about staying. Admittedly, it had crossed her mind to tie Kai up and stuff him away in one of the cargo crates, but she knew he would resent her for it. It was a decision he had to make on his own or else he'd always wonder the path denied him. He had to choose her.

"No . . ." she said, slowly. "You misunderstand. I'm not here to change his mind."

Nico frowned, and asked, "Then what is the point of this farce?"

"The *point* is that Kai cares about these sorts of things. We might never have a Naming Ceremony, but I can give him this, at least. I'm not here to convince him to come with me. He doesn't want to go."

"Then, can't you at least stay?"

"I've been trying to escape this place for years. I'm not going to pass up the greatest opportunity I've ever had to make it out of here alive. Kai wouldn't want that, either."

"You're his kulani," she said, harshly. Tea spilled across the table. She hadn't touched it. It sort of boiled and burst on its own. Nico glared at the mess, and right before the tea reached Rasia's side of the table to scald Rasia's clothes, she waved her hand and pulled it back. "Kai deserves better. He deserves someone who chooses him, and not just on a piece of paper."

"Maybe he does," Rasia bit out.

Nico huffed and got up for a linen to clean up her mess. She sopped up the spilled tea leaves and shook her head. "In the end, it was nothing but a Forging flame."

"He is my *kulani*," Rasia argued. No matter what, no one could argue she didn't commit. "I am to carry his name for the rest of my life."

"A name weighs nothing."

"A name weighs everything."

Nico gave a bitter smile, as if to say to herself, 'Of course, why would I think we would ever agree?' Then she left to discard the soiled linen. When she returned, she seemed to have cooled as tepid as the tea.

"I have tried to convince him to go," she said, insistent to keep trying. If anything, Rasia appreciated her capacity for stubbornness. It almost rivaled her own. "Kai can't walk out of the door without someone yelling to cull him. He can't go anywhere by himself. This place might never do right by him, and yet, he chooses this."

"Don't you?" Rasia asked. She drank the entire cup of tea in one gulp and leaned forward. "If the choice was between your kulani and the Grankull, which would you choose?"

Rasia knew Nico's answer. She had seen Nico war with her feelings for both Zephyr and Suri. She had seen Nico prioritize her agendas and her plans over her flames. Nico had always prioritized her purpose.

"You'd choose the Grankull because that is your fight," Rasia said. "Kai has his own battles, but they're not mine. Maybe it is selfishness to you, but I refuse to be shamed for choosing myself."

"The moment you signed his name, you owed a responsibility to him. There's no scratching that out like a mistake made in ink." Nico pressed a hand to her chest and clutched it there, like it hurt. "You made him so happy. I want nothing more than for him to go with you."

Same.

But there was no point mourning a choice already made. No point chasing after someone already set on their course. Rasia unslung the satchel from her shoulder and procured a hefty roll of leather. Nico straightened at the sight of paperwork, almost as excited as those administrative people when they get the chance to reject something. Nico cleared the table as she spread several of the scrolls that needed Nico's signature. No matter how far she traveled, Nico would always be her triarch. Rasia would have never imagined the day.

"I've arranged for my future paycheck to be dispensed to him, and to you by extension on his behalf. I trust that you will get the things that he needs." She shoved over a bag of bonechips. "That's what's left of my advance, and the rest needs your signature."

Nico's eyes scanned the pages with a speed Rasia could never hope to match. Then her eyes snapped up, almost incredulous. "You're giving him your windship?"

"He's my kulani. It belongs to him just as much as me. Since tah disowned me before she died, I didn't have a claim to the inheritance rights. Ysai inherited all of it, but he made sure the windship transferred over to my and Kai's name. As for the rest," she shrugged, "Ysai was adamant that half of it belongs to me. The administration is still processing the paperwork, but it's quite the sum. Albeit gained illegally, tah laundered a lot of it through legal channels due to her investments in several businesses. She also rarely ever spent any of her money." Kiba-ta was probably tossing in the wind. "Kai is now rich."

Nico's jaw dropped and dropped even further when she reached the number on the scroll. She tried to fix her face but couldn't entirely hide the fact that they needed the money very much. Knowing Kai, he probably would buy back everything they'd ever sold off—starting with everything Nico had sacrificed.

"I—thank you," Nico said finally. "I'll take care of this paperwork and get it filed. I do appreciate this, but nothing can replace a kulani. Hopefully, one day, you'll come back when you're ready to settle down."

"Nicolai," she said, gentle in ways she had never been before with the unerringly resilient face before her. "I am not ever coming back."

Over the years, Rasia had gotten the best of Nico several times, but nothing compared to this visceral gut-punch when pure emotion forced Nico to leave the table to stand arms crossed in front of the window.

"He's not helpless," she defended. "He can find me if he wants. Certainly, one day he'll be done here. The Grankull will betray him again, and he'll realize this place has nothing for him. He'll leave, and he'll find me."

Nico turned around, and with the sun washing over her, looked at Rasia as if this time, Rasia wasn't the one seeing the truth of things. She said with that same measure of awful gentleness that Rasia had used earlier. "Rajiani. If you don't convince him now, he'll never leave."

"I'm his kulani. He'll find me."

Nico saddened. She said, uncommittedly and unconvinced, "Maybe."

They'd hit that wall again, that wall neither of them could break down to reach a full understanding. No way forward.

Nico asked thoughtfully, "Dinner won't be ready for some time yet. Are you interested in one last spar?"

Rasia raised her brows, intrigued. Now, this was her type of Introduction Dinner. "As long as you tell Kai it was your idea, so I don't get in trouble for kicking your ass."

"From what I hear, nowadays, even a tent kid can defeat you."

She slapped her hands onto the tea table and pushed herself up to her feet. "You're on, Nico-ji."

⁙

Nico stepped onto the familiar reed mats of the sparring room, soaked with years of sweat and blood. This was the room where Ava-ta had beaten and cracked kata forms and breath control into her bones. For all of Kai's perceived weakness, tah demanded of Nico nothing less than strength.

She hefted one of the spears from the wall, the spearpoint sharp and reflecting her furrowed expression. For a moment, she remembered her last failed plea with Kai and the far-flung hope that even though she couldn't convince him to leave, maybe Rasia could.

She pivoted on the balls of her feet and faced Rasia. Rasia had chucked off her fancy pants and stripped to nothing but the wicked curve of her khopesh blades.

Of course, Rasia wasn't wearing underwear.

"Obviously, I had other plans," she said, wiggling her eyebrows. Nico had walked in on Rasia and Kai enough times to be completely unruffled by the two of them together now. Then, her shoulders dropped. She wondered the next time she'd experience Kai's embarrassed bluster or even Rasia's unrepentant laugh.

She hadn't realized it over the past blink, but Rasia had filled the maze of these halls with a life it hadn't had in a long time. There would no doubt be an emptiness in her absence. She couldn't help but to be illogically angry at Rasia's decision, even though she had bemoaned Rasia's general existence on multiple occasions.

Nico shook off her lamentations and anchored her focus on the present and the fight before her. Respectively, she shed the borrowed dress she wore for the formal dinner and folded it neatly and crisply on the sidelines. She unpinned the heavy bun, and it flowed down her back in her traditional ponytail. Stripped of all but the bare minimum, Nico and Rasia faced one another.

Nico braced for Rasia to strike first. Rasia rocked on her heels, right to left, but never made a move. Rasia grinned at her apparent wariness.

"You first, Nico-ji."

"Considering the circumstances, I hardly think you're entitled to use that address."

"We lived a whole blink together without killing each other. I think that entitles-" Rasia dipped under Nico's attack with the smooth motion of a snake—snapping fast and in enviable control of all that power. Rasia was far faster than any of their encounters in the Desert, and then she remembered that back then, Rasia had been nursing a broken rib.

Nico spun to cover her back and the snipping strikes of Rasia's blade vibrated against her polearm. Rasia's foot suddenly replaced her khopesh, and she was up and over Nico's defense.

Her kick slowed in resistance against a wall of water. Behind the blurry curtain of blue, Rasia smirked before being blasted back. She rebounded off the wall with both feet and charged forward once more.

Nico hoped to use her considerable reach, aided by both her height and weapon of choice to blunt Rasia's attacks, but Rasia's speed devastated that advantage, continually breaking through Nico's range to throw herself against Nico's wall of magic.

Because, of course, Rasia was used to going up against opponents far taller than her, considering Ysai was her usual sparring partner.

Nico heard tah's voice echoing off the walls, demanding perfection, demanding control, demanding strength, and excellence—because the world wasn't going to hand her anything, and it was up to her to fight for everything that she achieved.

Then a knee slammed straight into her chest, knocking the air from her lungs. She barely gathered herself before blocking Rasia's downward stroke with her forearm and then rolling under Rasia's right-handed thrust.

Nico straightened. Her jute string hairband snapped and wilted to the mat. Almost as if in shock, her hair took a while to realize what had happened, before it slipped down and collapsed around her face. Nico pressed a hand to her chest, where Rasia had claimed the first hit. It was a bruising reminder that Rasia was very aware of how the magic worked and where it was weakest.

Tah never taught her what to do against such an opponent—against the overwhelming force that was Rasia, where no amount of training and practice could prepare you to battle sheer talent. Nico's forms could be perfect, no movements wasted or squandered—and yet, Rasia would always be better.

Nico rolled her neck and sucked in a breath. The room darkened as clouds gathered, and it rained through the open slats of the ceiling. Like a gonda manifest, tentacles of water stretched around Nico to form a massive creature that casted shadows on the walls. She unleashed her magic and trusted Rasia to be good enough.

Rasia grinned at the oncoming onslaught, eyes alighting in challenge before ducking and dodging the whips of water. Nico glided up and over, following the curving wave, and jumped out of the water at Rasia's back.

The spear sliced through Rasia's forearm. Blood splattered across the mat. Nico jumped back to avoid Rasia's counterattack. Her vision blurred, and she emerged soaked on the other side of the room.

She doubted she could surprise Rasia like that again. Rasia smirked and dipped into a low fighting stance Nico had only ever seen out in the Tents, mastered by those of the Flock. Nico didn't give her the chance.

A wave crashed around the walls toward Rasia, and she broke her ground to sprint away from it. As it neared, she snatched one of the shields pinned to the wall. She jumped atop the shield and surfed the wave toward Nico's spear. Their weapons clashed, then Nico yelped when Rasia kicked a foot around Nico's hair to drag her across the ground as the wave stretched to an end.

She turned into water and slipped through Rasia's grip. Rasia and the shield crashed against the wall. Rasia and Nico both sprang back to their feet, circling, and once again, continued the dance.

Sometimes the strikes and clashes sang notes of pure joy and freedom, and at other times, anger and resentment. They sang a confusing litany: the freedom of unbridled magic versus the anger of Rasia leaving. The hurt of losing her title. The triumph of keeping up.

In a burst of realization, Nico noted the defensive turn of Rasia's movements. More evading than attacking. Rasia was trying to outlast her, waiting for the moment Nico had spent her magic. But Rasia didn't know that Nico no longer had limits, connected to the Elder as she was now. The Desert had been Rasia's territory, but the Grankull was undeniably Nico's.

Rasia dodged right where Nico wanted her.

"Shit," Rasia cursed when her blood from earlier, soaked into the reed mat, wrapped a vice around her ankle, and tripped her to the floor.

Rasia blinked at where Nico stood over her, holding a spearpoint to her neck. Rasia released her grip on her blades with a smirk. "I yield."

All Rasia ever wanted was Nico's everything. All Nico ever wanted was Rasia's respect.

Nico collapsed. She dropped next to Rasia with her chest heaving at the exertion. Their heads lay close, but their bodies pointed in opposite directions.

"Stay," she whispered. "We could fight together. We could be the greatest kull they've ever seen. The Grankull can't defeat us both."

Rasia pressed her hands to her face. "I can't breathe here anymore. I don't . . . I don't have any fight left," she said, with water choking her voice, "You win."

Tears streamed down Nico's temples, into her hair, and onto the mats. Rasia was the one with all the names. She was the one who slayed a dragon for her coming of age. She was the one the Grankull expected to do great things, who some said could be the greatest hunter of her age. They were waiting to write her pages and sing her songs.

Rasia wasn't supposed to . . . take herself out of the story.

Nico clenched her eyes shut with the shuddering realization that she might actually miss Rasia. Who was going to push Nico to be better? Who was going to critique Nico's mistakes? Who was going to be the foil for Nico to see herself clearer?

Then, she shook her head of those silly childish questions. Rasia never asked for those roles. They had been thrust upon her by Nico's doubts and insecurities. That wasn't fair to anyone. People should be allowed to be more than two-dimensional characters. Nico and Rasia and Kai could all be heroes.

"I've got things here," she promised. "Go. Write your own story."

CHAPTER SEVENTY-TWO

O

Kai threw Nico concerned looks when he came out of the kitchen with plates of food. Red rimmed her eyes, and she hadn't had the time to perfectly gather all her hair together before dinner. She gave him a strained smile when Kai placed the shared bowl of minced gonda meat, cooked with onions, peppers, and ginger onto the table. A golden poached heron egg crowned the dish.

"I'm fine," she mouthed as she sat at the head of the table. Kai pressed his head to hers, with guilt folded into his brow. Rasia imagined they'd had a lot of strained conversations these past few days.

From the fresh eggplants in Rasia's rations, Kenji-shi delivered another plate to the table—grilled eggplant cut in halves, salted and decorated with pine nuts and parsley. Then came another side-dish of goatpeas, okra, fresh grapes, and pomegranates. She raised her brows at the evident care and art that had gone into the cooking. Rasia remembered when she had helped Ysai prep the food the night before his Introduction Dinner. She had been sent on errands to knock on a neighbor's door to trade for Jilah's favorite food items. Not all rations contained the same ingredients, and it was normal to trade with neighbors. But for special occasions, neighbors and friends often banded together to hunt down the sought-after items, trading and trading until the entire neighborhood was as invested in the results of the Introduction Dinner as the person cooking it.

Rasia never imagined going through so much effort for anyone, but as she sat at the table, she thought of how her tahs were dead, and how all her extended family had ostracized her. She'd never get the chance to introduce Kai to her family. She'd never get the chance to show the Grankull that Kai was worth all the effort and more.

When he came out with the last dish and placed the honeyed dates onto the table, Rasia caught the strained laugh in her hands. There were far more dates than was usually allowed in a ration pack and had no doubt been traded for and hunted down specifically for her. She surged up and caught Kai's lips as he drifted down to sit beside her at the table. She reveled in the fact he didn't flinch away, but proudly stamped her mouth in front of his entire family.

She breathed, holding him, half in his lap, and wanting nothing more than to bundle him in her bags and keep him forever. She said against his skin, "I've got the windship back. After dinner, would you go on one last ride with me?"

He smiled. "Always."

"Dinner looks great," Nico said. Rasia rolled her eyes at Nico's attempt to steer dinner back on course. Even Kai shook his head, amused, by Nico's unsubtle attempts. They settled down and turned their attention back toward the food. Under the table, Kai held her hand, and beyond the Introduction Dinner, Rasia recognized the momentousness of the occasion. This dinner marked the first time this family had truly sat down together to eat around a table.

"Rasia Dragonfire, you are technically the guest, in so far this dinner is for you. The first bite is yours," Nico said.

A cheeky smile widened across her face, because she was an adult now, and no one could tell her what to eat first. She went straight for dessert and plucked up one of the warm sticky dates. Nico shook her head, while Rae narrowed their eyes from across the table. Kai gave a defeated nod, and Rae plucked their own from the plate.

Honeyed dates are a simple recipe, but the balance was so hard to get right. Rasia bit into the date, warm with honey and stuffed with walnuts and pine nuts, with the right sprinkle of salt to balance the overwhelming sweetness. *Perfect.* The taste erupted in her mouth, and she gasped, because she'd tasted this exact mixture of flavors before, even though she'd never physically swallowed it down. These are *the* dates—the ones she's dreamt of from the Lake of Yestermorrow since she was eight-years till, of which she thought she'd never taste again.

She stared, dumbstruck and confused.

"Do you like them?" Kai watched the minute details of her face.

"They're perfect," she mumbled as the room blurred. She wiped at her face and pushed toward the other bowls of food. She filled her plate and had trouble tasting the food with all the salt in her mouth. Stupid Lake. Stupid magic.

"Rae, how was school today?" Nico asked, expertly diverting attention from the fact Rasia was crying into her eggplant. Kai sat uncomfortably beside her, hardly eating.

"I like tah's class," Rae said excitedly. "We have class on a ship!"

"Truly?" Nico said and turned to Kenji-shi. "How did you manage that? They never let us have class outside. The teachers always feared we'd get distracted."

"The school is allowing me to build my own curriculum since I'm one of the most high-profile teachers they've had," Kenji-shi said. "Memorizing all the parts of a windship is fine and all, but for kids at Rae's age, I think it's more important to build the confidence of being around one. Even the older kids are enjoying it, now they're not stuck inside all day."

"I'm jealous. I had to memorize charts and all the parts of a windship before they allowed us to touch one," she said. "But I imagine it can't be easy to keep up with all those kids, especially the younger ones."

"Well, it's a good thing I've found myself an apprentice." Kenji-shi threw a meaningful glance at Kai. Rasia frowned at the way he looked at her nervously before setting down the piece of bread he used to scoop up the eggplant.

"I have an announcement," Kai said. "I have decided to accept an apprenticeship with Kenji-ta at the school. I'll be helping him with his class."

A stone dropped in the pit of Rasia's stomach.

"Is . . . the school going to allow that?" Nico asked slowly, wary.

Kenji-shi shrugged. "It's in my contract. I'm in charge of my classes. I can have any apprentice of my choosing. And it'll be good for the Grankull to see him around windships. Maybe by next Forging, they'll believe him."

Rae's face scrunched as they processed the implications. They looked up at Kai. "You're going to school?"

At that, a bright pleased smile stretched across Kai's face and confirmed, "I'm going to school."

Rae ran around the table and Kai caught the kid in his arms. Rae announced to the whole table, "We're going to school!"

Rasia watched Kai interact with Rae, and Kenji-shi, and Nico with that pit growing ever deeper. She belatedly realized what Nico must have concluded in the lounging room.

A night long ago atop a mountain, she had promised Kai what he wanted most in the entire world, but Kenji-shi had only been a missing piece. A small part of Rasia had hoped that once Kai accomplished all he sought to do, that he might find her afterward in the wide world, but as she sat at that dinner table, a brutal wind blew out that naive optimism.

Kai wasn't leaving.

His world was here.

CHAPTER SEVENTY-THREE

—

"Paths diverge, and split, and end. Till we meet once more again. Forever this ship ferry your name—" Rasia stabbed the windship mast before Kai could finish.

Below Shamai, below Ysai, Rasia wrote her names. She didn't need to dance to find the letters on her toes anymore, and instead pinned each letter with exacting accuracy and aim. Finished, she stepped back to inspect her handiwork—it would be the first signature of many for a scribe.

"This windship is yours now," she declared. "Take care of it, and it'll take care of you. I guess you can consider this ship your namesake since your last one was rudely destroyed."

It felt too much, but he knew not even the Grankull would question the inheritance. He was Rasia's kulani and the last member of her unofficial kull. It now unequivocally belonged to him.

"Not many people can boast a windship as a namesake," he said.

"You're damn right. When the Grankull becomes too much, or Nico gets too overbearing, you'll always have the windship. Something of your own." She held out her hand, and Kai gave her the gourd of date wine. She took a sip and then spat out bitterly, "It sucks. All I do is let people go."

"All hunters are hunted," Kai toasted.

Rasia huffed out a sigh and then tapped her calabash to his. "But the kull remains."

They drank deeply. She tossed her empty gourd over her shoulder and then gave him a hunter's scrutiny. She prowled backward toward the railing. She looked beautiful and he knew she had dressed up for him. He knew she liked the fact that he had dressed up for her. She sprawled back against the bow railing, and her brilliant red pants fluttered in the wind. Rasia's gaze sharpened.

"Fuck me, kulani."

Kai stormed across the deck and pressed her against the railing. At first, he didn't know if she would want to see him after that night when he had broken all his promises. He didn't know if she could forgive him, or if her anger would burn him if he tried to approach. But Rasia melted against him as if they were in their bed together after a long day and a good dinner. He gathered this creature of wind and stars in his arms. She met his mouth like the hunter's shroud to his elderfire, and they savored each dawn and dusk.

If only things had been different. If he hadn't been denied his face, if he had received his names, if . . .

Rasia would still leave.

If he had been born differently, if he had been born stronger and healthier, if . . .

Rasia would still leave.

This would always be their last ride together. She was of the wind, and he was too rooted. Too many things left unfinished. Too many names yet to earn. He would always be incomplete if he didn't go back into the forge. One day, he'd shape himself true. But Rasia couldn't stay, and the greatest of himself he had to give was the strength to watch her blow away.

His kulani was only for a season.

Sailing sand dunes, sometimes you forgot how tall they were until you're standing on top of one. Kai studied the sharp drop beneath his feet.

"Ready?"

"Rasia, wait-"

Rasia kicked off. She tightened her legs wrapped around his chest. Folded into the sand sled, he clutched at the edges as they went sliding down the vertical slope. Wind and sand battered his face. The speed thundered in his ears. He was no stranger to the high speeds of a windship, but it was always a little panic-inducing when you're going at any speed that could kill you. He couldn't control this crash with the turn of a steer.

They hit a smaller dune at the bottom and went flying into the air.

Kai's teeth clacked together as they landed heavily and slid to a stop. During the flight, his shroud had stripped off his face and Rasia's laughed at his windblown expression. She wanted to do something fun for their last outing, and Kai admitted he had always wanted to go dunesurfing. Of course, she had to choose one of the most advanced dunes whose size was so legendary it had a name.

"That was great, yeah?" she asked. "Come on. Let's go again."

Kai wobbled to his feet, shaken from all the adrenaline, as she reached for the sled. He dug his shroud out of the sand and wrapped it tighter around his face as they began the long march back up the dune. She glanced over at him.

"After I leave, I've made arrangements for my paycheck to be dispensed directly to you. I've given the paperwork to Nico-ji. She'll take care of filing it."

"Rasia, you didn't have to do that."

"Who else am I going to give it to? Ysai-ji and Jilah-ji are fine. You're my kulani. I've got to take care of you." She clutched the sled to her chest and took a deep breath. "When the time comes, you don't have to sign my name. The money will always be yours regardless of who you choose. I don't have to be your kulani, even if you are mine."

"Rasia, I'll never—"

"No, Nico-ji is right," she interrupted. "You do deserve someone who will be there for you. It sucks that it can't be me, and I selfishly hope that I've ruined you for all future flames, but I hope you find someone to make you happy."

He stopped. Rasia realized it belatedly and stopped two steps ahead. She glanced over her shoulder and stood like a scene woven into a tapestry, short hair blowing in the wind, while the dunes erected her throne, and the stars crowned her head. He couldn't imagine anyone else. He didn't care if they never saw other again, he would always know that she was the one. She was the star of his life.

"I'm signing your name."

It was windy out, and they both wore their shrouds to protect their faces, but her eyes watered with emotion. She turned on her heels and continued to march up the dune. She made it to the top several paces before him while Kai's thighs burned, and his breath came heavily while he pushed to keep up with her. They reached the second sled they initially left behind. He took a moment and drank some water. It made him feel slightly better knowing that most people in the Grankull would struggle with such a climb.

Rasia dropped her sled to the ground. He moved to sit, but she immediately hooked hands under his armpits to stop him. "Sitting is for budchildren. Now that you've got a feel for the drop, it's time to really dune-surf."

"Most of the Grankull have been sand-sledding with their families since they were budchildren. This is literally my first time," he said, concerned he was going too fast.

She slapped him on the ass and chided, "You trust me?"

He softened. "I trust you."

Her shroud stretched with her smile. Then she instructed, "Bend your knees. Lower your stance. Surfing is about balance, not power."

Kai stood upright atop the sled. Rasia took the lead, stepping in front of him, and they found their balance on the board together.

"Ready?"

"Rasia, wait-"

Rasia kicked off. He snapped his arms around her waist. She leaned forward, cutting the speed, and casually curving as they descended. He felt her move against him as she controlled the board with her body. She surfed around the small sand dune that they had jumped the previous ride and came to a slow easy stop. She looked back at him brows raised, then wiggled her hips, and brought attention to the erection digging into her ass.

"Had fun back there?" she smirked.

"I always do."

Rasia laughed, and her moved to press his face to her hair, to feel that laugh against his chest. He was going to miss it. She turned and pressed her face into his. They sort of stood there, like that for a while, holding each other.

"Kulani," he whispered, with finality.

She nodded, trembling, and pulled out of his arms. She turned away from him and grabbed the sled off the ground. They made the trek back up the dune.

"I'm glad you're taking that apprenticeship," she said after a moment. "I don't want you stuck in the house like some caged little bird. Kenji-shi better do right by you. I—" she stopped. He noted her clenched fists.

"What is it?"

She looked at him with fierce determination. "I already know the answer, but I've got to ask. I figure, at the least, you won't consider leaving this place until Rae has succeeded in their Forging. But... your magic. *You can fly*. You can visit me. You can find me, right?"

His chest heated at her questioning. He looked down at the grains of sand and remembered the sandstorm he had inadvertently created. So much power, but no control over it whatsoever. His magic was a work in progress, and he feared he had a long way to go to master it.

"I don't know," Kai said. "I don't want to make you any more promises I can't keep."

"Right," she muttered and then marched up the dune. He followed after her, finding the third hike even harder than the ones before it. He huffed and panted when he reached the top. Without waiting for him to catch a breath, Rasia dropped her sled to the ground. She motioned over to the second sled they had carried up.

"This time, we go by ourselves." She looked over her shoulder at him. "You're my best friend. I'll always miss you, but I can sail on my own."

Then she kicked and shot off faster than a windship. She bowed into the speed, and when she reached the bottom, she hit the smaller sand dune and flew into the air. He watched her spin among the stars.

Kai glanced down at the second sled. He was pretty sure it once belonged to Ysai. It had sat in the windship for so long gathering dust. He stepped on top of it and looked to where Rasia waited for him at the bottom. She was no longer here to push him anymore. He had to do that himself.

He kicked off.

It was utterly exhilarating. He always had a good sense of the wind, and he moved with it, in the same motions Rasia had pressed into his body. The speed bit at his face and ripped tears from his eyes. Ahead, there was that small dune at the bottom or the curving path around it.

He didn't approach anywhere near the speed Rasia had, who shot straight down compared to his winding curves, but he aimed for that dune. He crouched low as his heartbeat pounded in his chest. Then he shot into the air, flying truer than his magic could ever have propelled him.

He landed on his feet, but the ground caught him so jarringly, he over-rotated his hips. He fell, sliding, with the sand burning against exposed skin. He came to a stop on his back, under the stars.

Rasia said, running to him. "I thought you were going to—you weren't supposed to jump!"

She checked him for damage and jerked his arm up where a trail of linen, blood, and sand scraped down his arm. She pulled out her gourd and began cleaning the wound. She wrapped it with her shroud. He was sure once the adrenaline wore off, he'd start feeling the pain.

Then she kissed him.

"You stupid brave idiot," she said, with a mixture of fondness and exasperation. "You hit that dune with no fucking hesitation at all. That was fucking hot. And stupid. And hot."

Kai bucked his hips and rolled her underneath him. Then he rode her into the sand. She writhed under him, with all the fierceness and power of a gonda. Her limbs trapped him tight until they shivered and loosened about his waist. He breathed hot against her skin. "Let's go again?"

She smiled.

They hiked back up the dune with a lot more sand in their clothes. He glanced at her. He told her, softly, "I wish I could go with you. I wish our paths were the same. But if I go, I'd be leaving myself behind."

She glanced over at him. "I know, you brave stupid idiot."

"You were the one who taught me to never give up."

"I'm such a terrible teacher."

He laughed at that and hooked an arm around her, to pull her close as they walked. He kissed her sandy forehead. "You were the perfect teacher for me."

They reached the top again. Rasia and Kai stepped onto their boards. She looked over at him. "This time, bend at the back and crouch at your knees to better absorb the shock when you land."

He grinned, and she stared at him perplexed.

"Race you." He kicked off.

"Kai, wait—"

Rasia shouted after him. She caught up quickly and playfully curved in front of him, showing off. Then Rasia slowed to match his pace. For a moment, they surfed at the same speed side-by-side. Then he crouched, mimicking Rasia's earlier stance to gain more velocity. He laughed at her surprised shout, and then with a wink, she zoomed past him lying flat on her board. Rasia chose the curving route for the win. Kai chose the air.

They took their own paths and caught each other in the end.

CHAPTER SEVENTY-FOUR

⊢

An oil lamp glowed through the adobe brick hallways. Kai twisted through the maze and followed the light. He found himself unsurprised to stop at the library. Nico sat over the low desk, hunched over in concentration, as she swooped careful words across a page. He watched her with a hunched sort of defensiveness. Knowing his jih, she was not awake two drums from sunrise for no reason.

He wondered if this was another ambush, another last-ditch effort to convince him to change his mind. The past few days had been rather strained between them since he told Nico of his decision to stay. He was shocked she didn't bring the topic back up at dinner.

With a sigh, he announced, "I'm home."

Nico sat up startled, yanked from her focus. She blearily blinked at him, and he waited for the inevitable deluge of reasons why he should leave with Rasia. She probably had a whole list hidden under all that papyrus.

She looked around her at the orderly piles of scrolls and stacks and rubbed at her eyes. "I meant to go to sleep when I sensed your return. Looks like I got caught up again."

"You didn't have to stay up for me."

"I know," she whispered. "I know you're not completely

helpless, and you were relatively safe with Rasia but . . . It's hard for me to sleep when I can't sense you close. It's not that I don't think . . . it's for me. I worry."

"I worry," he said in turn. "You need sleep."

"I'll be fine," she said, right before a yawn. She sat down her quill. "Rasia? When is she due to set off?"

"She left for Ysai-ji's place to grab her stuff. She's supposed to meet up with the crew early, but they're not due to set off till first drum. From the Dawnward Claws."

She looked down at the paperwork with no doubt the same thought as Kai. No point going to sleep if they're going to see Rasia off in a drum. "Want to help?"

He nodded and stepped into the library. He unslung the ilhan off his shoulder and sat at the opposite end of the table. He was so familiar with Nico's organizational methods, he immediately identified what she was doing, where she had left off, and what each stack was for. He grabbed a blank sheet of parchment and began scribing a poster of Nico's campaign promises. She kept glancing at his bandaged arm.

"I thought you already made a bunch of these?" he asked.

She grabbed a blank sheet of her own and dropped her cheek onto her palm. "They're being ripped down. Someone on the Council is paying neighborhood kids to rip them up. I haven't figured out who it is yet. It's a petty move, in all honesty."

The peek of a list caught the corner of his eye. He reached for it, and in alarm, she snatched at it. It ripped, fluttering to the table with half of Nico's arguing points, and the other half pressed to her chest out of his reach. They stared, silent for a moment, at the ripped piece under his hands and the diagonal column of half-torn cons and the empty blank of pros between them.

÷

Nico clutched at her torn half. She never planned for Kai to see the talking points she had prepared for dinner earlier that evening. Rasia had been right. Nothing was changing that stubborn set of his jaw, but her eyes kept wandering over to his bandaged arm. She wondered what had happened. Had someone accosted him? She worried and her thoughts raced. She said soft, tired, and off-script, "I'm scared I won't be able to protect you."

"You protect me just fine. You give yourself too little credit." He grabbed the reed pen. He filled out his half of the list, the pros section, until it was longer than the cons.

She glanced over to look at it and then glared at him. "How is the Lakejaw a pro?"

"I haven't gotten the chance to swim in it yet. I'd definitely like to do that someday," he said.

"And the gardens?"

"If I leave, all our plants will die. You don't remember to water them. You can take care of whole wingfields but can't remember to water our plants."

"Give me that," she said. He raised the scrap of paper aloft so she couldn't reach it from the other side of the desk. She triumphantly sent a jet of water at it, until at the very last moment, the paper floated above the attack.

"Agh. What?"

He chuckled as he caught the paper in his hand and then handed it over. More seriously, he asked, "Is that what you really think? That I have nothing worth staying for?"

"What could possibly be worth more than your kulani?"

"Me," Kai said and caught her hands in his. "I know you're scared about this decision. You can do everything in your power, take all the precautions, implement all the measures, enforce all the rules—but Death is inescapable. It's coming for me anyway. I might as well live my life on my own terms."

"I know," she said, mournfully. She couldn't protect him from hate, rejection, or disappointment. Nor could she protect him from one of the most defining decisions of his entire life. He chose the hard road, and there would only be more potholes from here. All she could do now was to help him walk it.

"I'm always here if you need help," she promised. "Are you okay?"

He raised his arm. "Rasia and I went dune-surfing. I fell."

"Oh. That sounds fun," she said. "But I meant, generally, letting Rasia go. Are you okay?"

"It hurts," he admitted, staring vacantly at the bookshelves, "but we've both made our choices. I can't rely on other people to fix me. I've got to do that myself. I've got to stop running away and put in the work. Both you and Rasia taught me that."

She didn't think the work had to be done here, but Kai had chosen the Grankull to be his forge and only time would tell if it would break him or make him stronger. Regardless of the outcome, at least he chose it.

Nico sighed and leaned back against the table and looked over at the ilhan. "Did you serenade Rasia all night, too?"

He smiled. "I brought it just in case. With Rasia, you never know what's going to happen. Best to be prepared."

"I still haven't heard you play. Rasia has heard you play. Rae has heard you play. But I haven't."

"Do you want to hear me play?"

"You don't have to." She waved a dismissive hand, trying not to look too interested. "If you're embarrassed, I understand."

He gave her a flat stare and then placed the ilhan into his lap. She watched him set his fingers with intensity, fully alert and awake now. He glanced at her. "I only know the songs that I've seen played before."

Nico didn't understand why he would preface the performance with such a warning. Then, his fingers plucked the strings and a wave swelled through her chest at the chords of a song she hadn't heard in almost three years. Now, she understood the reason behind the warning. Kai only knew Kenji-ta's songs, so of course Kai would decide to play Nico's lullaby.

The melody overwhelmed her, and she closed her eyes to all the memories the song invoked. When the lyrics bubbled up her throat, demanding and insistent, she began to sing:

Sweet, little, caterpillar
It's time to sleep
Tuck your bones in starlight
Wrap your bones in dreams

Sweet, little, caterpillar
It's time to rest
Spin your heart a shield
Weave your heart a nest

Sweet, little, caterpillar
It's time to slumber
Adorn your head in dewdrops
Cloud your head in wonder

Sweet, little, caterpillar
I'll guard your sleep
Till you become the butterfly
You were always born to be

"You stopped singing too," he said softly, in a whisper, afterward. She hadn't thought it important, nowhere near as important as tah's universally lauded talent. Her singing was the joy of a child passing time as they did chores. She used to hum when she cooked. She used to dance in the bath. Her life had been one of music before Ava-ta's death had ripped all the notes away.

How hypocritical she had been, criticizing Kenji-ta when she had done the same. All this time, she had been mourning tah's songs when she and Kai have carried them all along. She could have always been singing.

"I've missed you singing through the hallways," he said. "I've always wanted to tell you that, but I feared hurting you."

They sat in their library, in their maze, in their home. Nico reached over to hold his hand. "No more chasing after each other or running away. No more afraid of hurting each other's feelings. No more keeping secrets. No more being too stubborn to listen. I may be the triarch, but this family is a kull, and this is *our* ship. We're in this together."

"Together," he promised, and squeezed her hand in turn, "We'll be okay."

CHAPTER SEVENTY-FIVE

⊢

Nico won the election. Not only had she won her seat, but she also accomplished what everyone thought impossible: she had orchestrated an overwhelming flip of the Council.

She had won her Wing-seat decisively, utterly destroying her opponent. The former Neck Councilor lost to Ashe-shi, which had become the big stunner and excitement of the election. Azan's family won back the Belly-seat. Her tajih retained the Heart-seat. The Hindlegs Councilor had flipped sides, and the Claws Councilor was a moderate she could sway to her side depending on the circumstances. True to their word, the previous Pelvis Councilor had stepped down to give the seat to the Tents' candidate. Only one conservative had triumphed, the staunch and bitter cousin of Kibari who had defeated Ysai and replaced her, but Ysai had already told Nico that he wanted to try again next year.

For the first time in a long time, Nico could breathe easier. It was a relief to know that those who wanted her and her family dead were no longer overwhelmingly in power. No doubt this win was the first step on a long road, but she was proud of the distance she had overcome so far. She was the first of the Ohan line to be voted onto the Council. She was the first to earn the right to be a voice for the people. She was the first to organize an overwhelming power flip within one voting season. Those were accomplishments none could ever strip away from her.

Nico slayed her dragons and prevailed. She couldn't be prouder of herself for it. All the insecurities and doubts that have plagued her, all the fears of never being perfect enough, all the exhaustion, stress, and anxieties from juggling so many responsibilities for so many people, sloughed from her shoulders like grime fleeing rain. On election night, confidence straightened her spine and self-assuredness adorned her neck. She smiled free of all the struggles weighing her down. She breathed free of the uncertainty squeezing her lungs. She danced free of that incessant guilt that had always come when feeling joy. Finally, Nico let her hair down.

Music and laughter poured over the branching roadways that bloomed out in every direction of the Heart, pumping life again into old bones. The veranda twined with conversations, and the roof glittered with excitement. The election party thickened with people who had come to offer her their congratulations, but most got waylaid by a rhythm in their hips or the alcohol in their steps.

"Butterfly, dance with me."

Tah swept her up in his arms, and Nico laughed as they spun to the music. They danced into the densest thicket of the crowd, where the heat quickened her heartbeat and the rowdiest stomped their heel against her front yard in celebration. The musicians beat drums, plucked at the strings, shook shakas, and strummed at their lunes.

"You've still got moves for an Elder," she teased.

Kenji-ta scoffed, faux-offended, and then swiveled his hips with the best of them. Something had changed in him since coming back from the Desert with Kai. A light had returned to his eyes, and she hoped it would become brighter in the coming seasons. This was the Kenji-ta she remembered: the one determined to enjoy every vibration of every day. Except now, she knew why he savored every moment. Because joy could easily be lost. When did the parents you idolize and put on a pedestal suddenly become . . . people?

She didn't know how long this phase of his would last, whether it was permanent or if there were more storm clouds on the horizon. Kai had sacrificed so much for hope, and she was wary about putting her heart back on the line. But that was the thing about kindness, and trust, and compassion. She didn't know if she would be wounded with disappointment or worse, but despite it all, she had to keep trying because there was always that small miniscule chance of joy. Kindness was not for the weak, and hope was for the brave.

"Kenji Ilhani! Come play with us!" One of the musicians called out after the current song ended. Suddenly, a great chant surrounded them that urged tah to play. She placed a supportive hand on his arm, but knew he was an expert at getting out of this situation. He'd scratch the back of his head sheepishly and bemoan how he was out of practice and didn't want to ruin anyone's fun. Even if he was never ready, Nico had decided that was all right.

To everyone's surprise, Kenji-ta rubbed at his chest, then glanced at her with a smile before striding forward. The crowd roared with cheers as tah dramatically flipped his hair back and replaced the musician who immediately vacated their seat. Kenji-ta grinned and Nico shook her head. A clash of riotous notes attacked the courtyard. People bowed under the horrendous sound and covered their ears.

Complaints and regrets bleated through the crowd, and tah threw his head back and laughed. She hadn't seen him laugh that powerfully and that true in a long time. Then her breath caught in her throat when tah hovered his hands over the strings. Time stood still and her ears popped at the tight hopeful pressure.

One swipe to test the chords, and then Kenji-ta played as if a comet burned through his fingertips. People cheered and danced. It was a song Nico had never heard before. Tah plucked notes out of the air and freewheeled with careless abandon through the sky. The rest of the musicians, friends from long ago, didn't bother keeping up, but instead kept him afloat so he wouldn't hit the ground ever again. The stars returned to his eyes.

Tah slayed a dragon, but there was a reason his last name was Ilhani. Aside from his unmatched technical skill, he had the sort of talent that came once in an epoch, a master storyteller who could control a crowd on the tides and crescendos of music. He brought people to tears. He lifted them on waves of buoyancy to last throughout the night.

It was magic, Nico swore. In the back of her consciousness, even the Great Elder shifted awake to listen.

She stood there, stargazing for a while, before catching sight of Suri leaving the veranda where the cases of alcohol were set up, some donated by goodwill, and some bought with her own paycheck. She zigged and zagged her way toward Suri. She extended her hand and fluttered her lashes with a smile. "Would you care to dance?"

Suri held a cup of alcohol, but her free hand accepted Nico's offer. They spun and twirled into the crowd, and for a moment Nico felt as if they were small children again, carefree and weighed down by nothing. But when they caught each other, they landed with all the weight of young adults.

"Thank you," she said. "For all your help with the campaign. It couldn't have been easy, fighting against your tah, and for something you don't believe in."

"I believe in you," Suri said. Nico's stomach did a flutter of flips, swooping at Suri's unwavering words. They came together, meeting in the middle with a kiss, hot and hungry.

Then she locked their hands and weaved Suri through the crowd. She deserved a break from all the politics and machinations. Tomorrow, she'd assume the role as the youngest Councilor ever elected, but tonight, she'd finally be that new face young adult she never got the chance to be on her Naming Night.

Nico drank the wine from Suri's gourd and led them into the darker corners and hideaways of the temple gardens. She rounded the persea trees and turned back at the sight of Ysai and Jilah going at it in the bending shadows.

Nico checked the next private pocket.

Azan and Ashe. Next.

Too many limbs to count. Next.

Nico and Suri reached the spiral rows of blooming jasmine. The chest-high bushes provided a barrier of privacy as they tumbled to the bed of soft soil. Soft petals of white crowned their heads. The fragrant flowers perfumed Suri's soft skin and hair. Even at this distance, the music buzzed through their bones. They danced with lust on their fingertips and swayed to rhythms of desire and aching need. They climaxed in turns. Then breathed together.

"Zephyrus Dragonblood offered me a job," she said softly. Nico curled a finger through Suri's hair while Suri pillowed her head on her breasts. "Or more accurately, his tah offered me a job."

Suri's tah might have lost her seat as Neck Councilor, but she had successfully fended off her elder child's play for her position. Suri's tah was still the Healer Han, which meant Suri was blocked out of that job.

"He says there aren't many healers in the Tents, and that someone who knows what they are doing is sorely needed, but has a kuller ever taken a job in the Tents before? I won't be eligible for the Grankull's rations, but Zara Scorpion assures me that she has the means to pay in rations and bonechips both. What should I do?"

"It doesn't come without its dangers," she admitted. "The other Tent Hans aren't going to like that Zara-shi has gained such an advantage. You'll be targeted because of it. I think it could work, but only if the job can cross territories with you beholden to no Han. An independent agent, if you will."

"I shouldn't consider it?"

"No, I think it's a great idea. The Tents desperately need healers. I'll talk to the Tent Hans when we next meet. I think an arrangement can be made."

"Thank you. And . . . Zephyrus Dragonblood has good bones. He's everything you said he was. I'm sorry I couldn't see that."

"Jealously makes unintended villains of us all," Nico said, understanding. She sat up and retied the straps of her dress. "I should be getting back."

"I'd carry your name if you let me."

Oh. She paused and looked over her shoulder at Suri, whose eyes looked soft, round, and vulnerable to hurt. She said, soft and gentle, "Suri, I've told you . . ."

"I know," Suri said, sitting up before she could complete her sentence. Suri dressed and the flowers trembled at the speed in which she rushed away. Nico picked up one of the fallen jasmine blossoms, a night blooming flower. All the long nights she stayed up working on her campaign, all the tireless drums, all the frantic rush from one place to another—she knew it was just the beginning.

She didn't have time for serious romantic commitments, and honestly, she didn't want them right now. She wondered if she ever would, because at the core of her, Nico enjoyed the work. She found purpose in the grind. She was the sort of person that wanted to give the best of herself and all her undivided attention to her endeavors. Change had the potential to be sudden and swift, but more often it was stacking one grueling weight atop another. She'd be balancing scales the rest of her life, and that potential of always having work to do . . . excited her.

She stood, surprised at how little regret or guilt she felt at hurting Suri, but she had always been clear with her boundaries and Rasia had been right all those days ago—Nico had always prioritized her purpose over her flames.

Something sharp stabbed into her back and an ominous voice whispered in her ear, "This is a message from the Tents. Don't forget your promises."

Nico turned and swatted at Kelin's pointed bare hand. He broke into an amused smirk and teased, "I could have assassinated you!"

"You wish." Then she dragged Kelin into a hug. Although he didn't wrap arms around her in turn, he was much less tense than the first time. "We did it."

"Yeah, well, we'll see if it makes any difference," he said.

"Kelin-kull, look at me," she said, and snapped her fingers to get his attention. "I'll never stop fighting for the Tents. I'll never stop fighting for you. Understand?" Kelin was too jaded to give her much more than a shrug, but she accepted it and wrapped an arm around his shoulder as they walked. "I've wanted to talk to you about something. My tajih is looking to hire someone for his windship-building kull. I suggested your name."

"The Flock wants me stationed in the bathhouses. Lots of gossip there."

"Anyone can keep their ears open at a bathhouse. Working with my tajih will give you valuable skills that no one can replace. It's not dangerous work. You won't be risking yourself out in the Desert, but it's a respectable job and makes good bonechips. It's also an easy sell—imagine the Tents with their own fleet of windships. Imagine the bargaining power it could give them and the resources it would allow you to gain. In the long-term, this job is more important than any general gossip you could overhear."

"Why?" Kelin asked, even now, after all this time, looking for the rot in the grubworm mash.

"Not everything has to be a belly bargain. We're friends. I want to see you happy."

"Well, excuse me, this friend thing has quite a learning curve."

She smiled at his sass. "Kelin-kull, people like you and me, we give so much of ourselves to our family, but we owe ourselves, too. It's okay to want something. I know you. You're too prideful to settle easily."

He kicked a pebble as they walked through the garden back towards the house. He shrugged, and they stopped abruptly when Ashe-shi smoothly walked from around the poinciana, with Azan pulling up his pants, hopping not too far behind. Kelin watched Azan, who had not noticed they were there. Azan had gotten home from drills a few days ago to participate in the voting, but soon he'd be gone the entire season with the hunting kulls.

"You should tell him how you feel."

Kelin scoffed. "I don't want to ruin his fun."

"Some friendly advice—you're a kuller now, whether you want to be one or not. If you ever intend to court someone, the number of your names matter. Your job matters. Perhaps not to Azan, but definitely to his tahs. There's nothing wrong with planning ahead."

"This place hurts my head."

She laughed. She patted him on the shoulder and parted as they reached the garden's end.

"Nico-kull," he called out before she receded too deep into the throng. She turned where he bit at his lip. Poor thing had a flame the size of a bonfire. He combed back his sleek hair and said finally, "I want it."

Nico nodded, a promise, and spun away into the crowd. She greeted a few more people she hadn't met with yet but noted the crowd had grown far larger than those she had initially invited.

Her mentor sat on one of the benches breastfeeding her newborn. A thin linen shroud hung over her mentor's shoulder to protect the child's face as they suckled. Nico had the honor to be invited to the birthpour—the celebration new parents held a blink after the birth to introduce the First Name and the face of their newborn to their closest friends and family. Most likely, she would never see the child's face again until their Naming Ceremony.

"Nicolai Councilor, I'm so proud of you," the previous Wing Councilor said, tired with that new parent exhaustion. "Would you like to hold them?"

"Yes. I'd like to."

Nico smiled holding the familiar weight of a newborn in her arms again. Rae had been this tiny not too long ago. Soon Rae would be hitting puberty, coming into their sex, and cocooned in a full shroud. She held the baby to her shoulder and burped them as her mentor dropped back against the bench, breasts out and tired.

"Never have kids," her mentor muttered.

"Where's your kulani?"

"She's off getting me some water." Her mentor waved off, then dropped her head back, and fell asleep. Nico smiled, amused, and patted the newborn's back. The babe burped loudly in her ear, spitting up on the shroud.

In the crowd of dancers, Nico spotted Loryn and Faris. They twirled around each other and various other partners. She had been proud to hear that Faris had joined the hunting kulls. She had also accepted Loryn's job application to work under her in the wingfields. She noticed some of the others from the Forging, too, all vibrant and flourishing and beautiful.

She closed her eyes and took a moment to soak up the sense of accomplishment. She built this. She fought for this. She bled, sweated, and cried for this. Even though the toil was difficult, nothing was more satisfying than watching a garden grow.

Kai and Zephyr sat beside each other on the roof and watched the festivities mill below their feet. Zephyr passed Kai his "water" gourd, and Kai took a drink of the beer, gulping it down with practiced ease. The crowd beneath them thickened, bolstered by newcomers attracted to the music and looking for a good time. Nico's campaign reception had turned into an outright party.

"I might need your help with something," Kai said, and passed back the gourd. Distant on the roof, no one paid attention to whether he was drinking underage and the deception was probably unnecessary but still, somebody would probably be a kulo about it.

"I've still got a few days before starting my apprenticeship, and there's something I need to do first. I need to go back to the Dragon's Coast. I was wondering if you wanted to come with me?"

"I don't have too many free days left in my sentry contract since I got stabbed and had to take a medical leave," Zephyr said.

"It shouldn't take long if we use magic," he suggested. "I've got a better handle on it outside the Grankull, and Nico has been pushing me to practice."

"What's so important about the Dragon's Coast?" Zephyr asked. "Did you forget something out there? It's got to be long gone by now."

Kai picked at the frayed strands of his shroud. Cautiously, he told Zephyr about the baby dragon and Zephyr's eyes widened at every sentence.

"And you just left them there?" he growled after Kai had finished.

"What were we supposed to do?" Kai asked. "I just . . . I want to make sure the dragon is okay. It's been weighing on me for a while now. With Rasia gone and Nico doing her own thing, I figured I should go check on them."

"Fuck it. Why not?" Zephyr shrugged. "I need a break from this place anyway."

Kai glanced at Zephyr's stomach where he had been stabbed not too long ago. He understood. They both could use a little time out of the Grankull, even if it was for a few days.

Zephyr took a long drag of the drink and then said to himself, awed, "*A baby dragon?* We should bring them some snacks. What do you think a healthy baby dragon diet consists of?"

"What baby dragon?"

Kai and Zephyr swiveled their heads toward Nico climbing up the last rung of the roof ladder. Zephyr tilted his head toward Kai, and Kai licked his lips nervously. Nico had been pushing him to take some time for himself, but he was sure she didn't mean leaving for somewhere as dangerous as the Dragon's Coast. She placed both feet on the rooftop and stared at him expectantly.

He confessed, "Zephyr and I are going to the Dragon's Coast to check on a baby dragon."

It was too dark to see the emotions that flitted across her face, but Kai could guess at them. She paused for a moment, took a deep breath, and released all those emotions out on a long exhale.

"Sounds good, but let's unpack the details of all that tomorrow," she suggested. "I need a drink."

Zephyr scooted to allow Nico room, and her hair pooled on the rooftop as she sat between them. He offered the gourd, and she drank from it without hesitation.

"It's so much nicer up here. Less hot," she said, pulling at her shirt and fanning her hand. She looked a little tipsy. Kai swept away a jasmine petal clinging to her hair and didn't need much imagination to guess what she had been up to in the temple gardens. It was good to see this Nico again, the *fun* Nico, who he had thought died with Ava-ta.

They settled into the new sitting dynamic and watched over the people Nico had brought together. Kai had always admired her ability to get things done, but her feat of overturning the Council had been truly impressive. He did wish that Ava-ta got the chance to see the brilliant person Nico had become, despite Ava-ta. He was so proud.

"What's next?" Zephyr asked.

Nico had an answer at the ready, and even with drink, her words were sharp and articulate, "I doubt anyone will have any objections to taking bones from the Graveyard. It's how we do it that will most likely be the point of contention. Convincing everyone to work with the scavengers instead of stealing from them is going to be tricky."

"If Timar doesn't double-cross you first," Kai said, hoping he never saw that scavenger again.

She nodded in agreement. "We'll have to send a diplomatic kull to assess the current situation in the Graveyard. But there's an even bigger problem ahead. Once we move the bones, we're going to need people to prepare the fields. More people than the Grankull currently has, which means that either the Grankull forms an alliance with the Tents, officially recognizing it as a legitimate territory, or we somehow roll everyone into the Grankull."

Zephyr's brows crunched at that. "The Grankull will riot with the former, and the Tents will riot with the latter. I don't see it happening. Even with all of your influence."

"What makes the Grankull the Grankull?" she challenged. "What defines us? The one thing that universally binds us together as a society is that we have all survived the Forging to come of age. But what if the Forging was open not only to children but to all who have no faces? What if when someone faces banishment as a punishment, it's not forever and after a certain period, they're allowed to regain their face? What if the Tents wasn't a permanent state but finally as fleeting as the name suggests—a transition? Not only will this open the Forging to both the Tents and the scavengers, but the ability to return home essentially cuts the knees off the no-face trade. There's a chance at redemption for everyone. Why does the Forging have to be something that sets us apart when it could be a tool to bind us together?"

Kai looked to the horizon, beyond the tall spires that jolted from the ground like fangs, toward the same direction Rasia had left a couple of days ago. He wondered if it'd become a habit or if the action would fade with time. He whispered, "The world is what we forge of it."

"Or what it forges of us." Zephyr shrugged.

"Or what we forge of ourselves." Her face burned bright with determination. "Together, we will sail toward a greater purpose—toward a shared goal to create something out of nothing, and to turn this arid bitter soil into an oasis. One day, the Grankull will be a place where everyone eats and everyone earns their faces." Nico lifted the gourd to the bones, to the Elder, and turned the page to the next story. "Tomorrow, the hunt begins anew."

CHAPTER SEVENTY-SIX

O

"Ready?"

Raiment looked down at Rasia from the bow of the windbarge. Just looking at the ship, weighed down with crates and barrels and her ticket out of here, she could barely contain her excitement.

"Almost!" she called up.

Rasia could delay her dreams, for just a moment, for the people who cared about her. She turned to those standing on the edge of the shipyard.

Ysai rushed her and smothered her in a hug that kept going and going. Her feet kicked uselessly off the ground. He swung her to and fro, and then with a tearful sniff dropped her to her feet. He knocked her on the head one last final time.

"I'm going to miss you."

"I'll write, because I can do that now," she said. "I have to send back reports of my travels, and they'll be stored in the Temple. You can read all about my epic adventures every time you miss all of this awesomeness."

"My poor bones are so comforted," he chuckled. They pushed at each other until Jilah swooped in and gave Rasia a hug of her own. Rasia might have lost a parent, but she had earned a sibling in Jilah. They were family now and Rasia knew her jih would always be in good hands.

Rae sidled up next and pulled on Rasia's pants. She crouched down, expecting another hug, and not at all expecting the disapproving glare out of the half-shroud. "You promised to protect him."

The words hit hard and unexpected. She stared at the child, lost at how to explain that some promises weren't indestructible. Sometimes they're broken, and sometimes they hurt. She leaned forward on one knee and told Rae seriously, "It's your turn now. Take care of your jih, and make sure he eats. You promise?"

"On my names," Rae vowed.

Kenji-shi scooped Rae onto his hip, and with the other arm, shoveled Rasia into a one-armed hug. "The hunting kulls are disappointed, but I know if Shamai-kull were here, he'd be proud of you, too. I am sorry I wasn't there for you after he passed. I should have been."

"Take care of my kulani and we're even."

"I'll take care of him," Kenji-shi promised, and retreated.

Of course, Nico was next.

The two young adults stared each other down. Rasia clicked her tongue and said, "I'm not wrong about a lot of things, but I was wrong about you. You're far stronger than I ever gave you credit for. If there's anyone who can change the Grankull, it's you. Make it better, Nicolai Ohan."

"I will, Rasia-ji."

They both nodded at the acknowledgment.

Everyone unsubtly pulled away to give her and Kai some semblance of privacy. He wore his shroud, both a shield and a cage. Sometimes the shroud protected against the wind and sand, or wiped at sweat as a rag, or hung as a belt tied around your waist. Sometimes it was a makeshift wrap or a flag flying the summit of a warship. It was a memento from childhood and embroidered with color in adulthood. It was many things to many people.

"Kailjnn," Rasia whispered, and the namesake glowed between them, illuminating their faces. She had thought long and hard about the last words to say to him, but they had said the important stuff already.

She moved for a final kiss over his shroud and at the last moment, he pulled back the linen. Their lips met in a kiss so long and dramatic it had the tent crew cheering by the boldness of it. She sucked in the warmth and a sweet honeyed-date longing that would never fade. He kissed her with all his everything, and then dared to surrender her wet and trembling with memories engraved all over her body. She laughed at the breathlessness of it.

He smiled, pleased. "Stay wary the Hunter."

"If he stays wary of me." Rasia winked.

She fastened her gaze to that smile as she walked backward toward the barge. She climbed the steps, crossed the deck, and leaned against the railing without ever breaking her view of him. The sail billowed. The anchor lifted. The wheels creaked. And Kai's face drifted away to a speck of sand.

Then she turned to greet the horizon. And didn't turn back around again.

Most kids took their palm sweet time with the bones. They rattled them in cupped hands, rubbed together sweaty hopes and dreams, blew on them four . . . five . . . forever times for luck, before *finally* tossing all that childish fat up to the air.

Rasia Dragonfire pitched her bones to the wind..

Ю

Her Names are Rasia the hunter, the wind-chaser, the horizon-seeker, the discoverer, the wanderer, the adventurer

a mane of wild horses, bones thrown afield, a map with no end, two blades and dragon-sail, swiftness and movement

the dark waters of the dragon's coast, a graveyard of bones, the today of yestermorrow

Kai-kulani

dragonfire

I'll remember it

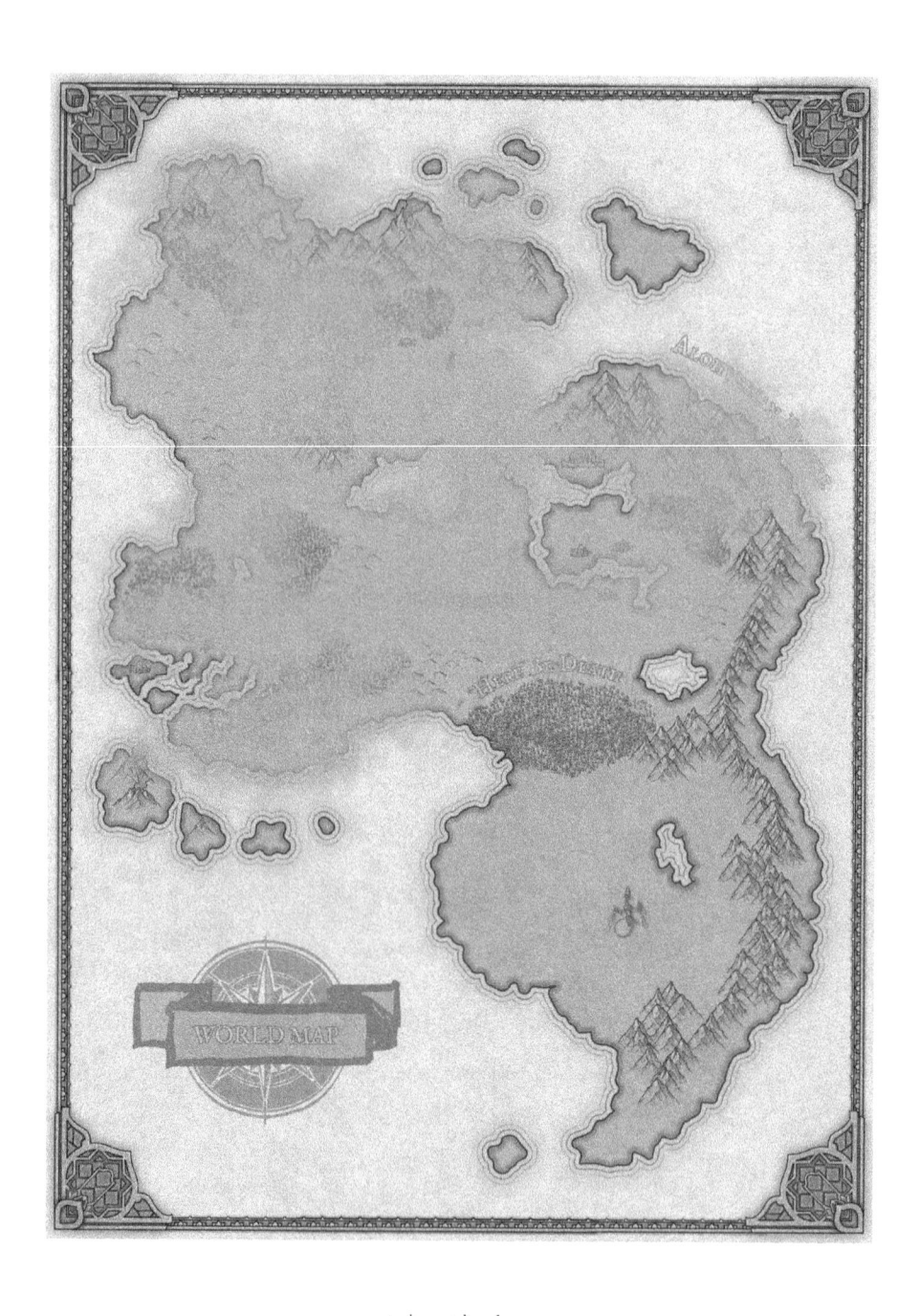

to be explored . . .

Other Works

Sistah Samurai: A Champloo Novella

JOIN MY MAILING LIST FOR NEWS AND UPDATES.

www.tatianaobey.com

FOLLOW

@obeytheauthor

AUTHOR'S NOTE

I initially wrote this duology as one long story. As I do not have the clout of Brandon Sanderson, or unlimited money to pay for editors and proofreaders who charge for every word, I had no choice but to split this tome into two parts. I do believe that both parts together are the best representation of who I am as an author and what you might expect of me in my career going forward. For those of you who have continued from Bones to the Wind to Dragon Your Bones, I am sincerely grateful. Thank you for allowing me the opportunity to tell you a story.

Online reviews are critical to an indie book's success. If you have enjoyed this story, please consider leaving a review on your preferred review site, or on social media.

ACKNOWLEDGEMENTS

Thank you to my family and friends who have supported me along this journey. Thank you for your excitement. Thank you for your love. Thank you for your encouragements. I wouldn't be here without you. I want to give a special acknowledgement to my father. He wasn't perfect, but his love for me was.

In addition, I have been so overwhelmed by the support of the self-publishing community and fellow authors who have embraced me since my debut. I thank you and I hope to one day have the resources to contribute to such an enthusiastic community. Thank you to the readers who have reached out to me and expressed their love for my characters and my story. It keeps me pushing forward despite the struggles of this industry.

I also want to give a special thank you to my beta readers: Agueda "Agatha" Lopez and Laura Montalvo. Thank you Agatha for feeding me and keeping me alive for the past year. Thank you to Lady Azulina, BookinItWithAhtiya, Trinity Gossage, Hilarie Anderson, AmyLola, Valéria Scholtzová, Shreya Pillai, and the rest of the ARC & Street Team for your support and help with marketing this book. I also want to give a special shout out to B²

Weird Bookclub! Thank you for the invaluable support and being such an awesome group of weirdos. Finally, thank you to Kristy Elam, my copy editor and proofreader, and to Asur Misoa for creating another awesome cover illustration.

Not all dragons breathe fire. Stay slayin'.

Printed in the USA
CPSIA information can be obtained
at www.ICGtesting.com
CBHW021529180224
4430CB00024BA/253/J